RYKER

By Briana Michaels

COPYRIGHT

All names, characters and events in this publication are fictitious and any resemblance to actual places, events, or real persons, living or dead, is entirely coincidental.

All rights reserved. No part of this publication may be reproduced, stored, or transmitted, in any form or by any means, without the prior permission, in writing, of the author.

www.BrianaMichaels.com

COPYRIGHT © 2024 Briana Michaels

Author Note

Please don't use this, or any other book of mine, as an educational tool. It might be inspiring, but always play responsibly and do your research. I take creative liberties because this is a work of fiction and I'm a chaotic creature in all aspects of my life.

Thank you for reading!

Dedication

For the ones who had to wrap themselves
in a red flag just to survive.

Chapter 1

Ryker

Watching people fuck each other's brains out is boring. It didn't use to be that way, but after five years of owning a sex club, I can honestly say not much gets me excited anymore.

The Monarch is known for quality service, exceptional experiences, and above all, supreme discretion.

Bottom line: I only cater to the elite.

Don't kid yourself into thinking this line of work is all whipped cream covered tits and blowjobs. It's hard work that never ends. I don't get vacations. I don't have a social life. Hell, I don't even have time to sleep most nights.

No amount of money I make now can relieve the tension that's been my constant companion for over a decade. While most men my age are having fun with their friends, going on vacations, driving to their nine-to-fives with a little wifey to go home to later, I'm in the trenches of the sex industry, forever defending my territory, making sure my club stays top notch, and all members are safe and respectful when they're within my walls.

This isn't just a business. It's a lifestyle. The Hell I've made sure to become king of. Between going over invoices, meeting with clients, and researching members to make sure they're staying on the up and up, the Monarch has a reputation to uphold, and so do I.

It's not easy to get into my club. It's even harder to remain in it.

I demand respect and the only way to ensure it is to make everyone obey my motherfucking rules.

One fuck up and I'll blacklist you. That goes for what you do in my club... and out of it.

"Good evening, Mr. Hudson."

"How are you tonight, Sophie?" I bring my employee's hand to my lips and kiss her knuckles like a gentleman always should. Tonight, she's wearing a black leather one-piece, stiletto thigh high boots, and a gas mask. Last night she was in a pink, furry bunny suit.

"I can't believe you recognize me under this." She pulls off her mask and laughs, but it's a nervous one. Most of my employees are a little scared of me, which I prefer. It keeps them in check and makes them damn good at their jobs because most don't have another place to go.

Sophie came to me during college, looking for a job. I gave her one cleaning the club, but that didn't last. She was too curious. Too young. Too talented and quick to learn. Four years later, she's one of my best entertainers. No one would guess this woman is a rocket scientist by day, and a Fem Domme at night.

"The Butterfly Ceremony is tomorrow night," she says, like I need the reminder. "Do you want me to come in for it?"

I shake my head. "I thought you had tickets to see Phantom of the Opera."

Sophie's bottom lip juts out in a pout. "I tried to score tickets but missed them, so I'm totally open if you need extra bodies to rev the crowd up and make them hungrier."

Reaching into the breast pocket of my suit, I pull out two tickets and hold them between my fingers. "Oh look. I just happen to have two box seats for the final showing."

Her eyes light up. "Oh my god, Ryker!" Then she back tracks quickly. "I mean, Mr. Hudson."

Good girl. Ryker is fine out of the club, but within these walls, I'm Mr. Hudson or Sir. Lifting a brow, I fan the tickets between my fingers. "Still want to work tomorrow night?"

Panic flits in her eyes because she's not sure what the right answer should be. Sophie's been pulling more than her weight here lately, and I'd rather she enjoy herself out in the wild than in here. "Have fun," I say, kissing her cheek. "Bring a friend with you, okay?"

She does too much by herself and I'm worried about her.

"Thank you so much!" Sophie leaps to hug me and stops herself. Clearing her throat, she drops her head and says, "I appreciate this, Mr. Hudson."

I know she does. "Get back to work."

Sophie tugs her gas mask back on her face and heads in the opposite direction of me, but I don't miss the way she fist-bumps the air as she scurries to the elevators. Okay, it's time to get back to fucking work. Throwing my weight into the heavy double doors of my office, I storm in, ready for the night.

"Good evening, Mr. Hudson." My best bodyguard, Dmitri, stands behind my desk with his hands clasped, and a four-thousand-dollar tailored suit stretched across his body.

"Who's on the radar tonight?" I drop into my chair and start scanning the monitors.

Running a tight ship means that nothing, I mean *nothing,* gets past me and my men in this club. If you make one wrong move, you're out. No second chances. When you have a room designed to suspend someone in the air with only their body modifications, you can't afford fuck ups. Same for the bedrooms used for gang bangs and machinery.

"Everyone's behaving. But it's early." It's six o'clock, which means the Monarch only opened two hours ago. "I thought you had an appointment?"

"I do." My gaze sails across the four monitors until it lands on a particular room with a small group of voyeurs. There's a blonde standing in the corner, closest to the door, watching a tied-up woman get fucked by two men on a bench in the middle of the room.

I've seen her here before—the watcher, I mean, not the threesome. She never takes part in the activities—because trust me, I've waited for it to happen. She reminds me of a Luna moth—graceful, ethereal, eye-catching, and doesn't stay long. Whenever she's here, she's a distraction to me. I follow her from room to room on my surveillance feed, but she only ever seems to observe. I've never caught her talking to anyone, fucking anyone, and she's never come to one of our BDSM classes.

"This woman..." I tap the screen. "You know anything about her other than what's on her file?"

Dmitri casually leans over for a better look. Bracing his hands on my desk, his lips press in a tight line and his jaw ticks. After a few tense heartbeats, he stands straight again. "No."

"Call Vault in here."

Dmitri quietly talks in his discreet headset and Vault walks through my door a minute later.

That's another thing I demand in my club—promptness and efficiency. Time is money.

"Do you know anything about her?" I tap the figure on the security monitor again.

Vault squints as he sifts through his mental filing cabinet. This man is a goddamn genius with a photographic memory. He sees it once, and it's locked in his mind's vault forever. Hence the nickname. He's also the one who does all the monitoring of our members when they're outside the club.

"Tara Reed. Age twenty-nine, Berkeley graduate, no known food allergies, enjoys baking shows and has both a praise and degradation kink."

My guys are worth their weight in gold around here, but Vault isn't telling me anything I haven't already memorized from her membership application.

I study her posture. Tara stands stick straight in the back of the exhibition room, as if holding herself back from joining in. Or maybe she's shocked by what she sees. Hard to say.

She looks like a little tart—sweet, decadent, and delicate.

Devour-able.

Leaning back in my chair, I steeple my fingers and continue staring at her. "Where does she work?"

"Not listed. And no socials either."

She could be a socialite of some kind. It wouldn't surprise me in the slightest.

"She's pretty quiet and reserved when she's here, which could suggest inexperience." Vault walks back around to the other side of my desk. "Or maybe she just loves to watch and takes the ideas home and puts them to use there. Hard to say. I can run more checks online and see what I can dig up."

For some disturbing reason, I don't want Vault getting the privilege of hunting down the details of this woman's life. "Don't bother." She's not doing anything wrong. No need to waste time on her.

I've done enough of that already.

Switching topics, I tap my mouse and open another program. "Are we all set for the Butterfly Ceremony tomorrow night?"

Vault nods. "For sure."

"How many are in the net?"

"Ten."

I cock my brow. Ten is good. Not the most I've had, but more than last year's selection. "Is her room ready?"

"Of course." Vault's grin makes him look like a wolf. "I've made sure all brackets, hooks, straps, and bolts are secure. Closets are filled, and the bath is stocked as well."

"How many are on the bidding sheet?" I look at the spreadsheet I've pulled up, but Dmitri answers before I can scroll down for the number.

"One-hundred and two."

I school my expression, hiding my shock. There are only two hundred members in my club, and most don't visit my establishment more than a handful of times a year. Tomorrow night will be *packed*. "Are we prepared to entertain that many at once?"

"Absolutely." Vault unwraps a lollipop and

shoves it in his mouth. "I'm betting most of them will leave once the auction's over with, though."

"Order ten more cases of condoms, just in case. And get another three cases of lube." Losers like to lick their wounds, or, around here, get them licked.

My gaze flicks back to Tara. She's left the exhibition room and I catch her on another camera, walking down a hallway.

Dmitri's low timbre rumbles behind me. "Need anything else, or can I get my night started?" D is always eager to pace the halls and maintain the safety of my guests.

"No. You're good. Thanks." My boys shut the doors behind them, plunging me into silence. I can't drag my gaze away from Tara on the screen. Her heart-shaped ass sashays in her tight dress to a rhythm I enjoy. Her heels are thin, tall, and expensive going off the dark soles. All that long hair cascading down her back in loose curls makes me want to pull it. My dick twitches at the thought.

I don't get involved with the members of my club. I'm off limits. Always. No exception.

It makes my growing obsession with this woman fucking pointless.

Where are you going now?

I pull up a camera from a different angle. Tara stops Sophie just outside the elevator. The two of them talk and then Sophie nods just before they split off again. Tara takes the elevator alone and I quickly pull up another screen to watch her descend to the ground level. Her head's down, damnit. I want to see her face.

"Look up at me."

I've got cameras everywhere in this place. Hundreds of them, in fact, to ensure everyone in my club remains safe — and behaves themselves. There's a well-paid team in another room, down the hall from my office, whose only job is to monitor every inch of the Monarch and alert security if something goes wrong.

So why am I doing their job instead of preparing for the small fortune I plan to make tomorrow night at the Butterfly Ceremony?

Because Tara fucking Reed keeps snagging my attention. And she hasn't looked up at the camera once. She's avoiding it.

Many of my clients are socialites and require the utmost privacy for the debauchery they perform in my club. Tara being in that pool of filthy-rich-high-and-mighties wouldn't surprise me.

What's a gorgeous creature like her doing with brains and a paycheck? Most women in this place have a trust fund, a sugar daddy, or both. They don't earn a dime unless it's on their knees.

Tara has officially piqued my interest. I might just have to greet her in person.

Shit, what time is it? Pushing away from my desk, I realize I only have thirty minutes to make it to my appointment. Looks like Tara's little meet and greet will have to be another night.

Taking the back exit, I rush over to my car and leave the Monarch's property and Tara behind. City traffic is a motherfucker tonight with the road construction, but I make it to my destination with two minutes to spare and pull up to an old building that stands like a megalith of doom amidst a dazzling city skyline. My heart thuds heavily in my chest.

Practicing my breathing exercises, I climb out of my car and button my suit jacket. With a charming, give-me-what-I-want smile plastered on my face, I head straight for the woman waiting for me.

"Mr. Hudson," the realtor says with a toothy smile. "I'm so happy you could make it on such short notice."

I shake her hand and maintain my charm. "It's incredible of you to fit me in like this. I can't thank you enough."

"Well, the owner is in a hurry to sell, and I remembered you mentioning once that if this one ever went up for sale, to let you know immediately."

My chest tightens. "Shall we?" I swoop my hand, gesturing at the door with the padlock.

"Oh, h-hang on." The realtor's eyes light up as she looks behind me. "Miss Reed, it's wonderful to see you again."

"How are you, Moira?"

The blood in my veins freezes when Tara Reed walks up and kisses my realtor on the cheek.

"Sorry," Tara says, shaking the loose curls from her face before flashing me a smile that's brighter than the sun. "I'm Tara Reed, from Brisbane Realty." Her gaze sails up and down my stiff frame. "And you are?"

Your biggest competition. "Ryker Hudson." It takes every ounce of strength to remain calm and shake her hand like a civilized gentleman. Her grip is much stronger than I expect. She smells sweet, like candy.

But now that I know who she works for, and that she might take what I want, I no longer want to suck on her. I want to chew her up and spit her out.

Being devour-able can easily be a woman's best trait and worst flaw. Tara better watch who she plays hardball with.

Nothing in her file said she was from Brisbane Realty. Either she hid the information, or she's a new hire and her file hasn't updated. Either way, I'm fucking pissed.

"Sorry I had to double book the two of you," Moira says sheepishly. "I'm leaving for a cruise in the morning, and this was the only way I could see you both."

Time is money, I can appreciate that. Except why do I feel like I'm about to get screwed somehow?

I want to expand. Invest. I've got the money, and this place is what I want. I can't let Brisbane Realty or even Clyde-Smith Properties get their claws in it first. They already own half the city. Why the fuck do they want this building? It's a shithole.

And it's going to be *my* shithole before I leave here tonight. I don't care what it takes.

"I'll keep this short and sweet," I say. "I'm ready to make my offer."

Moira's eyes round with surprise. "But, Mr. Hudson, don't you want to see inside first?"

"Yes, Mr. Hudson." Tara flashes me her pearly whites. "Let's take a tour, then we can play."

Play? *Play*? This isn't a game to me, but if Miss Reed wants to make it one, I have no problem giving her what she wants.

And I'm going to fucking win.

Chapter 2

Tara

So, this is the elusive Ryker Hudson. I've never considered myself a lucky woman, but tonight gives me hope.

"I'll keep this short and sweet," Ryker says, his chiseled jaw clenching as he obviously works to keep his composure. "I'm ready to make my offer."

Moira, bless her soul, gawks at him. "But, Mr. Hudson, don't you want to see inside first?"

I jump in because I'm vicious enough to fuck with my prey before devouring it. "Yes, Mr. Hudson. Let's take a tour, then we can play."

He glowers at me like I'm the one playing with fire here. Little does he know, I'm more than willing to get burned by him. I've been told he was untouchable.

Unfuckable.

Tall, tatted, and intense—he's not what I've imagined since joining the Monarch. He's even better.

This man looks like he could eat a woman alive, and she'd thank him for the pleasure.

But if he thinks he can charm his way into a deal with Moira while I'm here, he's about to get a lesson in humility.

I need to land this deal if I want to keep my job. It's not officially on the market yet, and I only found out this afternoon that it was going on the roster. I thought I'd have this deal in the bag with no issue tonight, but with Ryker Hudson willing to make an offer on the spot, I'll admit I'm confused. What could he possibly want with this place?

My family's company already owns most of the adjacent land and has big plans for this area. Brisbane businesses will quickly choke out anything he builds here.

So much for this being a quick, simple, cheap deal. My stepfather called me this afternoon, saying a little bird told him this building was going up for sale and that I better land it, or else.

My family and I don't get along. At all. I'm worried I'll get fired, which I won't let happen. When I leave Brisbane, it'll be my choice. Until then, I'll play nice. This deal seemed like a perfect way to ensure my job security—an easy win handed to me by my stepfather—but now that I'm here, I'm second guessing his intentions.

Maybe he's tricked me. Maybe he's testing me.

Maybe he's fucking me over.

This place is a shithole.

"After you," Mr. Hudson says, holding the door for us.

My Chanel dress is tight and short, making it difficult to climb the steps, and it's clear the elevator is out of commission and probably has been for decades.

"It has good bones," Moira says cheerfully, heading for the stairwell.

It smells like mildew and old cigarettes. The exterior wasn't so bad because it was brick, but the inside is awful. I already know what my family will do with this place. They'll tear it down. Level it. Turn it into a parking garage or something because they will not invest time and money to restore this place, even to turn it into luxury condos. It's a fucking dump.

We follow Moira to the second floor and my heel catches on a loose tile causing me to stumble backward. Mr. Hudson catches my arm with lightning speed, saving me from almost tumbling down the stairs. "Thank you." God, his grip is firm. Imagine what it would feel like as a necklace.

"Watch where you walk." He lets go of me and tips his head at Moira. "Continue, please."

"The owner has evicted everyone already," Moira explains.

"People were still living here?" I can't imagine. I've seen a half dozen code violations already and we're still only on the steps.

"Not everyone can afford a home on the East side," Mr. Hudson growls.

My blood runs cold. How the hell does he know where I live? Oh. Wait. My application to the Monarch has my address. Still, it's weird that he'd have that memorized.

Should I be freaked out or flattered?

Focus, Tara.

"The architecture is lovely." I mean it. This building might be a dump now, but it's clear by the engraved banisters and decorated ceiling it used to be a stunner. Too bad no one maintained it properly. I slow down to read some of the profanity graffitied on the wall. Someone's even carved *You're worth more than this* into the windowsill.

I stare at the words, my heart dropping because it feels personal.

You're worth more than this.

Am I? I make a lot of money with Brisbane Realty, but it comes at a cost I'm struggling to afford. My time, sanity, dignity, and energy are depleting fast. I hate my life. I hate what I've become. I hate that I'm here and I hate how it smells. My stepfather must be out of his mind to consider investing in this place. Or he was lied to about what a great property it is. Either way, it's my night wasted.

Fuck.

"Let me show you the rooftop." Moira pulls out a set of keys and we follow her up to what looks like a tetanus shot waiting to happen.

Mr. Hudson holds his hand out for me to take because there's no way I can climb these steep steps without some help. My dress rides up my thighs and I'm pretty sure I just flashed him my panties. Shit. This is so unprofessional.

I dressed for a meeting outside the building, not a tour.

No, I dressed for a sex club, not a realty deal on the down low.

Mr. Hudson keeps his hand gently pressed to the small of my back as I keep up with Moira. For someone who's my competition, he's acting incredibly civilized. It makes what I'm about to do almost criminal.

"I've seen enough," I say when we reach the outside rooftop that offers a phenomenal view of the glowing city. "My company, like Mr. Hudson, is also willing to make an offer tonight."

Moira's eyes light up.

"We're willing to offer—"

"One million," Mr. Hudson says, cutting me off.

"My offer is one million."

It's all I can do to keep my jaw from hitting the fucking cement. That's way too much for this property. Either he's desperate or an idiot, yet something tells me Ryker Hudson is neither of those things. Just as he rolls his shoulders back, assuming victory, I knock him down a peg. "Two million."

Oh. My. God. Talk about being a desperate idiot. What am I doing?

This place is a disaster. I had every intention of walking away and telling my family this place was a no-go, yet here I am, bidding way higher than any sane person would for this place. It's too late for me to take it back. I'm fucked.

My competition turns to me, his expression stoic. Good god, he's gorgeous. Dark hair clipped short and neat. Eyes a pale grey, like a storm with a little sunshine coming through. His mouth, so fuckable and kissable, gives nothing away as he stares down at me. Dressed in a pricey, cute little suit, he looks menacing and magnificent.

Mr. Hudson cocks his brow. "I don't have time to get into a bidding war, Miss Reed. What will it take for you to walk away?" With his hands stuffed into his pockets, he steps into my space and has me by a good five inches. My breath quickens as his eyes bore into mine. "Name your price and consider it done."

My heart slams to a stop.

Opportunities truly show up in the most unexpected ways.

I have an out... *and* an in.

Tipping my head to the side, I maintain an air of aloofness that's taken me half my life to master. "I want to be the Butterfly."

He stills.

My heart thrashes in my chest. My palms are sweaty. I've just made the biggest power-play of my life and it's not over property. It's for sex.

The Butterfly at the Monarch is a once in a lifetime opportunity. It's one of the things that makes the Monarch so special. Once a year, select women are caught *"in the net"* and put up for auction. The woman with the highest bid becomes "the Butterfly" and has her choice of lovers for the month—picking her Dom from elite professionals who work at the club.

It's the only way to get to them. The Monarch has several entertainers you can play with, but the elite pros are untouchable by anyone except the Butterfly.

"That's not possible," Ryker finally says, stepping back.

"Anything's possible when you want it to be." I close the space between us. "How bad do you want this place, Mr. Hudson?"

His jaw clenches. Maybe he's debating on pushing me off the roof. Maybe he's carefully weighing his options on whether this place is worth the price I want him to pay. I have no clue how versed he is in real estate, but it's not worth the price tag he's set on it. I wouldn't have offered more than six-hundred thousand for this mess. Instead, I ratcheted the damn thing up to two million and am ready to play hardball. I'm fucked no matter what.

If he caves, I'll be forced to pay the promised amount and my stepfather will have my ass for spending so much. If he takes my deal, I'll have to come up with a lie to explain how I lost this property when no one else was supposed to know it was up for sale yet. But at least I'll get what I've been desperately wanting for so long.

My body comes alive with adrenaline.

"What will it be, Ryker Hudson?" We stare at each other like two lions. I bet we both bite hard.

"Perhaps we should take this conversation downstairs," Moira says, nervously. She has no clue what we're referencing, but I'm sure she's aware of the growing tension between us. When neither of us budges, she turns around and busies herself on her cell.

Ryker's jaw ticks, his eyes dark and hard. "You have yourself a deal, Miss Reed," he finally says, holding out his hand.

That he's old schooling it with a handshake, like my word is gold, says a lot about him, and even more about me, because I'll shake it regardless of my trustworthiness. Slipping my hand in his, a thrill skates up my spine. My nipples harden. My mouth waters. I clench my thighs because all I keep thinking about is finally getting what I want.

Tonight is a major win.

I'll just need to talk myself out of losing my job in the morning.

"Um, I don't mean to interrupt." Moira almost trips over broken bits of stone and rubber as she rushes towards us. Her stenciled eyebrows knit together and her mouth cuts in a deep frown. "I'm so very sorry," she says. "I didn't check my emails ahead of time today because I had to pick up my grandkids from soccer and then I got stuck at the grocery store before I—"

"Spit it out, Moira. Is there a problem?" My hand is still in Mr. Hudson's and we're both squeezing tightly.

"Well, yes." She looks up at us and sighs. "I'm afraid the owner has already signed auction papers. Neither of your offers are valid. They slated this building to go up for sale on the thirty-first of this month. I'm so sorry to have wasted your time and brought you here last minute. The owner told me only yesterday that they wanted to sell, and I thought they were holding off on considering an auction."

Mr. Hudson slides his hand out of mine. "Looks like this was all for nothing, then."

My heart stutters to a stop. No, no, no. I've come too close to lose it all now. "A deal's a deal," I blurt.

"The deal was contingent on the sale being made tonight." He wipes his hand off on his jacket.

How insulting.

Instead of getting flustered, I get even. "The deal was for me to let this property go so you could have it without my competition. Now if you'd prefer I meet you at the auction, I'll happily do that," I step in close, giving him my best evil grin. "And I'll drive the price up higher than you can afford." I ease off a bit. "But I'm not a petty woman." I'm a horny one. "I assure you, Mr. Hudson, you don't want to play hardball with me. My pockets are far deeper than yours."

He arches his brow. "Says who?"

"That suit you're wearing." I turn towards the stairwell and pray karma doesn't push me down the steps for that low blow.

"For a Butterfly," he says behind me, "you sure know how to bite."

I look over my shoulder and flash him another wicked smile. "I assure you, Mr. Hudson, I never bite the hand that fingers me."

Successfully stunning him, I leave as fast as my Louboutin stilettos can carry me. By the time I'm out of the building, my knees are shaking and heart's racing. Sauntering over to my car, I wave without looking back at him. "See you tomorrow evening at the ceremony, Mr. Hudson."

A deal's a deal, and this man better not back out of it, or I'll take his ass to the cleaner and damn the consequences.

Chapter 3

Ryker

I'm fucked.

Storming back into my club, I weave through the tightly packed bodies and shove myself through the *staff only* doors to get to my office.

Tara. Fucking. Reed. Her name grinds my last nerve. I'm going to annihilate this woman by any means necessary for what she's done. Not only did that woman screw me with that deal, she's fucked my club out of making a lot of goddamn money tomorrow night.

And she's pissed all over my integrity.

Okay, that last accusation may be more my fault than hers. I let my pride talk for my bank account tonight. I didn't have to take the deal and could have walked away, refused to give her what she wanted. Instead, I shut my mouth and let her think she's won.

And while her sweet ass glided down the stairwell and back to her car, I imagined everything I'll make sure happens to her as the Butterfly. By the end of the month, she won't be able to sit, walk, or crawl.

Which leads me to my biggest problem.

The Butterfly gets to choose who they want as their Dom. That means not only do I have to rig this auction for her to win, but I'll have to coach whoever she chooses.

Or become her master myself. I shake the thought away before it turns into a full-blown temptation.

Too bad I'm not on the roster of available Doms.

She might have looked at me with those victorious Fuck Me blue eyes tonight, but the way she scuttled away from me suggests she's terrified of our little deal.

As she should be.

Grabbing Dmitri by the shoulder, I guide him down the hall. "Change of plans."

His stride matches mine effortlessly. "What's the problem?"

"The ceremony needs to be rigged."

He stops short. "That's…"

"Against my rules. Yeah, I fucking know." And I hate myself for doing it. "I need Tara Reed to be the Butterfly."

Dmitri's dark brow furrows. "You're not serious."

"It's important." My word is gold, and we made a deal. Tara's right. My pockets are nowhere near as deep as Brisbane Realty and they've bought up so much property already, I'll be damned if I lose this building to them.

The fuck are they going to do with it, anyway? Level it?

Jesus, what the hell am *I* going to do with it?

That's a problem for another day, I remind myself.

"Do I even want to know what you did in the past…" Dmitri glances at his watch, then back to me. "Two fucking hours that's turned you into a cheat?"

Getting called out by my best friend cuts deep.

"Tara Reed works for Brisbane Realty, and she

tried to go after something I want." It sounds pathetically childish even to my own ears. But my reasons for wanting that building are no one else's business. "There's got to be a way to manipulate this." Because I don't want to cheat.

My entire life, I've hustled, swindled, and done things most men wouldn't want to do. I didn't climb the ladder of success. I scraped, clawed, and fought my way to get where I am now.

Tara Reed just knocked me down a few notches, but it's nothing I can't come back from.

My integrity, however, says otherwise.

"Fuck." I pinch the bridge of my nose and drop into my chair while Dmitri shuts my office door. "I need to figure this out. I can't lose what I've built by cheating her way to a win."

"Maybe we can put a twist on it? Let the bidders go in blind so they don't see which woman they're bidding on. Then make it her at the reveal?"

"That's not a bad idea." But it won't sit well with my clients. Many of them bid on their own wives and girlfriends. They want their woman trained by my Doms in specific ways, so their new fuck toys turn into upgrades for them to play with after their month as our Butterfly is up.

As far as I can tell, Tara's not with anyone at the club. No one will specifically be there for her. She's also stunning and fucking ballsy. Maybe I can work all that to my advantage.

"Once she wins, however that happens, I need to make sure she pays for putting me in this position."

I want revenge.

Dmitri leans against the door and doesn't look happy. "How far you want me to go with her?"

Because we both know even he has his hard limits, as do I. We also both know that D is the top Dom in the club. Women would happily give their soul for a night at his mercy.

My god, I'm becoming a monster. And for what, some crumbling brick and mortar? "We'll have to see."

Imagining her under Dmitri's care shoots fiery ice through my veins. Not that I'll ever admit it.

If she chooses Dmitri, which most Butterflies do, we'll have to come up with a plan that meets both our requirements. He's not one to hurt a woman, and neither am I, but part of me wants to teach her a fucking lesson about… what was it she said? Oh yeah, never biting the hand that fingers her.

God. Damn.

She punched my pride tonight. I'd love a chance to return the favor.

…

"Good evening, Mr. Hudson."
"Good evening, Mr. Hudson."
"Good evening, Sir."

I'm too wound up to respond to any of my staff and all but storm through the growing crowd gathering in the club. Dmitri and I stayed up late last night devising a plan that will hopefully work. Time to put it into action.

I shoulder my way through the private doors to the suite where all the Butterfly competitors are getting ready. Tara's sitting between two women who are younger than her.

Perfect.

"How are you this evening, Stella?" I bend low and kiss the cheek of the twenty-four-year-old to the right of Tara. She's built to fuck, and her cuckold husband pays a lot of money to make that happen.

"I'm so nervous," she says, smiling. "I hope I win."

"Look how stunning you are." I practically purr against her ear. "The bidders would be insane to not pay top dollar to have you spoiled."

Tara's cheeks blaze red, but she doesn't say a word. Keeping my cool, I move onto the woman sitting on Tara's left. "Deseri, if you were my Butterfly, I'd spend hours with you on my tongue so I could gorge on your sweetness." I drag my thumb down her mouth, smearing her lipstick. "Keep it like this. The men will go feral for it." With a wink, I add, "As will Dmitri."

Her eyes darken with lust.

Giving them hope they might win weighs my heart down with guilt, but what I'm saying isn't a lie. There is an excellent possibility that either of them could win, just like any other woman here.

Because I'm not cheating tonight. Fuck that.

Nowhere in our verbal deal was it stated that Tara had to be *this* month's Butterfly. For all I care, she can compete every year until she finally wins or gives up and goes home. I'll be damned if I let my honor, or the integrity of my club, get smudged because little miss mouthy wants to play hardball with me.

I finally turn my attention to the woman who's gone from my little obsession to the bane of my existence. "How are you this evening, Tara?"

She may have to win this on her own, but that doesn't mean I can't nudge her in the right direction.

Just like I gave Stella a boost of confidence, and Deseri a tip to appease the bidder's desires, I'll give Tara a secret weapon too.

Dragging my gaze down her back, disdain drips from my voice when I say, "Your dress is a bold choice."

She stalls with her lipstick poised just in front of her mouth. "What's wrong with what I'm wearing?"

"Blue doesn't necessarily say fuckable. It's giving…" My gaze narrows and I frown with disapproval. "Frozen ice queen vibes."

She scoffs. "This is Dior."

"And that's Gucci," I say, pointing at the woman over by the three-way mirror. "That's Versace." I jab my finger at Deseri. "And that's…" I pause and contemplate what this other girl is wearing. "Jessie, what is that?"

"Balenciaga," she says, twirling for me. "Do you like it?"

"*Love* it," I purr appreciatively. Backing away from Tara, as if she's old news, I kiss Jessie's hand and parade her around the room. "You look like a goddess that every man and woman should fall on their knees for and worship."

Out of the corner of my eye, I see Tara throw her lipstick on the vanity.

Awww. That was too easy.

Making my way back to her, I stuff my hands in my pockets. "My clients like to make bold statements on behalf of their women, Tara. And going off these outfits, I think you can see they all have very, *very* deep pockets."

Not to mention the club fee is a cool two-hundred thousand a year, per guest, but Tara would have known that already since she forked that amount over herself to be here.

"Your competitors also have the advantage of bringing someone who is eager to throw money at this." I tilt my head and purse my lips. "Is anyone here for you tonight, *Miss* Reed?"

Her cheeks blaze red, and guilt wraps its hand around my throat.

Time to leave.

"I wish all of you good luck tonight." I step back from Tara again, but not before hearing her mumble something under her breath that's sounds an awful lot like, *"I'll show you bold, asshole."*

Taking my leave, I close the doors, knowing I've just set up the craziest game of mind fuckery of my life, and am left with one question.

How bad does Tara Reed really want to be the Butterfly?

Chapter 4

Tara

Mr. Hudson thinks he can play games with me? Fine. Let's play.

"Five minutes, ladies," a tall, dark, and insanely hot man says from the door. I'm still learning all the names of staff, but I'm pretty sure he's Dmitri.

The guy looks like he'd tear a woman in two and she'd beg him for a repeat.

"I hope I win just so I can climb that mountain," Deseri says wistfully. "My husband's tried to talk him into a ride between my thighs for two years and no amount of money or bribes have worked."

Smart. It ensures the highest bidding price during the ceremony. I wonder who came up with the no fucking the staff rules. Probably untouchable, unfuckable Ryker Hudson.

His reputation is part of what lured me here.

It's also what will make me win this competition.

I've studied the Monarch for months. Mr. Hudson runs the tightest ship I've ever seen. I can't get into half the rooms in the club without meeting certain requirements, and the clientele is top-notch executives, celebrities, and international entrepreneurs. And not a single person here makes a move without Ryker Hudson watching.

He's cultivated a lifestyle within the Monarch, and also a non-negotiable behavior strategy. Every member would bark like a dog if he commanded it. Hell, they'd piss on their own feet if Dmitri or any of the other Doms told them to I bet. Anything to get their approval. Whatever it takes to gain their affection and interest.

And I'm no better, it seems.

I can't help it. The Monarch is alluring and addictive. I'm forever on my best behavior just so I can get a little deeper down the rabbit hole. I can't imagine what it takes to run a sex club of this caliber, but I do know that requires a lot of time, money, and energy.

Compassion and ruthlessness too.

That's a heady combo—compassion and ruthlessness. I've spent many nights getting off to the image I've painted of the Club King himself. Ryker Motherfucking Hudson. Until last night, I thought my fantasy was pretty damn good. Then I met the real thing and Ryker doused imagination with a dark, delicious reality.

I'll stop at nothing to win tonight.

Stella leans forward and runs her middle finger along her bottom lip, dabbing on gloss. "I don't care how many times I have to try, I'll put myself on display for every member of this club knowing Mr. Hudson and his men are looking at me, too."

"Same, girl. I swear Mr. Hudson has the best fuck me eyes," Deseri says.

"I've orgasmed just fantasizing about him watching me on the cameras," chimes Jessie. "God, that man has the perfect mouth. I want to ride it. *Badly.*"

Deseri fans herself. "I heard his dick's massive."

"Can't be bigger than Dmitri's," Stella says. "I saw a leaked picture of it once. It's incredible."

"Wait." I hold my hand up. "You mean no other Butterfly has verified it before?" Surely these women have talked about what it's like to be the Butterfly afterwards, right?

"No way," Jessie says, her tits jiggling when she scoots up in her chair. "You sign an NDA and only get to win once. Most of the old Butterflies leave after they've become one."

Stella lifts her tits higher in the built-in cups of her dress. "Yeah, because all other dick is ruined for them after they have Dmitri's."

"Or Vault's," Jessie sighs. "I heard he fucks like a machine."

"I heard he even *uses* a machine," says someone else. "That's who I'm picking if I win."

A machine? I'm realizing that I know even less about this place than I thought. It only sparks my curiosity and lust hotter.

"I want all of them, if I win," Deseri announces.

"All of them?" Stella gawks. "You'd *die*!"

Deseri shrugs. "I'm cool with that."

I can't believe this is the conversation we're having. They're talking about these men like they're cars to take for a joy ride, not people. Is everyone here desperate for their dicks?

A part of me grows furious about it. These men are people, not toys to play with. They're humans. And maybe they're okay with being objectified and desired, but maybe they aren't, and that's the real reason they remain untouchable until the Butterfly ceremony. Maybe it's not to make them more desirable, but because it makes them less used.

I don't know how I feel about this anymore.

Stop overthinking it. They're grown men. They chose to be in this club, just like me. Nothing happens here without the full consent of all parties involved.

I can't imagine Ryker or Dmitri ever letting someone do something they weren't okay with.

No, Ryker Hudson makes his men hard to get so he can drive the price up when the time comes. It's simple economics. Supply and demand.

He's fucking brilliant.

God, that makes him even hotter.

"Has anyone ever been with Mr. Hudson?" Damn my mouth for opening.

"Not ever," Jessie groans.

"He's too good for us," a woman by the bathroom says. "I heard he used to be an escort. Maybe he's got a disease."

Someone throws a shoe at her. "You better shut your mouth. They can hear us, you know."

"And see us." Stella points at the camera in the corner by the door.

My cheeks blaze with heat. We're all on the meat market acting like we can't get good dick elsewhere, and putting on a show for a bunch of men who would pay us for the pleasure, regardless.

Still, my motives for wanting to be the Butterfly have nothing to do with good dick.

But my interest in Ryker Hudson has just reached a new level. If no one's had him before, why did he act like I could if I won?

Wait. Did he act like that, or did I make it up in one of my many fantasies I had last night while masturbating to the visual of that man's hand around my throat?

The door opens again and Dmitri, dressed in a black tux, announces, "It's time, ladies. Follow me."

All the women hurry to line up at the door and leave, squealing and laughing with excitement.

This is so weird and fucked up.

Dmitri holds the door and glowers at me. "You coming, Tara?"

"Give me a minute?"

He frowns. "One minute, sugar. Then you lose the opportunity."

Nodding, I watch him close the door and hurry to get my head in the game. At no point, since I made that deal with Ryker Hudson last night, did I think he'd rig this competition. If he had, I would have been disappointed because this club's reputation hinges on its owner's fealty and honor.

It's why I chose it.

It's also why I'll pick Mr. Hudson to be my Dom when I win.

So, if that man wants bold, I'll give it to him.

…

Ryker

As the women practically flutter down the hall, I notice I'm one short. No way. Did Tara back out?

Instead of relief, disappointment shoves into my chest. Christ, what's that say about me?

Dmitri shakes his head, whispering, "Tara asked for one more minute."

I'm sure it killed him to give it to her because it's against his rules. Excitement floods my veins knowing she's probably up to something. Again, I have no idea what this says about me. "Think she bought the bait?"

"No clue."

We split off once we're in the main room and I head to the stage used for larger exhibition scenes, while Dmitri and my other men take up their posts around the perimeter of the room.

Men and women murmur in their seats. The excitement is tangible. I wish I could bottle and sell it.

My hands grow clammy as I take the microphone and walk across to center stage. The entire club settles into silence, all my members waiting with bated breath for the ceremony to start. It's times like this I question how morally grey I really am.

I'm about to usher eleven women onto this stage, parade them around, and start bids as if they're cattle at the farmer's fair.

At least they volunteered.

And if I catch wind that any are here against their will, I'll blacklist their partner, beat the fuck out of them, and put the woman in touch with a counselor. Because if she was coerced into selling her body, God only knows what else she's been pressured into doing outside my club.

"Good evening, ladies and gentlemen." I stroll across the stage, the spotlights making me break out in a fucking sweat. "Before we begin tonight, I want to thank all of you, especially our potential Butterflies, for allowing the Monarch the honor of entertaining you."

A round of applause roars throughout the room.

"As you know, we anonymously donate every dime spent on these auctions to a charity of my choosing. This year's funds will go to Safe Access, an organization that helps women and children out of abusive homes."

Another round of applause ensues.

As part of the bidding process, they've each signed an NDA that's separate from their membership one, agreeing that what happens tonight, like all other nights, stays here, and the announced charity foundation also remains a secret.

I worry that if some of these charities know where the money is coming from, they'll deny my check.

After going over the rules and procedures, I give the signal and the lights dim, making only one shine on my stage. "May I introduce the first stunning creature of the evening. Stella."

The crowd hushes as she saunters on stage, looking like she lives for the attention and knows how to keep it. She spins in a slow circle, showing off her snatched waist and ample tits. Stella works the stage like she's in the running to win a beauty pageant.

No matter who wins or loses tonight, each of these women gets a bolster of confidence being up on this stage, and I love that for them.

Time to make some motherfucking money.

"The bidding starts at one-hundred thousand dollars."

Several paddles fly up.

"Two hundred thousand."

A few paddles fall.

This goes on until Stella has racked up a hefty price. "The Butterfly Bid ends at six-hundred-and-ninety-seven thousand dollars. Well done, gorgeous." I kiss her hand and watch her saunter off the stage. I hope she's proud of the money she just raised for charity and isn't pouting in the corner, hoping her competition trips and knocks their teeth out.

Next, I invite Jessie to the stage. Then another woman, and another, and another. Finally, I only have one left.

Tara's at the edge of the stage, but I can't see her all that well with this damn spotlight blinding me.

But I'd be a liar to say I hate being on stage where I'll showcase her like a blue-ribbon pig. Especially since I see she didn't take my bait and change her fucking dress to one of the available gowns hanging in the dressing room. Blue isn't going to win. Men like red. Black. White.

I tried to help her. Oh well.

"Our last in the net is Tara."

The room stills, and my breath catches as she walks onto the stage. She's stunning. I might have given her shit for wearing a light blue gown, but it's the perfect shade for her. Her hair cascades down her back, the layers playfully curling in different directions.

Her eyes are bright and bluer than her gown. Her lips glisten with light pink gloss. Her cheeks are rosy, not from blush but from nerves.

She's an angel standing in a den of devils.

And I've suddenly turned into the most devious one of all. My dick hardens, making my tuxedo too stuffy and tight. Desperate for composure, I turn my attention to the audience and work hard to ignore Tara as she sashays across the stage in a circle, giving everyone a good look at what's up for bid.

"We'll start the bid at..." I gulp, my throat suddenly dryer than the Sahara.

"Five-hundred thousand dollars," Tara says, leaning into my microphone.

Then she yanks the straps of her dress, severing them, and the whole thing pools by her feet, leaving her bare, decadent, lush body on display for everyone to see.

A collective gasp ripples through the room as I stand there, stunned for the second time in twenty-four hours.

Paddles raise into the air. The price for her goes up, up, up even though I can't drag my gaze off her to look at the crowd.

"Bold enough for you?" she mutters behind clenched teeth as she keeps her gaze locked on the men bidding for her.

Well played, princess. I cock my brow and flick my gaze back to the crowd. "One million," I call out. "Do I have one million dollars?"

More paddles go up, and something in me claws out of my chest that feels a lot like possessiveness. I'm no longer the man with everything. I'm the bastard who's about to lose a toy I've yet to pull out of the package.

When the price for Tara escalates to two million dollars, a vicious, old demon crawls out of my good senses and takes charge of my actions.

"Two million, one-hundred thousand."

The last bidder puts down his paddle.

It infuriates me.

Tara is perfection and if they can't spare her one more hundred grand, then fuck him. Fuck them all.

"Two million, two hundred thousand," someone says, shaking me to my core.

That someone…

Is me.

Chapter 5

Tara

"How *dare* you." Stella storms over and slaps me across the face. "You fucking *cheated*!"

"Dmitri, please remove Stella from the property." Mr. Hudson casually strides over to us with his head down. None of the contestants have made it past the foyer of the club, and I'm still naked, clutching my dress to my chest to hide myself from all the dagger eyes aimed at me.

"What? No!" Stella back tracks as Dmitri closes in on her. "You can't kick me out."

"We have a strict no violence policy here, Stella." Mr. Hudson's back hides her completely from my view as he shields me. The elation of becoming the Butterfly has already morphed into fear and guilt. Stella and the others might be upset that I won, but that's the way it goes. And as far as I know, there's nothing that says you can't go up there naked. Instead of playing on the mystery of what's under my gown, I showed them exactly what I'm built with.

If that's cheating. Oh well. I'd do it again in a heartbeat.

Sex clubs are the same as any other business. You're either a lion or a mouse.

I'm not a fucking mouse.

Besides, it's not like the members were bidding

to fuck me. They were donating to a charity and gifting me the chance at a few nights of fun with someone else.

I hardly see why my winning is such a problem. Swiftly stepping back into my dress, I safety pin together the straps I'd cut on purpose for my bold move on stage.

Mr. Hudson shoves his hands in his pockets and remains fixed on Stella. "Had anyone laid a violent hand on you, without your consent, they would suffer the same consequences you are right now. Get the fuck out of my club."

Stella argues and screams and cries as Dmitri escorts her to the door. "My husband will not stand for this bullshit, Ryker. Fuck you!"

There's tension in Mr. Hudson's shoulders when she calls him by his first name. That's a major rule here—He's Mr. Hudson or Sir. Not even his friends call him Ryker that I know of.

The door shuts, cutting off Stella's screeches as Dmitri escorts her off the property. The rest of the room plummets into icy silence.

"The Butterfly's boldness will cost her," Mr. Hudson says to the other women. His dark gaze cuts to me and I almost shrink back. "Thank you for putting yourselves on display tonight, ladies. The money you raised is tremendous and will make a great impact on others less fortunate than yourselves."

No one says a nasty word. In fact, their attitudes lighten.

Then they all start purring and flirting, smiling and melting. "Of course, Mr. Hudson. It's a privilege to be a contestant at all."

"I'll happily try again in six months. This was so fun."

"What a wonderful cause. Tonight was great, Mr. Hudson, thank you so much."

I'm sure no one else wants to risk Stella's fate, but the ass kissing is giving me second-hand embarrassment for them.

Deseri sidesteps Mr. Hudson and comes straight at me. "Congratulations, girl." She gives me a hug that's about as fake as her eyelashes and tits. "Enjoy being the Butterfly."

"Yeah," says Jessie with a pouty lip. "Guess it's good you can't compete again, so maybe I'll have my shot next time."

"That's a good girl," Mr. Hudson says, tipping Jessie's chin up. "How about you and the others enjoy the penthouse tonight? My treat. I'll send some of my staff to spoil you."

That seems to appease her. "Thank you, Mr. Hudson."

Well, now I want to know what the hell's in the penthouse.

"Butterfly." He turns and holds out his arm for me to take. "Allow to me escort you to your new quarters."

After a shaky exhale, I loop my arm in his and we leave. He doesn't say a word to me. Not when we cross the club. Not when we're in the elevator. Not when we arrive at the Butterfly Suite.

But the instant the door shuts, he yanks off his bow tie and starts pacing. "You're going to cost me a lot of fucking money, Miss Reed."

Two million-two-hundred thousand dollars, to be exact.

I'm floored he bid on me, honestly. If he's never bid on a Butterfly before, it makes me feel special that I was the one he had to have. "I didn't expect you to—"

"Shut your fucking mouth and let me think." He fists his hair, ruining its perfect style. Just before I can snap back, there's a knock on the door. "Damnit." He rushes over and swings it open. "Get in here. Fast."

While I'm still trying to understand why Mr. Hudson's making such a big deal about this, a line of men file into the room. Panic takes hold because although they're all spectacular and here for me to choose from, none look happy about it.

My pussy dries up on the spot.

Victory only feels good when it's rightfully earned. Shame assaults me. I should have never made that deal with Mr. Hudson.

And now I can't back out of it.

Dmitri storms into the room last, taking his place at the end of the line. Seven men and two women stare at me, waiting for me to make a choice.

"As the Butterfly," Mr. Hudson says, "the master, or masters, you choose will be who you obey for the entire month. You must live in this suite, and we'll have all your personal effects brought here for the duration of your stay."

Wait. Whoa. A *month*? I didn't realize it was that long. And to admit how little I truly knew about being the Butterfly would only make me look like a fool now. "What about work?"

Mr. Hudson's sinful mouth curls into a wry smile. "Surely you knew the conditions of being the Butterfly before you went through all the effort to become one?"

Shit. Shit. SHIT.

I didn't realize I'd be a prisoner in the club. I thought the Butterfly had free rein in all rooms of the club at her leisure. But if I can't get to work tomorrow, I'm royally fucked. I may have evaded my stepfather today, but that won't fly a second time.

How am I going to get out of the hole I've just dug myself into? Fuck.

"Make your selection, Butterfly."

He never answered my question about work.

"Quickly, Miss Reed, we have a club to run."

"I…" Glancing at the lineup of Doms, my mouth runs dry. I'm in over my head, which is absolutely my worst toxic trait. I always get myself into situations I later wish I hadn't. But if I'm honest, there is only one man in this room that makes my regrets tolerable.

"You." I turn and face him. "I choose *you*, Mr. Hudson."

He won't even look at me. "I'm not in the line."

Confusion rattles my voice. "But… you bid on me."

"It's a charity, Miss Reed. Every man out there bid tonight, and none of them are in this room. It's not the winner who chooses who the Butterfly gets as a Dom. She decides for herself, which is a privilege, I might add, that was paid for by the bidder. Now choose from the Doms presented, Butterfly, I have work to do."

I'm not budging on this. "I chose already. I want *you* as my Dom." When he opens his sexy mouth to argue with me again, I get in his face. "You're a Dom, too, *Sir*. And *you're* in this room. *You* paid for me to win and for the privilege of picking who I want. If it's the Butterfly's choice, then you have my final answer."

Someone snorts from the other side of the room. Dmitri ducks his head, so I assume it was him.

The one named Vault gets this lopsided grin on his face next to him.

Two more are giving each other *Oh shit* smirks.

Dmitri clears his throat. "According to club rules, any Dom in the room is available." His mischievous gaze flicks at Mr. Hudson. "You've just never been in the room while she's chosen before, *Sir*."

Someone else fights back a small laugh and it looks like Mr. Hudson wants to beat them all to a pulp. His face turns red and the veins in his temples stick out.

"You've made your choice then," he says in a growl. "Everyone, get back to work."

Dmitri is the last one out the door. Just before he closes it, he flashes a smile in our direction and mumbles, "Have fun, you two."

The door closes and we're plunged into an airless, soundless space that seems to have become an anti-gravity chamber because I swear, I'm floating.

"You didn't have to bid," I whisper like a little mouse.

"And you didn't have to get naked."

"You said to be bold."

His jaw clenches. We stare at each other and the urge to kiss him is strong. But I can't. I won't. Not until I know he won't strangle me for putting him in this position.

My heart thuds in my tightening throat. "Is being my Dom so awful?"

He doesn't answer.

Now I'm pissed. "You didn't have to stay in the

room." I toss my hands in the air. "You could have let Dmitri or someone else escort me here while you went back to ruling over your club. No one forced you to stay."

I don't believe for once second that he doesn't remember what his own motherfucking club rules are. He stayed on purpose, whether he'll admit it or not.

We glare at each other for a long time.

I'm not scared of him. I think Mr. Hudson is all bark, no bite, and if I'm wrong, I don't think I'll mind letting him sink his teeth into me.

"Why did you do this?" He seethes. "You've set me up and I want to know why."

I've done no such thing. "I only wanted to be Butterfly. Last night I saw an opportunity, and I took it."

"An opportunity to tear down what I've built." He slowly prowls over to me.

"I'm not here for your club. I'm only here to learn about myself."

"You don't need to be the Butterfly to do that, Miss Reed." He's dangerously close to me now. "Why couldn't you have just walked away from that building?"

"For reasons that no longer matter since we made this deal."

His eyes darken. "Until you tell me the truth, I will not make this a pleasant experience for you, Tara."

My heart skitters to a stop. Keeping my expression impassive and voice calm, I tip my chin up and deadpan him. "I told you the truth."

He'd never hurt me. It's against his rules. I'm also certain it's against his nature. He's just lashing out because he's mad I got the best of him.

Mr. Hudson holds my gaze for a long time, then he exhales in a half-growl and steps away from me. "I'll have a driver take you back to your house. You'll have fifteen minutes to pack your things. You will not have access to your cell phone during your stay here."

The club has a strict no cell rule, but how the hell is that supposed to work if I'm here for a month?

Ryker pulls out an envelope from the breast pocket of his tux. "This is an NDA you *must* sign before you leave this suite. Take your time going over it. If you chose to not sign it, the woman who came in second during the ceremony will become the new Butterfly. Since you won this time, you cannot be in the ceremony ever again, which means this is your one and only chance."

He heads to the door while I'm left holding the NDA in my clammy hand.

I feel like he hates me. And maybe he has a right to, considering I put him on the line and made him bend his morals to put me in this position. I live in a dog-eat-dog world, and part of me assumed he did too.

No one knows anything about Ryker Hudson other than he started an elite sex club and has become extremely wealthy from it. But no one in the sex business is an overnight success.

Unless you're the Butterfly.

I can't help but want to scratch at this man's hard exterior to see how the self-made millionaire has done so well, so fast. I'm guessing he's about the same age as me and even with my family's name, I don't have his prestige.

Then again, I'm a woman. We always have to

work harder to get less.

When he reaches the door, I suddenly feel awful for things that shouldn't matter. "I'm sorry," I say. "I should have never exploited your weakness for my gain."

Mr. Hudson halts mid exit. Then he looks over his shoulder. "I have no weakness, Miss Reed. The only thing you've exploited is yourself with that stunt you just pulled."

"I only wanted to be the Butterfly." The rest of my confession dies on my tongue when he faces me again.

"So does every other woman in here, Tara. You had no right to demand special treatment."

"And you had every opportunity to refuse me." If he thinks he can make me feel shitty for what I've done, he doesn't know who he's dealing with. I'm kicked down daily by my family and peers and especially myself. Mr. Hudson will have to sharpen his tongue if he ever wants to cut me. "You also didn't have to bid on me."

I'd already won without him doing that and we both know it.

Ryker's jaw clenches and I swear he's going to crack his molars with how hard he's chomping down on them. Without saying another word, he wrenches the door open and slams it shut behind him.

Chapter 6

Ryker

What have I done?

Being impulsive is not okay. Losing my cool is dangerous. Becoming a Butterfly's Dom is strictly forbidden.

Even if it's not in the club's rule book.

"You're all fucking fired," I announce, entering my office. My men stand in a semi-circle, waiting for me like it's a goddamn intervention.

"Whatever, Ryker," Vault says. "You'd be fucked without us."

I'm fucked no matter what.

Dropping onto the couch, I scrub my face with both hands and groan. "This is a disaster."

"Not necessarily." Dmitri sits next to me and squeezes my shoulder. "This might be what you need, man."

What I need is to get these assholes away from me, soothe the busted egos of all my members, and give Tara a spanking severe enough that she can't sit for a week. "Vault, Bull, can you make sure the penthouse guests are completely satisfied? And I do mean *completely*."

"No problem," Bull says as he leaves with Vault.

I can only imagine the tricks they'll pull tonight to make Jessie and her party happy. No bump in pay would likely be big enough to make it worth it for Bull and Vault either. *Fuck my life.* "She's cost me too much, and it's only been ten minutes."

I don't know what came over me on that stage. I pushed this woman to be bold, and she delivered. Then I lost my composure and wanted to…

Wanted to what?

My answer makes my skin crawl.

I've just paid for sex. Took my power and aimed it at her. I don't even know this woman and here I am, offering two-point-two million like its chump change, have accepted to be her Dom, and kicked out one of my best member's wives from my club, all in one evening.

"I've lost my damn mind."

Dmitri's cocky smile vanishes. "What made you bid on her?"

I've never bid on a Butterfly before. Part of my reputation stems from the fact that I'm unavailable and untouchable. Why does it feel like everything I've built over the past five years is about to crumble like a house of cards?

"I have no fucking clue." My chest hurts. It's hard to breathe.

"Relax," Dmitri says. "I'm sure we can fix all this."

"I'm gonna need you to shut your fucking face." I stand up and start pacing. "You made it so much worse pointing out that she could pick any Dom in the room."

"I'm just adhering to the rules, boss." I don't appreciate the amusement in his tone.

Someone else clears their throat. Another shuffles their feet.

I feel like the butt end of a joke, and my anger comes to a rolling boil. "Everyone *out*!"

They leave without being told twice. Except for Dmitri. Stretching his massive arms across the back of the couch, he makes it clear he's not going anywhere yet. "You pay me to keep my eyes on everyone in the club."

I keep pacing.

"As part of my job, I also keep my eyes on *you*."

I flick my gaze to him, then drop it back to the floor while I act like a caged tiger.

"The look on your face when you saw her spoke volumes, Ryker."

"My expression was the same for every woman who came on the stage."

"I'm not talking about the stage. I'm talking about when you're in your office watching her from the security cameras. I'm talking about when you were in the changing room where they were doing hair and makeup."

I stop short. Dmitri was watching us? It shouldn't surprise me. "I didn't look at her any differently than I do the others."

"Yes, you fucking did." He stands up and storms over to me, jabbing me in the chest with his finger. "You always have the same expression, Ryker. All business, all flirt, all bullshit. But with Tara?" He huffs a laugh and I want to punch him. "You looked at her like she was yours to play with."

"Because I *was* playing with her." Dmitri knew the plan. I was to go into the dressing room and make her jealous, make her feel insecure amidst her competition so she'd either walk out and forfeit her chance to be the Butterfly, or be bold enough to do something that would ultimately win her the title on her own. He and I worked all night on that strategy, damnit. "That was the plan!"

"The plan was to make her feel some kind of way." He licks his lips and that smirk of his comes back. "Instead, it was you who felt something, Ryker. I saw it."

"You don't know what you're talking about."

"I'm your oldest friend. I know you better than anyone else here."

"That doesn't mean shit."

"You want her," he presses. "And so does the rest of the club."

I know.

"You didn't have to bid on her. She'd already won, man."

I know.

"Swooping in at the last minute and upping the bid wasn't necessary for her to become the Butterfly. It was only necessary for you to assert dominance."

He's right and I hate that he knows me this well. "Fuck."

"You also did it because the thought of someone else not paying her worth wasn't something you would tolerate."

Double fuck.

"You bid on her because you've seen the way others drool over her at this club and you weren't going to let that shit stain, Blake Rittenhouse, have the bragging rights—and ultimately the power—over Tara when her month as Butterfly is over if he was the highest bidder."

Triple fuck.

Dmitri is slinging truths, and each one feels like

a whip across my chest.

Tara's drawn the attention of every member in the club. They'll want to either fuck her, be her, or break her.

"We all know you stayed in that room because you wanted her, Ry."

"So?" Maybe, on some level, that's true. But I can't afford to indulge in what I want. This is a business. *My* business. "I've wanted plenty of members before. She's hardly the first."

Dmitri's brow arches. "When you escorted Tara into the room for her to choose her Dom, we all felt the possessiveness roll off you."

Doubtful.

"You could have left immediately, like you always do." Dmitri shrugs nonchalantly. "You could have told me to shut up when I reminded you of the rules."

But I didn't.

"You've been really tense lately, Ryker. I haven't wanted to pry, but maybe..." He pauses and sighs. "Maybe this woman will help you blow a little steam off, yeah?"

If I blow any steam off on Tara, I'll likely break her.

"Look at it this way," he says. "The next Butterfly Ceremony will be the best one yet, now that everyone thinks you're on the roster as a Dom."

It's the one thing I never wanted to have happen. "God damnit."

"Don't worry, we'll use it to our advantage."

The hell we will. "I'm not—"

"We'll take care of it," he says, cutting me off. Probably because he knows where my head went.

"Trust me, okay? I got your back. Now if you don't mind, I've got a club to run, and you've got a Butterfly to play with."

Chapter 7

Tara

After signing the NDA and going home to pack my things, I left my cell phone as instructed. There's something freeing that comes with leaving that ball and chain behind, even though I'll have to use some other method to conduct my meetings. Look, I can't just drop off the planet for a month, and it's frustrating that I didn't know about that part of the deal beforehand. I could have made arrangements ahead of time, if I'd known.

I should have researched more about what it means to be the Butterfly, damnit. What else don't I know about this deal?

I've only been a member of the Monarch for three months. That ceremony was the first one I've seen in action. I knew the winner got to pick her Dom or Domme, or multiple, and is given the time of her life, which was all I needed to hear to want it for myself. Come on, a night of debauchery—let alone an entire month—where I'm fucked in ways better than the missionary position? Yes, please and thank you. No way would I willingly give up on this privilege until I won.

I need this. Fucking *hell*, do I need this.

My life is one big hustle. The stress of my job, my family's constant degrading, and the assholes who run in my social circles always picking at me nearly had me at a breaking point last year. The more they pushed, the harder I fought to hold my ground.

I've turned into a cold-hearted killer in the conference room, and an ice queen in the bedroom.

I hate it. I hate myself. I hate that I can't see a way out. I hate why I started and how I can't stop.

Hell, I'm not even sure why I grind so hard every day anymore. Is it out of love or spite?

I need a break. A time out. An escape.

It's not all about hot sex and thrills at the Monarch. It's about submitting to someone safe, knowing I have the power, and freedom, to explode if I need to. Ryker's club is renowned for being a safe space, and the Dominants here are top tier.

Or so I hope.

All the entertainers are gorgeous, and the men who stay so close to him are all absolute thirst traps, but Ryker Hudson is in a league of his own.

And he's mine for a month.

I think we can teach each other a lot.

As a private car pulls up to the front steps, I take a minute to appreciate the position I'm in. This isn't going to be easy. I have no clue how I'm going to handle this man. It's clear he detests me, and I don't blame him, but I'm still going through with this. And as I'm escorted inside, up the elevator, and to my private suite, I see Mr. Hudson is still going through with this too, considering he's sitting on my couch with a scowl.

Does the man ever genuinely smile?

"Have a good evening, Butterfly." The driver places my two suitcases just inside the door instead of taking them into my new suite. Dipping his head at

Mr. Hudson, he leaves, and I'm left alone in the dimly lit suite with my new Dom.

After a long pause, Mr. Hudson stands, smooths out his tuxedo jacket, and stuffs his hands in his pockets. "From this point forward, you will call me Sir. *Only* Sir." He slowly makes his way over to me. "Strip."

Keeping my gaze locked on his, I take off the gown I'm still wearing by simply unfastening the safety pins used to hold the straps together. Just like on the stage, it falls to my feet in a glittery pale blue puddle, leaving me bare for his pleasure.

Sir walks slow circles around me like a wolf observing its meal. "We will use a light system. Green for good. Yellow for borderline. Red for stop."

My heart rate kicks up, and a chill skates down my bare flesh.

"Trust and honesty are the most important things between a Dom and his sub. I will not lie to you. And I have to trust that what you're saying is truth, especially with the light system, just like you will have to trust me to know how to bring you…" He stops in front of me and wraps his hand around my throat before leaning in until our mouths almost brush. "Exquisite release through pleasure." His hot breath warms my lips. "And pain."

I swallow hard.

"Your file didn't give me much to go on, Butterfly. You like both praise and humiliation?"

My heart thuds. "Yes."

"What are your hard limits?"

"I don't know of any," I say carefully.

He cocks his brow at me.

"Sir," I tack on quickly.

"Then we'll find them together." He runs the tip of his nose along my cheek until his breath tickles my ear. "Do you enjoy my hands on you like this, Butterfly?"

"Yes, Sir."

"Do you understand I am your master for the next thirty days?"

Quick math tells me that's a week beyond when the building goes up for auction. There's a strange satisfaction knowing I'll still be reaping the benefits of my deal, even after he's gotten his end of the bargain.

I also know that all because I said I'd make sure Brisbane Realty didn't bid on the property doesn't mean another company won't outbid him at auction. Mr. Hudson could still lose the property, but I've already secured my reward. "Yes, Sir."

"Get on your knees."

My legs buckle and I not so gracefully descend like a good girl.

"Stick out your tongue."

I obey, feeling equal parts turned on and humiliated. He's got me on the ground like a dog, and I swear, if he asks me to give him a paw, I'm going to punch him in the dick.

Or suck him off.

Christ, this is confusing.

I can't tell if I like it or not. But when he shoves his thumb into my mouth, I decide it isn't so bad.

Until he tries to gag me with it.

"Suck." He presses down on the back of my tongue, and my gag reflex kicks in.

"Relax your tongue." His lips curl into a cocky smirk. "And *suck*."

I know how to give head. This is harder. The

pressure is different, and my eyes keep watering. Squeezing them shut, a tear slips free as I wrap my lips around his thumb and draw it in till my cheeks hollow.

"Good girl. Open." I obey, and he replaces his thumb with three big fingers instead. My lips wrap around them, and he snaps his fingers by my face. "I didn't say close your mouth, Butterfly."

More tears prick my eyes, but I keep my gaze locked on him and open my damn mouth again. He shoves his fingers down my throat and I gag hard and ugly.

"Breathe through your nose," he growls, unyielding. With his fingers in my mouth like this, I can't get my throat to stop convulsing. Saliva builds up, and I choke on it. He pulls out and wipes his fingers on his pants, then walks away from me. "We'll work on that."

Jerk.

I'm stuck between wanting to throw something at him for humiliating me just now and begging him to do it again.

"You will stay on your knees until I return, Butterfly." He shuts the door and leaves.

With. My. Belongings.

Chapter 8

Ryker

After carrying Tara's suitcases into my office for safekeeping, I quickly pull up the suite cameras, expecting to find her walking around, likely cussing me out for my behavior. Imagine my surprise when I see she's right where I left her.

"Good girl."

Her obedience won't last. It's early. She'll get up soon, I'm sure of it.

I'm good at reading people, finding little cues that let me into their deeper desires. Trained in the art of sex, I'm a master at working a body over until it's puddy in my hands. She'll break sooner rather than later. Especially with me as her Dom.

Pulling my cell out, I hit the security system app and expand the video feed so I can leave the office and carry on with my evening while monitoring her.

Tonight is all about damage control.

Tara fucked shit up for me and I've made it so much worse by letting myself get swept up in her game. If I don't act fast, the Monarch's prestigious reputation will go down the drain like cum in the private sauna.

"Excellent ceremony, Mr. Hudson. The tally was the highest to date."

I stop long enough to shake the hand of the

politician talking to me. "Thanks, Ryan. It's always humbling to see the generosity of my club members."

"Generosity is a bit of a stretch. Though watching you reach into your wallet for that prize piece of pussy was the highlight of the night. Some of us were wondering if you were a eunuch."

"I still might be," I joke, flashing a fake smile. "All I did was donate to a charity that's dear to me. Nothing more. Nothing less."

Blake Rittenhouse joins the conversation. With a cigar in one hand, the other in his pocket, his impassive expression leads me to think he's hiding his anger over being beaten as the highest bidder. "Who did she choose as her Dom?"

"That's confidential." Which he knows.

Blake's gaze sweeps the lobby. "I saw Dmitri already, which means it wasn't him. That man never leaves his Butterfly, even to take a piss." He puffs on his cigar and blows the smoke a little too close to my face. "Or so I was told."

He wasn't told shit. The NDA contracts prevent any information from leaking.

Vault, Bull, and three of my female entertainers stroll past us to head to the elevators. They're each carrying large cases with them, filled with high end sex toys to play with.

"And there goes your other two prized stallions." Blake smirks at Ryan before facing me. "Maybe no one wanted her."

My fists clench. "Have a good evening, gentlemen. And thank you again for your contributions to tonight's ceremony."

As I take a step away, Ryan's next statement holds me still. "Yes. Well, I have a very pouty mistress waiting for me in room seven." He glowers at me with no hint of the friendliness he just showed. Typical.

Dipping my head, I feel my chest tighten with dread. "And what do you think you'd like done about it?" I'm not into granting requests, but tonight's a special circumstance.

"Send Sophie up to play with us."

If this motherfucker thinks he can order me around in my own club, VIP or not, I'll knock him the fuck out and blacklist his ass. He better remember who the fuck he's talking to.

"I didn't hear a please," I warn. Perhaps humiliation is in order, so he learns his goddamn lesson. "I'm waiting, *dog*." He might be a Senator outside these walls, but in here, he is a pet. He enjoys being called Pup. I've seen him crawl on all fours, bark, and wag his tail. To each their own, but he will not act like the animal who calls the shots up in here. That's my privilege and mine alone.

His cheeks redden as he looks away from me. "Please." he says harshly.

Blake Rittenhouse stands beside us, slack jawed. I hope he's taking notes, but if he needs a lesson too, I'll give him one next.

"Please what?" At six-foot three, I have Ryan by only a couple inches, but I've never needed height to make others feel small around me. Taking a slow step forward, I look down my nose at him. "Please. *What*?"

I love watching people choke on their audacity.

"Please, can you send Sophie up to us for the evening, Sir?"

He won't even look me in the eye at this point. "She's already taken for the evening."

Ryan's head snaps up. "Then can you make her

un-taken, please, Sir."

It's up to Sophie if she wants to play with that couple or not. I doubt she will, though. Brushing the invisible dust off his shoulders, I smile and say, "I'll see what I can do."

"Thank you."

"Can I also get one of those fuck machines brought into room ten?" Blake asks with a wry grin. "And a taser, *Sir*." At the last second, he tacks on. "Please."

My smile is tight enough to split my bottom lip, but I keep my mouth shut and fists to myself. This is the price I must pay to keep the peace. But the reality of it is, I'm not the one paying for it at all.

My employees are.

Without saying another word, I leave Blake and Ryan to their quiet chatter, and for the first time in my life, I dream of burning this club to the ground.

...

In the penthouse, Jessie's having a lot of fun with her playmates.

Crack!

Moan.

Crack!

Moan.

Jessie's in her glory—her glassy eyes shining with a subspace induced high. A lusty smile ghosts her face as she's bent over a bench, her hands tied to the bottom front, and legs tethered to the floor. Bare and streaked with red, her ass glows from being spanked hard with a paddle. Her back sports several red streaks from a flogger, too.

"You wanted to be the Butterfly?" Sophie practically growls as she lifts the flogger and cracks it down on Jessie's ass again. "You think someone else knows how to give you what you need like I do, slut?"

Crack!

Jessie's arms shake even as she melts onto the bench. "No, Mistress."

"I didn't think so." Sophie's leather outfit gleams in the dim light, but she's taken off her gas mask. Hair in a high pony, some of it sticks to her temples from sweat. She sinks a finger into Jessie's cunt and pulls it out to inspect how wet she is. Sauntering around the bench, Sophie crouches down to look Jessie in the eyes and smears her lust-coated finger across Jessie's cheek. Then she walks around and spanks her again. "No one gets you wetter than me."

"No, Mistress. Yes, Mistress. Mmph." Jessie's words become unintelligible once Sophie lowers down, spreads Jessie's cheeks, and rims her asshole.

"That's my good little whore." Sophie glances over at me while she finger-fucks Jessie and gives me a wink.

I tip my head ever so slightly, signaling we need to talk.

Sophie snaps her fingers, cuing Jessie's husband to come crawling across the floor with his ball gag firmly in place. "Shove your nose to her soaked cunt and stay like that until I come back." She makes her way over to me, ignoring the others fucking around us, just like I do. Sophie's voice is low and quiet when she asks, "What's up? Everything okay?"

Jesus, I'm not sure how to answer that. "Ryan's asking for you to join him and his mistress in suite seven." No need to say more than that. We all know Ryan's tastes, and we all know his piss poor attitude when he doesn't get his way.

Sophie's brow crinkles and she looks over her shoulder at the scene she's already in the middle of. Her features soften as she sighs. "Give me ten more minutes with them to have fun with, then I'll go."

"You don't have to." I force no one to enter a scene with someone. My loyalty is to my employees, not my members.

"I know." She wipes the sweat from her brow. "But tonight's rocky and if my participation makes them less agitated, I don't mind. Ryan's not a violent lover."

That doesn't make the ache in my chest ease in the slightest. "I'm going to deny his request."

When I turn to leave, Sophie grabs my arm. "No. I want to go. Seriously."

My gaze flits over hers, desperate to read her expression. "You're absolutely sure?"

"Yes."

I'm still deciphering her expression to make sure she's telling me the truth when Jessie calls out from the bench. "Mistress! I want to come now."

Sophie doesn't break eye contact with me when she raises her voice and yells, "You'll come when I want you to come, slut. Someone shove a cock in her mouth and keep her quiet until I say otherwise."

A man from Jessie's circle eagerly makes that happen, and we continue our conversation. Sophie crosses her arms and smiles up at me. "You made a bid on a member. What made you do it?"

Damnit. "I don't know." That's the truth. I think. "Impulsivity got the better of me tonight."

"Mmm." She tips her head to the side, studying me like a bird with a worm. "I hope she's worth it. I have a feeling we'll all be bending over backwards to soften the egos of these animals."

I lower my voice and plead, "Don't do *anything* you don't want to do, Sophie. *Ever*." It's a major rule here. "I'd rather lose every member than lose one of you."

She smiles and I hope she knows how much I mean that. "Don't worry, Mr. Hudson. I've got things covered here. Now go do whatever boss men like you do and leave me to my fuck toys." Sophie shoves me back playfully and saunters over to Jessie, and strokes her hair. "Suck his cock harder, slut. I want to hear you gag on it."

I leave Sophie to work her magic. One problem solved, onto the next.

Chapter 9

Tara

After an hour of kneeling, my knees hurt. I'm not getting up. Mr. Hudson—*Sir*—is going to learn just how far I'll go to get what I want. My knees can grind holes in the floor for all I care. I will do whatever he says, so I can break out of the cage I've been in for far too long.

The suite is huge and built for seduction. The king-sized bed looks like a cloud-puff dream, the white chaise, leather couch, and sex bench all scream *fuck on me*. Hell, the hooks and brackets secured to the head and footboard were so discreet, I almost missed them. Wow, this is going to be fun. I can't believe I'm staying here for a month. There's even a kitchen, living area, and I'm sure the bathroom is just as exquisite. I wouldn't know for sure since I'm still on the floor by the door.

Glancing up at the camera mounted in the far corner, I sigh.

Is Mr. Hudson watching me?

I sure hope so. Otherwise, this show I'm about to put on will be a waste.

Look, he said to stay on my knees until he returned, but he didn't say I had to stay in the same spot. Nor did he say I couldn't have some fun while I waited for him to come back.

Biting back my smile, I crawl over to the bed and angle my body for the best camera view with the bed at my back. Dragging my tongue along my middle finger, I get it good and wet while keeping my gaze locked on the camera mounted in front of me. Spreading my legs wide, I finger myself while still on my knees.

I alternate between rubbing my clit and delving my finger inside my pussy, trying to hit my g-spot. It's a slow process. I've experimented with several ways to get off on my own, but without a toy, or other forms of stimulation, I rarely orgasm from only my hands.

Still, I'm no quitter.

Closing my eyes, I imagine what it will be like to have Mr. Hud—*Sir*—take me from behind. Will he grip my hips and rail me until I can't catch my breath? Will he bite my shoulder and scratch ribbons down my back?

My nipples harden to little buds, and I pinch one hard enough to make me gasp.

With one hand between my legs, the other pulling and twisting my nipple, a weight settles in my lower belly. My arousal becomes slicker. Using it as lube to rub my clit harder, I stare up at the camera.

I want you to watch.
I want you to see what you've paid a fortune for.
I want you to want me.
I want you to fuck me.
I want you to own me.
I want you to break *me.*

Will Sir tongue fuck me like I'm his last meal? Will he pull my hair and choke me out? Will he make me beg for his cum or paint my face with it while I sleep?

Fuck, I'm getting hotter. My pace quickens until I'm rubbing my clit hard and fast. My other hand drops between my legs and I shove more fingers inside myself. My knees dig into the floor painfully.

Will he fuck me like a whore? Treat me like a princess? Tie me to the bed and use my body to get off with?

Oh God, I'm so close... so damn close...

Will he spit in my mouth and slap me as he fucks me? Will he make me gag on his dick like he did his fingers? Will he spank my ass so hard I can't sit for a week?

Pressure builds. My breaths turn ragged.

Will he use a spreader bar and make me lie on display in obscene positions? Will he smack my cunt and fuck me with whatever is within reach?

My body coils a moment before it explodes. The orgasm's long and mild, but oh so relieving. I fall forward, my knees spreading wider as I buck against my hand, rubbing my clit long enough to ride out the last pulses of my needy pussy.

Panting, I stare up at the camera, even as I rest my head on the side of the bed.

It's been a long day and an impossibly long night. To think this morning I went for a five-mile jog, had a three-hour long conference with my stepfather and his cronies, settled on two properties, followed by a meeting with the permit office, a conference call after that with my stepbrother and assistant, along with completing a pile of paperwork and drafting emails to go out so my family thinks I'm working when I'm not, all before a quick mani/pedi and finally the Butterfly Ceremony. I'm fucking exhausted.

And now that I've accomplished everything I

wanted to today and finally took the edge off a little, my eyes close and I drift off.

Still on my knees.

Still waiting for Sir to return.

...

Ryker

It's four in the morning before I've put out every little fire, soothed every whiney rich fuck's complaint, and checked the last occupied room to make sure all is well. My damn eyes burn, legs are like heavy lead pipes and this tuxedo is suffocating.

I've been too concerned about the well-being of my employees and the satisfaction of my members to check on Tara. She's probably in bed, all tucked under the expensive silk bedding, sound asleep with no worries in the world.

The filthy rich are carefree people, right?

And Tara thinks she's entitled enough to weasel her way to being the Butterfly without having to suffer any of the consequences.

Must be nice.

Unlocking her suite door, I step inside and quietly shut it behind me with a soft click.

Of course, she's not where I left her. No surprise there.

I make my way across the room and freeze. Tara's on the floor, propped up against the bed, with her mouth open and head tipped back as she sleeps. She's naked. And still on her knees.

I'll be damned.

It's rare for me to underestimate someone. This

woman keeps delivering the unexpected. Looming over Tara, I take in her long, blonde waves, the cupid's bow mouth, full tits, soft belly, slender waist, and dark patch of hair between her thighs.

I was struck stupid on the stage when she dropped her dress, not only by her boldness, but because I pegged her as a waxer. I'd have put money on Tara being as smooth as a baby's ass everywhere. To see she's gone for a more natural look makes the blood flow directly to my cock.

Tara's hand flinches while she dreams.

Squatting down, I brush the hair from her face, and she immediately pops her eyes open and smacks my hand away on reflex. I stay where I am until she realizes who she hit. Something in me stirs and a growl nearly slips from my throat. That's a vicious reaction to have. Are her instincts from abuse or paranoia?

Wait. Why the fuck do I even care?

With a sleepy smile, she mumbles, "Mmmph. Sorry. I didn't know it was you."

"It will only ever be me in this room, unless you invite another in."

She rubs her eyes and yawns. "What time is it?"

"Four fifteen."

"Mmph." Her head flops back, and she stares at me with sleepy eyes. "I'm still on my knees, Sir."

There are a hundred responses I could give, but there's no way I'm saying any of them. Tonight was long, this woman is too new, and I'm fucking exhausted. Scooping her into my arms, I gently lay her on the bed and see how red her knees are. Pulling the covers over her, I whisper, "Sleep. You'll need your energy for what I have planned for you, Butterfly."

"Yes, Sir." She closes her eyes and is out almost immediately again.

Massaging my brow, I stare down at her. What the hell have I gotten into with this woman, and why she was so bent on being the Butterfly? Every woman has some level of desperation for the title, but none sank low enough to trap me in a deal to get it like Tara has.

I can't figure out if she's resourceful or pathetic. Regardless, she's gorgeous and I can't seem to break away from her. The moment I first saw her in my club, she enthralled me. Always quiet, always alone, she flutters from one scene to the next, gathering all the knowledge and entertainment offered by the other couples and groups in my club. But why?

Many members here prefer an audience. Tara's been within her right to admire each scene at her leisure. That she has, as far as I know, stayed away from participating is what intrigues me most.

For her to want to be the Butterfly, only to never indulge in debauchery before now, doesn't sit well with me at all.

And Vault's done his homework on her, even though I told him not to. He filled me in while we took care of more little temper tantrums and pouty man-babies about three hours ago. There is no mention of a Tara Reed across any social media. She works for Brisbane Realty but isn't listed as a top employee, which probably means she's a bottom feeder. A grunt worker.

It would explain why she was sent out in the late night to look at a property under the radar.

My protective instincts light up thinking of how dangerous that could get. Is she sent out to meet strangers to make under-the-table deals on other properties on behalf of Brisbane Realty? What kind of sleezy ass dirtbag bullshit is that? I'd never send a woman out on her own at night. It's unsafe. Unnecessary.

Look at her. She's so fucking *delicate*.

A dark part of me wants to make her crawl to me on her sore knees and beg to suck my cock. I want to make her come so much that she passes out from dehydration. I want to ruin her for any other man or woman.

Which is exactly why I better do the bare minimum. I don't want Tara to enjoy her time with me. I don't want her to last the thirty days either. The faster I get Tara out of here, the better for all of us.

Tonight, I made concessions. That won't happen again. This woman is bad for business.

Miss Tara Reed has got to go.

Chapter 10

Tara

Waking up every hour, in an unfamiliar bed, in an unfamiliar space, frustrated me all night long. I've slept in plenty of hotels and beds that weren't my own before, but being in the Monarch overnight was surreal. It's dead quiet in here and the blackout curtains combined with plush bedding keep me in darkness, as if I'm in a big, soft cocoon.

The only light shining is from a small light over by the chaise.

"You're awake."

I roll over and barely make out the silhouette of Mr. Hudson. He must press a button on a remote because the curtains slowly open, illuminating the gorgeous suite.

"Sleep well, Butterfly?"

"No." I sit up and stretch my arms over my head. I'm still naked, and when the sheet falls around my lap, Mr. Hudson gets a superb view of my tits. His jaw clenches and he drops his gaze to the foot of the bed. It hurts my feelings a little. When I shift to get up, he says, "Stay there."

"I have to use the restroom."

"You'll piss when I tell you to. Now stay there."

As he swaggers over to a closet, I roll out of bed and head for the bathroom.

He can be mad at me for disobeying, I don't give a fuck. To make it worse, I flip him the bird over my shoulder.

Look, I'm all for being uncomfortable and obeying orders like a good girl, but I haven't peed since before the ceremony last night and my damn bladder is killing me. Slamming the door shut, I lock it in case he tries to come in.

My heart beats against my ribs as I make my way across the marble tiled floor. It's cold in here. My nipples harden and I shiver even when sitting on the toilet. After taking care of business, I wash my hands and face and try to get most of last night's makeup off. Then I brush my teeth with one of the unopened toothbrushes I find in a drawer.

There are a lot of things stocked in here. Gels, lotions, shampoos, and bath salts in large glass canisters, and first aid stuff, too. After finger-combing my hair, I head back out with my head held high. I should take a shower while I'm at it, but something tells me if I don't hurry back out there, Sir will make me suffer for it.

After stepping one foot outside the bathroom, I know I've made a mistake.

Shit.

Sir stands just outside the door, his mouth cut in a straight, thin line. His glower almost makes me shrink back. "Get on your knees, Butterfly."

Arching my brow, I defy him. Fuck this man if he thinks he can wake me up and order me around like a goddamn dog. I know he's supposed to be my "master", but I refuse to submit to every little thing. And some part of me worries he's being this cold, controlling, and degrading because he's mad at me for my stunt last night at the ceremony.

He'll get over it.

"You've already racked up more punishments than your body can handle." His tone rings with warning bells. "You do not want to piss me off any more than you already have."

Maybe I do.

Can't be worse than I've already suffered in my miserable life.

In this club, I'm at his mercy. This is his kingdom, and he calls all the shots. I glance up at the camera quickly and he chuckles. "Think you're being watched, Miss Reed?" He leans in and the heat of his breath sends a shiver down my body when he whispers, "You are."

You. Are.

Those two little words make me go from defiant to compliant.

Had he threatened me with "no one's coming in here to save you," I would have laughed. The Monarch is likely the safest place in the city. Nothing gets past Ryker Hudson and his men. And I know he might be mad at me, but he'd never hurt me unless I wanted him to. Even then, he'd probably deny me.

Instead, he told me what I long to hear.

I'm being watched.

Just like I'd hoped Sir was watching last night when I got myself off, I love that he's watching me right now. And if he is the only one, and no one else is staring at us from a monitor right now, then I pray this is being recorded so he can rewatch it later.

Leaning into his face, I snap my teeth at him, and keep my satisfaction hidden when his eyes flash with surprise. Lowering onto my hands and knees, I wait until he steps out of my way, then I crawl like a cougar back over to the bed and climb into it.

There's a spreader bar waiting for me. And a ball gag.

Oh my god.

I force myself to remain impassive, even though my nerves are in a panic, and rest my feet on the spreader bar, playfully eyeing Sir up as he comes closer.

"Disobedience will cost you, Butterfly."

Fine by me.

I don't make a peep when he straps my ankles on the bar. But I do gasp when he cranks the goddamn thing until my hips ache. Fuuuuck. Lifting onto my elbows, I stare at how wide I'm spread.

Without saying a word, Sir climbs onto the bed with the ball gag in his hand. "Open your mouth."

Licking my lips, my mouth dries up as fear sets in. He doesn't look turned on. He doesn't sound dominating as much as he sounds annoyed.

Without giving him more to be angry about, I open my mouth and let him set the gag in place.

"Is it too tight?" he asks, pulling the strap and buckling it around my head.

I shake my head.

"Good girl." His tone's slightly softer. "Lay back for me."

My eyes water as I obey. I signed up for this. I manipulated for this. I dreamed of this. To be used and pleasured and given a chance to play with my darkest desires.

I didn't know it would feel this terrifying. The vulnerability, I expected. But the fear and shame hits harder when I can't tell what he's thinking. I squeeze my eyes shut as old insecurities fill my head with voices I'd be happy to never hear again and yet one in particular still infiltrates my walls.

What kind of monster likes sick shit like this, Tara?
Only whores open their legs for strange men.
You're a disgusting slut.

My hands tremble as I wipe the tears off my cheeks.

Suddenly, my body slides to the edge of the footboard and legs raise into the air. I squeak with fear as Ryker, Mr. Hudson—*fuck!*—Sir, attaches the spreader bar to a chain that's dangling from the ceiling. Tipped so far back, I feel like a prize fish hanging for inspection. Panic sets in and I try to twist myself so I can see what he's doing. It doesn't work.

"Nothing will happen that you don't want to have happen." He runs a hand along my calf, as if to soothe me. It doesn't work. "Remember the light system. Green for good. Yellow for unsure or uncomfortable. Red for stop."

How the hell am I supposed to say a color with this gag in my mouth!

"You will nod when I ask," he says, like he's read my mind.

When he climbs onto the bed, his head crests between my thighs. "Good morning, Butterfly." He lowers his mouth to my pussy and licks me. When he drags his tongue across my cunt, I tense and watch his pupils blow wide.

I wonder if mine have too.

When he licks me again, he targets my clit and is rough with my tender flesh. I like it. A lot. But it's not enough to get me to climax. I feel too empty.

Click. A loud buzzing noise starts up and

suddenly, he's pressing a huge vibrator against my cunt.

"Are you still green?"

Hells yes, I am. How can I not be? It's just a vibrator, for fuck's sake.

I nod, relaxing into the sensation of the toy on me.

Sir runs it along my slick pussy and shoves something else inside me. Pumping whatever it is in and out of my cunt, I notice he's still in his tux from last night. His hair looks like he's raked his hands through it a dozen times. There's stubble across his jaw that the morning light hits just right.

My belly feels heavy. A light sheen of sweat spreads across the back of my neck. Relaxing into the moment, I let the sensations consume me again.

The vibrator's speed kicks up a notch.

"Still green?"

I nod.

Whatever he's got inside me quickens, and my body coils around the pressure and pleasure. It builds, builds, builds, then—

I scream through an orgasm that has me seeing stars. My body erupts in goosebumps, chills, heat, and bliss. My voice cracks as I scream, my pussy clenching around whatever he's got stuffed inside me. The lower half of my body sways, suspended in the air by the hooked spreader bar. I'm dizzy. Heart hammering, I lift onto my elbows and try to tell him to let up on the vibrator. I need a minute to climb down from this euphoria, but another orgasm assails me instead.

I can't catch my breath.

I can't see straight.

I can't move.

Crying out around the silicone ball in my mouth, I choke on my spit. Sir doesn't relent. In fact, he keeps me coming until I'm in the yellow.

My thighs shake, my hips are sore, my body feels too hot and strung out. I can't breathe, my head's spinning, and dots sprinkle in my vision.

"Are you still green?"

I shake my head.

"Are you yellow?"

I nod.

The bastard turns the vibrator up and makes me come over and over until I'm sobbing. Fat tears fall down the sides of my face and soak my hair. I'm covered in sweat. I can't feel my cheeks. I can't feel my ass. I can't feel my pussy.

Everything's a violent combination of overly sensitive and completely numb.

He's broken me before breakfast was served.

Mr. Hudson doesn't stop.

I try yelling at him through the ball gag to give me a minute to recuperate. With barely enough strength to prop myself up, I cuss him out with my ball gag.

"I'm sorry, Butterfly. What was that?" He presses the vibrator harder against my clit and my next orgasm makes me nauseous. My thighs shake as I buck against it and my head hits the mattress again. Fuck!

"Are you green again?"

I shake my head fast.

"Yellow?"

If I go to red, he'll stop. If I say yellow, he'll continue, and I might die.

I don't know what do to because I don't want him to stop, and I can't let him continue. My body's mush. My head's a foggy mess. My pussy tingles and feels pulverized.

"Butterfly, are you yellow?"

I don't have an answer.

"Fuck." The vibrator shuts off, and he tosses it to the side. Quickly unhooking my ankles from the spreader bar, he lowers me down slowly.

I cry out because my muscles hurt. Fumbling with the buckle on my gag, my hands tremble too much for me to unlatch it.

"I've got it," he says in a gruff voice. For someone who did nothing but play with toys, he sure sounds as exhausted as I am. Sir releases the gag from my mouth and my jaw aches from being open for so long.

I can't keep my eyes open. I can't feel the bed anymore. I'm neither floating nor sinking.

I'm… gone.

Chapter 11

Ryker

God damnit.

I set out to make her exhausted and I think I just fucking broke her.

That's disappointing. I thought she'd at least make it to lunchtime.

Tara passes out the instant I lift her body into my arms. Mouth open, head flopped back, she's completely unconscious.

Shit, shit, shit. I should have known better. I lost focus on what mattered most and now look what's happened.

"Miss Reed." Tapping her cheek does no good. "Butterfly." I smack her face a little harder. "Tara!" I shake her.

Her eyes crack open. "Mmph."

"You need to drink some water." And eat. And get cleaned up.

After that many orgasms, she's not just a quivering mess, she's soaked and boneless. She'd squirted twice while I had my fun with her, and it's all over the front of my tux and bottom of the bedding. Good thing I'd placed a waterproof blanket under her before we started—not that I think Tara noticed.

Christ, this woman is going to destroy me. First her little brat move of defying my orders to stay in bed, then snapping her teeth at me before getting on her hands and knees.

But the way she looked at me when I tied her legs to the bar shook me the most.

Tara made me feel like I was her escape from Hell.

As if being bound and used by me was the salvation she craves.

It made something inside me turn feral. And now she's suffering the consequences of both our actions. Rushing to get her something to drink, I work hard to keep my composure and grab her a bottle of water. I have a business to run, and what I just did to her was only to exhaust Tara enough to get her to sleep a while longer so I could leave, but I wasn't expecting to feel bad about it.

Technically, the Dom never leaves their Butterfly. The forced proximity ends with one of us spent and the other transformed. My men often need breaks after being a Butterfly's Dom because they sometimes allow their emotions to get involved. It's hell on the psyche if you get attached because at the end of the month, the Butterfly will leave, and she won't return.

No matter how many times I tell my men to keep a line in the sand and remind them this is a job, not a relationship, someone fails to remember.

I'm in danger of blurring that line already with this woman.

Don't get this wrong—I'm not in love with Tara. Not even close. I might have been infatuated with the vision of her on my surveillance feed, but that's it. After she put me in this fucked up position, I now loathe her more than lust after her.

But when she looked at me with those big, beautiful blue eyes shining at me with unshed tears, and put her feet against the spreader bar so willingly, so eagerly, like this was all she's waited for, what she needs to escape the voices in her head, I'll admit a part of me felt protective and possessive of her.

"Drink, Tara." Using her real name isn't smart. It's like naming an animal you know you can't keep as a pet. It fosters attachment. Butterfly is most acceptable. But there's also slut, whore, princess, and a bunch of safer options. Still, she's so out of it, only her real name seems to penetrate her brain fog and sub drop. "Tara, take a few sips for me."

Her glassy eyes flutter open again when she attempts to drink the bottle of water I'm holding to her lips. After a couple of small pulls, she grows greedy and starts chugging. Snatching the bottle from my hands, the plastic collapses under her grip and she drains the whole thing.

"That's my good girl." Relief makes my head spin.

Tara wipes her mouth and lays back on the pillow. "I need sleep," she says in a raspy voice.

Good. That's exactly what I want to hear. I didn't think I'd be able to scare her off with a single course of intense orgasms, but it buys me time to come up with a better plan.

And it gives me a chance to shower and rest.

After tucking Tara in, I close the curtains and head out. The club is empty of members and housekeeping is in full swing. The rich scent of fresh-brewed coffee invades the air. My stomach growls. My head's pounding.

"Didn't expect to see you here." Dmitri stares up

from my desk monitors as I enter my office. "She didn't last very long."

"Do they ever?" Yanking on my bow tie, I head to the bathroom, desperate to scrub last night off me. "Can you have the kitchen staff bring her up a high protein meal, water, and chocolates?"

Not bothering to wait for his answer, I kick the door shut and lean against the counter. I barely recognize myself this morning.

"Fuuuck." Squeezing my eyes shut, I slip into an old memory...

"The trick is to keep them so satisfied, they're too exhausted to keep track of the time, and you."

"How do I do that?" I shove the hair out of my face for the tenth time since I've been in here. It's getting too long. Tonight, maybe I'll chop it myself with the kitchen scissors. Or shave it.

"First," Natalie says, "you must learn to use that tongue of yours better." She spreads her legs while I stand across from her. "Start practicing, Ryker."

I swallow the bile rising in my throat and stare at the escort's pussy. Natalie lives in the same building as me, and always wears nice clothes, and has her hair and nails done. I bit the bullet and asked her if she could help me. She said yes.

Now here we are.

I stand on her wooden table, my combat boots landing heavy on the wood. Staring down at her, I wish I felt intimidating, but her non-reaction tells me I'm not. I step down on the other side and position myself between her legs. My jaw aches from how much I've clenched it. My stomach is in knots because I'm ashamed and hungry. I haven't eaten since yesterday morning but what little food is left in my house isn't for me.

I have to learn how to make money fast, and this is the best way. I mean, I've eaten girls out before. I like pussy. I just don't like Natalie's waxed up cunt. She's twenty-six and I'm sixteen, even though I told her I was eighteen. Most guys my age would give their left nut for a chance to be with a skilled slut like her. I should be grateful she's willing to be with me at all.

"Stop overthinking it, Ryker, and get on your fucking knees like a good boy."

Hate and anger consume me until my vision darkens. I drop to my knees, wanting nothing more than to smack that smirk off her face. But what would that say about me? No man should raise a hand to a woman. Ever.

Besides, she's doing me a favor.

I need money and she's going to teach me how to make it.

"See this?" Natalie runs her finger over her slick pussy and spreads her lips, exposing her clit and fuckable hole. "This is where you need to concentrate your efforts."

"I know how to tongue fuck, and I know where the goddamn clit is." *The smell of her cunt makes me hard and nauseous all at once.* "This isn't my first time."

"Women are different than girls, Ryker. We expect more. We demand more. If you want me to teach you how to get the most bang for their buck, you better do exactly as I say."

My throat tightens, and it hurts to swallow.

"Now eat me like a good boy, so I can teach you how to improve."

Humiliation makes me shiver as I lower my face down and make her orgasm in less than ten seconds because I want this over with as soon as possible. And like I said, I'm not new to eating pussy. I know how to get a girl off.

"Holy shit." *Natalie laughs, even as she struggles to*

catch her breath. "Again," she orders me. And when I don't automatically comply, she grabs my overgrown hair and yanks my head down to her pussy. "Again, Ryker."

Splashing water on my face barely brings me out of my headspace. I can't believe I'm thinking of that old bitch again. Tara's nothing like her and yet I haven't been able to stop thinking about Natalie for weeks. Her memories, and what came afterwards, keep me up at night. They make me lose focus during the day. They cause me to—

I barely make it to the toilet before I throw up.

Heaving until my already empty stomach aches and muscles burn, I flush the toilet and rinse my mouth out. Then I brush my teeth and shave before getting into the shower. Scrubbing as hard as I can, I want to peel layers of my skin off, but that's never helped in the past.

Braced against the tile, I let scolding water rinse off my issues and reset my emotions back to zero. Tara needs a Dom who can handle his shit, and hers. I have to pull myself together long enough to get her out of my system.

I mean out of my suite.

Shit. Why'd I just say that? Tara's not in my system. She's not under my skin. She's nothing but a cheater who used me to win the Butterfly privilege.

But goddamn did she look divine in that bed.

Why did she have to choose me as her Dom?

Why didn't I leave before she made her selection?

Why can't I stop thinking about her?

Last night, instead of catching some much needed shut eye, I stayed up staring at her.

Fantasizing about every little depraved thing I wanted to do to her, I jerked off twice into her discarded dress. Then I set up a plan to make her miserable, so she'd quit early and walk away from me.

The sooner the better.

That plan backfired before I even had it set in motion. I want more of Tara. I want to play with her. Pleasure her. Break her and remake her. Mold her into a perfect masterpiece of sexual depravity.

That look in her eyes when I strapped her to the spreader bar has burned into my soul. I've never had a woman look at me like that before in my fucking life. I'm not someone's salvation. I've been their toy. Their paid for fuckboy. And then I became their desire and prize they'd never win. Now I'm untouchable.

At sixteen, I learned a hard lesson about how low life can drag you. Now, at thirty-two, I can honestly say that life has a basement, and at least fifteen floors below that.

Hell, maybe even more. I'm still digging.

Wrapping a towel around my waist, I step out of the bathroom and head straight to a closet where I keep spare suits. Dmitri still hasn't left. "Don't you have work to do?"

"Yeah. And instead, I'm doing *your* job."

I arch my brow at him while stuffing my legs into a pair of pants. "Vault's team can monitor the club."

"I'm talking about watching over your Butterfly." He leans back in my chair as if he's the owner of this place. "You shouldn't be out of that room, Ryker."

"I shouldn't be *in* it."

"The rule is you don't leave her side. She's had

to give up her life for a month. So do you. That's what's been paid for."

Paid for.

Bile rises in my throat again, but I swallow it down. "It's *my* money that was spent. *My* rules. *My* club."

And I'll change them as I see fit.

"Don't do that." Dmitri stands and makes his way over to me. The man's got me by two inches and a good fifty pounds. Where I'm all lean muscles, Dmitri is brute strength. I spent my teenage years on my knees, while he spent his swinging his fists. We both have scars that only we know about.

"Don't do what?"

"Don't weasel out of this somehow."

"I can't let the club go to shit for some princess's cunt."

"Then negotiate."

The terms and conditions of the Butterfly's time here are always negotiable. But I don't want to give Tara the power to allow or deny me time to do my business.

"She's not going to be a Sleeping Beauty for thirty solid days."

I deadpan him. "Then you've forgotten how harsh I can be with pleasure."

"Oh, I'll never forget it." Dmitri's smile is more scary than sexy. "And that's what I'm worried about. She's not Natalie, Ryker."

"Never said she—"

"I heard you puke in the bathroom."

My gut sinks. "I ate something that didn't agree with me for breakfast. That's all."

He grips my shoulder and squeezes. "The only

thing you've eaten in the last fifteen hours was Tara's pussy. Want to try another excuse? Let me guess, you're nervous? No, maybe it was the pasta from the night before? Bad milk in your latte?"

I smack his hand off me. "Fuck you."

"I'd allow it if I thought it would do you any good."

Raking my hands through my hair angrily, I rip a shirt from the closet next. "How much did you watch?"

"All of it."

Possessiveness flies out of my mouth with a growl. "Don't watch us again."

It's hypocritical. I know that. I keep my eye on every Dom that's with a Butterfly in that suite—including Dmitri. To act like him following protocol is wrong makes me a dick. Still, I don't care. I don't want anyone seeing Tara's body, or the things I'm going to do to it, except me.

"Rules are rules, Ry. You'll be watched."

"Then you're fired."

"No, I'm not." He crosses his arms over his chest. It makes me want to punch him hard enough to break his fucking jaw.

But I promised to never do that again, so I settle for, "She's got to go. She's fucking me all up."

"Or she's making you face things you haven't been willing to work on in a while." He doesn't budge, so I have to walk around him. *Asshole*. "What's up with you lately, man? You've been more tense than usual. Got a dildo stuck up your ass or something?"

If only. "23 Greene Street is for sale."

That changes his mood entirely. Dmitri drops his arms and his shoulders droop. "What are you going to do?"

"I'm buying it."

"Jesus Christ, Ryker, that's—"

"I don't care. I'm fucking buying it."

"And then what?" He tosses his hands up. "What the fuck are you going to do with that shithole? Turn it into another sex club? Think that'll calm your demons? Because I know you're not going to tear it down."

He's right. I won't. "It's got potential."

Dmitri stares at me like I've lost my mind. Maybe I have.

His voice drops to a low whisper when he says, "You need to let it go."

My hands ball into fists. I don't need his opinion or his approval. "Get the fuck out of my office, D."

He tips his head back just to look down at me a little more. *Fucker*. I'm vibrating with the need to hit something, and I know damn well Dmitri is fantasizing about knocking me the fuck out right now, too. He always gets this extra vein in his temple when he's furious enough to fight, and he's got it now.

"You're making a mistake, Ryker."

"You're making a bigger one by standing here when I said to get the fuck out."

Dmitri shakes his head and mumbles something under his breath as he walks out my door. Once he's gone, I get a goddamn grip and regain some composure. Pouring three fingers of whisky into a glass, I take one sip and the burn hits my gullet, making my stomach clench.

Furious, I throw the glass against the door. It shatters, splashing bourbon all over the place.

A gentle knock makes me storm over and swing

the door wide open. "Dmitri, I swear to fu—"

Sophie stands in front of me with a tray of food, her eyes wide with fear as she takes a step back. "I'm sorry. I thought Dmitri was in here."

"Why aren't you home, Sophie?" Her shift ended hours ago.

"I… I'm bringing Dmitri breakfast."

"He's not here." Knowing him, he's in his "office" which is nothing more than a dark room in the basement with a punching bag hung in the center and a cot against the far wall.

She slumps a little. "Oh."

Fuck my life. Running a hand down my face, I sigh heavily. "Leave it here for him. I'm sure he'll be back." I step out of her way, then wait for her to drop the tray on my desk. "Go home and get some rest, Soph."

"I will." She yawns and stuffs her hands in the back pocket of her jeans while she steps towards me. "You okay, boss?"

No. And I won't be until Tara fucking Reed gets out of here.

Chapter 12

Tara

Holy shit, what time is it? Rolling out of bed, I can't see much of anything because the curtains have been drawn again.

I feel boneless. Stretching my arms and legs, the memory of what Sir did to me with that spreader bar floods my mind. My thigh muscles hurt like a motherfucker. Don't get my started on my pussy. "Shit."

Ding!

Something lights up on my end table. It's not my cell, since I left mine at home, but it's definitely someone's.

And the only person in here besides me has been Sir.

Rolling over takes more effort than it should. Christ, my body is Jell-O. Plucking the phone off the end table, I tap the screen and see a message.

Take a shower, Butterfly. We have lunch reservations at two.

I'm not that hungry, honestly. But I'm dying for a drink. My head's throbbing and my pussy aches. Just getting out of bed and walking to the bathroom makes me stumble and whimper.

The lights turn on automatically once I enter the bathroom, forcing me to squint against the brightness.

"Turn off," I groan, smacking the heel of my palm against the light switch. "*Please*, turn off." I smash it three times before the lights dim.

That's good enough.

The shower's huge and has more buttons in it than a space shuttle. It takes me forever to figure out how to get the water running the way I'd like. Just standing under the rain showerhead, letting the water fall over me, feels incredible. I take my time, enjoying the heat and relaxing atmosphere. The shower lights are a dim blue hue, which is lovely. And so extra. Bet there's a switch to make it beat with the music on that control panel too.

Not that I'll mess with it.

By the time I'm done in the bathroom, my headache isn't so bad. Nothing a few cups of coffee can't fix.

But now I've realized that I don't have any clothes or makeup with me because my suitcases still haven't returned to my room. Shit. Going back over to the nightstand, I pick up the cell phone and type a message.

Can you please bring me my clothes, Sir?

A ding sounds from the sofa, and it scares me half to death.

"Jesus fucking Christ," I say, holding my chest. My heart gallops and head pounds with renewed force. "You scared the shit out of me!"

The curtains automatically open, revealing Mr. Hudson stalking towards me. I squint against the light and automatically cover my tits and pussy.

"Put your arms down," he says.

I obey easily enough. There's something strange about submitting to a Dom. I learned how much I liked it back in college, though it didn't end well the first time. Or the second.

Or the third.

I have shit taste in men and even worse taste in Doms, I guess. My track record doesn't bode well for Mr. Hudson. But his reputation supersedes my past lover's inability to Dom safely and correctly. I'm hoping to learn more and explore myself without the backlash of being abused in the process this time.

Lowering my arms, I keep my gaze locked on his. I might be submissive lately, but there's a powerhouse in me too, and that part of me won't cower. Maintaining eye contact is something I need.

"Good girl." Sir runs his hands through my dripping wet hair. Hard lines etch his handsome face as he cocks his brow at me. "We have a hair dryer and all other styling tools in the bathroom closet for you to use."

"I saw them." Shuddering under his gaze, I add, "I didn't use the blow dryer because my head's pounding. I didn't want to make it worse."

Sir's expression softens, and suddenly he's escorting me back to the bed. "If you're unwell, we can hold off for a day or two."

"No." It's a headache, not a bullet wound. I'm not letting him get out of another day or night with me. "I'll be fine. I just need some coffee and food."

He looks around the suite, confused. "You haven't eaten?"

"No." Anger dances across his face and his jaw clenches. It makes me think I've done something wrong. It makes me nervous. "I only just woke up. I haven't had a chance to grab a bite to eat yet."

"I had food sent up to you hours ago." He looks

around again. "I don't see it."

No one's been in my room that I know of. "No one can creep in and out of here, can they?" My heart races, which makes my blood pressure rise, and that causes my headache to worsen.

"Absolutely not. They'd need your permission first."

Thank God. Although, part of me is hurt finding out that he's been gone this whole time. It's like he keeps trying to get away from me and that's not fair.

"Well..." I shirk away before he makes me sit on the bed. "How about you go grab me some coffee and my suitcases and then we can start our fun day together." It's already twelve thirty in the afternoon. "Where are our lunch reservations?"

His mouth forms a thin line as he stares at me. "Downstairs."

"Oh." My disappointment is made clear by my tone. It's silly of me to think he was going to take me out and show me off. I'm nothing but a fucktoy with an expiration date, right?

And I signed up for this.

The devious part of me takes over and I storm over to the door. "I'll get my own coffee then. See you in the kitchen for lunch." I walk out and let the door slam shut behind me.

"Hey!" Mr. Hudson yells behind me. "What the fuck are you doing, Butterfly?"

"Getting shit done, *Sir*." It's not lost on either of us that I'm completely naked. I have no problem showing off my body—I made that perfectly clear last night at the ceremony. My only real issue is I have no clue where to get a fresh cup of fucking coffee in this big place.

Mr. Hudson's on me in an instant. Grabbing my arm, he swings me around and presses my back against the wall. His pupils are blown wide, his breaths controlled and heavy. If it wasn't for the way his veins stick out in his temples, I'd say I've turned him on. But I'm pretty sure I've just pissed him off again.

Well, I've got news for him. He's pissed me off too. "What is your problem?"

"I'll not have my Butterfly on display for anyone else but—" He catches himself before finishing that sentence.

"Anyone else *but*?" I arch my perfectly manicured eyebrow at him. "But *who*, Mr. Hudson? You?"

His gaze darkens.

"Because you seem to be doing anything *but* paying attention to me. In fact…" I shove him back. "You don't seem to want anything to do with me."

"I literally gave you so many orgasms this morning that you passed out, Miss Reed."

Miss Reed. Not Tara. Not Butterfly. If he keeps that up, his defenses will be all mine to manipulate, and that's annoying, honestly. He's calling me names to keep me at a distance. The more personal things get, the more open we'd be, and it's clear he wants none of that connection.

I don't either, really. But I *do* want to be treated with more respect than what he's given me so far.

"I can do that myself, Sir. You did me no favors."

He scoffs.

The audacity of this motherfucker. "You knocked me out with pleasure just so you could go back to work." I poke my finger into his hard chest. "You didn't do it for me. You did it for yourself."

"As a pleasure Dom, my only concern is making you come."

"As your Butterfly, my only purpose is to..." My words trail off because my headache's making a righteous comeback. Clutching the side of my head, I groan and close my eyes.

"Fuck."

Before I know it, Mr. Hudson has scooped me up and is carrying me back to my suite. He no sooner lays me on the bed than pulls out his cell and makes a call. "D, I need you in here now."

"I'm fine." Honestly, he's overreacting.

"You're not fine. You can barely open your eyes."

A gentle knock interrupts what I want to say, and Ryker leaves me so he can open the door. I hear low whispers and the fresh scent of coffee wafts through the air and into my nose. My mouth waters for it.

"Here." Ryker sits on the side of the bed and hands me a mug.

Steam trails into my nose, making me perk up a little more when I take it from him. "Caffeine addiction is a bitch." I can drink my weight in coffee on a bad day. I can drink a river of it on a normal one.

"Take these," he says, handing me two little pills. "It's over-the-counter shit."

"Thank you." I pop them in my mouth and chase them down with another sip of this amazing coffee.

"Don't you burn your mouth doing that?"

"Sometimes. But it tastes too good for me to care

about the pain." I take another small sip. "What's in this, heavy cream and cinnamon?"

"Fuck if I know. Dmitri makes it."

"Had I known the club had an expert barista on staff, I'd have joined last year instead of waiting so long." Man, this is good stuff. My stomach growls and Mr. Hudson hands me a pastry. It's only after I take it from him that I notice my hands are trembling.

"When was the last time you ate, Tara?"

The way he says my name makes me melt. I like it. "I guess yesterday morning."

"You *guess*?"

"Mmm." I chomp down on the pastry Dmitri brought too and take another sip of my coffee. "I don't keep track."

There's that look again. Mr. Hudson keeps dropping his mask, which makes me want to see what it would take to tear it off for good.

"If you get me my suitcase, I can get dressed and be ready for lunch in twenty minutes." My head's still not okay enough for me to use the blow dryer on my hair, but I can braid it if he wants me to. "We can go out somewhere."

"No."

My heart drops, along with my stomach. "Why?"

He reaches up and I think he's about to touch my face, but stops himself. "I…" His hand falls again. "I'll be back later."

With that, he gets up and leaves me again.

Chapter 13

Ryker

What the hell am I doing?

I couldn't get out of her suite fast enough, but now that I'm in the hallway, I can't seem to drag my sorry ass away from the door. Bracing against the wall, I take a deep breath.

What the fuck is wrong with me?

My heart's pounding a mile a minute. My dick's a steel rod in my pants. Squeezing my eyes shut, I lock down on my emotions and shove them right back where they belong—in the black hole where my heart once was.

This woman is fuckery personified. She's messing with my head.

I'm messing with my head.

The sheer force of will it took not to rip the door off its hinges when Tara left her suite, in nothing but her skin and attitude, rocked me to the core. I think I would have gouged out the eyes of everyone who saw her had she made it all the way to the kitchen.

I can't afford to lose that much of my fucking staff.

And Tara might as well have kicked me in the balls for saying she was "getting shit done," as if implying I'd slacked in taking care of her.

She was right.

I might have ordered food to be sent to her suite, but I should have known it wasn't going to happen. It's my job to take care of the Butterfly, no one else's, which Dmitri took great joy in reminding me when he brought the coffee and meds for her. That motherfucker had the nerve to tell me she was my responsibility and mine alone.

He's also right.

That I let Tara go this long without the basic necessities is unforgivable.

Jesus fucking Christ, I've been her Master for less than twenty-four hours and have fucked up so much, I should be fired.

And beaten.

And left out in the desert for dead.

I know better than this. Why am I losing my decency and head?

Fucking hell, I can't stand the thought of Tara going hungry. Her headache only added salt to my reopened wound. *And she didn't have meds she needed to get better faster.*

It hits too close to my past that I can never escape.

Logically, I could tell Tara I can no longer be her Master. But what good would that do other than get me off the hook as her Dom?

And put someone else in my place.

The notion makes my blood boil.

Part of me fears if I walk away from this arrangement with my tail between my legs, the bricks holding this place up will crumble and bury me alive. And a very feral, territorial part of me can't imagine her with another Dom.

What the fuck have I gotten myself into?

"You okay?"

I don't bother looking at Dmitri when I answer with a ragged, "No."

"You want to go down to my room for a while?"

Beating the shit out of a punching bag sounds amazing, but I'm too drained for it. And I still can't move from this spot on the wall, three feet from Tara's door, either. "This is a mistake," I whisper.

"Only if you make it one."

Sighing, I push away from the wall and scrub my face. Now I'm getting a headache too, for fuck's sake. "You knew what she needed." It's a warning, not a statement.

Dmitri doesn't deny what I'm implying either.

He was watching us from the video feed in her suite. Just like he said he would, even after I told him not to. For once, I'm grateful he followed protocol instead of whatever possessive shit I'd said to him earlier about it.

"Look," he sighs. "Maybe this is a good thing."

"Maybe. I didn't have to cheat and lose my integrity for Tara to win. We raised a lot of money for the charity. My reputation is still intact. My club is still running."

"That's not what I fucking mean, Ry."

"I know..." I rake a hand through my hair. "Fuck, I know."

"She's really gotten to you, hasn't she?"

And just like that, Dmitri's words suck me back into the past...

"She's really gotten to you, hasn't she?"

"Shut up, D." I pace back and forth in the doctor's office.

"Poor baby. You have a gorgeous woman bouncing on your dick every week."

"If you don't shut your fucking mouth, I'm going to break your jaw and have it wired shut."

"I'd love to see you try." He chuckles and then groans in pain. Holding his side, he leans back in the folding chair and rests his head against the dingy wall. *"Shit, I'm pretty sure I broke a rib last night."*

"Serves you right for fighting a man twice your size."

"Earned me triple the normal payout. I had to shoot my shot."

"And you lost."

Dmitri shrugs. "Still had to try."

I get it. I'm also doing things I have no business doing for good money. And D's right, Natalie is getting to me. I hate it so much I want to tear the skin from my body and set myself on fire. I'll also come running to her the second she calls me to her apartment again.

I fucking hate myself.

"Ryker Hudson?"

I spin around so fast, my foot hits the leg of a chair and knocks it over. "Yes?"

"She's all set."

"Okay." I glance at Dmitri for a hot second, then follow the nurse back into the examination room. *"How's she doing?"*

"I'll let the doctor talk with you."

That's not good. Every time they say shit like that, it always goes from bad to worse. I can't let them think I'm not doing anything at home for her. "She's eating more. Her appetite has definitely improved."

"That's wonderful. Her weight hasn't dropped since her last visit," the nurse says. *"That's a good thing."*

Good as in she's going to be okay? Or good as in,

that's the only bright spot in her dark life? I'm not sure I want to know the answer.

"She's right in here, sweetheart."

"Thanks." *I slip past the nurse as she holds the door open for me. Mom's rolling down her sleeve and I see the cotton ball taped to the crook of her elbow. They've taken more blood from her.* "Is she doing better?"

I can't look at the doctor when I ask that. My gaze remains locked onto my mom so I can read her expression when the doctor gives me his answer.

"Her levels are the same, but we're running a few more blood tests," *he says from a stool.* "We're going to have to run more scans next week, too. I've told your mother —"

"No more scans, no more tests," *Mom says firmly.* "And no more chemo."

My heart falls out of my ass. "Mom."

"I'm done." *Hopping off the examination table, her legs give out and I lunge forward to catch her before she crashes onto the floor.* "I'm fine," *she lies, patting my arm.* "He just took a lot of blood. Nothing a lollipop and juice box won't cure."

Fuck, I can't stand this. My mom doesn't need a juice box, she needs a miracle.

"Ashley, please reconsider what we've discussed today."

She puts her hand up to silence the doctor. "I've made up my mind." *Squeezing my arm, she looks up at me and says,* "Take me home, baby."

My legs feel like weights are strapped to my ankles as I half-carry her out of the office. Once we reach the waiting area, Dmitri hops up and gently grabs her other arm. Together, we get her outside and to the bus stop. Panic chokes me. I know damn well she'll never step foot in this side of town again if I can't get her to change her mind about treatment.

"Shit, I forgot to pay. Wait here with D, okay?" I *dash back, feeling guilty for lying–because I'd paid up front for the visit the instant my mother went into the room for her exam – and I book it straight back to the doctor's office.*

Out of breath, I grab his arm, stopping him before he enters the next patient's room. "What's wrong with her now?"

His frown deepens, making him look ancient. Holding the clipboard to his chest, he takes off his glasses and stares up at me. "It's spread to her bones, Ryker. I tried to convince her to be in a clinical trial, but she's not having it."

"Will it save her?" *Because if so, I'll do all that's in my power to get her into that study. Why won't he fucking answer me? My voice shakes as I yell,* "WILL IT SAVE HER?"

"No."

The floor opens and swallows me whole. My legs buckle. I fall to my knees. "Why…" *I can't breathe.* "Why would you have her in the study, then?" *For more money? Because these treatments have cost me all I have and then some. For hope? Because that shit's worthless. Because they need a goddamn guinea pig? She's worth more than that.*

"For more time," *he says.* "It'll buy her time to be with you, Ryker."

My gaze falls to the linoleum floor. I can't feel my face. "Time spent sick in the bathroom or passed out in bed." *Rage coils in my gut. I understand why my mother would refuse to do it.*

But I also desperately want her to be with me for as long as possible.

It's the selfishness that snaps me out of my sorrow. How dare I think of myself when she's the one suffering.

It doesn't matter that I quit school a year ago and lie to her every day about it. It doesn't matter that I work in construction by day, and as an escort by night. It doesn't matter that I've managed to put food in our bellies and pay our rent. It doesn't matter that all the medical bills are on a payment plan so I can manage them as best I can since my mom lost her health insurance because she also lost her job. I'd forged a letter from the company, saying they were giving her a severance package and allowing her to keep the health benefits as a thank you for her years of dedication. She was too sick at that point to question it. I'm not even sure she cared.

My mom's lived a hard, brutal, awful life. Abused by her father, then battered by her shit husband, only to run off with me when it got too unbearable, too painful and dangerous, to stay in her marriage to my dad. She's done nothing but struggle to keep us safe and happy ever since. I'll be damned if I make her life any harder by not giving her the choice and respecting her decision.

No matter how much it hurts me.

"I'm so sorry, son."

"Fuck you." I growl as rage rips through me. "Fuck every single one of you who said she'd be saved." I lift onto shaky legs and storm out of the office, knowing I'll never come back here again. By the time I return to my mom and Dmitri, I'm so numb I can't even hear the traffic honking around us.

"You good?" D asks.

My gaze lands on my mom. She stares at me with watery eyes and a stern expression that dares me to defy her. Dares me to beg her to do something she doesn't want to do.

I drop to my knees in front of her and hold her hands. My palms are sweaty. Hers are ice. "Make a list," I say firmly. "We're going to check it off and do everything you want until you can't anymore."

She closes her eyes as a sigh leaves her cracked lips, and the weight that seems to lift off her shoulders now lands heavily on mine.

Our bus pulls up and the doors open. D and I get her on board and into a seat where she rests her head against the window and closes her eyes.

D sits in the empty row behind her, and I sit next to him so my mom can stretch out on the bench seat if she wants. "What's going on, Ryker?"

"She's dying," *I say, admitting it out loud for the first time.* "And she's refusing anymore treatment."

"Shit." *His head slams back on the headrest and I know his heart is breaking just like mine. My mom's been a mother to us both for years.* "What can I do?"

I don't have a clue. I can't think straight.

The bus takes off and as we get further and further away from the doctor's office, it's like I didn't just leave the building behind, but all my hope too. It's done. It's over. I can't do anything but move forward.

"When she makes a list, I want to check everything off, no matter what. It might get expensive." *I have no clue what my mom might want to do, but I swear to God, if she says she wants to eat a croissant in front of the Eiffel fucking tower, I'm going to make sure I take her there and get her the best pastry in all of France.* "She deserves happiness before she dies."

Especially since she's had none her whole life.

"Money we can make easily enough," *D whispers.* "I'll enter a few more heavyweight fights."

"And I'll suck a lot more dick." *Because that pays better than servicing a woman around here.*

We both fall into silence with my mom passed out in the seat in front of us.

"Hey," Dmitri snaps his fingers in my face. "Ryker."

"Yeah." I clear my throat. "I'm good."

"Don't pull that shit, okay?"

"What shit?" I'm sweating like a sinner in church. Yanking on my collar, I pop the top button and it rolls across the floor. "I'm not doing anything, D."

"You're blurring the past and present. Tara's not Natalie. And your mom is—"

I wrap my hand around his fat neck and squeeze. *"Don't talk about her."*

We promised the day we put her in the ground, we would never talk about my mother again. All the blood, sweat, tears, and other fluids we drained ourselves of just to make her shortened life a good one blew to smithereens too fucking quickly. I don't think either of us have recovered from it yet.

"You've got to move on," D says with a strained voice. His face is a lovely shade of crimson and I have no intention of letting him get air. "Everything… happens for… a reason, Ry."

My long-leashed fury breaks free. I draw my fist and smash his face.

Chapter 14

Tara

What the hell is that noise? It sounds like two lions attacking each other in the hallway. I peek my head out the door and —

Oh shit!

Racing over to the bed, I grab a blanket and tie it around myself, then shoot out the door to stop the fight between Mr. Hudson and Dmitri.

"Stop!" I yell.

They're pounding each other. Or rather, Ryker is walloping on Dmitri, who's doing the bare minimum to stop him. When Dmitri finally pushes back, Mr. Hudson slams against the wall so hard, it leaves a dent in the drywall. Mr. Hudson shoves Dmitri, screaming as he drives him backwards, and now there's a Dmitri sized dent in the other wall.

"Stop it!" Getting closer to them will likely risk an elbow to my face, so I look up and wave my hands at the camera in the corner down the hall. "Someone help!"

"Don't worry about it, Sweetheart." Dmitri grunts as Mr. Hudson punches him in the gut. "He hits like a little bitch, anyway."

Ryker swings a left hook that makes Dmitri spin around and fall to the floor, blood spraying out of his mouth.

A door opens down the hall and Vault runs towards us. Instead of pulling Ryker off Dmitri like I expect, he manhandles *me* instead and starts pulling me back towards my suite. "Get back inside, Butterfly. You don't need to be here for this."

"Get off me!" I yank my arm out of his loose grip and turn back to the fight.

"Butterfly," Vault growls. "It's for your own safety."

"I'm not the one bleeding all over the floor!" I jerk away when he grabs me again. "Get off me!"

"Touch her again and I'll tear your fucking hands off, Vault."

We both freeze and my eyes widen when Mr. Hudson slowly rises to his feet. His chest expands with his heavy breaths and blood drips from his split lip. Dmitri rolls over and stands up, swaying on his feet even as he laughs.

Crazy motherfuckers.

My gaze bounces between them, but I back up when Mr. Hudson storms towards us growling, "Back away from her."

Vault's hands fly up, and he takes several paces back from me. "I didn't hurt her."

Mr. Hudson doesn't look like he believes him, not with how his eyes lock on my arm where Vault's hand just was.

I shake my head. "He didn't hurt me. He was only trying to keep me safe."

Ryker doesn't seem to hear me. Or see me. It's like he's in some other headspace, too far away for us to reach. He wraps a gentle hand around my throat, his gaze sailing across my face, down my neck, and to my chest where I'm clutching the bedsheet wrapped around me.

"He didn't hurt me, Ryker. Mr. Hudson. Sir." *Fuck*, I can't think straight with him on me like this. It's hot and scary at the same time. "I promise."

His eyes drop to my arm again, like he's checking it for red marks or something. Then he snaps back to my eyes and leans into my face. "Go back to your suite, Butterfly. *Now*."

"Not..." Oh my god, why am I so turned on right now? "Not without you."

"She's not the one," Dmitri says from several feet away.

It makes Mr. Hudson's grip on my throat release and his hand fall to his side.

"She's not the fucking one, Ry."

Mr. Hudson moans and leans into me, pressing his forehead against mine. His eyes close. His breaths punch out, fast and hard. His shoulders shake with what I assume is fury.

She's not the one. I have no clue what that means. Should I be insulted or grateful? It doesn't matter. "Come back to the room with me," I whisper. "Please, Sir."

Ryker's voice cracks. "He didn't hurt you?"

"No." It's like the fight, or what started it, no longer matters to him. All he seems to care about is my safety. "I'm fine. Come see for yourself."

Mr. Hudson doesn't escort me back to my room. He grabs my hands and squeezes them tight, then presses his forehead to mine harder, and starts walking, driving me backwards until we're both back in the Butterfly suite. He eases up once we're inside, but his gaze never stops burning into mine.

Holy shit, my heart's forgotten how to beat.

The door shuts behind us and he continues to drive me through the suite and towards the bed. The bedsheet wrapped around me is too long, and he accidentally steps on it. I realize too late, and step back more, making the sheet unfold and fall to the floor.

He continues maneuvering me, manipulating and guiding my footsteps until my ass hits the side of the mattress and I drop onto the bed. Then he falls to his knees and spreads my legs. "You're not hurt."

"N-no." I don't understand why he's acting like a bizarre animal.

He shoves his nose against my pussy and stills. His shoulders tense and I'm not sure how to respond. I press my hand against his head in encouragement, but he jerks away from me. "Don't do that."

"Okay. I'm sorry."

Running his hands up and down my calves, he looks up at me again and we stare at each other. "Don't be afraid of me."

"I'm not."

"You are. Your eyes give it away."

"I…" Okay, I'm a little scared because I don't understand his behavior. And more pressing is the fact that it's turning me on when it's probably a big red flag. "I just don't understand you."

"You're not supposed to, Butterfly." He spreads my pussy lips and shoves his tongue inside me, licking and tasting. "You're just supposed to enjoy me, Tara."

My name on his lips is a spell. I'm certain of it. And when he stares at me like he is right now, I forget all about my worries and focus on his mouth, his gaze, and the way his hands run up my inner thighs. He tongue-fucks me until I'm a writhing mess. My orgasm comes so fast, I'm almost ashamed.

"That's my good girl," he says in a low tone. "Lay back and enjoy it."

My brain fritzes for a second before I'm able to collect my thoughts and take the reins. Fool me once, Mr. Hudson, shame on you. Fool me twice, shame on me. I'm not about to let him play the "Make Tara come until she passes out so I can leave" game again.

"Red." Part of me feels like it's an abusive way to use my safe word, but it has the outcome I need. Sir pulls away from me immediately. His gaze searches mine, likely seeking an answer for why I'd call Red when all he's doing is giving me much wanted pleasure. "You're hurt, Sir."

"I'm fine."

He's far from it.

"Your knuckles," I say quietly.

Looking down, it's as if he's just noticed how busted they are. Maybe his anger made him numb earlier. Maybe using my body as a sexual distraction dulled his senses, too. But I'm not about to let him pretend he didn't just have a major tantrum outside, and then come back in here to play mind games with me.

"Come into the bathroom so I can clean you up." I slink off the bed, hoping he'll follow me, which he doesn't do until I call for him again from the bathroom.

Mr. Hudson enters cautiously, confusion making his mouth turn down.

"Sit." I get the first aid kit from the cupboard.

He plops down on the edge of the massive tub. "This isn't necessary."

"Neither is making me come until I pass out, but

here we are." I get on my knees between his legs and grab his right hand first. "Looks like we both go the extra mile for each other."

His hand is rougher than I thought it would be. I'm used to being with men who sit behind a desk all day. It makes me wonder what Ryker does when he's not pleasuring a woman, running a sex club, or beating the shit out of his friends.

He inhales sharply through clenched teeth when I dab a soapy washcloth to his cut knuckles.

"Sorry." I make sure to be as gentle as possible.

"No, I'm the one who's sorry. I shouldn't have acted like that out there."

"I think that apology should go to Dmitri, not me." Looking up at him, I tack on, "Sir."

Mr. Hudson takes his hand back before I'm finished cleaning it. Shoving up to his feet, he storms out of my bathroom without saying a word, leaving me on my knees in front of the bathtub, gawking after him. Part of me fears if he walks out my suite door right now, he won't come back.

I'm not willing to risk that.

"Ryker!" I scamper to my feet and dash out of the bathroom, only to find him digging around the trunk behind the chaise.

His gaze snaps to mine and his eyes narrow. "What did you just call me, Butterfly?"

This man's mood shifts are giving me whiplash. Instead of answering him like a good little submissive, I cross my arms over my chest and lean against the doorjamb. "You heard me."

He walks over, carrying a flogger that has red and black leather tassels, and a smirk creeps across his handsome face. "Are you familiar with a flogger,

Butterfly?"

Yes, but I've never used one of those before. And in his current state of mind, I sure as shit don't want him using it on me right now. "I don't want that."

"That's not what I asked, Tara."

Again, the way he says my name makes my pussy clench. It's like the word itself is something he wants to spit out yet savor on his tongue at the same time. Or at least that's what my overactive imagination thinks. "Only a little."

"Give me more than that. Have you been flogged before?"

"No." My cheeks heat. "I did use a riding crop once, though."

"That's not the same as this." He swishes the tassels. "But did you like the crop when you used it?"

"No." My heart pounds in my chest. "It stung too much and left big welts."

He combs his fingers through the tassels and approaches slowly. "It only hurts if you want to make it hurt."

Shaking my head, I'm not sure I believe that. Getting flogged isn't something on my bucket list, but I also didn't come here for vanilla sex. I wanted to be the Butterfly so I can experience things no one else will share with me. Still, Mr. Hudson isn't in the headspace for happy fun times with a whip. Unless…

"Let me use it on you." The words fly out of my mouth before I can stop them.

"There's an art to flogging someone, and I'm not about to let you whip my back or any other body part without experiencing it yourself first." He points to the floor. "On your knees, Butterfly."

When I don't budge, he surprises me by taking a step back. "Would you be more comfortable if I used this on someone else first, to show you what it's like?"

"Yes." But I have no clue who that might be.

I also don't think he's in a good space to be using that thing on anyone. He just threw hands with his security guard for crying out loud. Now he's calm as a cucumber and wanting sex? I don't get it.

Mr. Hudson walks backwards, keeping his eyes on me while making his way to my suite door. Reaching behind him, he opens it and simply says, "Come in here."

I had no clue there was someone on the other side of our door this whole time. My jaw drops when Dmitri enters. He's got a swollen left eye, a split lip, and his thick neck still has Ryker's handprint around it. But he doesn't act hurt at all. In fact, he's just as calm, cool, and collected as Ryker is.

These guys are fucking crazy.

Why am I turned on by that?

"My Butterfly wants to use this flogger on me," Mr. Hudson explains. "But she's never used one before."

Dmitri chuckles. "Then let's give her a beginner's lesson."

"Is that okay with you, Butterfly?"

I'm baffled. Did these two not just have a fist fight five minutes ago? Why would Ryker ask him to be in here?

"I asked you a question, Tara."

I fix my gaze on Dmitri as he pulls his black t-shirt off. Christ this man's stacked.

And scarred.

"Yes," I finally say to Ryker. "I'm totally okay

with this. I want to learn."

Guess what's just been added to Tara's sex-filled bucket list, boys and girls.

I try to not stare at Dmitri's scars, but when he drops to his knees, he grants me a genuine smile and says, "They're from a long time ago."

Like that makes it any better? I also notice there are fresh bruises on his ribs. "Did you give him those too, Sir?"

"No," both men say at the same time.

"I like violence, Butterfly. It gets me off." Dmitri jabs his finger into his ribs and hisses with a pain, even as his eyes roll back in ecstasy.

My mouth waters and pussy clenches, while my mind screams that this is a bad idea. "That's... not helpful to me if you're now about to convince me that a whip won't hurt."

"She's got a point, D." Mr. Hudson's smile is a little bigger now. And more real. "How about we switch."

The men change positions. Mr. Hudson carefully unbuttons his white dress shirt, rolling his shoulders back as he takes it off and lays it on the floor beside him. Dmitri looms over Ryker's back, and both are staring directly at me.

These two men are powerful.

Bloody and powerful and here to teach me.

Why is this such a fucking turn on?

"The tassels on this one are soft," Mr. Hudson explains. "Feel them, Butterfly."

My hand trembles when I touch the whip Dmitri holds out for me. The leather is super soft, like fringe.

"Hold your palm flat," Dmitri orders. When I do, he hits me with the whip. It doesn't hurt at all.

"How was that?"

"Green," I say, automatically fixating on Ryker. "*Very* green."

"Show her how to swing it." Ryker stays on his knees with his hands resting on his thighs. He doesn't break eye contact with me. Not even when Dmitri makes the first strike across his back.

The sound of impact isn't hard or sharp like I expect. It's almost lazy and slow. "That's not how it works," I say, more to myself than them. Every time I've seen a toy like this used downstairs, the strikes are so harsh, I always flinch hearing them.

"It is when you first start and you're new." Ryker keeps still while Dmitri hits him again and again, moving the strikes back and forth across his shoulder blades. Each hit gets a little faster, and a little harder as he keeps a steady rhythm. The tassel's rustles grow louder and become more uniform. Mr. Hudson's eyes soon glaze over. A calmness takes over his body, his posture sagging as his mouth parts and expression relaxes.

"Your Dom drops into subspace fast like this," Dmitri says to me. "Does he look hurt to you?"

I shake my head, unable to pull my gaze from Mr. Hudson. He looks sublime. *Beautiful.*

"That's because he chose a very sweet flogger for you, Butterfly. He's not going to hurt you. Not unless you negotiate ahead of time and give consent first."

"Pain isn't my kink." Shit, I shouldn't have said it like that. "I mean, no offense. You do you, but…" I still can't pull my eyes from Ryker. It's like his head has shut off.

I want that for myself too. But more so, I want

to give Ryker this level of euphoria. I know he's hurting, even if I don't know why, and if I can help ease that pain for him by doing something like this, I want to learn how.

Dmitri continues flogging him, harder, faster. Ryker lets out a small groan and tips forward. My mouth waters at the sight of his back—it's got small pink welts and a few red slash marks.

"Does it hurt yet?" I ask, dropping down on my knees, dying to run my hands across his sweaty skin.

"No," Ryker confesses in a deep tone. He arches when I run my fingers along his back. "Fuck, woman."

I pull away instantly. "Did I hurt you?"

"Not at all. Your cold fingers feel incredible on me."

I run my hands along his back again, loving that my touch may offer some relief.

Dmitri leans down and grumbles in my ear, "Would you like a turn, Butterfly?"

Considering Dmitri could have very well whipped the hell out of Ryker for what just happened outside, but instead gave him only pleasure, and the way Ryker is still glassy-eyed and groaning? I can't imagine a better way to experience this for the first time.

"Yes, please." My hands wrap around the soft leather corded handle of the flogger.

"Swing just like I showed you."

My strikes are nowhere near as precise as Dmitri's. I don't think Ryker cares. The power I feel is astounding. Ryker trusting me like this means so much, I'd never fuck it up. To know each slash I make across his back somehow brings him relief, makes my chest crack open.

There's so much pain. So much aggression. So much *everything* inside him.

Does flogging shove those emotions back down in their hole, or does it give them a way out of his body?

My voice drops to a sultry tone as lust floods my body. "What color are you?"

"Green." He runs his hands over his thighs. "Very green, Butterfly."

"Do you want to feel what he feels?"

Dmitri's icy blue eyes connect with mine, pulling me under his spell too. I don't know what's happening to my head right now, but I feel light as a feather. "Yes." God, yes.

"I'll do you both together, if you wish."

Holy Hell. "Okay." I mirror Mr. Hudson's position, and brace for Dmitri's first strike.

"Relax, Butterfly. Trust your Dom to keep you safe."

"Light system," Ryker reminds me as he threads his hand in mine. "All you have to do is say green, yellow, or red, remember?"

"Mmm hmm. I remember, Sir."

"That's my good girl."

Such a small phrase, just a minuscule bit of praise, has me willing to let both these men destroy my body.

But they don't.

Dmitri starts slow and soft, just like he did with Ryker, and before long, I'm yearning for more impact. These hits don't sting at all. They're more of a thud. A light pounding against my muscles. "Harder, *please*."

"She begs so beautifully," Dmitri says darkly.

Mr. Hudson's hand is still on top of mine, but

it's damp. "What color are you, Tara?"

"Green."

"Good." He lets go of me and stands. "Will you allow me to have a turn with you now?"

"Yes." I'm dying to know if there's a difference between their methods. My body is hot and flushed. My pussy is slick and aching with need. I feel so good. So floaty.

Dmitri squats down in front of me. "Eyes on me, Butterfly."

I lock gazes with him just as Mr. Hudson's flogger lands on my left shoulder blade. It's not nearly as hard as I want it to be. "More."

He strikes again and again, his rhythm eventually speeding up, his force builds and builds. I'm not sure if I'm in subspace or not, but I like the way this feels. A lot.

"What color are you, Butterfly?"

"Green."

His next strike is noticeably harder.

"Keep your gaze on me." Dmitri holds my chin between his fingers. The flogger lands harder on my back again. "You're doing so well for us."

My eyes flutter shut. This feels so fucking good.

"Open for me," Dmitri says.

Does he mean my eyes or my mouth? Or is he talking about my legs? I'll open all three at the same time if they want me to. I want more than my back lashed. I *need* more. I want to be overwhelmed and taken to some faraway place where I can escape my reality. My brain feels so fuzzy. I want to be fucked and overpowered.

Dominated.

"*Eyes on me,*" Dmitri says again since I've yet to

obey him.

The delicious impact on my back suddenly stops. Ryker's body heat sinks into my skin when he gets on his knees behind me and presses his bare chest against my back. Wrapping his hand around my throat, he tips my head. "Open your eyes, Tara."

It's harder than it should be to obey. I feel sleepy and foggy headed. "I'm-with-you," I say, my words slur together. "I'm still green."

They get me onto the bed.

"She's perfect." Dmitri swipes the hair from my face and kisses my cheek. "Thank you for the privilege, Butterfly."

He leaves just as Mr. Hudson unbuckles his belt.

Chapter 15

Ryker

I'm vaguely aware of the danger I'm in as I remove my belt. Tara stares up at me, seemingly unbothered that I could just as easily choke her, tie her up, or beat her with this leather strap as I could cast it aside and be sweet to her. "What do you want, Butterfly?"

"For you to stop staring at me like that."

I don't have to ask what she means. I know the way I'm looking at her because it's the same way I've looked at every person who's ever made their way into my bed. Settling between her legs, I hover over Tara and kiss down her neck. She tilts up to give me better access to her throat.

Fuck, her trust makes me grip the belt in my hand even harder.

Cupping the back of her head, my lips almost brush hers when I say, "Tell me what you want done to your body."

Since she likes the flogger, I bet she'll enjoy some of the other toys stashed away in here too. I'm determined to make her stay in this suite absolute Hell, yet my actions swing closer to divine pleasures every single time I'm in the room with her.

I crave this woman on a level I can't understand. Since the moment I first saw her in my club, and even now as she's putty in my hands, I want to do things to her I haven't indulged in for a very long time.

Maybe it's because I see something in her eyes that matches the ache I carry in my chest. Like draws to like, isn't that the saying? But even if we have nothing in common, and my instincts are completely off this time, Tara's still a beautiful creature to worship.

And to break.

Christ, I need to get a grip. I feel a thousand times better now that I've had a decent fight and flogging, but rage still burns in my body and needs an outlet.

"Everything happens for a reason, Ry." Dmitri's words seep into my bones, melting my resolve. Tara's not Natalie. She isn't here to betray me or ruin me. She's only here to use me.

As all whores are meant to be used.

And I chose this, whether I want to admit it or not.

"I want you to kiss me," Tara whispers.

That's an easy request. I bend down and press a gentle kiss on her collarbone.

"On my mouth, Sir."

Not happening. I cock my eyebrow at her and smile like a devil. "My mouth could be better used in other ways." I run my thumb across her fat bottom lip. "And yours can be stuffed with something to keep it better occupied, Butterfly."

The room flickers. I blink a couple times. Shit, what the fuck is wrong with me?

Tara sits up, startled. Her eyes widen. "What was that?"

Alarms suddenly go off.

"Shit." It's the fire alarm. I rush over to the closet and yank it open. "Put this on and come with me." Tossing her a robe, I barely give her time to get into it before yanking her out of the room.

Vault runs out of the back hall where our offices are and runs into Dmitri. "What the fuck's going on?"

"Don't know," he says, running towards the steps.

"I'll check the server room," Vault dashes down the hall.

Keeping Tara protectively under my arm, I quickly escort her to the stairwell. My mind races with a million situations. How many staff are here right now? Are they all safe? If something in the kitchen's caught fire, is it repairable by this evening? What's the damage going to cost? I don't smell any smoke. Did someone pull the lever for shits and giggles?

My heart pounds along with my footsteps as I descend another flight. Tara's bare feet slap against the concrete as she keeps up. Fuck. She doesn't have on shoes!

I should have *never* taken her clothing from her. I'm such a dick.

We hit the first-floor landing and I scoop her into my arms.

"Ryker!" She yelps, smacking my shoulders. "Put me down!"

I'll let it slide that she's using my real name right now. She can protest all she wants, but there's no goddamn way I'm going to let her outside in the back alley barefoot.

Dmitri breaks through the back door. "There's nothing in the basement," he says, out of breath. "I'll check the kitchen. Vault took the server room and offices."

Shit, maybe the fire started in the walls or a bedroom? "Is everyone out?"

"It's only me, you, Vault, and Sophie." Dmitri runs a hand over his shaved head. "And Tara."

Sophie should have gone home already, so the fact that she's still here worries me because who else might be here, unaccounted for? My employees always go above and beyond for me. It wouldn't be surprising if some of my staff were already setting up scenes for tonight. Besides, the cleaning staff might still be finishing up somewhere we haven't accounted for yet.

The faster I get Tara to safety, the faster I can help my friends.

At least she's stopped kicking her feet and smacking my shoulders.

"I'll be back," I say to Dmitri. Hurrying out of the alley, I carry Tara to my car and set her down once I'm sure the road is clear of debris. "Sit in my car and wait for me." Digging my key fob out of my pocket, I unlock my Audi s6 and open the door for her. "If you get scared or if you see smoke, drive off, okay?"

"What?"

"Do what I say, Tara." I'm not sure if there's really a fire or not, but worst-case scenarios creep into my mind and I don't want Tara injured from an explosion or something. "Get in."

She obeys — *thank fuck* — and I slam the door shut to seal her inside before running back to my crew.

Chapter 16

Tara

Ryker Hudson is unpredictable. I don't think I like it. As he runs back into his sex club, I take a deep breath and blow it out. Leaning back in the leather seat, I grip the steering wheel and stare down at my lap as I try to make a plan. The silk robe I'm in barely covers my goods. The pedal and brake both feel rough against my soft, pedicured bare feet.

This is ridiculous.

I'm leaving.

Starting the engine, I feel a slight pang of guilt. What if Ryker needs my help?

He has Dmitri and Vault, dumbass. He doesn't need a woman in a barely there silk robe and no shoes coming to anyone's rescue.

Realizing how very useless I've become, especially dressed this way, only flares my anger more. This is Ryker's fault. If he hadn't been such a controlling dicktwat and let me have my fucking clothes, I could be helping instead of running.

Now I'm really fucking pissed.

If there were flames shooting out of the windows, I wouldn't hesitate to run in there to help — silk robe be damned. But there's *nothing*. I didn't even smell smoke while he rushed us out of there. For some reason, it makes this situation feel even lamer. Not that I want his place of business to burn to the ground or anything, but being carried out, then instructed to sit tight while he leaves to make sure everyone's safe and handles this chaos himself, while I'm wrapped in a white silk robe in a dumb car, makes me rage.

I'm not a delicate butterfly, no matter what my temporary title is here.

Did someone pull that lever and fake a fire?

Wait a damn minute…

Did Ryker set this whole thing up to distract me and separate us again?

"Fuck this." I slam the car in drive and take off.

Twenty minutes later, I pull my, I mean Mr. Hudson's car, up to the front of my condo complex.

Garret glares at me from the front door of the building.

Great. Just fucking perfect.

Humiliation finds me wherever I go.

My stepbrother storms around the front of the car and the urge to run him over is strong enough that I have to put it in park, so I don't actually commit murder this early in the day.

"The fuck," he yells, standing at the driver's side door and attempts to yank it open. Too bad it's locked. I sit back and smile at him. He looks like a fucking idiot.

"Open the fucking door, Tara!" The heel of his palm slams against the window and my heart leaps into my throat.

Garret has a bad temper and considers himself better than everyone else. Especially me.

I suck in a deep breath and mask my expression. Confidence gets me out of jams often and I've perfected my bullshit game to where sometimes I even fool myself. Opening the car door, I hit him with it because he won't back up. "Do you mind?" One bare foot, then two, land on the cold asphalt as I climb out of the Audi.

"You've got to be fucking kidding me." Garret snarls, stepping back with a disgusted expression that makes him twice as ugly as usual. "You're an embarrassment, Tara."

Swallowing a million usual comebacks, I decide to flaunt past him and head inside.

"Don't walk away from me!" Garrett yells, storming after me.

Making sure my robe is tightly wrapped around me, I keep my gaze straight ahead and make it to the elevator before caving. "What are you even doing here, Garret?"

"You missed our meeting this morning. I called your cell, and you didn't answer."

"So?" My heart thuds in my chest. "That hardly warrants you coming here."

"Did you get the Greene Street property or not?"

"I decided against it."

Garret grabs my arm and jerks me. "*What?*" His voice is clipped. Low. Seething.

Ignoring the dizzying fear that's gripped me, I cock my eyebrow at him and calmly say, "Let. Go."

He doesn't.

"That was your last chance, Tara." His smile makes my throat tighten. "You just fucked yourself better than I ever could." His icy gaze drags down my body as he huffs a laugh. "Bet you didn't even bother to go to Greene Street, you lazy whore." His gaze rakes up and down my form. "I can only imagine how many dicks you sucked last night."

"Angry none of them were yours?" My palms are sweaty and chest aches.

His grip tightens on my arm, and he slams me against the wall. The back of my head cracks on the marble tile and his hand wraps tightly around my throat. "You stupid fucking cunt."

Two people step out of the elevator, take one look at us, and rush out the front door. *No one ever helps me.*

Garret chuckles because he's used to no one interfering with his temper tantrums. "You're pathetic." His mouth gets closer to mine. "I hope you get fired for sinking the deal. Hell, maybe you'll get cut off for good. *Finally.*"

My eyes fill with tears because he's squeezing way too hard. He sees me struggling to breathe. That smug smile of his also tells me he likes it.

"If you want to keep your motherfucking hands, you better remove them from her throat."

I'm robbed of breath when Ryker casually walks towards us. He looks calm. Unfazed.

But his dark gaze is vicious.

Garret doesn't let go. "Mind your business, asshole."

Ryker doesn't hesitate. The instant he's within striking distance, he punches Garret in the back of the head. My stepbrother drops to the ground with a grunt. "She *is* my business," Ryker says, kicking Garret in the ribs next.

Two more hits and Garret's splayed out on the ground, face down. Ryker straddles him and uses Garret's own tie to strangle him with. My stepbrother's eyes bug out, his face turning a spectacular crimson, and he chokes with his tongue out like a fucking dog.

"When I let you go," Ryker growls, "you will apologize and never touch her again. Is that clear?"

Garret sputters and kicks his legs. "Yessss."

Covering my mouth with shaky hands, I'm terrified, angry, and relieved all at once. No one has attacked Garret like this before. It'll either put him in line or make him act out worse later.

"That's a good boy." Ryker lifts Garret off the floor with his suit jacket. My stepbrother has never looked so scared, disheveled, and pissed off before. It makes me want to take a step back, but I can't since I'm already against a damn wall. "Now what do we say?"

Garret glowers at me.

I roll my shoulders and take back a little of my power. "Yes. What do you have to say to me?"

Never mind how my knees wobble. I'm just glad my voice is still steady.

"Sorry," Garret spits out.

Ryker manhandles him out of the lobby like he's taking out the trash. Shoving him through the glass doors, he says something I can't make out, and then calmly turns around and stalks back to me again. "Are you okay?"

Yes. No.

"I'm fine."

His jaw clenches as he stares at my neck.

"I…" It's like the world stopped spinning. "Can I go up to my place for a minute?"

I don't know why I'm even asking permission. Ryker's not my master, not outside the club. But when he nods, I can't describe the relief it gives me. I click the button, calling the elevator and hate how my hands shake.

Holy shit. Holy shit, holy shit, holy shit. This is bad. All of this is so bad. Garret will retaliate, and I have no clue how I'm going to handle it.

And how did Ryker get here so fast?

The silence is deafening on the ride to the seventh floor. When the elevator doors open, we both step into my living room.

I gave Garret the code to my place a couple months ago because I needed him to swing by and pick up paperwork for our father while I was away on a business trip. I never bothered to change the code afterwards, but I do now. God, the thought of him coming here whenever he wants sends shivers down my spine.

There was absolutely no reason for that asshole to show up here today. He doesn't care about me, and he definitely wouldn't give a shit about that Greene Street property. Still trembling, I reset the passcode while Ryker watches from a short distance away. He's not speaking. Then again, neither am I. What's there to say?

Jesus, I can't believe just a few short hours ago I was having some of the best orgasms of my life and now here I am, my throat sore from being squeezed, my nerves shot, and my anger simmering in my belly.

"Who was that man, Tara?"

I don't owe him answers and I didn't ask him to step in and save me just now—even though I'll be forever grateful that he did. "I'm guessing your club isn't burning down."

"There was a small fire in one of the bedrooms from a fucking candle. It's being handled." With arms crossed over his chest, he glowers. "Who is he?"

"No one that concerns you."

"It very much concerns me." He blocks my way again. "You're mine for the next twenty-eight days."

He's counting? Anger simmers under my skin like hot coals. "I'm not something that can be owned."

"Yes, you are." Ryker steps in my way again, his hand outstretched like he wants to touch me, or grab me, or hold me down, or I don't even know what because I can't see past my tears. "You're mine to pleasure," he says in a softer tone. "And mine to take care of."

My chest cracks open, letting my heart plop out between our feet. Sure, I'm his for the next twenty-eight days, but not past that. Coming home for two seconds is a harsh reminder of what I have to look forward to when I'm no longer the Butterfly.

I'm just so grateful Ryker showed up when he did to stop Garret this time. I'm not even going to ask how he got here so fast, or how the hell he even knew where I lived. Knowing Ryker, he probably has a tracker in his car and my damn address memorized.

Ryker tips my chin, his brow furrowing as our gazes collide. "Who is he, Tara?"

"Why does it matter?"

"Because I want to know who I'm planning to murder." He looks serious. "But really his name doesn't matter. I just want to know who he is to you, so I know exactly how fucking brutal I should be when I get my hands on him again."

My chin trembles. I almost confess everything I've kept inside since I was twelve. Then survival mode kicks in and I toughen back up. "He's not worth the prison sentence." I brush past Ryker and go into my room, shutting myself inside until I calm the hell down.

I have twenty-eight days left with this man and I refuse to let my personal struggles influence what I want from Ryker.

God, that look in his eyes? The one Ryker wore when he came up behind Garret and punched him in the back of the head? It was the same vicious, possessive darkness he had when he thought Vault might have hurt me in the hallway.

That look.

That *look*!

I don't think I've ever seen someone possess such a brutal, feral, murderous gaze in all my life. I bet Ryker holds himself back from shredding the world to ribbons every day.

What has he gone through to make him this way?

The terrifyingly possessive and vicious gaze that made Ryker seem like he'd gladly bash the brains in of anyone who ever tries to hurt me, is absolutely terrifying.

Because the sickest part is…

I want Ryker to always stare at me like that.

Chapter 17

Ryker

I have no business being this possessive and protective over a woman. Let alone someone like Tara. She's using me the same way every client in my past has used me. She wants a good time.

Only I've paid her for her privilege to fuck me.

How shit-tastic is that?

Ever since this woman's been in my crosshairs, she's head-fucked me. I go from craving her, to wanting to kick her out, to fighting the urge to protect her at all costs, and even contemplating murder.

I wasn't kidding about that. No man should lay their hands on a woman in anger. That motherfucker's only still breathing because I wanted Tara safe and away from him first. Even now, the urge to take the elevator back down to the lobby and hunt him down is fucking strong.

But unlike my best friend, Dmitri, I have enough control left in me to table it for now.

If D was here, and this was his woman, the lobby would be soaked in blood and Dmitri would be on the news, getting hauled away to prison with a life sentence. I have people who need me, and I've hesitated because of it. Well, that and I don't know this woman at all.

Just like I don't know who that guy was

downstairs.

Was that her husband? Lover? Friend? Enemy? Co-worker?

I hate not knowing the answer. Why does she refuse to give it to me?

Scrubbing my face with both hands, I familiarize myself with her apartment. It's swanky. Smells feminine. Most of her furniture is white with splashes of turquoise. Her kitchen looks like it barely gets used. In fact, the only thing that looks used is her desk positioned in front of an enormous window. Stacks of papers and folders litter the top. One drawer is half-open. Most of the letter keys on her laptop have all worn off.

It's quiet in here. You can't hear the busy street below since the windows are high quality like the rest of the place. I can't even hear Tara in the other room. The silence makes my balls clench. I like noise. No, I need it. Chaos is very much my comfort zone, and this place makes me feel like I'm walking around a graveyard no one visits.

Knocking on her bedroom door, I hold back from barging in. "You okay in there?"

No answer.

"Tara?" Did she climb out the window or something? "Tara, answer me."

Still nothing.

"I'm coming in." Shoving the door open, I expect it to be locked, but it isn't. Her bedroom is white on white—from the cushioned headboard to the bedding, curtains, and rug. It's like an empty canvas. There are no photos or art hanging on the walls. No plants. Nothing that makes it seem personal.

It's a hollow shell.

"Tara?" Her closet door is open, so I head there first. It's not until I see her bare feet in the corner and hear sniffling when my heart falls out of my fucking ass. *Jesus Christ.* "Tara," I say softly, kneeling in front of her.

"Just give me a minute." She keeps her face hidden behind several thousand dollars' worth of couture.

I can't bear the thought of her huddled in the corner of her closet like this, crying, and me useless to fix it. God, I don't even want to know why I *want* to fix it. She's not my wife. She's not my lover. She's the club's Butterfly and nothing more. Still, I can't stand seeing her like this.

"Take all the time you need." I lick my lips and add, "I'm not going anywhere."

Tara lets out a slow breath and wipes her cheeks. "I'm sorry I left the club."

"Don't be." Fuck, how did we get to this? "Sorry I held your clothing hostage." If she'd had them earlier, a lot of humility and vulnerability could have been avoided. "I was a dick to keep them from you."

"Yeah, you were."

Tara eventually takes my hand and I lift her to her feet. She's no longer in the robe from the club, but what she has on isn't much better. Her dress hits just above her knees and the sheer sleeves hit mid-forearm. There's a belt cinched around her waist, showing off the flare of her hips.

She still hasn't let go of my hand. I've yet to stop staring at her perfect-for-me body.

Before I know it, I draw in closer until our bodies are flush against each other. Her eyes are a brilliant shade of blue that has me drowning. I wet my lips. Lean in.

Then catch myself.

Shit. Nope. Time to step back and take a breather.

Only when I do, she looks like I've just kicked her in the crotch. "Sorry," I say, rubbing the back of my neck. "I should give you space. You just had a scare, and the last thing you need is someone else in your face."

Cop out.

"It's fine." Tara scoops her hair up to put in a low ponytail. That's when I get a good look at her throat.

A clear red handprint marks the front of her neck where the skin's already bruising.

My anger flares to life all over again.

Instead of insisting she tell me who that was, I turn on my heels and head to the kitchen for ice. There's only a bag of frozen strawberries and a bottle of vodka in her freezer. I pour her a shot in case she needs it and smash the frozen bag of fruit on the counter so it's more pliable. Heading back to her, I stop when I see she's now at her desk, rummaging through papers.

"Lay down," I say, handing over the frozen berries. "Work can wait."

"No, it can't." She rifles through more of her folders.

I assume she's like me and dumps her energy into work instead of finding a better outlet for it.

"Who was that guy, Tara?"

"Just another asshole who thinks he owns the world."

He doesn't own Tara. I do. That motherfucker will pay for what he's done to my girl. But that look she's giving me is pleading for me to drop it, so I will for now. I've got plenty of time to wear her down about it later.

"Look..." She says after a heavy sigh. "I know the rules of the club state I can't have outside contact while I'm the Butterfly. But that's not going to work for me. I have a business to run and shit to do."

"The rules clearly state—"

"That the Butterfly and her Dom or Doms will be locked in for a month together. Yes, I'm aware." She tosses the bag of berries onto the desk. "But you've already left me three times to run your club. You'd be a hypocrite to make me follow the rules you, yourself, are breaking."

Where is this coming from? Five minutes ago, she was crying in the corner of her closet. Now suddenly, she's ready to pick a fight and get back to business? "If you don't like it, you can always relinquish the title and honor, Tara."

"*Honor*?" She stands up, seething. "It's supposed to be an *honor* to be treated like I'm just a chore? I'm not something on your to do list."

Ahh, I get it. She doesn't swing punches like I do, but she still knows how to pick a fight so she can unleash her anger. "That's not at all what I—"

"Oh, it is, *Sir*." She gets all in my personal space. "You act like you can just make me come until I crash, and that should be good enough. You keep me locked and naked like a prisoner."

She wants a fight? Now she's got one. "I've *never* locked you in that goddamn room."

"You might as well have," she tosses back. "And you took all my clothes!"

"I said I was sorry for that." Shoving a finger in

her face, I add, "You said you knew what you were getting into by being the Butterfly. And you fucking chose *me* as your Dom. Don't get shitty with me now just because you suddenly have buyer's remorse."

"Buyer's remorse!" She tosses her hands up. "I'm not the fool who paid two million and change to make me the Butterfly, asshole. You are."

"Tell me about it," I roar back. "You're just a spoiled little princess who swindled me into a deal. I should have *never* made that bargain with you the other night."

"Then nix it," she says. "Give me back the rights to buy that property, and I'll cease to be your Butterfly."

My heart stops beating. In fact, my entire body freezes. There's no air in my lungs. There's no thought in my head. I just stand there like a goddamn stone.

"In fact, I'll sweeten the deal." Tara crosses her arms. "I'll never step foot in your club again if you let me out of our deal and give me a chance to bid on that property."

My hackles raise. She went from not giving a shit about that old ass building, to suddenly making it sound like she's desperate to get it.

Her offer is perfect. It gets me out of my bind and still allows me a chance to purchase that building. But since she works for one of the largest firms in the city, her pockets are, and always will be, deeper than mine. I can't risk it. I'm already going to have trouble bidding against the other investors for it at auction. Besides, I may have hated the idea of Tara being my Butterfly, but I'm not ready to let her go yet.

And that might just be the most fucked up thing about us to date.

"You want to walk out? Fine, Miss Reed. Walk. But I'm not voiding our deal. That building is mine." *And so are you*.

"Why do you want that stupid thing so much?"

"Who was that man in the lobby?"

We both know we're not willing to give up our secrets, so it's a standoff that will get us nowhere.

Finally, she caves a little. "He's not my husband, if that's what you're worried about."

"I'm not worried. It doesn't matter if he's your husband or not."

"Then why ask?"

"Because I like to know what kind of person I'm fucking."

She scoffs, and it makes her face twist with an ugly expression. "You haven't fucked me yet, Ryker."

"Sir," I correct her. "You *will* call me *Sir*."

"Not in my house, I won't." She closes the distance between us and cranes her neck to look up at me. "You might be king of the Monarch Club, but that's not where we are now."

Her defiance turns me on. "You will address me how I say, whenever we're together, Butterfly."

"I just told you I'd walk. I'll give up being Butterfly."

"But we both know you won't." If she wants to play games, I'm down. Being a Butterfly comes with rewards she can't get easily elsewhere. Tara was desperate enough to ensure the title was hers before. There's no way she'll just give it up so fast now. "You *need* this."

"Like Hell I do." She rolls her eyes. "I've never been so fucking insulted and humiliated in my life. And your oral game is *not* that spectacular."

She and I both know that's a lie.

Getting down on my knees, I trail my fingers up her thighs and hook her underwear with my thumbs, peeling them down slowly to give her time to tell me to stop, which she doesn't.

"Let's make another deal." I can't believe I'm doing this. "I'm going to eat your cunt until your knees buckle. If you can stand longer than five minutes, I'll let you bid on the building. If you collapse, you will call me Sir wherever we are, and you will obey my every command until your month is up."

"I hope you like shopping, *Ryker*." Tara lifts her dress and rests her foot on my shoulder, as if showing off that not only will she stay standing, but she'll do it on one fucking foot. "Because I intend to snag that property and turn it into a goddamn strip mall."

Arching my brow, I stare up at her and ignore the glorious scent of her pussy that's mere inches from my mouth. "Is that a deal, Miss Reed?"

Chapter 18

Tara

Having a man like Ryker Hudson on his knees for me is the single most empowering experience of my life. I've been in conference rooms with men twice my age and size who boom their voices and slam their fists on the table when they wheel-and-deal and I can storm out with my head held high and their balls in a jar by the time I'm finished with them.

In those instances, I'm untouchable.

But here with Ryker?

I want to be touchable. No, fuck that, I want to be edible. I want this man to devour every inch of me — with his mouth, his hands, his gaze.

One flick of his tongue along the seam of my pussy and I feel it over my whole body. A heated gaze from him and lust explodes in my bloodstream. All my anxiety evaporates when he puts his hands on me. If we're enemies, that's fine. I don't care what we are as long as we're *something* together.

He's a powerful man. A strong, quiet, calculating man. He's got dark secrets, and my demons want to drag them out and play with his vicious side.

"Put your hands on the wall for me and keep them there."

I lean back and spread my arms wide as if I'm a

butterfly pinned in a display case. Sir's gaze penetrates me the same time he plunges a finger in my pussy.

"Stay steady for me," he says before leaning in to lick my clit with fast, precise strokes of his tongue. The first orgasm builds deliciously, and I hold out for as long as I can. It's hard to keep myself pinned like this when I want desperately to hold his head, dig my nails into his scalp, and grind against his mouth.

While he worships my body, my mind flashes to the way he took Garret down. How he was harsh and brutal when protecting me. How he was soft and patient with me afterwards. I hope he's the same when he fucks.

"I'm close," I say in a rush.

He doesn't speed up or double down like I expect. Ryker just keeps his own pace, and I'm so very happy he does. I can feel each notch of pleasure build in my body, coiling until it reaches a crescendo.

My release is euphoric. Steady. Strong. But it's not those sensations that does me in. It's the way Ryker looks up at me as I come in his mouth. His grey eyes flutter open, his pupils blow wide, and he devours me like a starved animal that won't let his meal escape.

And that's what makes my motherfucking legs give out.

He catches me easily. I expect him to brag. Laugh at me. Say something annoying like "I told you so" but he's still on the chase. Ryker lifts me up and cups my ass in his hands. With a growl, he shoves my back against the wall again and a breath tears out of him.

I want him to kiss me. I want to know if his

mouth is diabolical on my lips or only my pussy. I want to know what he tastes like. What he feels like. I want to fuck him and get fucked by him. I want to see that animalistic, dangerously possessive look in his eyes again, and I want to put him back in that glassy-eyed subspace just like earlier with that flogger.

"Fuck me."

His voice drops to a gravelly tone. "As my Butterfly wishes."

Ryker carries me into my bedroom and lays me down amidst the million blankets and pillows I have. The swish of his belt, the rip of his zipper, the swoosh of his pants falling down before he steps out of them are all loud as screams. My heart's rapidly beating. My pussy's sopping wet.

When he crawls between my legs, he peppers my thighs with tiny kisses before licking my cunt again.

"No," I say. "I don't want your mouth. I want your cock."

He glances up at me and I see it then—the feral animal is gone. The cold, distant man that was in the Butterfly suite with me just this morning is here. The one who looked at me like I was just a chore to do.

How did that happen?

Why?

"Ryker."

He rolls me over on my belly. *Slap!* He spanks my ass hard and fast. "I told you to call me Sir."

The sting renders me speechless. I'm mad and embarrassed and confused because what the hell? I reach behind me to shield my butt from another spanking, but he grips my hands and holds them both in one of his.

"If you want my cock, Butterfly, you have to be ready for it." He spanks me again, only this time not nearly as hard. The air whooshes out of me as I give into him. "That's my good girl." He runs his hand over my ass cheeks, greedily, hungrily.

Smack! Smack!

I melt into the mattress. This is different than I've experienced, and I think it's solely because of the intention behind the impact.

And the man.

Squeezing my eyes shut, I try really hard to erase the thoughts infiltrating my good mood.

"Talk to me," Sir says. "You need to let me know where your head is, Butterfly."

"Green." I roll over so I can see him. "I'm green."

He stares at me for a beat, probably deciphering if I'm telling the truth or not, then he smiles. "Good." After taking his shirt off, Ryker crawls back on top of me, and my thighs spread wide to give him room. "Your ass looks gorgeous with my handprints on it."

"You like marking your territory, huh?"

"Understatement of the century." He nips my skin, working his way up my neck to lick the shell of my ear. "Do you have condoms?"

"Top drawer, just there." I point at my end table.

The instant he lifts off me, cool air blows across my skin, hardening my nipples even more. I'm still wearing my dress. Reaching around to unzip it, Ryker stops me.

"Don't take it off," he orders, peeling off his shirt.

"Why not?"

He arches his brow at me. "You lost the bet.

Now you better hold up your end of the deal and obey me."

I lay back and pout. Damnit, I should have never made that deal with him. But really? He's right. I was never going to walk. He called my bluff. Honestly, I'm not sure why we even made the deal in the first place. Especially Ryker.

This man is chiseled but not bulky. He has various tattoos all over his tanned body. When he crawls between my legs again, he shoves his pants down and rolls the condom over his length. I'm suddenly hyper aware of how big his dick is. It's above average in length and has some serious girth.

I hope it fits.

"Your needy little pussy is so pretty." He reaches between my legs and shoves two fingers inside me. Sir hits my g-spot and smiles. "I need you to come again for me, Butterfly."

I don't do on command tricks. But if he doesn't stop whatever he's doing in there, I just might come close. "Fuck, that feels good." My gaze locks with his as breaths turn to pants, and I lift my leg, pressing it against his shoulder. He holds my ankle and lifts it away from him, holding me half suspended in the air at an angle that makes his fingers inside me that much more intense. "Oh my god."

"Be my good girl and let me get you ready." His rhythm changes. So does his speed. I think he adds another digit inside me. Everything's tight. Sensitive. On fire. I feel so full. "Can you take another?"

Wet noises fill the room. My body burns. Blood swishes in my ears. Something in me coils tightly. "I… Yes." I can try, right?

Ryker slips another finger inside me. "That's it.

You're doing so good for me."

If that's the praise I get for taking another finger, he can shove all ten up there.

He pumps into me again and it's so intense I have to breathe through the pain for a few seconds until pleasure takes over again.

"Look at you, taking this so fucking well, Tara."

My name in his mouth sounds sinful and decadent. My thighs shake, back arches, and eyes squeeze shut. "I'm gonna come again," I groan, just as my orgasm hits.

He pulls out, jerks me forward, and impales me with his cock, robbing me of breath. I'm so full, so stretched, it fucking burns. Instead of giving me time to adjust, Ryker moves his body over mine like an undulating wave. I swear to all that's unholy he's able to hit that same spot inside me with his dick and my almost-lost orgasm renews and barrels out of me like a fucking hurricane.

"That's a good girl," he thrusts harder. "Fuck you're so tight. Clench my cock with that pretty cunt."

We fuck slowly, intensely, until he's driven us both up to the headboard. Then he gathers my dress and balls it in his hand, before shoving a bunch of the fabric in my mouth. "Ready to scream?"

I nod, desperate for him to not stop, even if I'm not sure how much more I can take.

Head spinning pleasure rolls through me, again and again. My vision's blurry too.

What the hell is he doing to me?

Ryker presses his hand on my lower belly, rocks back, and slams into me. I lose all breath. He repeats this again, and again, and *again*. I claw down his arms. My teeth grind as I bite down on the fabric stuffed in my mouth as hard as possible while he fucks me. And I do mean F-U-C-K-S me. It's brutal. Fast. Hard. My headboard slams against the wall so loudly, I'm shocked drywall hasn't crumbled down on us yet.

He fucks me like he hates me.

I love it. Like I said, I don't care if we're enemies as long as we're something.

My body coils again and pain, pleasure, and vertigo hit me all at once. Gravity doesn't exist. The world doesn't exist. Floating in subspace, I come again and scream until I don't remember who I am anymore.

Chapter 19

Ryker

Shit! I've gone too far.

Tara's screams went from music to my ears to a goddamn nightmare. She started hyperventilating as I lost my mind, railing her sweet pussy, and she passed out.

I've never had this happen before.

Pulling out, I'm so furious with myself. The only thing that stops me from cutting my dick off is the need to get Tara conscious again. She's my priority. My *only* priority.

"Tara." I pat her cheek. Her head's slumped, and my gaze drops to the fingerprint bruises on her neck again. Anger spikes in my bloodstream. I'm a monster. She was attacked less than an hour ago and I've gone and fucked her like a raging beast with no control. "Tara, wake up, baby."

Baby.

I've never called a woman *baby* in my fucking life.

My cheeks tingle as panic sets in. Lifting her out of the bed, I carry my girl into the bathroom and step into the shower, sitting down with her in my lap. Hitting the lever, cold water pours over us and Tara sucks in a shocked breath.

"There you are." I brush her hair back so I can

see her better. "You had a moment there."

Tara's brow pinches, and she tries to crawl out of my lap. "Not yet," I say. "I'm not ready to let you go yet."

The familiarity of those words stops my heart in its tracks. Instead of acknowledging the pain in my chest, I ignore it and stay focused on Tara.

"I'm so sorry," she says, sounding half high. "I don't know what happened."

I do. I went too far, and she's suffering the consequences of my actions. Apologizing won't make it better. Explaining myself won't help either. I just need to make sure it never happens again.

But, damn did it feel good to let loose for once.

Jesus Christ, I'm an asshole.

Sitting on the floor of her sizeable shower, cold water rains down on our heads, and I rock her.

"Feels good," she mumbles.

When Tara cups my face, I think she's going to kiss me, and I can't let that happen, so I keep her talking. "What feels good, Butterfly?"

"My body." Her words slur together as if she's half-drunk. "The way you…ffffuck me. Feels ssssso good."

She'd passed out. That's *not* good. In my club, that would put you on notice unless the person specifically requests, and gives consent in advance, to be fucked out of their mind until they collapse. Or choked out until they fall unconscious.

Tara hadn't asked for either of those things.

Still, some of the tension eases from my shoulders because, honestly, she looks thrilled. There was no buildup to what we just did. No playing, teasing, foreplay with anticipation. We clashed and tore at each other as if we both needed to explode, and inside each other was the fastest way to make that happen.

My eyebrow arches. "You liked being used hard like that?"

She wraps her arms around my neck and smiles up at me. "Yeah. It's all I've wanted. For a really, *really* long time."

I can't swallow past the lump in my throat. I can't swallow *period*. My instincts kick into action, and I reach back to turn the water off. We've cooled down enough, and she needs specific attention. "Does anything hurt?"

I fisted her before I fucked her. She's got to be sore as hell.

"Nothing hurts." She laughs a little. "I'm boneless and a little numb."

Which means I've got time to tend to her, so the sub drop won't hit too hard. "How about a warm bath, Butterfly?"

"Okay."

With my arms firmly locked under her, I lift us both up and carry Tara out of the shower and into the adjacent claw-foot tub.

The cool off in the shower did wonders for my system, but the combination of coming down from my headspace, the cardio of fucking so hard, the terror of my sub slumping unconscious on me at the end, and then getting in a cold fucking shower has me all wonky again. Normally, I wouldn't join my subs in a soak, but I think we both need it today.

Shit, I'm still wearing a condom. "Lean forward for me, baby." She obeys, and I pull the rubber off and toss it in the trash beside the sink. I didn't come, but

Tara doesn't notice. Not that I expected her to. I climb into the tub and help her inside. Turning on the water, I check in. "Too hot or cold?"

"It's perfect," she says, resting her back against me again. "I just want to sleep."

Kissing the top of her head, I relax and let the warm water relax us both. Her weight feels good on my chest and holds down my galloping heart. While her breaths slow and steam billows around us, my past claws its way into my present again...

"That was really good, Ryker." Natalie's bent over, drying her long hair in a towel. "Can you go again?"

My dick's going to fall off. Either from an STD or extreme use — this appendage isn't going to last long in this business. "Yeah, if you want."

"Veronica, ride him."

The camera's still rolling, and I've been in Natalie's bed since eleven o'clock this morning. This has turned into a seven hour fuckfest and I'm dehydrated, sore, and exhausted.

"I'm too tender to go again, Nat. Ryker should have a girth certificate for that thing."

Natalie swings her gaze to the other girl. "Erica?"

She sighs. "I'm done, too."

"The camera's still rolling. We're making a lot of money today, guys. Don't stop now."

"Then you fuck him," Veronica snaps.

Embarrassment tightens my throat, making it difficult to swallow what little pride I have left.

"Fine." Dropping the towel, Natalie climbs onto the bed and wiggles her ass for the camera.

I don't want to fuck her. I can't. She makes my dick limp because no matter how beautiful she is, I hate her. She's helped me gather clients and has shown me how to make a lot of money, but the cost is becoming too high.

I don't know who I am anymore.

The other girls here are in the same boat. She's trained us all. Broke us all. Uses us all. Getting down to business, she grabs a condom from the pile on the floor and straddles my hips. There's no hiding the loathing in my gaze when she looks at me.

"There it is," she says, smiling as she puts the wrapper between her teeth and rips it open. "I want that Ryker tonight."

That Ryker? *What the hell does she mean?*

Reaching between our bodies, she grips my dick and strokes it, coaxing it to harden again.

It doesn't.

"Come on, kid. Don't quit on me now."

I hate when she calls me kid. I'm eighteen—even though she thinks I'm twenty. Growing up poor, scared, and desperate made me a man a long fucking time ago. I'm the one taking care of my family and handling business. Speaking of which... "I have to get out of here in twenty minutes."

"She's probably sleeping," Natalie whispers, still jerking my cock to get the blood flowing.

My mom's pain levels have elevated lately, and she ran out of her prescriptions last week. I told Natalie about it, and she gave me some pain meds for a fraction of the price I pay at the pharmacy, but they make my mother comatose, which scares me.

"Come on, big guy."

I knock her hand off me. "No."

"Jesus, Ryker." Natalie's shoulders slump and she tilts her head, inspecting me like I'm nothing but a cockroach in her cereal. "You have a great thing going here and you're being really ungrateful."

"Ungrateful?" I grip her waist and move her off me. "I've made you a lot of fucking money too, bitch." Natalie takes a cut of all the clients she brings to me. Plus, most of what we make when we do these live streams.

Natalie tosses her head back, acting up for the camera and live audience we can't see.

"Someone's asking you to slap her," Veronica says, reading the messages on the screen. "He'll pay a thousand bucks."

Natalie's grin goes a mile wide. "Do it."

I can't. Hitting a woman isn't something I'm capable of, even if they beg. No dollar amount will change my mind either. "No."

"God, Ryker, you're ruining this!" She sits up and slaps me instead. Then she laughs. It's a cackling, obnoxious, anger inducing sound that makes my blood rush.

I grab her wrists and pin her down. "Shut the fuck up." I pitch forward and shove my half-hard cock in her mouth. She chokes on it. Now it's my turn to fucking laugh. "You talk a lot of shit for someone who chokes on a semi."

She shoves her finger in my ass, and I grunt in surprise. Then I pull out of her mouth and truly debate on what to do. This is humiliating. I can leave. Walk right out and never come back.

But I hear the dinging of money coming through on the live stream and I need every fucking penny, so I'm not going anywhere yet.

Glaring at the camera, I concentrate on all my hate, my hunger, my fear, and my torment. I cling to the idea that I can fuck my way out of this hell and snag the condom from Natalie's hand. With a growl, I roll it down my length.

Then I give our audience a fuck they'll never forget.

Tara lightly snores against me. The water has cooled down but I'm too exhausted to move. Using my toe to unplug the drain, I let out some of the water and refill it with fresh hot stuff. We've probably been in here for about an hour. I've massaged her shoulders, arms, and scalp. I ran water down her chest to keep her warm. I kissed parts of her body I could reach. She slept through every bit of it.

When I finally try to reposition myself—because my back hurts like a sonofabitch—Tara jolts awake.

"No!" Water sloshes over the rim as she fights nothing but herself.

"Easy," I say calmly. "It's just me."

She twists towards me, her eyes wide as she takes in her surroundings. "Holy shit." Rubbing her temples, she sighs. "Sorry."

"No need to apologize." Gripping the rim, I stand and the water level drops considerably. "I'm a prune."

And also hard as a rock.

Tara stares at my dick like it's the prettiest thing in her bathroom. "Don't get out yet."

She gets on her knees, wincing, and that makes me feel bad. "You're still sore?"

"A little, but it's nice. I like it."

Doubtful. "I'm sorry for earlier."

"Don't be. I wasn't lying when I said it's what I needed. Getting hate fucked has to be the greatest exorcism ever."

Her words confuse me. "You saying I exorcized your demons with my dick?"

"Something like that." She grips my hard cock and wraps her pretty little mouth around my head to suck on it. "You have a really veiny, fat dick."

"Thanks." I try to not enjoy what she's doing to me, but her hot tongue sends goosebumps erupting down my arms and chest. And when she looks up at me with her mouth full and lips stretched with my cock, I shove it in until it hits the back of her throat.

Tara doesn't grunt or pull back for air. She holds that position, her nostrils flaring as she breathes steadily, until I pull back to give her more air. Then I thrust into it again and repeat the shove, hold, release act over and over until my balls tighten.

"I'm going to come on your tongue. You will show it to me before you swallow."

She nods and moans her consent while continuing to suck me off.

I fuck her mouth slowly. Carefully. And when she pulls on my balls and makes obscene slurping noises, I give up the fight and finally give into my long-awaited release. Gripping her hair, I tip my head back and empty myself in her mouth, then pull out. "Show me."

Her jaw drops as she sticks out her tongue. Some of my cum drips out and she catches it in her palm.

"Swallow." I gently wrap my hand around her throat so I can feel her gulp it down. Then she surprises me by dragging her tongue along her palm and licks the cum off her hand too. *Impressive.* "You're such a good fucking girl, not wasting a drop."

The way she looks up at me like I'm a god, her salvation, her motherfucking master, makes me falter. The way she let me fuck her like a mindless animal also makes me second-guess what kind of woman she is. I thought Tara was a precious little petal, but now I'm beginning to think she's unbreakable.

Like me.

Jesus. My cock's hardening again with the image of her body bent in half so I can rail her until her throat's raw from screaming my name. Hearing her do that earlier, until she passed the fuck out, will forever live rent free in my brain.

I wasn't Sir. I wasn't Master. I wasn't Mr. Hudson.

She screamed Ryker and made it sound like something *good*. I can't shake it off. Not her voice echoing in my head, not the way she felt sleeping in my arms, and not the way she's staring up at me right now with her heavy-lidded eyes, pink swollen lips, and nipples hard as rocks.

I want to cradle the back of Tara's head and kiss her mouth. I want to confess why I treated her all the ways I did and beg her to let me do some of it again. I want to—

Shit. Time to snap out of it and put space back between us. I can't afford to lose any more to this woman. "Get dressed, Butterfly. Time to get back to the club."

Before I change my mind, I leave the room first and get dressed. We don't speak, but that's okay. Not every minute has to be filled with noise.

Tara eventually heads over to her desk again and starts stuffing shit into a Birkin bag. "Make an exception for me, and I'll make one for you."

"The fuck's that mean?"

"You can't run the club and spend the next twenty some days with just me. Besides, you had a literal fire to put out. How much more chaotic can your day get?"

"It was a false alarm fire."

"Well, that's good. But you still have a club to run. I know you're my Dom, but you're still king of the club, too. You can't abandon your duties."

"What are you saying?"

"I'm saying I get it. I'm a businesswoman who cannot let her work slide for some mind-blowing cock. I know what a Butterfly is supposed to do, but make an exception for me."

"I've made plenty already."

She puts her hands on her hips. "I'll make you another deal."

"This is getting old, Tara."

"So is your hot and cold attitude," she slings back. "Let's both adapt and adjust, Mr. Hudson, so the careers we've built don't burn to the ground while we're fucking each other's brains out."

I'm going to regret this, but she has a point. "What is it you want this time?"

"One hour." She holds up a manicured forefinger. "*One* hour a day, we both get actual work done."

Looking at the piles of folders on her desk, I'm sure Tara can't afford to take an entire month off like she's supposed to. To deny her this request would make me a hypocrite because I can't afford it either. "Fine. But it happens in my office. You can't have work in the suite."

Tara's smile lights up the room. "Deal."

She thinks she's won this negotiation, but I'm the one who's making out. If I watch her work, there's a good chance I'll be able to figure out who that motherfucker was who attacked her, and I'll go after him once she's asleep.

Chapter 20

Tara

Time holds little weight in the walls of the Monarch and it's easy to forget there's an entire world outside. It's been a whirlwind of orgasms, sleeping, eating, and now checking our emails in Ryker's office together.

This victory feels weird.

I can't tell if I've made Mr. Hudson rethink how our next three weeks can work amicably or if I've just made him more frustrated. He doesn't like me. That hate fuck in my bedroom yesterday was proof. But Mr. Hudson is a man of his word, and this is a solution that can benefit us both.

I get a safe space to figure out how to get what I want, in and out of the bedroom, as well as keep my motherfucking job.

And he gets to keep his beautiful club running smoothly while enjoying easy pussy that's at his beck and call.

He's a liar if he says he doesn't want me. And Ryker doesn't seem like the kind of man who would fuck just anyone—even out of obligation. At the very least, he wouldn't enjoy it. Mark my words, Ryker *loved* hate-fucking me.

And I loved every second of it, too.

The way he overpowered me was intoxicating.

Seeing him turn into an aggressive, greedy animal, chasing his release. The man was relentless and savage and borderline monstrous. It was fucking amazing.

My foolish heart almost wishes there was a deeper reason for his actions, but I know better. He thinks I'm a princess who gets what she wants, when she wants it. I've already put him between a rock and a hard place by using that building as leverage, which would only solidify his suspicions of what kind of ruthless piece of shit he thinks I am.

The real truth is I'm a stepchild who had to claw my way up to reach the same level of respect everyone else gets for just existing. I work hard to stay in my stepfather's good graces so my mother doesn't have to choose between us, and I will work myself to the ground on her behalf, and my stepbrother's, and everyone else who's on my ass all the time about doing what's best for the company.

But I hate it.

"I'm sorry," Ryker says into his cell as he runs his thumb lazily along my inner thigh. "But seven doesn't work for me tonight."

One caveat of getting work done is he insists it be in his office. Together. With me in his lap. Trust me, I'm not complaining. I'm still shocked he said yes to me. But ever since we came back here yesterday, he's stuck to me like glue. It's like he's done a complete one-eighty in attitude. No matter how badly I want to ask why, I won't.

"No. This entire month is booked solid."

I lean back against his chest to whisper in his ear. "If you need to leave, you can."

He doesn't need my permission. But I enjoy

giving it, anyway.

Ryker's eyes cast down to mine. "Hold on a minute." Muting his cell, his brows dig down. "Are you sure? I won't be long."

"It's fine. I'll likely need to meet my mother for brunch Sunday, so..."

Tit for tat.

Wow, this is weird.

Ryker's jaw clenches. After his gaze lingers a little longer on me, and I suspect he wants to object, he hits the mute button on his cell again and responds to whoever is on the other end of the line. "I can do nine o'clock tonight." He keeps staring at me. "Two of us will be there." He swallows and I watch his Adam's apple bob up and down. "No, not Dmitri. Someone else. See you then." He hangs up and leans back with a sigh.

Instead of prying, I lean forward to concentrate on my emails. Ryker's hands slide across my belly until he's wrapped his arms around my waist. I furiously type my email and smash the send button. Then my cell goes off.

He's allowed me to have that back as well. But only if it stays, with my laptop, and my files, in his office.

"May I... Sir?" I look over my shoulder at him.

Jesus Christ, I can't believe I'm asking permission to answer my own fucking cell phone.

"Yes."

I quickly snag it. "How's Paris?"

"Dreadful," my mom says. "I came back early because I was bored."

Biting my lip, I refrain from saying what I want. My mom and I grew up poor and she somehow snagged one of the richest men on the planet — well, at least my stepfather acts like he is — and ever since, my mother's taken the rags to riches concept to a whole new dramatic level.

"Did you meet any friends there?"

"Everyone's on holiday that I'd want to see. The weather was awful. It rained most of the time."

"How was fashion week?"

"Dreadful. The styles this season are atrocious."

Oh my god, I can't even. My mother used to buy her clothes at Wal-Mart and thought Macy's was for fancy people. Now look at her. Pretentious as fuck.

Ryker's hands slide between my thighs, and he spreads my legs. My body automatically melts against his chest, giving him easier access to the rest of me. Look, I don't know what's going on between us, but I'm not missing an opportunity to receive pleasure. I've been starved of it for most of my life and my time with him is finite. I'll take all I can, please and thank you.

"Maybe look at the new…" I suck in a harsh breath when he shoves a finger inside my pussy. "The new Dior line."

"Mmm." My mother sighs. "I'm tired of them too."

He plunges a second finger inside me. "Um. Well." I grind myself against his palm, seeking friction for my clit. He nips my earlobe with his teeth, the sensation sending a sharp jolt of lightning to my pussy.

"Want to meet for lunch, sweetie?"

"I c-…" *oh my god, this feels so good.* "I can't today. Let's stick with brunch on Sunday."

"About that. William wants us to have it at

home."

My thighs slam shut immediately, and I pitch forward. "Why? What's happened?"

"I think he just misses us all being together."

Lies. We never do family things.

"Your father's been working himself to the bone lately."

"*Step.*"

"Tara. Don't start. You know he hates it when you call him your stepfather."

But that's exactly what he is. "Okay. Then I'll see you two on Sunday."

"Garret's coming as well."

I should have known. "Great!" I fake my excitement. Ryker's still as a statue behind me, but I can feel his hard on against my ass. "Sorry, but I have to get going. My next meeting's about to start."

"Okay, sweetie, love y —"

I hang up immediately.

Shit. We only have family meals when someone's in trouble. I'm pretty sure that someone is me.

What am I going to do?

Chapter 21

Ryker

I'm in fucking trouble. With Tara in my lap, my dick is hard as a rock, but my hands want to pummel something. Tara's incredibly easy to read, even with her back turned to me, and whoever was on that phone call meant something to her.

They also made her frightened.

While she talked about designer clothing and Sunday brunch, my mind raced with arguments about whether or not I should pry.

She's just a Butterfly.
She's a temporary toy.
She's only a member of the club.

Those facts aren't what has me head-fucked though. It's that I can't stop worrying about her.

What's her life like outside of my club? Who was that man I threatened yesterday? Why did Tara's entire body go from languid to stiff with just the mention of brunch? Who is her family and how do they treat her? Who is her fucking boss and why is he sending her out to make undercover deals on shitty properties in the middle of the night?

This is a major problem. I shouldn't give a shit about Tara or her life outside the Monarch. Once someone steps out of my club, they're no longer my responsibility. And Tara will be out of here at the end of the month and who knows if she'll ever come back.

I don't like the way it makes me feel.

"Stand up." I tap her thigh.

"Yes, Sir." Tara's only wearing my button-down shirt from yesterday. The front is completely open to reveal her beautiful breasts, hard nipples, and perfect pussy.

I rub my forefinger across my lips. It smells like her cunt.

It's making me crave another taste of her again and that's a rarity. I usually eat a woman out to get her to leave me alone. Just like I used to do it so they'd give me money for my bills. But Tara? She's quickly becoming an indulgence.

I get it now.

The reason my men like to be Doms for the Butterfly.

Before, I could never understand why they looked forward to being with the same woman for so long. I don't have long-term girlfriends. The few lovers I bring to my bed are brief and serve a very specific purpose.

Tara meets every qualification for being a lover of mine, except she's starting to get under my skin. I stayed up and watched her sleep again last night. I jerked off into her dress again, too. Once I couldn't stand not having her attention, I woke her up, eating her pussy, because I could not, for the life of me, wait another moment to taste her.

She's lucky I didn't give into my desires and fuck her while she slept.

"Sit on the desk and put your feet here." I tap the armrests of my chair.

Her eyes widen a fraction before she does as she's told. Tara playfully spreads her legs for me, a wry smile extends across her sweet face. This woman runs hot and cold, just like I do. Aggressive one minute, shy the next. Scared, then brave. It's an act that took me years to perfect just so I could keep my inner peace and protect myself. To see her with the same traits makes me want to save her. Protect her.

"You have a beautiful pussy." I watch her closely. "Are you still sore?"

"Not at all."

"Good." Leaning forward to run my nose along her wet, swollen lips, I love how she melts for me. "I want to play with you, Butterfly."

Her body language has changed again. Gone is the tension from her back and shoulders. She's already panting at the mere promise of being played with like a little fuck toy.

Perfection.

I pull her off the desk, making her follow me out of my office, down the hall, up the elevator, and to a special room that's always booked solid at least six months out.

One of the many perks a Butterfly gets is an all-access pass to every room in the club. Since they live here for a month, and the club is only open in the evenings, she can have all the fun she wants with the club's many amenities.

Her eyes widen in shock when we step inside.

"Holy shit, Ry… Sir."

I let the mistake slide. Honestly, I want to hear her call me Ryker again, but in order to maintain our dynamic, that's not happening. Striding to the center of the room, I pat the cushioned leather bench that's the main attraction. "Hop on."

Tara lights up. "What are you going to do to

me?" She looks too excited to care what my answer might be.

"I'm going to play, Butterfly." Sauntering over to the wall of various ropes, I pluck two off a shelf. "If you'll let me."

"Yes, please. Sir."

"Have you experienced Shibari before?"

"No."

"Would you like to?"

"Yes. Please." She tucks her hair behind her ear. "Sir."

"We'll start slow and simple." I escort her over to the bench. I don't ever take on a newbie, but Tara's been an exception to every fucking rule I have, it seems. Honestly, I'm a little excited to see how she handles being tied up for me. "This particular rope is made of jute. It's soft and easy to tie and untie." I let her feel the threads. "May I bind your torso?"

She swallows hard and smiles. "Yes."

"Get naked for me, Butterfly."

"Tara," she says softly. "Please call me Tara."

I shouldn't give her what she wants, but... *fuck it*. Getting up close and personal with her, I say, "Take my shirt off your body, Tara."

Using her real name instead of calling her Butterfly makes this connection between us in jeopardy of getting stronger. But I can't deny that my heart skips a beat when I see the effect it has on her. I understand wholeheartedly because my body reacts the same way when she calls me Ryker.

Have I mentioned how much danger I'm in with this woman?

She gets naked and pulls her hair up into a low ponytail, securing it with a hairband from her wrist.

"Shouldn't we negotiate some things first?"

Yes. But I'm sick of making deals with her. "I've watched you closely since you stepped foot in my club, Miss Reed."

Her mouth drops a little.

"I see you go from room to room, always watching, never participating. You linger in the places where sex is… intense."

"You mean brutal."

"Subjective." I flash her a stiff smile. Did she think I was brutal when I fucked her until she blacked out yesterday? Maybe. But that's not what I'd call it. "Did you like what I did to you yesterday, Tara?"

She relaxes a little. "Yes."

"How much did you enjoy it?" I lean down and kiss her collarbone.

She sucks in a breath before answering. "Probably too much."

"You like being used."

"Yes," she whispers.

"You like being in a position where you can unravel."

She gulps and looks down at her feet. "Yes. I think."

Tipping her chin with the bundle of rope in my hand, I make her look at me. "You think, or you know?"

"I…" She bites her bottom lip. "I've never experienced it before yesterday. But I loved it. I want it again."

Fuck me sideways. She's too perfect for her own good. Before I confess shit I shouldn't, my mind scrambles to keep control of the situation. "You like being fucked like an animal, Tara?"

"I like being fucked by *you*, Sir." Her eyebrow lifts as she looks down at the rope. "Are you going to tie me down and do it again?"

God, do I want to. "Something like that."

Unraveling the rope, I get down to business and set the scene. "I want to put you in a quick release compression corset. You can easily get out of it if the sensations are too much for you."

She smiles. "Okay."

"Then I'm going to make you lie on this bench and eat your pussy."

Her smile grows bigger. "Okay."

"After you come three times, I'm going to use that." I point at a piece of machinery. "And fuck you with it."

Her smile crumbles. "A machine?"

"Yes."

The blood rushes out of her face.

"If you don't want to, just say so. And know that you can change your mind at any point." Cupping her chin to make sure I have her full attention, I remind her what's most important here. "You're in control. Always. Just call red if you want to stop and it all ends."

"Why do you want to fuck me with a machine?"

"Because I think you're going to like it, Butterfly." And she's going to like what I'll do to her while the machine is on, too. "What do you say, Yes or No?"

Chapter 22

Tara

I want *him* to fuck me, not a machine. But I'm not about to deny the fact that letting Ryker watch me get railed doesn't turn me on. If it's with a machine, so be it. I've always wondered what it would be like to have two men at once.

Could I make that happen while I'm here? Yes. I know damn well I could request to have Dmitri, Vault, or anyone else who works at the club fuck me with Ryker. Christ, imagining Dmitri and Ryker taking me at the same time?

I'd need stitches by the end of it.

Too bad I'm not attracted to anyone at the club other than the Dom I chose. Dmitri's hot, but Ryker is so fucking sexy it should be criminal. Now that I've had his dick, I'm certain addiction has set in.

Staring at the ropes, then the machine, then the bench, I'm suddenly eager to give this a shot. I'll call red if it's too much, even though I don't want him to be mad at me if I chicken out. I feel like the wall between us is finally cracking and the last thing I want is for him to reinforce it if I disappoint him.

"Hey." His voice is softer. "Look at me, Tara." My gaze lifts to his. "This is all about you, baby. Nothing happens without your full consent. I only brought you here because I truly think you'll like it. If

I'm off base, tell me. Or if you don't want to try anything in here just yet, tell me that too. Whatever decision you make is completely fine."

I look around the room again. This suite has been off limits for as long as I've been a member. I feel like I've just gotten a golden ticket and there's no way I'm walking out of here without trying *something*. I didn't want to be the Butterfly just for good dick. I want to explore myself, my limits and different kinks, so I know what to go after once I'm out of here. "Go slow?"

"I'd do it no other way."

Ryker places the two bundles of rope on the bench and slips out of his shirt. Today, he's wearing dark blue jeans and a black shirt that hugs his form. Most of his tattoos are on display, and I want to ask about them. Now isn't the time, though.

"How about you go choose a dick."

I freeze. "Excuse me?"

Ryker smiles, and it's probably the first genuine one I've seen from him. It makes his eyes crinkle on the sides a little and his jaw squares off. "Go pick a dick."

I walk over to a large wooden box he's pointing at. Lifting the lid, I'm dumbstruck. "Holy cow." There are a lot of options, all of which are still in boxes, unused.

The toy inventory for the sex club must be massive.

Glancing at the machine, it's surprising how small it is. There's a long steel rod on the end where I guess you attach the dildo somehow. I don't know.

Okay. Fine. I'm actually a little excited to see how this thing works. Plucking a reasonably sized toy out of the box, I set it down beside the machine and blow out the breath I've been holding.

"Good girl. Now come back to me."

I'm getting really horny.

Why am I like this?

A familiar voice echoes in my mind, ripping through my lust with an answer. *You're a disgusting little whore, Tara.*

My stomach plummets.

"Hey. Woah." Ryker's suddenly holding my shoulder. "What just happened?"

"Huh?"

His face contorts with concern. "You just went all pale on me."

"Oh." I touch my cheeks. "Sorry." I'm not about to tell him I heard my stepbrother's voice in my head calling me names and slut-shaming me. That's what therapy sessions are for. "I'm just nervous."

He stares at me a little longer, then seems to accept my lie. "You sure?"

"Yup." I slap on a big smile. "Let's do this, Sir."

He flashes another grin, but this one doesn't make his eyes crinkle. "Okay."

Ryker unravels the first bundle and makes a huge loop, then places it around my neck, with the circle hitting my bellybutton. He moves behind me and knots it at my neck. Then he brings my hand up so I can feel it. "Pull this at any point and it'll all come undone. Understand?"

My heart skips a beat. "Yes, Sir."

He takes another bundle of rope off the bench and unravels it. I want to fill the silence between us with words, but my head's a little jumbled. Shame's setting in because I feel awkward.

"Talk to me, Tara."

"What should I say?"

"Whatever's going through your mind."

That's not happening. "I feel silly being here."

Ryker stops rigging. "Why?"

My stomach knots. Tears prick my eyes. This was a mistake. "I feel like I'm using you."

He stills and I watch his Adam's apple bob.

A mountain of guilt dumps out of me. "I'm sorry for causing you so much trouble at the ceremony. I know you didn't want me to be the Butterfly. I shouldn't have leveraged the property to get to you. And I'm sorry you're stuck in this position."

"I'm not stuck. I chose to be here."

"No, *I* chose you to be here because I picked you to be my Dom." Before he can argue, I add. "I don't trust anyone. And I'm not well-versed in kinks. I just know vanilla doesn't do it for me. Ever. I can barely get myself off, much less have some boring office manager pull missionary on me and expect me to come. I need chaos turned all the way up. I think I need to be overpowered so I can shut down my brain and let loose. Joining the Monarch only reinforced the desires I have." I can't believe I'm saying all this now. "And you're the one who can give me what I need."

"Any of my Doms can give you what you need, Tara. It's why they're here. It's why I built this place. So people can explore kinks safely. My staff are trained to pleasure members safely."

"Do you wish I'd chosen one of them and not you?" My voice cracks when I ask this. I feel sick. I can't read his expression at all.

Ryker stares at me for what feels like a long

time. "No," he finally says.

Does he mean that?

Instead of elaborating, he goes back to his ropework. The silence between us makes me want to scream. "I watched you," he says quietly. "Every time you came into the club, I'd watch you."

Our gazes collide, and I don't say a word.

"I couldn't pull away from you." He pulls the rope taut and keeps rigging. "I think if you'd picked someone else to pleasure you, I would have killed them."

It doesn't sound like a lie.

We both stare at each other again. He blinks and the intensity of his words shifts, as does his body language. He pulls the rope snug again and clears his throat. "What color are you, Butterfly?"

"Green." Getting tied up isn't scary or claustrophobic like I thought it would be. "Super green."

"How's the pressure?"

"Nice." It's like getting a big hug.

"Good." He continues working on the knots and tension. Every once in a while, he has me hold the rope, which I like because it gives me something to do and makes me feel like I'm part of the process.

"You're doing really well, Tara."

God, the way he says my name. He could bind in me barbed wire if he said my name like that while doing it.

"There." He tightens the last knot at my lower back. "All done."

Spinning around for him to appreciate his handiwork, I catch a glimpse of myself in the mirror to our left. "Oh wow." My boobs are still out, nipples hard. My waist is snatched. I look and feel amazing.

"Fucking stunning," Ryker says, admiring me. The ropes line up perfectly and are a combo of rose gold and black. It's really pretty. "Lay back for me, Butterfly."

Climbing on the bench is easy. I still have use of my arms, hands, and legs.

"God help me, Tara. You're a fucking knockout in every position I put you in."

Ryker leans down and licks my pussy. I can't believe how much he enjoys oral. The man has feasted on me so much, it must be his favorite form of sex. My toes curl when he plunges two fingers into my pussy and sucks on my clit.

"Go slower." Otherwise, I'll come too quick, and I don't want that yet.

He chuckles against my sensitive flesh. "As you wish, Butterfly."

His pace changes over and over, edging me until I'm sweaty and shaking. Cranking my body up and then letting it relax back into a chaotic buzz, he works my lusty body until I'm whimpering with need for a release.

I think I'm dying.

"Please, Sir." I lift my head to look at him. His eyes flutter open from between my thighs and he looks at me. "*Please* make me come now."

He snaps his fingers and points to his left. I turn my head and see our reflection in the mirror.

Holy hell, this is hot. Ryker's on his knees, hard dick out. He's pumping it with one hand while using the other to play with my pussy. His mouth is firmly sealed over my clit and he—

"RYKER!" Arching my back, I come so hard I

shake from head to toe. The ropes stretched across my chest hold me together while I rattle apart. The pleasure's so intense, stars burst in my vision. I lose my mind and buck on the bench, screaming, as he continues to bring me out of one orgasm and straight into another. "FUCK!" I can't take in a full breath. My thighs clamp around his head.

He growls and snaps his finger again. I immediately look back into the mirror he points to and watch myself come undone a third time. I barely recognize myself. Riding out this ungodly wave of pleasure, I gyrate my pussy against his mouth until I feel his teeth on me. The pain is sharp and delicious. I easily orgasm again. "Ryker." Tears spring to my eyes. "I can't take your mouth anymore."

It's a miracle I haven't fallen off this damn bench.

"You did so well, baby." Ryker rubs his cock against my slick pussy.

I'm desperate for him to shove it inside me. I want him to fill me. Stretch me. Come all over me.

"My Butterfly wants dick, doesn't she?"

"Yes. God, yes. *Please*."

He walks away.

No, no, no, where is he going?

Ryker picks up the machine and, without saying another word, unboxes the dildo and hooks it to the end of the rod. "What color are you, Tara?"

"Green." Bright, glorious, vibrant green.

He carries the machine over and positions it between my legs, pressing the tip of the dildo against my opening. "Breathe, baby."

"I... I am breathing."

"No. I need you to breathe slower. You're

starting to hyperventilate."

"Well, if... I am... it's your fault."

He smiles down at me. "Inhale." He sucks in a big breath. "Exhale." He blows it out.

I want him to kiss me and steal the air from my fucking lungs. Breathing isn't necessary if I can suffocate in Ryker instead.

"We can't proceed until you do as you're told, Butterfly."

I suck in air from my nose and blow it out through clenched teeth. Clinging to the side of the bench, my fingernails dig into the leather and it's like my whole body is about to rattle apart again. "I'm still green."

"Put your feet here," he says, and I realize he's popped out two footrests from under the bench.

Oh. My. God. I've never felt so desperate and vulnerable and terrified and turned on. This is confusing.

"Tell me when you're ready." Ryker waits by my feet, holding a remote. His dick is still hard, out, and unused.

"I want your dick in my mouth while this machine fucks me." I can't believe I just let that fly.

"As the Butterfly wishes." He gradually walks around to stand by my head. Our gazes lock again. "If you can't say red, tap my leg twice and we stop. Understood?"

I can't believe we're going to do this. "Yes, Sir."

Smiling, Ryker hits the button on the remote. The machine kicks on and the dildo shoves into me slowly. It pumps in an out with a boring rhythm that almost annoys me. I'm too needy for it to go this slow. "Faster."

He speeds it up and I lay my head back to enjoy it.

Being locked in this room, bound with rope, with only Ryker, makes it feel okay to be overwhelmed by my desires, curiosity, and needs. What happens in the club, stays in the club. No one will ever know that I'm being used like this.

Or that I like it so much.

My head's buzzy and the ropes around my chest feel like they're the only thing holding me together. "Faster." This bit of chaos almost makes me forget my life. But it's not enough. "*Faster.*"

Ryker's eyes darken as he clutches the remote. "What color are you?"

"Green." The rope knots on my back dig into my spine. I like it. "I'm green. Please make it harder, faster, *something.*" I must look obscene the way I'm trussed up and splayed on this bench with a dildo ramming my cunt. Shame heats my face.

Ryker must hit the button because the machine fucks me a little harder.

But it isn't enough and I'm so frustrated, I scream.

Chapter 23

Ryker

Tara's scream freezes my heart. It's agonizing. Furious. Soul-shattering. *Relatable*. Something possessive claws out of me because of it.

I press the stop button on the remote and drop it to the floor. The machine slows down while Tara continues screaming. Fuck this. Ripping the damn thing away from her and letting it crash onto the floor, I lift Tara off the bench.

Her eyes widen with shock, but at least she stops screaming.

My heart pounds in my chest. I think I'm going to have a fucking stroke.

"What are you doing?" She rasps when I set her on a chaise and pull the quick-release rope in the back, making it unravel. "Ryker!"

I can't respond. My hands tremble as I pull the rope away from her torso, letting it fall in her lap.

Her legs are shaking. Her skin's clammy.

I've fucked up. I'm downward spiraling and I can't let her know it.

"Ryker, why did you do that?"

She sounds gutted.

Why did I do that? She'll have to be more specific. Why did I agree to let her be the Butterfly? Why did I put myself in this fucked up situation? Why did I bring her to this room? Why did I try to make her so frustrated she'd leave? Why did I let a machine do what I can do better? Why did I stop it? Why did I untie her? Why did I think I could get through this unscathed?

Which why is she asking about?

"As your Dom…" Fuck, my chest hurts. "It's my responsibility to make sure you don't cross your own lines. If I see or think you're in trouble, it's my duty to stop the scene and see to your well-being."

Tara wraps her arms around herself, casting her gaze to the floor. I hate it. She's all over the place — happy one moment, demanding another, passionate and frustrated all at the same time.

She's exactly like me.

Okay, I'm reading into this too much if I'm drawing similarities between us again. Tara's nothing like me. To pretend she is only insults the woman who came here to explore her sexuality.

"Hey." Placing my finger under her chin, I try lifting her head up, but she jerks away from my touch. "*Butterfly*," I snap and she flinches. "Tara." My softer tone finally gets her to look at me.

I hate what I see in her eyes. I know that look well because I see it even when I close mine to sleep at night. *Shame*.

Her voice cracks when she says, "I didn't call Red, and I didn't tap your leg either, Sir."

"I know." Pulling her into an embrace, I feel like I'm floating out of my body. There's no way I care for this woman, but my actions say otherwise even though my brain and heart both have massive walls up. "But your screams were…" *heartbreaking, terrifying,* "Concerning."

"I just need to fall apart," she whispers. Tara's shoulders droop, and she backs away from me again. "I like the rope. I like being fucked hard. I like being used."

I believe her about the rope, and the intensity of being fucked. But the last part? She's lying. Either to me or both of us. I'm good at reading my subs and though Tara might enjoy Shibari, she doesn't like to be used as a hole. Just the way she said it has my hackles raising. Being used can be fun, but I can't imagine she actually enjoys being used as a fucktoy.

She's not you, asshole. Stop trying to find similarities that do not exist. If she likes it, then good for her. Don't let her be ashamed of it.

But I can't. If I do, something far more dangerous is going to creep out of me, and I refuse to let that demon out to play.

I should have never brought her here. Never used this machine on her. I only did it in the first place because I thought it intrigued her. God knows she seems so curious about everything in this club, and I didn't realize until this very moment how much I've watched her while she explores the rooms and scenes I've created for my guests.

If I'm really honest with myself though, I think I did it for my own selfish reasons. "I'm so sorry."

Her gaze lifts to meet mine. "Why?"

A Dom/sub relationship won't work unless there's trust. Tara clearly trusts me, but I don't trust her. Not enough to confess my reasons. They shouldn't matter, anyway. This isn't about my hangups, it's about celebrating, worshipping, and exploring her.

"Why are you sorry, Ryker?"

My fists clench along with my jaw. She should call me Sir, but I can't seem to find the strength to correct her. I like the way my name sounds from her mouth. My gaze roams her beautiful features. I should explain why I'm sorry, but I won't. I can't. But I can be honest about something else. Confess something just as damning. "You fascinate me."

There. I've just handed over the one thing I shouldn't: My power.

She knows I've watched her. She knows I'm possessive of her. But now she knows I'm fucking obsessed with her. That's what fascination is for a man like me.

The way her eyes widen, the sound of her breath escaping, the sight of her cheeks pinking, has me uneasy. She's flattered when she shouldn't be.

She's going to exploit me again with this. Use this new weakness of mine to get something she wants. And I'll have no one to blame but myself.

Her expression softens, and she smiles while cupping my face, trapping me. Then she lifts on her toes to kiss me.

Fuck that.

Knocking her hands away, I step back three paces and scoff. "Don't get the wrong idea, Tara. I'm not a hero or your boyfriend. I'm just a dick you'll ride until your time is up."

I've got to get the fuck out of here so I can get my head back in the game and remember my purpose here. Because what almost just happened *can't* happen at all. Turning to head out of the room, I make it all the way to the door before something hits the back of my head.

Chapter 24

Tara

I'll admit, I have a short temper. I let things pile up until something finally makes me snap and then I lose my shit about everything. So, when Ryker had the audacity to walk away after what he said, I did the first thing that came to mind.

I threw a dildo at his head.

Hey, it was the closest weapon within reach. And it's still in the box, so it's perfectly reusable.

Ryker pitches forward when the box makes contact with his skull, and the impact is *loud*. My heart hammers in my throat when he slowly turns around and glowers at me.

If looks could kill, someone would be reading my obit online right now.

Oh well. I don't care. He's making me crazy. Thrusting my chin out, I scowl back and put my hands on my hips.

"You're going to pay for that, Butterfly."

I hope so. I hope he spanks my ass until I can't sit. "Well, if you're going to act like an asshole, I'm going to treat you like one."

I enjoy about two seconds of pure satisfaction until I'm suddenly stumbling backwards because of how fast he comes storming over to me.

"So. Fucking. Naughty." His aggressiveness

overshadows any dominance I've gained as he backs me against the bench. "Do you know what happens to bad girls in my club, Butterfly?"

His mouth is incredibly close to mine, and that burning intensity is back in his eyes. Will he rail me hard enough to make me boneless again? Will he teach me a lesson in manners with spankings and forced orgasms? I want that Ryker back. No, I *need* that Ryker back. The one who maneuvered me into our suite after he beat the shit out of Dmitri. The one who pinned me at my apartment and fucked me until I couldn't breathe. My body unfurls and mouth waters thinking about it.

Being used like a fucktoy is addictive. Getting fucked by a machine unlocked a new kink. Having Ryker as my partner is going to be my undoing. There's a reason he picked this room, and it has nothing to do with me and a lot more to do with him. I want to know more.

I'll get it out of him even if it breaks me to do so.

"What happens to bad girls, Sir?" Because I'm going to be the best bad girl in this motherfucking club.

His eyes roam over my face and finally lands on my mouth. I want him to kiss me. Why hasn't he done that yet? Tipping my head back, I sweep the tip of my tongue along my lips to dampen them. His hold on my waist tightens while he watches.

"You will not enjoy it, I assure you."

I arch my brow. "Try me."

Huffing a little laugh, Ryker pushes away from me, leaving me cold where I'd just been burning. "Get your ass up to our suite, Butterfly. This scene is over."

His punishment leaves me wanting.

Literally.

I expected him to fuck me hard and mercilessly up in our suite. Spank me. Shove his cock down my throat until I gag. *Something*.

Instead, I'm left with this ache between my thighs and a sinking sensation in my belly that resembles rejection. I'd completely forgotten we were meeting someone at nine tonight, but Ryker hasn't. We got to our suite, and he headed straight for the shower. I shamelessly pressed my ear to the door, hoping to catch him jerking off, but I couldn't hear anything other than his music playing. He got out and dressed in a suit that Dmitri hung outside our door for him.

The drive was dead silent, too. Hell, I'm shocked he even took my hand to help me out of the fucking car once we arrived at our destination, which is a dilapidated night club.

"You will not speak, Butterfly. And you will keep your eyes cast to the floor at all times unless I give permission otherwise. Understood?"

My mixed emotions swirl in my gut, making me queasy. "Yes, Sir."

I know what anger feels like—both from the receiving and giving end. Ryker's attitude makes me believe he actually *loathes* me and, somehow, that's a million times worse. Maybe this is my punishment for talking back, for challenging him, for pushing the idea that I might very well like whatever depraved shit he has in his mind.

Fine.

He wants to play. I'll play.

I'm no stranger to being seen, not heard. In my line of business, I'm usually the only female in the conference room, which means I go unacknowledged and underestimated often. I prefer it that way. It's better than being the center of some old man's attention and undervalued as the powerhouse I really am.

He places his hand on the small of my back, ushering me through the red double-doors, and we're met with the stench of stale cigarettes and cheap leather. As far as night clubs go, this one seriously sucks. I don't even think it's running anymore.

Without saying a word to each other, Ryker brings me into the back, through an impressive sized kitchen, down a flight of steps, and into a small room. My heart's pounding at this point. Where the hell are we going? What kind of meeting has to happen in a room this far removed from the land of the living?

I squeeze his hand nervously. Ryker looks over at me, his tone calm and low when he says, "I'd never bring you someplace that wasn't safe, understand?"

I hear what he's saying, but I don't trust him. I don't even know him. Everything he says and does is contradictory.

It makes me want to bolt.

Ryker knocks on another red door three times before opening it.

Holy. Shit. There's a whole different club in this basement. This one is leaps and bounds better than the version we just walked through. Music pumps through the overhead speakers, and the entire place is low lit with the warm scents of vanilla, cigars, and something sweet like cherries. Plush leather seating arrangements are everywhere, clustered in groups of four and six.

Ryker leads me to the back of the massive room where a man in a white t-shirt and jeans smokes the cigar I smell. He stands when we approach and Ryker growls, "Eyes to the floor, Butterfly."

Gritting my teeth, I do as he says.

"Holy. Fucking. Shit." The man laughs. "Mannn, I wish I'd known it was date night."

"Shut it, Knox." Ryker slides into the booth first and then pats the leather cushion, signaling for me to sit next to him.

It makes me feel like a dog.

I obey anyway.

Ryker's hand rests possessively on my thigh. "Dmitri couldn't join us."

"Guess that's why D ain't here, huh?"

"Something like that," Ryker says.

I stare at the mahogany table. It's nice quality. Everything in here looks brand new from what I've seen so far. What the hell?

"You gonna introduce us, Ry?"

Ryker grips my leg a little more. "Tara, this is Knox."

"Hey, sugar."

I don't respond. It makes me feel awkward and powerful, which is such a weird combo.

"Ah," Knox says, chuckling. "I get it. Well, then, let's get down to business so you two can do whatever the fuck you two are doing."

While they start talking about construction, permits, people and contracts, I study the tattoo on Ryker's hand. It's a monarch butterfly with wings spreading across the top of his hand, the antennae twirling while the lower part of the body morphs into a skull. The bottoms of its wings drip down towards his wrist like poison. His veins are pronounced and disappear under his dress shirt where I know there's more ink.

"—need at least another five hundred thousand."

"What?" Ryker lifts his hand off my leg and rests it on the table. "That's more than we projected."

"Inflation's a bitch, man."

"What about another loan?"

"I'm tapped out. It's why I asked you and D to both be here. If we split it, we can cover the rest easy."

"We've already given you more than enough to cover it, Knox."

"Yeah, but that was *before* I had to pay off the taxes my pops owed, plus two permit officers to grease the wheels so I could get the liquor license rushed. I've also had to deal with an outsider influencing my old man."

"Who?"

"Someone from Brisbane Realty."

Ryker stiffens, and his reaction makes me edgy. "The fuck do they want?"

Knox shrugs before leaning back in his seat. "They've offered Pops a lot of money to sell this place to them under the table."

"Shit." Ryker swipes his mouth. "Did he accept?"

"Not yet, but he's given me a deadline. If I can't make the necessary changes to the club and have it up and running in the next sixty days, he's selling it to them." Ryker curses and Knox puffs on his cigar. "What a kick in the fucking balls, right? He's not giving me a lot of time to work with here."

"He's given you an impossible deadline, just to make you fail so he can get rid of it." Ryker blows out an angry breath. Then I feel his eyes on me. "Butterfly. How about you go grab us a couple drinks from the bar?"

Being called Butterfly sounds less and less like an endearment each time he fucking says it, too. I want to slap him. I'm not a server, nor am I his lap dog. But I obey if only to give myself a minute to let what they've said sink in. "Yes, Sir."

Sliding out of the booth, I tense when Ryker adds, "On your hands and knees."

I'm going to kill him.

Biting back my fury, I sink to the floor and do as he commands. The worst part about it is, I know how good I look and I'm certain he's watching. He said I fascinated him before. Let's see if I can annihilate him now.

I crawl like a cougar towards the bar and hear Knox say, "Damn, she's got an ass for days. Bet it's nice and ti—"

"Finish that sentence, and I'll cut your tongue out of your big fucking mouth."

I had no idea threats could be such a turn on until this very moment. Once I reach the bar, I get up and wrap my hand around the closest bottle of booze.

Grey Goose Vodka.

Snagging two crystal glasses next, I dump some ice into each, pour three fingers worth of vodka, and finish them both with a lime. If they don't like it, tough shit. Keeping my gaze on the floor ahead of me, I return, *on my feet*, and slide their drinks across the table. Though my eyes are still cast down, my brow arches when I ask, "Anything else you need from me, *Sir*?"

My question's loaded and we both know it.

I bet Ryker needs a lot. I bet he *needs* me.

You fascinate me.

He snaps his fingers. "Sit."

I'm going to kill Ryker when we get out of here. Head down, I drag my tongue across my teeth and slide back into the booth. The dress I'm wearing is a black Armani from last season and it suddenly feels too tight and hot. My red sole ankle-straps are also hurting my feet but are worth wearing when I make sure to step on Ryker's foot as I adjust my dress in the booth.

He grunts, but makes no other move to escape my painful, silent "fuck you".

It's one thing to be someone's sub, but I'm not sure that's what I am here. And the fact that they're talking about my family's business makes me queasy. My stepfather isn't in the market for clubs. And if he's changed his mind without letting me know, that's bad news for me. I have a lot of questions that I won't ask Knox, like who came to him and what the offer was, because Ryker still has no clue that's my family's company, and I'm only here as eye-candy apparently, not a business advisor.

Knox takes a hefty chug of his drink and smacks his lips. "Fuck, that's good."

Ryker doesn't touch his at all.

"Not to bring up more old history, but uhhh," Knox puffs on his cigar again. "I heard Greene Street was up for auction."

"I know."

"'Bout time. I hope they level that p—"

Ryker's on him in an instant, grabbing him by the throat and slowly shakes his head.

Knox puts his hands up, and Ryker lets go, grumbling, "We have to leave."

"Wait." Knox's brow furrows. "We didn't even have dinner yet. I made your favorite."

"We're not hungry. Let's go, Butterfly."

Knox smacks the table. "Damnit, Ry. What the fuck's gotten into you."

"We're done." He shoves me gently, signaling me to get up and out of his way. I'm shocked when he takes my hand and laces our fingers together once we're both standing. "I'll tell Dmitri about all this, and we'll work something out." His tone softens again. "I won't let you lose this place, okay?"

I sneak another peek and catch Knox staring at the two of us like we just kicked his puppy. "You're really not going to stay and have a bite?"

"Can't." Ryker clears his throat. "The club's in full swing and I have to get back to it."

While I'm led out of the nightclub's little speakeasy in the basement, my mind reels with questions.

What does Brisbane Realty want with this place? Why didn't my stepfather tell me the company was expanding its portfolio to include nightclubs? How will Knox be able to pay for the renovations if he's already tapped out and coming to Ryker and Dmitri for money? How long have they known each other? And why on earth did the mention of that property on Greene Street make Ryker so volatile?

That dilapidated apartment building means something to him. It's more than a shitty, cheap piece of property to invest in. It's personal.

Personal enough to make a deal with me.
Personal enough to make him attack his friend.
Personal enough to make him shut down.

I suddenly have a burning desire to crack this man open and see what spills out.

Chapter 25

Ryker

I'm stuck between a rock and a hard place. My fucking head is pounding. My stomach's in knots.

"How do you know Knox?"

Tara's question comes out of left field. It takes me a minute for my brain to make my mouth function while I drive us back to the Monarch. "He's an old friend."

"Like Dmitri?"

She's too nosy. I hate it. Ignoring her prying questions, I focus on the road ahead of me. Not just the asphalt and red lights, but my future. I don't have endless money. It took me years to build the Monarch and the cash I've set aside has now been wiped clean—thanks to the apartment building going up for sale, and the bid I put on this woman who drives me insane.

"If you need permits pulled fast, I know someone," she says.

I'm not taking her bait. It's a lie to get me to open up so she can learn shit about me. There's no reason for that level of bonding between us. I'm her Dom. She can bond with my dick and aftercare. Not my future, and sure as shit, not my past. "He'll handle it."

Turning right, I step on the gas and weave through traffic. The sooner I'm back in my own space, the better.

"I didn't realize there was a speakeasy in that club," she says. "It's leaps and bounds better underground than it is above. Why didn't he renovate that first, then work on the basement as a bonus?"

Gritting my teeth, I don't answer her.

"You know, if you—"

"Since you like using your mouth so much, how about I give it something more to do besides spew bullshit no one wants to hear, Butterfly?" My heart pounds in my chest and I feel sick talking to her like this. But I need to think, and she needs to shut up. I unbuckle my seatbelt and pull out my dick. "Stuff my cock in your mouth."

"You're joking."

The hell I am. Swerving in and out of traffic, I'm only a couple blocks away from the club and she's yet to follow my orders. "Butterfly, your defiance in the club is already going to cost you. Want to keep racking up the penalties?"

"Racking up the penalties?" She has the nerve to laugh. And I do mean this woman tips her head back and cackles. "This isn't a hockey game. And if we're racking up punishments, you'll be getting your own fair share when we get back to the suite, *Sir*."

My dick turns hard as iron.

I slam on the brakes before accidentally running a red light. We both pitch forward, and she yelps in surprise. But not me. I'm speechless. How the hell can this woman turn me upside down all the time?

Glowering at her, I can't decide if I want to kiss her or kick her out of my fucking car. It pisses me off. And even though she has every right to say what she's saying—because I'll also admit I'm being a grade A asshole here—it makes me see red.

She's not at all intimidated by me.

God, this woman has a spine made of steel.

Unfazed, Tara maintains eye contact with me while I'm mentally locking down my fortress and putting my temper back on a short leash. I have no right to speak to her the way I have. No right to treat her the way I have either. The Dom/sub dynamic was never to be taken outside of the Monarch. In Knox's club, I humiliated her and made her serve us like she was there for our bidding, which isn't true at all.

The crazy part is, I think she fucking liked it.

And damn me straight to hell, because so did I.

Tara's right. If anyone deserves to be punished, it's me for my repulsive behavior. I have no excuse for my actions. I can't explain to her why I act certain ways sometimes. I can't tell her that I'm almost positive Knox will lose his business and that it terrifies me. I can't tell her that Greene Street is my undoing. And I definitely can't tell her how jealous and possessive I felt when she crawled away to get us drinks and Knox gawked at her ass like he wanted a bite.

I brought her there because for her to come with me today, means I'll get to go with her to something later. But I didn't think Knox would disrespect her like that. I hope she didn't hear him talk about her ass. Fuck, if she did, she might have also heard my threat to him afterwards, and that will only give her leverage over me later.

She'll read into this. She'll think I care about her more than I really do.

BEEP!

The car behind us honks, jarring me out of my

thoughts. "Shit." I step on the gas and bring my focus back to the road, where it belongs. Tara doesn't say another word for the rest of the ride. And when I park, she's out before I can get the car door for her. In fact, she marches to the back entrance of the Monarch and yanks that door open, too. Or tries, at least. "You need a key or a code," I grumble, ashamed of myself. I pull a key card from my wallet and hand it to her. "Keep it."

What the fuck am I doing giving her the keys to my kingdom like this?

Doesn't matter. I'd rather she have a way in and out than be a prisoner here. Besides, it's not forever, it's just for now. "Don't lose it."

She looks like she wants to slap me.

I kind of hope she does.

The door unlocks and I open it for her, just so she can storm inside and head back to her suite. Christ, she's sexy when she's mad. Her hips sway more when she's in a bad mood, too. My mouth waters at the fantasy of fucking every ounce of aggression out of her body and mine.

When we reach her suite, I'm still five steps behind her, slowly reeling in my thoughts and closing all the open tabs in my brain. Tara deserves a big fat apology, and that's all I should focus on right now. Knox's club can wait another day or two. Greene Street isn't until the end of the month. And Dmitri will understand if I lock myself in with my Butterfly for a while.

Tara opens her suite door, slips inside, and promptly slams it in my face. Then I hear it lock.

What. The. Fuck.

"Tara!" I slam the heel of my palm against the

woodgrain.

"Leave me alone, Ryker."

God damnit. "Let me in."

"Fuck you."

I deserve this and so much more. "I'm sorry," I say, pressing my forehead against the door. "Please let me in." When she doesn't answer, I apologize three more times. Embarrassment heats my cheeks because I know this is all being caught on video. That means D and Vault will know I've acted out of line and they're going to give me shit for it, too.

As they should.

I'll suffer the consequences of my actions, but first I want to apologize to Tara the right way—face-to-face—not behind a god damned door.

Is she crying in there? Setting the room on fire? Watching TV? Taking a nap? Or is she pressed against the other side of this door, listening to me grovel? I could pull the surveillance app up on my phone and watch her from my cell, but I don't. I think knowing the truth will gut me no matter what she's doing in there.

An hour goes by, and I haven't budged or uttered another word. Then something in me breaks a little. Dropping my head in defeat, my arms braced against the doorjamb, my shoulders sag. "Tara, *please*."

She swings the door open, and a ragged breath rattles out of me. "I'm so—"

"That's not an apology. You better *beg*," she says, with her perfect plucked eyebrow arched.

I'm falling down a motherfucking rabbit hole. Rendered speechless, I take three tries to find my voice. "I'm sorry. Please, forgive me."

"On your knees, Ryker."

Anger flares in me, but I drop to the floor, anyway. "I'm sorry. Please forgive me."

She hugs herself even as she glowers down at me. "Sorry for what?"

"For being an asshole." Tara rolls her eyes and tries to shut the door in my face again, but I thrust my arm out, slamming my palm into it and knocking it wide open. "I'm sorry I snapped at you. I'm sorry I made you serve us at Knox's and made you crawl on that fucking floor. I'm sorry I told you to put your mouth to good use and suck my dick in the car."

"And?"

And? What the hell else did I do? What am I forgetting? "And…" At a loss, I stare at the floor and scramble to come up with what more I should apologize for.

"Say you're sorry for not letting me speak."

"I'm sorry for not letting you speak." Wait. What? "Butterfly, I didn't silence you."

"Yes, you did."

When I try to stand, she steps forward and shoves me back down. "Stay on your knees."

Now she's pushing it. "I didn't silence you, Tara."

"You did. When I tried to offer my help in the car regarding the permits, you cut me off and acted like the only thing I was good for was giving you road-head."

"I already apologized for that."

"Not properly, you haven't." She steps back and sweeps her hands. "You can come in. But you'll do it on your hands and knees."

"You want me to crawl like a fucking *dog*?"

She looks triumphantly down at me. "Well, since we're treating each other like animals who *Sit* when they're told to, and get drinks when they're told to, I figure you can appreciate the art of obedience between a pet and their master."

Oh shit. I did tell her to do that back at Knox's, didn't I? And though the pet/Master dynamic is totally fine and a lot of fun, that wasn't something we discussed prior to my treating her that way. Fuuuuck. I've never botched a situation with a lover so badly in my life.

I crawl into her suite with my head down. If she wants me to bark, I will.

Tara shuts the door behind us, and I won't move from this point on the carpet until she tells me.

"Good boy."

The molten anger bubbling in my veins cools quickly when she sinks to her own knees in front of me.

"Look at me, Ryker."

God, my name on her lips brings me peace when I deserve torment.

Our gazes lock, and that's when real shame hits me like a sledgehammer. I've been a piece of shit to her this whole time. No amount of pleasure I've given her was because I wanted to please her. It was to pacify her. To distract her. To relieve some of the pressure from my own body, not hers.

"Tara." I reach up to cup her cheek, but she shies away from my touch. Jesus, I have a lot of work to do if she's already flinching away from me. "I'm so fucking sorry for my behavior. Everything I've done with you, since the minute we made our first deal, has been one-sided, petty, and unfair."

She gasps, clearly not expecting me to say that.

"I understand if you want to get a new Dom. Shit, I'll understand if you want to call this whole thing off and walk away from the club entirely."

Her soft eyes harden again. "Is that why you've done all this? You think it's going to make me walk away from you?"

Time to be brutally honest. "Yes."

Because even though I let her in a little, I have got to shove her out. She doesn't belong in my world. She's too good for it. Too sweet.

I don't deserve her.

And that means I'll drive her out by any means necessary. She told me she didn't know her hard limits the night we first started this tryst, but I definitely have mine. I can't let her in. I can't keep her. And if there's even the smallest chance that my last, and strongest demon, discovers that she likes certain kinks...

There will be no saving either of us.

Tara laughs. "You'll have to try a lot harder than that if you want to run me off, Mr. Hudson. I'm not easily intimidated."

Tell me about it. And I think that's one of the main reasons I'm so drawn to her. It would take a special kind of woman to be with a mongrel like me.

"You're a smart woman, Tara. A smart woman would run from me."

"Well, I must be an idiot because I'm staying."

I tip my head back and sigh. "You have no idea what you make me feel like."

"Explain it to me then."

"Obsessed." My dark gaze latches onto her bright blues. "I have to shove you out because if you stay…" I shake my head. "I won't let you go." I crawl closer to her. "But I'm stuck, because if I let you go, you'll fuck someone else." I pinch her chin. "I will commit unforgivable crimes if another person touches your sweet body." I lean in, almost brushing my mouth against hers. "I hate that you like to be humiliated, because I very much like to humiliate you." I move over and kiss her jaw. "And I hate that you like to be my good girl, because it makes me want to spoil you." I nip her earlobe. "I hate that everything I do, you take, and it makes me crazy for you."

Her breaths quicken as she presses her hands on my shoulders. "I'll be your good girl, Mr. Hudson. And I'll be your naughty brat too." She swallows hard. "I love being your fucktoy, Sir."

If she's trying to get me to snap, it's working. "Tara," I warn her. "You're playing with fire, woman."

"No, Mr. Hudson." She stands up and heads over to the collection of whips kept at her disposal. "You're the one playing with fire." She plucks a large flogger from the collection and runs her fingers through the tassels. "And I want to know how hot you like to burn."

A smile spreads across my face. "Do your worst, Butterfly."

Because I'll certainly do mine.

Chapter 26

Tara

Ryker wants me to do my *worst*? That's a hunk of bait I'm tempted to take. Look, I'm not a Domme. At least, I don't *think* I am. But I don't really consider myself a sub either. Maybe I'm a combo? Lord knows I can be aggressive when it's called for, and obedient when I want to be. They say there are two wolves inside everyone—one of mine wants complete control, the other desperately wants to lose it.

Right now, I want control.

Ryker does nothing without purpose. There was a reason he treated me like that at the club. I just wish he'd told me why first instead of just acting like that.

But damn does this man look good on his hands and knees. He might be smiling, but I know it's a mask. There's a war going on in him and he probably thinks no one else sees it. But I do. I saw it in his eyes when we met the realtor at that apartment building. I saw it at the ceremony when he placed his bid for me to be the Butterfly. I felt it when he fucked me at my place. And I heard it in his apology outside my door.

"Everyone has their demons." Closing the space between us, I tip his chin with the end of my flogger, forcing him to look up at me. "And I want to be introduced to yours."

His eyes darken as he slowly unbuttons his shirt

and pulls it off. God, his body is perfect. Defined muscle lends the perfect canvas for his tattoos and the way he sits makes his abs flex. It's hard to tell how old he is, but I'd say late twenties, early thirties.

"What's this date for?" I run the handle of the flogger along his chest where there's a tattoo and a jagged scar.

"That's none of your business, Butterfly."

He's right, but that won't stop me from pushing him. "What's the scar from?"

Ryker doesn't answer that either. I sink to my knees in front of him for a better look. It's a thick, raised line and must have been a painful injury. Without another word, I lean over and press my lips to it.

A breath shudders out of him. "Don't." He drops his head, shaking it. "Don't ask me personal questions."

"How are we supposed to trust each other if we don't know personal things about one another?"

"You don't need to know my past to enjoy my present." His mask is firmly back in place. "And trust is something earned, not given."

My gaze lingers a little longer on the scar before moving down to his abs again. Ryker sits back on his haunches, his hands pressed against his thighs. So much tension. So much ink. So much pain. This man is a mystery—one I'm not sure if I should leave unsolved or not. There's appeal to both.

"I trust you." My voice holds steady even though I'm trembling. "I wouldn't have let you back in here if I didn't."

"You shouldn't," he argues. "I've proven over and over that I'm not a good man."

"Who said I wanted a good man, Mr. Hudson?" Tipping my head, we're suddenly very close again. "Maybe I want a great man instead."

He barks a laugh like that's the dumbest thing he's heard all day. "You're more fucked in the head than I am if you think I rank any higher than the dog you've turned me into."

"I didn't turn you into a dog. And you *are* a great man."

"Not hardly."

"You protect." Grabbing the flogger from the floor, I stand up. "You care for people." Circling him, I run the tassels along the backs of his shoulders. "You work hard to keep everyone in here safe, happy, and healthy."

I can't see his face, but his body stiffens at my words, which means I've struck a chord.

Good.

Swinging the flogger down on his back, it falls flat, the impact sloppy. To recover, I keep talking. "You're a great man, Ryker." I swing again, this time making the tassels land solid on his skin with a thud. "Say it." Swing. *Thwack!* "Say it, Ryker." Swing. *Thwack!*

His back mottles with redness in no time.

"You're a great man." Swing. *Thwack!* My hits come harder. Faster. Stronger. Before long, my voice raises to a shout. "Say it!" Swing. *Thwack*!

Ryker shakes, and he pitches forward. His fists and knees dig into the carpet. I'm not sure if I'm hurting him or not, but he isn't calling Red, so I'll keep going. Swing. *Thwack*! Swing. *Thwack*!

The dynamic between us is morphing. I like it.

"Crawl over to the bed and bend over." Head

down, he does as I command. Part of me feels bad for him. A bigger part is so fucking turned on, I'm swollen between my thighs. "Good boy," I coo, stepping up behind him.

Biting down on the handle of the flogger, I hold it between my teeth so I can use both hands to run up and down his back. His skin is hot and damp. Red lines are everywhere, chaotic and temporary. Reaching around his waist, I unbutton his fly and yank his pants down. "Step out of them."

He obeys.

And he's gone commando.

My heart skips a beat at his perfect, round, firm ass. His thick thighs. The way his waist tapers.

Gripping the flogger again, I land a perfect strike on his ass that makes him grunt. His hands ball into fists. "Again."

"Say it." I run my hand over his ass cheeks, soothing the burn. "Fucking say it, Ryker. Say *I'm a great man*."

He shakes his head, defiant as ever.

"Think about when Vault grabbed me in the hallway just to drag me away from your fight with Dmitri." I run my fingers along his abs. His muscles tighten. "Think about what you felt when you saw that man wrap his hands around my throat at my apartment." He tenses even more. "You want to protect me." Swing. *Thwack*! "Say it, Ryker. I want to hear you say it."

"No."

Swing. *Thwack*! This last strike makes his knees buckle.

"Think about how it makes you feel when I suffer."

"Tara."

Swing. *Thwack*!

"I want you to acknowledge what I already see in you." Swing. *Thwack*!

"I'm not..." Ryker shakes his head. "I'm not what you think."

"Yes, you are." Swing. *Thwack*! "Say it."

He spins around before I can land another strike and catches my arm. "I'm *not* a good man." He knocks the flogger out of my hand and drives me backwards. "I'm sure as fuck not a *great* one." He presses his body flush against mine, driving me further away from the bed.

I've got him back in that wild state of mind I love so much. "Then what are you, Ryker?"

"I'm a *whore*, Tara." My back slams against the wall, and he brackets his hands on either side of my head. Dipping down, his eyes deadlock with mine and I feel his breath on my mouth when he growls. "I'm nothing more than a *fucking whore*."

I shake my head, unable to speak.

"Yes, Miss Reed. I was an escort before I became the owner of this club. I fuck people and take their money. Take their secrets. Take their favors, too."

"That doesn't change the fact that you're still a great man."

He scoffs. "You're delusional if you really think that."

"Then I must be a whore too," I say quietly, with my heart slamming against my chest. "Because you paid two-point-two million for me."

"You have it all wrong." Ryker gets a wicked, angry smile. "I paid that amount to save you from being a whore like me."

I'm confused. "What?"

"You didn't do enough research before making our deal, Tara. The Butterfly will owe the highest bidder after her time is up in this suite. For the clientele I cater to, that's okay, because it's their husband or sugar daddy that's paying for the privilege of them getting our special treatment for a month. But you? You're the outlier. You joined this club solo. You have no one claiming you. No one to protect you from the monsters that fuck within my walls. And the man who nearly won, Blake Rittenhouse? He would eat you alive, little girl."

My knees nearly give out and he catches me by my waist. "Ryker."

His eyes squeeze shut. "Stop it," he whispers. "Stop saying my fucking name like that all the time."

I don't want to call him Mr. Hudson or Sir. I want to call him by his real name because this feels like a real goddamn problem. "Why can't I call you, Ry—"

He claps his hand over my mouth. "Every time you say it, you make it sound like a good thing. Like I'm some kind of hero coming to your rescue. Like I'm a fantasy come to life for you."

You are.

"I'm a whore, Tara. Nothing else. And when our month is up, you'll never be in my bed again."

Knocking his hand off my mouth, I want to cry. "Why not?"

He doesn't say anything, so I push. Not just the subject, but also him. Shoving my hands against his chest, my fury unleashes. "Am I not good enough for you? Not rich enough? Pretty enough? Smart enough?" I drive him backwards until his ass hits an armoire. "*Fuck you*, Ryker."

"That's what we're here for, isn't it? For you to get fucked until you can't walk, can't think, can't move? It's what you pay your membership dues for, Miss Reed. To be railed by a whore like *me*."

My temper gets the better of me and I slap him. Well, almost slap him. He blocks my strike, then pins my arms to my sides. "You wanted to play with fire? You said you wanted to see how fucking hot I'll burn, and I warned you, Butterfly. What did I fucking tell you?" He clamps my hands behind my back. "Say it. What did I fucking tell you when you got me on my knees?"

"To… to do my worst."

"And why was that, Miss Reed?"

"B-because you would also do your worst to me."

Oh shit.

Ryker's entire demeanor changes. Any cracks I made in his armor have somehow welded closed again. Lifting his chin, he glares down at me with a victorious grin. "Get on your knees and open wide, Butterfly. It's time to put your fucking mouth to work."

Chapter 27

Ryker

If I don't reel myself in, this very instant, I'll explode and there's no way I'll be able to clean up the damage. This woman has unraveled me.

Groveling, check.

Flogging, check.

Forcing me to say I'm a great man? Hard stop.

I appreciate her effort—my back and ass haven't felt this good in a while—but I'm not about to lie to this woman. There's nothing good left in me. Those things she said about me being a protector and all? They don't make me great; they make me a decent human being.

Fuck, my body feels boneless. The impact of her strikes with that flogger grew harder and harder and now I'm melting. She did it perfectly, which is incredible for someone who's just learning basic methods of impact play. My girl's a natural.

When Dmitri flogs me, I'm already well-versed on how it will go, how it will feel, and the only sound between us is the crack of the whip on my back. There's no talking. The silence grounds us both and he's never gone too far. D knows the rhythm and pace I love that will ultimately drop me into a glorious subspace in a matter of minutes.

I trust him, implicitly.

Tara, on the other hand, just tipped my world upside down. She threw the importance of trust in my face and when I gave her some of mine, she bent it into something more.

Bless her heart.

It almost fucking worked, too. In the dark recess of my mind, I almost believed what she said could be true. *Almost.* She's sweet to think I'm all greatness and strength, but if she knew me — the real me — she'd run for the hills. I'm not a hero. I'm a villain. I came from nothing, and I still have nothing. I'm a piece of meat, a fantasy, a luxury. My anger and torment fuels everything I do. The need for ultimate control comes from years of not having any.

I've made my fortune off sex and being objectified while maintaining a club that's safe for my members to indulge in their most intimate desires. Tara's the first member of the club I've taken to my bed. She'll be the last one too. I can't put myself through this shit ever again.

"Say it. Say you're a great man." Her words have cut me bone deep, and I'm bleeding out. With every lash of her flogger, I sank deeper into my darkness, where I sit with my demons in peace. Now I have to claw my way back to the light. The only problem is my demons are going to come with me.

I warned her. I said to do her worst, because I wanted to return the favor.

This woman awakes a side of me that hasn't been touched in a long time…

I'm so fucking exhausted. Between patching up Dmitri's injuries, being up all night with my mom while she puked, and then getting a random call from one of my clients saying they wanted to meet up at four in the morning, my damn eyes are blurry.

Everything hurts. My head. My heart. My legs and back.

Pulling out my cell, I check to make sure I don't have any new messages. I should catch the bus back home, but I slowly walk towards the butterfly conservatory instead. It doesn't open until nine am, but sometimes I'm able to sneak in early and have the place to myself.

Ryker*: You working today?*
Knox*: Yeah. Already here. U good?*
Ryker*: Be there in five. Let me in.*
Knox*: k*

Massaging the back of my neck does little to ease the pressure. By the time I reach the employees only entrance of the conservatory, Knox is already waiting with the door open. His brown staff shirt isn't even tucked in.

"You look like shit."

"Thanks." I pat his cheek and slip by him to head inside. "How long do I have?"

"'Bout forty minutes."

I can't stay that long.

The heavy door slams shut, plunging us into darkness. Stuffing my hands in my pockets, I navigate through the lockers, tables, and greenhouse area for new plants, and push open a set of beige doors that dump me into the conservatory. Humid, warm air hits my face, and though the morning light streams in from the glass ceiling, it's still a little dark in here.

Or maybe it's my mood.

Fuck, I wish I was in my hoodie and jeans right now. I'm sick of wearing suits. Sick of sewing buttons back on my shirts and reinforcing my pockets. I make a lot of money, but none of it goes to shit for me. Every dime is for my mom and her medical bills, our rent, electricity, and groceries.

The rest is for her pills, which I've begun to rely too heavily on Natalie to get for me.

My ass drops onto a bench and the last of the air leaves my lungs with a heavy sigh. It's so quiet in here. So calm and peaceful. Bright flowers and large green leaves surround me. If I try hard enough, I can almost trick my mind into thinking I'm in a faraway jungle where no one can touch me, and my life isn't real. But that's not happening today. The soreness in my ass and roll of twenties in my pocket verifies that I'm a whore.

Little plaques with information about different butterfly species are scattered around. There's a painting of a yellow brick road on the concrete floor, paving the way through the building. I've wandered that path a million times. It never takes me anywhere except right back to where I started.

Knox sets out bits of fruits on small pedestals, but he doesn't look at me or talk.

I love that about him. He always knows when to speak and when to leave me the hell alone. Dmitri's the same. The three of us have been through some shit, and we're still praying we make it out to the other side of our personal hells. Vault has already. His survival gives the rest of us hope.

Unlike my mom.

She's so much worse now. How has she hung on this long? Why?

Tears prick my eyes as dark thoughts crowd me. I'm torn apart. One piece of me wants to spend as much time with her as possible, so I feel guilty sitting in my sanctuary right now. Another piece of me wishes I could do more for her. Another piece of me hates what I've already done for her. And there's even a part of me that wishes she would die so this could be over.

I double over and hold my empty stomach. What kind

of son am I to think shit like that?

I'm a fucking bastard. A piece of shit.

Squeezing my eyes shut, I force my emotions back into their boxes and scrub my face. Jesus Christ, I think I'm going to puke. I'd walk out into oncoming traffic if I didn't have to go home to take care of my mom. But without me, she has no one, so suicide can't happen.

Yet.

Will I want to die after she does?

I can't imagine my life without her. Fuck, I can't imagine my life at all. Is being a sex worker all I'm good for? Fucking isn't a skill I can put on a resume. After being laid off from my construction job last month, the struggle to find something new has really put shit in perspective for me. I can't make our bills flipping burgers or stocking shelves. I can't go back to school to get my diploma. What's a GED going to get me, anyway? It's not like college will be an option for me. I need fast, big money, not minimum wage and long hours away from my dying mother.

I'm so fucking stuck. I'm so fucking exhausted. I'm so fucking defeated.

Anger and sorrow fill me to the brim. It builds, builds, builds until I tip my head back and roar.

My voice cracks. My throat hurts. Tears fall down my cheeks as I fucking sob like a baby. I hate myself. I hate my life. What the fuck did I do to deserve this shit? The tears won't stop. I don't even try to wipe them away. It's like the floodgates to my soul have blown to smithereens and what flows out is uncontrollable.

I sob for my mom. I sob for myself. I sob for Dmitri and Knox and even Natalie.

We're all in Hell.

We're all fucked.

We're all destined for a lifetime of misery.

By the time I have nothing left in me to cry with, my

head's banging and I feel numb. Jesus fucking Christ, I'm a mental case. I can't think straight anymore.

Leaning back on the bench, I close my eyes and pretend I'm anywhere else but here. I let the humid air fill my lungs. The sound of water trickling is my solace.

Then my ass vibrates with an incoming call. Pulling it out takes work because I'm still shaking from my meltdown. "Hey." I clear my throat and try again. "Hey, what's up?"

"Oh good, you're awake."

Resting my elbows on my knees, I pinch the bridge of my nose and close my eyes. "Just out for a walk. What do you need, Natalie?" I'm not telling her about my client this morning. I got her on my own, and there's no way I'll split the payout with Natalie. In fact, I've grown my own secret client list without her and have every intention of keeping her in the dark about it.

"Jackson Barre wants you for lunch."

Jesus. That man's golden shower fetish annoys me. "You take him."

"He's specifically requesting you, Ry."

"I'm busy."

"He figured you'd say that. Says he'll pay triple for one hour."

Triple? That's... shit, that's more than I've made in the past two nights. "My mom's —"

"I'll sit with your mom, sweetie. Go and do this. It's only an hour. You can do anything for an hour."

Scrubbing my face, I groan. I need sleep. Food. And apparently a lot of water now. "Fine. Tell him I'll meet him at eleven at his place." That will give me about two hours to get home, shower, feed my mom, and get there. "Can I borrow your car?" If not, I'll have to take the bus and walk the rest, which will eat up more precious time.

"Yeah, sure. But I get a third of your cut."

God. Damnit. "Fuck off, Nat."

"It's only fair. I've been the liaison between you and Jackson every time."

Because I won't give that asshole my personal cell number. I think he likes how evasive I am — maybe he considers me more valuable because I'm not easily accessible. Who knows?

"Fine." *Even if I didn't have Nat as the middleman, she's still helping me take care of my mom when I'm on these dates. Her time costs money, too, even if she's never asked a dime to look after my mom.*

"Are you at the conservatory?"

Leaning back on the bench, I sigh. "Yeah." *She only knows that because she's likely pulled my location from Snapchat. We try to keep tabs on each other for safety reasons.*

"Don't stay long," *she chides, even though her tone is soft and understanding.* "And make sure you drink a lot of water before you go. Make it rain, Ryker. Make it rain."

She hangs up and I've suddenly lost my desire to stay here and find my peace of mind.

Standing up, I stretch my arms over my head and half the bones in my body snap, crackle, and pop. A monarch butterfly lands where I was just sitting, her little wings open and close slowly as she crawls across the slats of the bench. Holding my finger out, I wonder if she'll climb on.

She doesn't.

Instead, the orange and black beauty flutters away and I lose sight of her amidst the greenery.

"They're poisonous, did you know that?" *Knox slowly approaches from my left side.* "They eat milkweed, which has toxins that's harmful to animals. But the toxins don't ever hurt the butterfly, so they gobble it up, build an immunity to it, and taste bad to animals that try to eat them."

I have no idea why Knox is telling me this. "Cool."

"Yeah. It is. Maybe we all need to take a page outta their book, right? Like, just be toxic. No one will fuck with you if you are and you can flutter around and live your life being just out of everyone's reach. If someone gets too close, they'll taste how awful you are and leave you the fuck alone."

Knox's hand trembles when he places another piece of fruit on a pedestal. "Hey man. You okay?"

"Of course." *He pulls a what the fuck face on me.* "I'm always good, Ry."

No, he's not. "You still clean?"

His face contorts with anger. "The fuck kind of question is that? Yes, I'm clean."

Putting my hands up, I step back. "Just checking, bro. You know how we worry."

"Well stop. You and D have enough on your minds as it is. I'm not using again. I swear."

"What's with the shaky hands then?"

"Too much caffeine."

I can't tell if he's lying or not. "You sure you're okay?" *He looks too thin, especially now that his shirt's tucked in.* "When was the last time you had a decent meal, Knox?"

"Yesterday. Morning."

Damnit. "Here." *I dig out my earnings from earlier and pull off two twenties.* "If you need more, tell me."

"No, man. I don't need that."

"Take it." *I shove it against his chest.* "Consider it my early entrance fee to the conservatory."

Knox shakes his head. "You know that's never necessary."

"Yeah, well, eating is. So, get yourself something good and hearty today, understand me?" *If he takes this money home and puts it with his paycheck, his pops will find the cash and blow it on blackjack or something. Knox is all I care about in that house and, given how he's a couple of years younger than me, I feel protective of him like he's my little brother.*

"Thanks, Ry."

"No problem." *Slapping him on the back, I head out through the employees only area and leave the conservatory, my friend, and my peace of mind behind. The world is awake, hungry, and needy.*

And I've got what it wants.

"Get on your knees and open wide, Butterfly. It's time to put your fucking mouth to work."

Tara sinks down without a word and opens her pretty pink lips and sticks out her tongue. Stroking my dick with one hand, I stick my thumb in her mouth and love how she closes her lips around it.

"Suck," I say calmly. The flat of her tongue is soft as she sucks me like a pacifier. That's not something she can do with my dick. It's too thick for that. "Good girl." I push my hips forward. "Suck on my balls."

Tara releases my thumb and goes in for the heavy weights I'm offering. She pulls one into her mouth, making me groan. While she works my balls over, one at a time, I lick my wet thumb.

It's the closest I'll get to tasting her saliva because I refuse to kiss her on the mouth. Kissing is for people who care, which I do not.

"You feel so good, Butterfly." She flutters her eyes open to look up at me. "Now I'm going to face-fuck you, and if you can't take it, tap my leg. Understand?"

Tara pulls away long enough to say, "Yes, Sir."

I'm disappointed with how fast she changed from Domme in charge to a little submissive kitten, but I'm also relieved. Looks like she's a Switch, like me.

Cradling her head in my hands, I thrust into her mouth. Tara gags and gurgles and makes all kinds of sweet, messy noises while I ram my dick down her throat. She taps my leg and I pull out, even though I'm so fucking close to coming that I'm shaking. "You good, Butterfly?"

Her breaths saw out of her. Drool coats her chin. Her eyes are glassy and cheeks beautifully flushed. "My jaw hurts."

Too bad. "Open."

She does, and it makes me pause. "How bad does it hurt?"

Tara's brow furrows. "Bad. But I want to keep going. I want to taste your come, Sir."

I don't want her in pain just to chase down my pleasure. No kink shaming, but that's just not for me. "I'll give you a taste, Butterfly." Swiping the drool off her chin, I add my own spit to it and jerk myself off with her waiting impatiently for my load. "Tell me you want it."

"I want it. I want all of it." She leans forward and sucks on one of my balls again, pulling it into her mouth until my eyes cross.

"Fuck, woman." I jerk off faster. "Stick out your tongue, baby."

She releases my balls and does what I ask. I come all over her tongue and lips. One rope lands on her chin and I swipe it, gathering it on my thumb before I stick it in her mouth. "Suck it clean."

Tara does everything I say.

"Did you swallow every drop?"

"Yes, Sir."

Cupping her chin, I stare down at her. "Let me see." The room spins when she opens her mouth and sticks her tongue out. She swallowed my entire orgasm. "Such a good girl."

"I want more." Tara leans forward and grabs my balls again. I pull back. "Please?" she begs. "I want you to sound like that again, Sir."

Sound like what? "What noise did you like?"

If I know what makes her melt, I'll figure out what makes her freeze too.

"My name," she says, paralyzing me.

I didn't say her name, did I? Wait. No. Wait. Did I?

Fuck.

"You just screamed my name like it was..." She clams up and backs away. Pulling up to her feet, Tara shakes her head. "Never mind. It's stupid."

I grab her arm, stopping her from walking away from me. "How did I say it?" Morbid curiosity alone has me almost begging to know her answer.

"Like... you've been in Hell and..." Her gaze softens. "And I was the angel that pulled you out."

She rips her arm out of my grip and disappears into the bathroom, leaving me naked and alone in the suite with my heart in my hands.

Shit.

Chapter 28

Tara

It's stupid to read into anything Ryker says and does. He's a cunning hustler. It's a mistake to ever consider the possibility that he'd fall for someone like me. I'm a temporary problem with an expiration date, not his salvation.

And he sure as shit isn't my savior, either.

I should have never tried to dominate him. No matter how great it felt, I messed it all up. I just wanted him to grovel and worship me and admit something he's probably never said to anyone else.

I'm so fucking stupid and arrogant.

I used the flogger as punishment, when it was really a reward. I can't even tell if that's okay or not. I'm in over my head and this is *not* the place to "fake it till you make it" like I can out in the real world. In here, with these tools at my disposal, someone could get hurt.

I fear it'll be me.

But it might also be Ryker, because how he said my name as he came? The way he looked? The intensity of it all? I almost cracked his fortified armor again. I was so close, it made me ache. But it made me crack open too, because I now know what I want, and I'll *never* have it.

I want a Dom to discover who I am with. I want

a safe space to fall apart while I'm fucked to pieces and held together by strong arms and rope. I want to be the Butterfly forever so I can stop feeling like a freak and find myself. I want to find my peace. Embrace my kinks and banish my shame. I want to find someone who understands me and knows how to be with me. I want a protector, a provider, and an equal. Someone who will open the door for me and slap my ass as I walk through it. I want someone who will see me enter a room and simultaneously love and loathe the fact that I turn heads. I want someone who will give me independence while putting me in my place.

What I want doesn't exist. How could it? They'd have to be a walking contradiction.

They'd have to be Ryker.

He teeters between humiliating me one minute and worshiping me the next. I have no idea which is the real him. I'll go mad trying to figure it out. Maybe that's why there's only a one-month rule to being the Butterfly. Any longer and it would cause permanent damage to the woman's psyche.

"Tara." He softly knocks on the bathroom door. "Can I come in?"

"Give me a minute." After splashing cold water on my face and blotting it dry, I fix my hair and blow out a deep breath. Then I swing the door open. "What?"

He looks... devastated. "I'm so sorry. For everything."

I'm sick of his apologies. And seeing him grovel again will lead me right back down the path of bad decisions and hopeful heart bubbles that are better left popped and gone. "There's nothing to be sorry for."

My stomach rumbles. Christ, what time is it

anyway?

"Want pizza?"

"Pizza?" I turn to look at him. "*Seriously*?"

"Unless you don't like pizza. I'll order whatever you want."

"I'm not hungry." My stomach's too twisted with emotions for food, no matter how noisy it's being. "I have work to do in your office."

"Come on," he says, pulling out all his charm. Grabbing my hands, he lures me towards the bed. "Get comfy and I'll feed you anything you want."

What the hell is this? "I said I have work." I rip my hands out of his.

"Not today, you don't."

"Ryker, I'm given one hour a day to get my shit done. Just like you."

"And I'm not working today either."

That's not helpful. "Well good for you for taking the day off. I can't."

"Yes, you can."

"No. I can't." That's not true. Whatever's sitting in my inbox can wait, but I'm too mixed up in my head and want some space between me and Ryker. An hour of banging away on my laptop sounds like a viable plan, even if he makes me sit on his lap to do it.

"Tara."

"Ryker."

"Tara!" He's gone from sweet to frustrated again. I honestly don't know which I like more. "Damnit, let me take care of you."

"I take care of myself, Mr. Hudson. I don't fucking need you."

"Please." Lifting my chin with his finger, he tips my head up, so I'll look at him. I don't want to. He'll see my vulnerability and I can't let that happen. "*Please*, Butterfly." His voice cracks this time. It makes me wonder if he wants to take care of me, for me, or for himself. "Let me do this."

Pizza won't show his intentions. I want something better. "Kiss me."

He flinches back. "What?"

"Kiss me. On my mouth. Right now."

Ryker shakes his head. "How did we go from pizza to kissing?"

"You said you wanted to take care of me. Prove it. I'm sad and confused, and I'd feel so much better if you would just *kiss* me."

My heart sinks as he backs away from me. "That's not happening. I don't kiss club members."

Figures he'd pull that card. It's absolutely bullshit. "Fine. Consider me no longer a member then." I storm towards the door, hoping he'll fall for my bluff and give me what I'm asking for. "I'm done being the Butterfly."

I'm halfway out the door when he grabs my hand and yanks me back. Slamming the door shut, he rears up on me. "What are you doing?"

"I just told you, I'm done. I quit being the Butterfly."

His gaze narrows. "Because I won't *kiss* you?"

"Because you won't show me who you really are!" I scream in his face.

"Oh, and you have?"

"What?"

"I know nothing about you, Miss Reed. And though you may have won this…" He flicks his hand around the room, "*privilege*, that doesn't mean you've earned the right to know things about me or demand me to give you things I'm not willing to give."

"And yet I'm supposed to trust you."

"You can trust that I would never hurt you."

"That's where you're wrong." I jab my finger in his chest. "You keep hurting me. You make me feel like I'm a thing. A job. An obligation."

His shoulders sag. "How? By giving you orgasms and fulfilling your fantasies? Boo fucking hoo, princess."

"You have no idea what my fantasies are."

"Then tell me and I'll make them happen."

A cold, cackling laugh bursts out of me. "I just did, and you shot me down."

"You don't come to my club for a kiss. You come to get railed."

He's right. Sort of.

"Tell me your other fantasies." Ryker tries grabbing my hand again, but I pull back before he can touch me.

"Oh, so now who's being demanding? Do you honestly think I owe you my personal information? My secrets and desires? God, you're the biggest hypocrite on the planet." I shove him back and he stumbles until his legs hit the bed where he catches himself.

"Hypocrite or not, I'm here for your pleasure, Tara. That's all. I'm your Dom who will see to your sexual needs safely and fulfill all your fantasies before you leave at the end of the month."

If my eyes roll any harder, they'll detach from my skull. "That's not all a Butterfly needs, you insufferable dickhead."

"That's *exactly* what she gets here, Miss Reed. It's what every woman in this club would sell her soul for and you're shitting all over it."

My blood chills. "Well," I say, fanning my hair over my shoulder. "I guess I'm not like the other women in this club. And you being my pleasure Dom *isn't all I fucking need.*"

We scowl at each other so hard I swear the toxicity between us makes it hard to breathe.

"Maybe you're right," he finally says. Picking his shirt up off the floor, he tugs it on. "Maybe you should leave."

Good. Glad we're on the same page. Never mind that hearing him say that makes me dizzy and sick to my stomach. I've handled rejection before, and I can certainly handle this. Ryker doesn't deserve a woman like me and I'm sick of trying to prove my worth to men who don't want to see it.

Fuck this guy.

Fuck every guy.

I'm. Done.

Spinning on my heels, I march to the door again, but Ryker beats me to it. Slamming his hand against the door, he presses his chest to my back. "Don't." His hot breath tickles my neck. "I… don't want to let you go yet, Tara."

"You don't get to make that choice." I elbow him in the stomach and when he doubles over, I open the door and run.

Chapter 29

Ryker

I've never been this fucked up before. When Tara runs away from me, I let her go because she's right. The choice is hers, not mine.

It's never been mine.

I'm nothing more than a monarch butterfly—a pretty creature who's poisonous to others. Tara just got a taste of me and ran. Good. It's nice to see her self-preservation skills work. I'm almost relieved that it's over.

Almost.

Listening to her feet beat the carpet as she dashes down the hall, I brace my hands on the doorjamb to keep from chasing her down.

This isn't love I'm feeling. It's not even lust.

It's just a connection. One I haven't had in a long time. I need to let her sever it for us both.

The stairwell door creaks and slams shut. My heart rattles in my chest, trying to burst out of my body to go after her. She's probably racing down the steps, clutching the banister, her hair flying behind her as she flees far, far away from here.

I can't breathe.

My knees buckle and down I go.

Air. I need air. I can't see right. My vision tunnels until everything's black except for a pinprick of light. My throat's closing up.

"Call D!" Someone yells. I think it's Vault. Of course, it's Vault. He's the one who monitors the cameras most. He would have seen the entire shitshow from his desk.

I don't need him here. I don't need anyone here. I don't need—

"Hang on, Ry." Vault nestles down behind me and wraps his legs and arms around my torso, caging me. It makes it worse. "Breathe with me, man. Come on. You got this."

I don't got shit. Fears tumble out of me. Feelings. Emotions. All my hang-ups twist into a noose that tightens around my neck. I'm choking. Suffocating.

"What happened?" Dmitri's voice filters through my wonky hearing even as my pulse quickens to a deafening roar.

"Don't know. They got in an argument, and she left. Then this."

"Hey." D pats my face. "Ryker. Breathe slower."

"I… I can't… I can't see anything." I can't hear or think or breathe or move. The room's spinning in too many directions. The voice in my head screams, *RUN, RUN, RUN*. But I'm frozen.

Dmitri claps his hands on my face and presses his forehead to mine. "You gotta inhale and exhale slower, man. Come on. I'm right here. We're both right here."

"I can't let go." My cheeks tingle. My hands go numb. "I can't… I can't let… her go."

"She's gone already," D says in a broken tone. "She's been gone a long time, Ry."

He thinks I'm talking about someone else. He has no idea I mean Tara.

"You have to breathe." Vault loosens his hold on me. "Come on. In with the good shit. Out with the bullshit."

I'm going to be sick. "I... I can't...."

D stays in my face. "You can and you will. *In...*" He sucks in an exaggerated breath. "*Out.*" He blows out an exhale that hits me in the face. "In..." He inhales. "Out." He exhales.

I finally manage to get with the program and my panic lessens, marginally. It's enough for me to ease my grip on Vault's thighs. My vision clears too. "Your breath stinks."

"No, it doesn't," D laughs.

He's right. It doesn't. He's smacking on minty gum. "Thanks." It's been a long time since I had an episode like this.

"You want me to help you, uhhh, relieve some more pressure?" D tips his head where the floggers are.

"No." I think that's part of the reason my head's so fucked right now. I'm having a drop. Too many emotions have popped up at once because of it.

Tara has been the best worst thing to ever walk into my life.

I fear I'm the same for her.

After a few more minutes of calm breathing, I tap Vault's leg. "You can let me go now."

"Awww, but I like it when we cuddle."

Dmitri holds his hand out and pulls me to my feet. The room spins a little. "Shit. I'm dizzy." Stumbling to the couch, I drop in it and cradle my head in my hands. "I'm a fucking mess."

"You have a lot going on," D says. "The club, your Butterfly, Greene Street."

"Knox needs more money," I blurt. "Brisbane Realty offered his father a lot of cash for the club, so he's given Knox two months to get the rest of it up to code and running, or he's selling it."

"Jesus Christ." D plops down next to me. "That asshole will make him do all the work and sell it off anyways, probably thinking he'll get a higher price if it's updated."

"My thoughts exactly."

"How much more does he need?"

"Five hundred grand."

Vault whistles. "On top of what you've already contributed? That place is not even worth it."

"It's all he has," I say. But Vault is right. That club is a dump and even though Knox managed to turn the underground level into something great, the biggest part of the building still needs serious work. His father ran it into the ground and no amount of paint or leather seating will fix it. "We're in too deep to let him fail now."

As silent partners, Dmitri and I have given a lot of our savings to him already.

"Do you have any extra cash, Ry?" D rests his elbows on his knees. "'Cause I don't."

"Not after bidding at the ceremony," I admit. The room finally stopped spinning and my perfect hearing is back. "I need the rest of my money for the auction of Greene Street."

I'm not even sure I'll have enough to cover it. Loans are out of the question. I refuse to ask for outside help.

"Maybe you shouldn't bid on it, Ryker."

There goes the joy of having my hearing back. Or maybe I'm hallucinating because I swear Dmitri just said that I shouldn't buy the building. "Maybe you should mind your business."

"Oh, it's like that now?" He stands, stretching every bit of his six-foot-five self as he towers over me. "You just ran your Butterfly out of here, had an anxiety attack on the motherfucking floor, and you're still stupid enough to not see what's causing all your damn problems?"

"That building isn't—"

"Oh, it is. You can't let go of *shit*." D marches towards the door. "I love you, Ryker. You know I'll do anything for you. But you've got to stop being your own problem. You literally sabotage everything good in your life."

"What good?" I yell. "I'm a whore who runs a sex club. I have nothing and no one."

And now I'm flat broke.

"Nothing and no one, huh?" D nods his head. "Okay." He walks out the door and Vault follows him.

Shit. I didn't mean that. These guys have been there for me since the beginning. I don't have nothing, I have *them*.

It's just that I want more.

I love my club. I love offering a safe space for people to get their kinks on. I love working with my best friends. I love helping people. But there's a huge hole in my heart that nothing has been able to fill. I grab onto things—people—and try to mold them into the shape of the cavity that's inside me. They don't ever fit.

Tara probably won't either, so it's a good thing she's gone. I would have tried to morph her into that missing piece. I did it to Natalie. And I did it to—

"Hi Ry!" Kenzie leans over the coffee shop counter and flashes me a huge smile. "I was hoping I'd see you today."

"Oh yeah? Why's that?"

"I've missed you." She grabs my t-shirt and yanks me in for a kiss. Each time she does this, it injects joy into my black veins. Kenzie looks at me with these little puppy dog eyes and is never not smiling, which helps my black heart smile too. She's the sun in my stormy life. We've been dating for three months, and I haven't told her what I do for a living yet. It makes me feel like a fake and a liar.

I hate myself for it.

I'm just not ready to let her go yet. She makes me feel good. Happy. Normal. D says it's a mistake to string her along without being upfront with her, but I just need this fantasy to last a little longer. My mom's disintegrating and being with Kenzie comforts me, even if she doesn't know I'm battling a war for my mom's life. And mine.

"Where have you been? I tried calling last night, but you didn't answer."

"I was working," I say, tucking a lock of hair behind her ear. She has the cutest earlobes ever. "Just left the butterfly conservatory."

"Awwww. I'm so jelly. I wish I could have gone with you."

I flash her a smile, then bite my bottom lip once her gaze drifts to my mouth. "When do you get off work?"

"One."

That will give me time to meet with Jackson Barre, piss on him while he gets off, then I can grab something to eat and catch the bus back here. "How about I scoop you up and we can go to the conservatory together this afternoon?"

She lights up. "Really?"

"Yeah." I chuckle. God, she's so bubbly and happy. I love it.

"Oh shoot. I have to study for an exam." My girl's in college and smart as fuck. *"Can we make it a quick trip?"*

The quicker the better, because I need to get home to my mom. *"However long you want to stay, that's how long we'll be."*

"Okay!" She beams me another killer smile, and I swear my heart pounds harder every time I see her happy.

"I'll see you soon, Kenzie."

"Hey!" she yells, when I turn away. "Don't you dare walk away from me like that, Ryker Hudson."

Biting back my laugh, I turn towards her and grin. "Did I forget something?"

"Damn straight you did." She hops on the counter and grabs me by the back of the neck. Then she kisses me like it's her last act on this earth. The other baristas hoot and laugh. Pure joy bubbles out of me because of it. "I love you," she says against my lips.

My heart explodes.

That's who I've compared Tara to. The first and only girl who said she loved me. The first and only girl who, once she found out the truth of my life, looked at me like I was shit on the bottom of her shoe. The girl who ran and never looked back.

Just like Tara has now.

The night Kenzie found out I was an escort was a bad one. We'd been together for a little over four months, and I was escorting a forty-year-old woman to the theater…

"Ryker?" Kenzie stops on the sidewalk, with her friends in tow, and gawks at me. "Hi!"

Oh fuck. Oh fuck, oh fuck, oh fuuuuck. *"Hey,"* I lean over and kiss her cheek. *"How are you?"*

"Um." Kenzie's brow knits with confusion as she regards the woman I'm with. *"Hi, I'm Kenzie."*

She probably thinks this is my mom. Only my mom is too sick to walk to the bathroom by herself, and Kenzie has no clue about any of that either. The client on my arm has flaming red hair, heavy lipstick, and drips in Tiffany.

"Pleasure to meet you," my client says. *"Come on, Ry. We're going to be late."* This woman is a jealous creature. I don't blame her. Her husband fucks anything with a hole, including me, and is never there for her like I am afterwards. She cries in my lap some nights and pays me five hundred an hour for the privilege. But she also thinks she owns me. I'm her property when we're together. *"Tell the girl goodbye."*

"Bye," I say, feeling like a complete clown.

She drags me down the sidewalk, and I have no choice but to let her. I need the three grand she's paying me for this date. Wincing when my client grabs my ass and sinks her manicured talons into my skin, I growl between clenched teeth. *"Let… go…"*

"Not until that little bitch knows who you belong to," she claps back.

Regretfully, I glance over my shoulder and see Kenzie staring at us. Her jaw falls open. Her eyes are locked on where my client's hand is.

"He fucks me like a machine, too," my client calls over her shoulder. *"That's what you get when you pay the premium price, sweet pea."*

It's the last straw. I remove her hand from my ass. *"We're done."* *She tries to touch me again, and I smack her hand away.* *"I said we're done. Don't call me again."*

"Ryker!" she seethes. *"Don't you dare walk away from me, you ingrate!"*

I spin on my heels and rush back to Kenzie. *"I can explain."*

"Oh, this should be good," one of her friends says, folding her arms.

"That's not your mom." Kenzie points at my furious and humiliated client marching away in her six-thousand-dollar red heels. "Is it?"

"No. It's not." So many confessions sit on my tongue because I don't want to do this here. Especially not in front of an audience. "Can we go someplace more private for a sec?"

Kenzie shakes her head. "Anything you have to say, you can say it in front of my friends, too."

"Yeah, Ryker. Let's hear you charm your way out of this one. Or does that come with the premium price tag too, sweet pea?"

I don't even know who Kenzie's friends are, but they're surrounding me like a pack of wolves. My heart gallops in my chest. "My mom's sick. She's been dying of cancer."

"And you're going to the theater to find her a cure?" one of them asks.

"Shut your fucking mouth," I snap back. Shit, I shouldn't talk like that to anyone here. It's not their fault I'm a liar and a cheat. "Her meds and stuff cost a lot of money. Money, we don't have."

"Oh my god." Kenzie holds her cheeks. "Are you serious right now, Ryker? Are you a…" She looks around like she's embarrassed being seen with me. "Are you a fucking hooker?"

"Escort," I correct, knowing how stupid it sounds. "And it's not – "

"I'm going to be sick." Kenzie stumbles away from me like I have the plague. "You fuck people for money? You're a whore?" Her voice rises. "Oh my god. How many diseases do you have? Oh my god, oh my GOD!"

We've never slept with each other. I've never done

anything but kiss her for these four months. I gave her the only thing I haven't *given anyone else.* "Kenzie, please, just hear me out."

"There is absolutely **nothing** *you can say that will make this okay. Back off right now." Her friend shoves me, but I don't budge.*

All I can do is stare at the one ray of sunshine I have and beg for her to stay. "Kenzie, please."

She takes off running and even though I try to hold back from chasing her down, my feet start moving. "Kenzie!"

I run across the street, screaming her name, her body the only thing I focus on. I have to get to her. I have to stop her. I have to make her understand I don't want to be like this. But halfway across the street, I stop because what's the point? She deserves better than me. I'm not going to change. I can't. "KENZIE!"

A horn blows and wheels screech. I'm blinded by headlights and the chaos of my life crashing into me.

SLAM!

I fly into the air and land hard on the asphalt while Kenzie keeps running farther and farther away from me...

I feel like I've been hit by a car again. Everything fucking hurts.

Tara left. All she wanted was a kiss and I couldn't give it to her. How pathetic is that? But how can I give that one piece of myself to a woman who can't stay.

You're a great man. Say it.

I told her I wasn't a great man. I told her I was a whore.

You're a great man. Say it.

I told her I was a whore, and she didn't run or

look at me like I was garbage.

You're a great man. Say it.

I told her I was here only for her pleasure and that I would give her anything she wanted. I said I'd make all her fantasies come true. All she had to do was tell me what she desired, and I'd make it happen.

She wanted a kiss.

I'm not a great man, I'm a fucking coward.

Chapter 30

Tara

Ryker is an asshole. It's the only thought that circulates my brain as I leave the club. Then I realize all my shit is still inside, including my goddamn cell, laptop, and car keys.

Fuck my life.

Head high, I march my sweet ass right back inside and straight to Ryker's office. I hate how good it smells in here. The way this motherfucker affects me should be criminal. Rushing over to his desk, I grab my phone first and start piling my files on top of my closed laptop.

Then I see it.

One of the computer screens shows my suite with Ryker sitting on the floor and my stomach drops. He looks like he's suffocating. His chest heaves and he's clawing at his legs. Is he having some kind of attack?

Vault barrels into the room and quickly attends to him.

Oh my god, what the hell is happening?

Dmitri storms in next. They sandwich Ryker on the floor. Is Ryker having a seizure? Should I call 9-1-1?

My hand trembles as I try to find the volume. I'm not even sure if there is sound on this camera system, but I need to know what's happening and I'm not going back down there to find out.

I don't even know why I care.

Clicking a volume button on the laptop, sound filters through the tiny speaker.

Dmitri's in Ryker's face. "Breathe slower."

"I... I can't... I can't see anything." Ryker sounds terrified and something inside me fractures.

Dmitri claps his hands on Ryker's cheeks and gets in his face. "You gotta inhale and exhale slower, man. Come on. I'm right here. We're both right here."

"I can't let go." Ryker's voice cracks. "I can't... I can't let... her go."

Muting the sound because I can't bear to hear anymore, I drop into his chair. What do I do? Listening to the rest would be such an invasion of privacy, but also, it'll make me want to go back to that suite and try again with this guy.

I refuse.

If he can't let me go, then he'll have to come get me. On my turf. On my time.

Although, who's to say he's even talking about me at all? That possibility makes my stomach twist. I've heard Dmitri say weird shit to Ryker before—during their fight in the hallway—where he said, "She's not the one."

There are too many possibilities in what any of this means, and since I don't know Ryker Hudson intimately, I'll likely never find out what his issues are. But seeing him break down like this? Watching a grown ass man crumble in such a drastic way?

My god. I can't put it into words.

I also can't seem to pull away from the computer. Not until I see both Dmitri and Vault leave.

Okay. He must be better now, right? They wouldn't leave him alone if he was still suffering, would they?

No. They wouldn't.

Okay, I gotta get out of here. Grabbing my things, I head for the door.

Maybe I should check on Ryker one more time before I go, though. Just to make sure he's all good.

Creeping back over to his desk, my heart sinks. He looks absolutely broken.

The office door suddenly swings open. *Shit*! On reflex, I slam the laptop closed like a teenager caught watching porn. Dmitri halts when he sees me behind the desk. "I-I was just getting my stuff."

He steps inside and shuts the door, locking us both in together. "How much did you see?"

"Nothing. I saw nothing."

Dmitri slowly closes the gap between us. "Don't lie, Butterfly. Tell me what you saw."

"I barely saw anything. Just a group hug."

He sits down in the leather chair facing me. "Sit."

"God, what is up with you guys always barking orders at me like I'm a dog?"

"*Sit.*"

I drop my ass into Ryker's chair. Damnit. No part of me would take orders outside of this club, and I think the only reason I'm willing to do it now is because I desperately want to know more about Ryker and I'm betting if I play nice, Dmitri will share.

He crosses one leg over the other and leans back in the chair, arching his brow at me.

"What happened in there?" I ask quietly.

"That's not for me to say."

Well, this chat just became worthless. I open the

laptop and the cameras all come back to life. I watch Ryker stand up and head towards the bathroom. "Will he be okay?"

"Do you honestly care?"

I drag my gaze away from the screen once Ryker's gone from view. "Yes."

Dmitri's expression softens. "Do you really, Tara?"

"Yes. And I hate it."

"Good." He gets up and opens the door. "Get the fuck out of here."

...

It's been a few days since I left the Monarch. I haven't heard from Ryker at all. Not that I expected to, but my heart won't listen to my brain. I'm not in love with the man, but I could easily see myself getting there if he wasn't such a prick. A prick who didn't want me. A prick who wouldn't even kiss me.

Lord knows I have a type. The ones who don't give me the time of day are the only ones I work harder for. Talk about toxic traits. I really should consider therapy.

What time is it? Shit, I've got to leave in fifteen minutes if I'm going to make brunch with my family in time.

My doorbell rings, and dread consumes me. Earlier, I got a message from the Monarch's concierge service saying my bags would be delivered this morning. It's the finale. The last cord to sever between me and that club.

After Dmitri told me to leave, I washed my hands of the place and refuse to think of it ever again.

"It's open!" I yell, while applying another layer of lipstick in the mirror of my bathroom. "Just leave my bags at the door."

Fixing my hair one last time, I smooth down my sundress and sigh at my reflection. Talk about trying hard. My stepfamily is another group of people I'm not good enough for. No matter how hard I try, I can't win them over.

I hate bowing down to men, and it's all I've done since I was a teenager.

When my mom married William Brisbane, I was fifteen. I went from having a tiny dresser stuffed with t-shirts and shorts, to a walk-in closet overflowing with designer dresses, bikinis, and jeans. Don't get me started on the shoe collection.

I loved it.

I still do. Who doesn't like nice things?

What I don't like—and never have—is the expectations that come with having those nice things. I have to sit pretty. Be sweet. Stay polite. Pretend I don't notice old bastards eye-fucking me while I sip champagne at fundraisers. Play along with clients when they flirt atrociously with me over dinners at stuffy restaurants when my stepfather isn't paying attention.

He's never once treated me like his clients do. In fact, he almost values my work and opinion like I'm his equal. It makes working with him easy—and working with Garret, his son, impossible. Garret's been jealous of me since the day our parents got married. No amount of time has changed the way he loathes me. And ever since we graduated college, and both took heavier roles in Brisbane Realty, Garret's done all he can to make my work life hell.

"Looks good," I say to my reflection. This floral print will make my stepfather happy. He loves flowers on me and my mom, even though I have no idea why. But I'll forever do my best to stay on his good side because I don't want my mom to have stresses in her life because of me. William can be a bear when he's angry. My mom's the one who has to put up with his attitude.

Clasping a bracelet on my wrist, I enter my living room and see two suitcases in front of my coffee table.

And Ryker sitting on my couch.

"What are you doing here?"

Dressed in a black suit, he stares at the coffee table with his elbows on his knees. His jaw clenches several times before he finally looks up at me. Then he stands up and saunters over to me. The intensity of this man is off the charts. Ryker silently wraps his finger around one of the curly tendrils I made to frame my face. "You look stunning, Tara."

Tara. Not Butterfly. Not Miss Reed. Not baby or good girl or any other thing he's called me this week. I want to slap him. I want to hug him. I want to cry and laugh and melt into him. I'll never understand why him saying my real name stirs so much emotion in me, but here we are. Enigmas.

"You shouldn't be here." Stepping back lets me find my courage. "And I have to go."

He swallows hard. Then silently takes a step back from me, too.

"I have an appointment."

Ryker nods. "Brunch. I remember."

Whatever. I'm not delusional enough to believe he memorized any part of our time together that didn't somehow suit his motives. Moving towards the door, I look over my shoulder to make sure he's with me. He's not. Ryker's gone back to my couch.

Damnit.

"You have to leave," I say. "I have to go."

He sits down again.

"I mean it! You have to leave!"

He stares at me.

"God damnit! If you don't leave, I'm calling the cops."

He leans forward and steeples his fingers, resting his elbows on his knees again.

What a stubborn asshole. "Why won't you leave?"

"Because I don't think you really want me to."

The arrogance in this man! "I never want to see you again. Get out."

His Adam's apple bobs in his throat. "Do you want me to get on my knees and beg again? Because I'll do it."

My cheeks tingle. "What? No. I don't want that at all."

"Then tell me what you want, Tara. How can I…" He looks away from me and sighs. "I don't know how to do this."

"Do what? Be anything other than a fucking asshole?"

"I don't know how to be…" He looks around the room. "Normal."

Seriously? What a dumbass. "Do you know someone who's *normal*?"

"You are."

"You don't know anything about me, Ryker."

"You're right." His gaze captures mine. "But I

want to."

My palms sweat. "Why?"

"Because I feel something with you."

I bet he does. "Yeah, you feel hate, frustration, obligation, and disappointment. Funny, I'm not one to kink shame, but I didn't see that coming from a man like you."

He frowns. "I don't feel any of those things with you, Tara."

Crossing my arms, I hug myself and look away. "Could have fooled me, *Sir*."

"Don't do that. Don't use honorifics right now."

Fuck this guy. "Bye, Ryker. See yourself out." I walk out and slam the heel of my palm on the elevator button, grateful that it opens immediately. Stepping inside, I muster what's left of my confidence and turn to face him so I can flip him the bird.

He's already out of my apartment and slams his hand on the closing elevator door, forcing it to reopen. His intensity is back too. Tenfold. I back up until my spine hits the wall. He's on me in a flash, caging me in. His forehead presses to mine as his hands remain braced on either side of my head. My heart races. I can't feel my feet.

Ryker looks down at my mouth.

He leans in a little more. I feel his breath on my lips and his soapy scent tingles in my nose. Ryker's overpowering everything that's mine. This elevator, my thoughts, my heart, my lust, and my brain.

"I'll kiss you," he whispers, and I float a little higher. "Just... let me earn you back first."

Pop! The hope floating inside me bursts like a balloon, and little pieces of it flutter to the ground as garbage. Slipping out from under him, I smash the lobby button and hug myself again. Damnit, I left my keys!

A headache starts creeping in. Massaging my temples, I wait until we hit the lobby and the door opens. I don't get out. Neither does Ryker. "This is your stop."

He doesn't leave.

I hate him.

Ryker hits the close button and pushes the number for my floor again.

"Turn around and face the corner," I grumble. To my surprise, he does as I say. The elevator starts moving. He doesn't budge. Not even when we're back at my apartment, and I step out to grab my keys and purse. He doesn't even move once I step back inside and hit the lobby button again.

He keeps his nose in the corner, back to me even when we're dumped back out at the lobby.

"You can turn around now," I say. Holy shit. I have no idea what this is, but… I like it.

Ryker turns around and smooths his suit jacket down. Then he lets me step out first and makes sure the door remains open for me as I do and grabs my arm to stop me from going out the main door.

I look down at his hand with the monarch tattoo. "Let me go, Ryker."

"I don't want to," he says quietly. "Not now. Not tomorrow either."

Oh look, my stupid heart has found fresh hope. Can't wait to see how long it takes for this one to pop too. "I don't understand you. And I'm not willing to play your games anymore."

His grip remains on my arm, even if it's loose. It's both grounding and unsettling.

"I know I started it," I confess. "I put you in a bad position with that building and used your interest in it as leverage to get me what I wanted. That's my fault."

"Making your stay with me miserable is mine."

"It wasn't miserable all the time." Holy shit, why can't my mouth stay shut?

"No?"

"No." Look, if there's any chance of fixing what we both busted, maybe I should try. He once said I was his obsession, but after the three days I've been away from him, I'm strong enough to admit I think he's mine too.

We have chemistry. I just don't know if it's explosive and damaging, or precarious and precious. But there's something between us I've never felt with anyone else. I want to explore it. I want to learn. Ryker could very well be the biggest mistake of my life, or the greatest chance I'll ever take.

"I liked us together when you weren't being a shithead."

"Yeah." He lets go of me and rubs the back of his neck. "I'm a massive prick sometimes."

"It's good that you're self-aware." I hate the torment in his gaze. "But it's not sometimes. It's most times. And I know it's a mask, Ryker. I wear one too. Take it off for me, like I have for you."

"If I do that…" His breath rattles out of him. "Will you please give me a chance to make things up to you?"

"Depends." I cross my arms. If I give him another chance, it'll be on my terms. "Are we going to trust each other with more than a flogger and dildo?"

"Yeah," Ryker nods.

"Then tell me something about yourself. Something really fucking personal."

"Right now?"

"Bye, Ryker." I storm off and he grabs my waist to stop me again.

"Okay, okay, okay." He spins me around to face him. "I've only had two girlfriends in my entire life. One when I was fifteen. And one when I was eighteen."

"How old are you now?"

"Thirty-two."

"How many lovers? Not clients, *lovers*." I don't give a shit about his stupid high school girlfriends or the people who've paid him for sex. I want to know how many women he's brought to his bed. Not as an escort, but as a man who wanted pleasure and comfort.

The silence is suffocating.

"Six." His face turns red. "I've had six."

I'm not making Ryker say this to humiliate him. I just wanted something open and honest to come out of his mouth for once.

"That includes you," he adds.

"Me?"

"I never counted how many clients I had back when I…" He drifts for a moment, then shakes his head. "Back then. It would have killed me to know the exact number. And when I opened my club, I stayed away from everyone. I only take a woman to my bed when my nights turn too dark, and I can't see the light anymore."

Oh my god. How awful.

"And you… you just came into my world and shook it all up, Tara. Like a fucking snow globe. Only all the little snowflakes are pieces of me. They're swirling around and I can't catch them all and shove them back under my feet."

My mouth runs dry.

He runs the back of his hand along my cheek. "You don't treat me like everyone else has. You don't look at me like everyone else does."

"How..." I clear my throat. "How do you think I look at you?"

He steps into my space and is so close to me, I can barely breathe. "Like I'm the devil your demons have hunted for their whole life."

A tear slips free, and he swipes it away from my cheek. Unable to deny his words, I whisper, "This could go really, really bad, Ryker."

"Or it could go really, really great." His expression softens as he stares at me. "Give me another chance. *Please*, Tara."

"Okay," I say after a few heartbeats.

The relief that washes over him saturates me, too. I have no clue how this is going to work, but I'm willing to give it a try.

"Come on." I grab his hand and ignore the sinking feeling in my belly. "We're going to brunch."

"Are you serious?" He sounds concerned.

I lead us over to where my car's parked. "You just opened up and gave me a very personal truth. Now I'm going to do the same."

Here's hoping this doesn't blow up in my face before mimosas are poured.

Chapter 31

Ryker

No one's ever taken me to meet their family before. I can't cut off the overflow of wild, insecure thoughts blowing around like a blizzard in my mind. What if they hate me? What if they recognize me from somewhere like the porn sites I used to be on? What if they ask questions I don't want to answer? I think if it was for anyone else, I'd turn this car around and say fuck it.

But Tara's worth putting myself in the line of fire for.

I wasn't kidding about how she looks at me. I know she mentioned I say her name like she's an angel coming to take me out of hell, and maybe I *do* say her name like that. But it's not my intention. Her name isn't a prayer answered. It's a fucking summoning.

I'm the devil and her demons adore me.

I think I'm in love.

Shit. Wait. No, that's too far. But I'm close. I could slip on a banana peel and fall down the rabbit hole with Tara, and if I do, I'll be glad. This woman has done the impossible. She sees me for what I am and accepts it. I don't pretend with her. She knows who I am, what I am, what I've been. She hasn't made me feel shame for any of it.

Talk about a one-eighty.

Every person I brought into my bed was a temporary thing. I never told them what I did for a living before I owned the Monarch. Hell, they didn't even know I own a sex club. My career was none of their goddamn business. They were with me for a dickdown, and I used them to relieve some tension. That's it. I've always been clean, health-wise, because I faithfully use protection, regardless of them begging for me to raw dog it, but there's always been this darkness in my mind reminding me how filthy I am.

That reminder comes often, and now that I'm about to meet Tara's family, it's screaming at me. I need to pull my shit together.

Tara truly has me in pieces. Will I come out of this a better man or a bigger monster?

"Tell me about your family," I say, to keep my mind busy.

"My stepfather is a no-nonsense man. He's really stern and work focused. He spoils my mom like a queen, though. Same for me."

That's wonderful. I'm glad she's treated right by her family.

"My mom's changed."

"How so?"

"She used to be carefree and goofy before she got married. Now she's prissy and too good for everyone."

Interesting. "Do you guys get along?"

Tara's quiet for a moment before saying, "Sometimes. We've drifted apart over the years, but I guess that's what happens when you grow up. Are you close to your family?"

My palms get sweaty. "My dad's been out of my life since I was a ten. My mom died when I was nineteen."

She looks over at me with puppy dog eyes. "I'm so sorry, Ryker."

"Don't be. She was really sick. It's good that she's not in pain anymore." I want to throw up. I don't discuss my mother with anyone. Not even Dmitri anymore.

It's kind of hard to talk about the perfect parent who was murdered by someone you thought was your friend.

We drive in silence the rest of the way to her family's home. When we pull onto a road lined with oak trees, my muscles tense. Holy shit, Tara's family is filthy rich. I mean, I knew she had money, considering she's a member of my club, but her family must be gazillionaires to own this piece of land.

Jesus fucking Christ, the home could fit five of my clubs in it.

Tara's voice trembles when she says, "You ready for crab cakes, Bloody Mary's, and animosity?"

I don't get a chance to respond. She opens the door and heads up the fancy marble steps where a man holds the door open for us.

"Good morning, Charles." Tara taps the gentleman's cheek, and he chuckles.

"It's a stormy day," he says in response. Something tells me he's not talking about the weather since there isn't a cloud in the sky.

Her eyes widen but she doesn't say anything, even after Charles quickly looks at me and clears his throat.

Suddenly, a woman's honey-dipped voice rises from inside. "Tara? Is that you?"

"Hi, Mom." Tara saunters over, all bubbly and

airy, to hug a woman who could easily pass as her older sister.

"I'm so happy you're here! Let me look at you." Her mother cups her face. "God, Tara, couldn't you have at least put on a little concealer? When was the last time you slept?"

My girl turns to me and holds out her hand like I'm a lifeline. "I want to introduce you to Ryker Hudson."

Her mom freezes. "I didn't realize we were having more company today." She shoots a pointed look at Tara again. "Honey. You should have told me."

"I didn't think it mattered." I can tell she's lying.

Tara's mother schools her expression and turns her charm all the way to one thousand. "The more the merrier, I always say. Mr. Hudson, it's wonderful to meet you." She glances at Tara again, her smile getting faker. "Your brother also invited an extra guest. You two need to let us know when you're bringing guests, so I can make sure the cook has enough food prepared for everyone."

"I'm sure it's fine. It's brunch, Mom. What's on the menu, crab cakes and quiche?"

"Of course, they're your favorite." Her mom turns back to me and holds her hand out. "I'm Rebecca."

"Lovely to meet you." I take her hand and kiss her middle knuckle. "You have an incredible daughter."

Rebecca looks back at Tara. "Now I see why you aren't getting any sleep. Good for you, sugar."

"Oh my god, Mom." Tara rubs her temples.

"Bec, where are my—oh Tara. I didn't hear you

come in." A man with broad shoulders and thinning salt and pepper hair approaches. "You look beautiful, sweetheart."

"Thanks." Tara gives him a hug. "I want you to meet Ryker Hudson. My boyfriend."

Her *what*?

"William Brisbane," he says, holding out his hand.

William *WHO*?

It's like I've been hit in the belly with a battering ram while someone pulls the rug out from under me at the same time. *Brisbane*. As in Brisbane Realty. I knew Tara worked for them, but I had no fucking clue she was *related* to them. I swallow the betrayal I feel and shake his hand. "Nice to meet you, Sir."

Then I shoot Tara dagger-eyes. How could she not have told me this before now?

Maybe it's because she has no idea how much I hate this company. Or maybe it's because she does know it and didn't want to put another hot coal on our burning relationship.

Fuck me running.

"Well, come on. These mimosas aren't going to pour themselves!" Tara hooks my arm with hers and leads us into a dining room the size of a fucking basketball court. "Sorry for not saying something sooner," she whispers.

I can't respond because I'm too busy grinding my molars.

There's no way she brought me into this circus as a punishment. She's not vindictive like that. At least, I don't think she is. Tara said she wanted to give me a personal truth and brunch was it. She wants me to see her life. And going off of the warning from the doorman, and the way Tara's attitude is overly bubbly and sweet, I don't like what I'm seeing.

Pulling a chair out for her first, I make sure she's settled in before taking the seat next to her.

"Garret will be late. As usual," Rebecca fusses, placing a napkin on her lap.

William glowers. "He's been in my office with an associate, Bec. It's not like he slept in."

"I know," she pouts. "But I want a nice family meal for a change with no talk about Brisbane business."

"Brisbane business got you this house and that ten-thousand-dollar necklace you're wearing," William growls.

The tension in the room thickens, and I instinctively put my hand on Tara's thigh. She looks over at me and smiles, but it doesn't reach her eyes.

Yeah. She wants me to see something alright, and it's not the fancy curtains, expensive furniture, or line up of art on these walls.

Two men enter the dining room, laughing, each holding a glass of amber liquid. One halts the instant he sees me.

Son of a bitch.

"You're just in time." William motions at the two empty seats next to him. "Travis, I hope you like crab cakes."

"Love them."

"Garret, get our man's plate loaded."

My hands curl into fists. Garret stares me down from across the table. It's cute. If he thinks he can intimidate me, he's about to learn a valuable life lesson. Again.

"This is Ryker Hudson. Tara's friend."

"Hi, *friend*." Garret smiles at me like a jackal as he drops into his seat.

Tara's leg bounces with nervous energy. I rub her thigh to give her a sign that I'm not mad, nor am I going anywhere, and that she's safe.

"Have you two met before?" Rebecca asks cheerfully.

"Yeah. We ran into each other at Tara's the other day when I stopped by." Garret grabs the asparagus with a set of silver tongs and drops some onto his plate. "You look nice today, Tara. Was it hard to put on clothes for once? I know you like to stay easily accessible for your dick-of-the-month."

Rebecca's fork clatters on her plate. "Garret! Don't talk to your sister like that!"

He shrugs and goes for a slice of quiche next.

Tara smiles and tips her head. "I'm sure you know all about the dick-of-the-month club, Garret." She winks at Travis. "I assume this one's Mr. June?"

It's nice to see Tara's not intimidated by him. Still, anyone talking to my girl with this much disrespect needs his fucking teeth knocked out. I'm just waiting for the perfect time to do it.

Rebecca huffs. "Stop it, both of you."

William rests his elbows on the table, steepling his fingers. "Where are we with that Greene Street property, Tara?"

So, he's going to let his son talk to Tara like that too? This is bullshit.

"Ugh, William," Rebecca pouts. "Can we *please* eat first before you get into this? We have guests! Let's not bore them through the entire meal by discussing old buildings and demolition projects."

"It's okay, Mrs. Brisbane," Travis says with a

warm smile. "I'm here for business, too."

"But can we just discuss something, *anything* else, for a moment?"

"Tara said you were just in Paris." I keep my hand on Tara's thigh, feeling more possessive and protective of her than ever. "How was the weather there?"

Rebecca looks shocked I knew about that, and relieved for the subject change. "It was wonderful."

Lies. I know she hated it, but I also realize she could be putting up a front for her husband since Tara seems to do the same. I'll keep playing along for now. "Isn't fashion week soon? I bet the spring line's nice."

She eases into the conversation, gratefully. "I'm not crazy about this season's styles at all. Too many bold prints, not enough florals."

William takes a sip of his bloody Mary. "I love my girls in flowers."

"I've never been to Paris," I say, casually spinning the stem of my champagne flute. "My work keeps me too busy for much else."

William leans forward and faces me. "And what is it you do, Mr. Hudson?"

"I'm in personal luxuries."

Garret mumbles something under his breath I don't hear. Travis snarfs his drink and quickly grabs his napkin to blot his tie. Then he chokes on whatever bourbon he hadn't spit out, and Rebecca jumps up to whack him on the back. "Are you okay?"

I take the distraction as an opportunity to slip my hand under Tara's dress and enjoy how Garret turns a mottled red because he knows where my hand is. My girl stays extra still for me, even as I plunge a finger into her cunt.

"Pass me a crab cake," William orders just as his phone goes off. He answers it while Rebecca rushes to cater to his needs.

It's fucking ridiculous.

But this brunch is about to become my new favorite meal.

Tara's breath hitches when I pull my finger out of her pussy and bring the glossy digit up to run around the rim of my champagne flute. I haven't taken my eyes off Garret yet. He's fuming, and it makes me want to fuck with him even more. After dipping my finger into my champagne, I bring it to my lips and suck it. It's my middle finger too.

He gets my message loud and clear.

Keeping Garret's gaze, I tip my flute back and take a sip. "Fucking delicious."

Sometimes knocking a man's teeth out isn't nearly as fun as watching him implode. His furious gaze leaves me and lands on Tara.

Go ahead. Say one more thing to her, motherfucker. I grab my fork, ready to stab his eyes out just for looking at my girl.

William yells at the person on his cell, shooting up out of his chair and marching out of the dining room. Rebecca sits back and crosses her arms like a petulant child. Travis brings up how lovely the gardens are and asks her for a tour. They both hop up and leave like they can't get out of here fast enough.

Putting my fork to use, I stab something on my plate and put it in my mouth, not tasting whatever it is. My attention remains solely on Garret.

I can't believe Tara didn't tell me who he really was to her when he attacked her the other day. Of all my guesses, not once did *stepbrother* register in my head as a possibility. And I'm willing to bet he's treated her like shit since the minute their parents got together. His animosity and ugliness couldn't have happened overnight. They have a well-seasoned hatred, by the looks of it.

Why?

"Tara!" William yells. "Get in here!"

"Shit," she whispers. Springing into action, Tara stands up, smooths out her dress, and scurries out of the dining room.

"Uh oh." Garret grins like a Cheshire cat once it's just the two of us. "Looks like *Daddy's* girl is in big trouble."

William's voice booms from the other room. "Garret! Get in here."

"See you around, lover boy." He tosses his napkin onto my plate of food. "Show yourself out, mmkay? I'll send Tara back to you when we're done."

I'm on him so fast, he doesn't have time to back away. Climbing over the fucking table, knocking the drinks and kicking a platter of scones over as I go, I hop down and back him up against a wall.

He doesn't have time to move or yell. I hold him pinned against the wall by his motherfucking throat and stare at him until he trembles under me. Then I inch closer, taking up all his fucking space, all his air, all his fake ass bravado. Our mouths are so close I can practically taste the bourbon fumes on him.

I hold his gaze for a long moment, and as I grab his tie, his pupils shrink. Ah, so he remembers what I did with his last one. Good. For a minute there, I thought he was delusional enough to believe I'd be civilized just because I'm in his territory.

Instead of wrapping the tie like a noose around

his neck again and finishing the job I started the other day, I undo it. Keeping my smile tight, I re-tie the fucking thing, making it extra snug around his stringy little neck. "Better get going, Garret. Don't want to keep *Daddy* waiting."

He doesn't move until I take another step back and let him go. Then he rushes out of the dining room and I'm pretty certain there's a wet spot on his pants.

I finally get why Tara didn't want to tell me about her family.

They're absolute scum.

It's infuriating to know she grew up with every luxury money could afford and was deprived of the one thing everyone should have in spades. Her words come back to haunt me now.

"You protect. You care for people. You work hard to keep everyone in here safe, happy, and healthy."

Tara saw me for exactly who I was because it's probably something she's hunted for.

Well, she found me.

And I'm not letting anyone hurt my girl or make her feel less than incredible ever again.

Buttoning my suit jacket, I head for the office.

Chapter 32

Tara

"I thought you said you handled the Greene Street property, girl?"

"I did. I met with the realtor last week and did a walk through. It's not worth the investment, Daddy." God, I hate calling him that.

William slams his fist on his desk, making me flinch. I've never seen him this angry before. Yes, he has a temper, but he's never aimed it at me before.

"I told you to get that property, Tara. God *damnit*!" He drops into his seat and pinches the bridge of his nose. "I'm sorry. I shouldn't have yelled."

"It's okay." No, it's not. "You're under a lot of pressure." I sound like my mother. "I went to close the deal, but the owner decided to put it up for auction at the end of the month and refused all offers."

William stills. "How many offers did they have already?"

"I don't know exactly."

"Fucking Clyde-Smith vultures. They've managed to get every single property I want, and I don't understand how. If we hadn't already signed the contracts for the two hotels, they'd have them too. They're working faster than us." William runs his finger along his bottom lip while he thinks. "I was told a third party is interested in it, too. Do you know anything about that?"

"I'm sure there are several investors who want it." I'll never tell him it's Ryker. I'll protect that man at all costs from my stepfather's vindictive strikes. "It's the last cheap piece of real estate on that side of the city."

"And yet you couldn't close the fucking deal."

His angry disappointment makes me cringe. "It's garbage. You'd have to level the place and turn it into parking spaces."

"Don't fucking tell me what I should do!" He slams his fist on the desk again.

I take a step back. Holy hell, I've never seen him so mad before.

"Travis can investigate who the other interested parties are," Garret says behind me. I didn't even hear him come in. "I'll take care of it."

"No." William stands. Leaning on his knuckles, he bends forward and glares at me from across the desk. "*Tara* will take care of it." His dark eyes rake down my body and lands on a specific body part. "By any means necessary. Is that clear?"

The blood drains from my head. He... he can't possibly be referring to what I think he is, right? "Daddy, I—"

"You want to keep that trust fund, sweetheart? *Earn* it. Get me that fucking property or kiss your money and your job goodbye."

I can't believe he's doing this to me. "But it goes up for auction at the end of the month."

"Then you have two weeks to seal the deal before that happens." My stepfather straightens up and walks over to me. "I thought you were a smart woman, Tara. You've never disappointed me before now." He runs his finger along the strap of my dress. My stomach twists. I'm going to throw up. "If your brains can't seal the deal, use what's between your legs. It worked wonders for your mother."

I slap his hand off me and step back. I'm so done with this. I've spent too much time and energy trying to prove myself to William, to prove to his whole side of the family that I'm a valuable asset. That I'm smart and skilled. But I'll never be good enough. I'm only a woman who's worth to the company is valued when I spread my legs to seal a deal a man can't get on his own.

It makes me sick.

Seething, I can barely keep my tone level and calm. "I'm done." My chin trembles and I hate it. "I fucking quit."

William blanches.

"Nothing I do is good enough." Fisting my hair, I want to pull it out. "The degrees, the deals, the work and time I've put into making you happy and proud. I've busted my *ass* to help your company grow. And you've never seen me as an asset at all."

"Ass, asset." Garret shrugs. "Tomato, tomahto."

William doesn't say a word.

I've never felt this used before. So slapped in the face. All the work I've done to be a member of the Brisbane family, all the shit I've put up with from Garret over the years, all the digs I let slide from the company employees… I've been trained to keep William happy for my mother's sake.

Fuck. This. I know my worth and if they don't, that's their mistake. "I'll have my assistant transfer all accounts to Garret."

William's brow furrows. "Tara, you're not

serious."

"Oh, I am. So, fuck you," I flip him the bird. "And double fuck you, you arrogant piece of shit." I flip both middle fingers up to Garret and then spin on my heels and storm out the door.

Only to run smack into Ryker in the foyer.

"Let's go," I say, fisting the lapels of his suit jacket and spinning him towards the front door.

"Tara, what the—"

"We're leaving. *Now*." If I stay any longer, I'll commit murder. "I need to get out of here."

He must see the desperation in my eyes because his jaw clenches. Then he glances at the door to my stepfather's office and his eyes darken. Without asking me why, he wraps his arm around my waist. "I've got you," he says, escorting me towards the front entrance. "Let's go, baby."

We make it outside and I all but stumble down the steps. I swear to God, I've never been this mad before in my life. Of all the things I've put up with, William's just crushed me with one fucking sentence, and I refuse to roll over and take it anymore.

Nostrils flaring, I look over at the garden—tempted to tell my mother what's just happened. But what's the point? I know exactly what she'll say. *Tara, you need to apologize. He's under a lot of stress and says things he doesn't mean. Don't make a mountain out of a molehill. It's no big deal.*

Well, it's a big fucking deal to me, damnit.

I no sooner reach our car, when something catches my attention. The black Mercedes parked behind us in the circular driveway is rocking.

My blood chills.

"Tara, get in the car," Ryker commands, but I

flick my finger up at him, silently telling him to hold on. Then I creep closer to the vehicle.

Mom's bouncing on Travis's lap in the backseat, making loud porn star noises.

My last fuck burs to cinders.

Stalking back to Ryker, I drop my ass into the passenger seat and slam the door shut. "Get me out of here."

Chapter 33

Ryker

Tara hasn't said a word since we left the house. I think she's still processing whatever happened in that office. If I'd been just a minute quicker, maybe I could have stopped whatever went down in there from happening.

But when I headed for the office, I couldn't figure out which direction to go. I went into the first door I saw, only to land in a huge, pompous library. I was about to try door number two when Tara barreled out of it, looking like she wanted to set the house on fire, with her inside it. My decision to handle her family turned into a rescue mission to get my girl out of that house as fast as possible.

"I'm sorry." Tara sits in the passenger seat with her hands in her lap. "I didn't want to tell you he was my stepbrother the other day when you asked."

"I don't blame you. If he was my stepbrother, I wouldn't want to admit it either." Yielding onto the highway, I check my side mirror before crossing two lanes. "What happened in there, Tara?"

"I don't know," she says. "William's acting more assholey than usual."

"So, yelling and throwing things are standard household activities?"

"Yes. He didn't use to be that way, back when

my mom and him first got married. But over the years, his temper's got way worse. Garret just feeds his fire."

She runs her hand up her arm, soothing herself.

"You're afraid of him."

"I'm afraid of what he can do. My mom's in that house with him."

I grip the steering wheel and choke it. "Will he hurt her?"

"No," she whispers. "I don't think so."

Think is not the same as *know*. "What did he say to you that has you ready to burn his house down?"

She wipes her nose with the back of her hand. "He told me to get the Greene Street building by any means necessary. As in use my body if I have to."

"Jesus fucking Christ." The highway turns red with my anger. My chest constricts every time I draw in a breath. Rage grips my throat, making it hard to swallow. "What kind of asshole says that shit?"

"He's acting stupid," she murmurs. "His need to have this stupid building makes zero sense for profitability. I've run all the numbers. Even if we have every piece of property around it, it's not worth more than a parking garage at best. I think he just wants it so Clyde-Smith can't have it."

"Competition doesn't make someone say shit like that to their daughter."

"Stepdaughter." Tara leans against the window. "I'm done. I fucking told him I quit. He can suck dick to get the deals he's so desperate for because I'll never do it. The Brisbane's can all kiss my ass. Including my mother."

I grip the steering wheel harder and stay quiet. I'm glad Tara knows her worth. I'm proud of her for standing up to those pricks and walking away. My respect for this woman grows by the day.

"I can't believe he wanted me to sell my body for a fucking building." Her eyes round and she sits forward. "I'm sorry. I didn't mean—"

"I get it." Tapping her leg, I smile to let her know I'm not offended. "I can't believe he'd ask you to do that either." Swallowing my pride, I shove down the fact that we both know I've sold my body for much less. "It's one thing to make the decision yourself. Quite another to have someone force it on you."

"Is that how it was for you?"

"Whoring?"

"Escorting," she corrects.

"I started that for other reasons. Continued it for different ones." Dread consumes my thoughts, and I glance over at her. "Has William ever asked you to do something like that before today?"

"No, but sometimes he would request me in certain clothes for meetings. I didn't like it, but nothing I wear in the office is very risqué. It's hard to be taken serious in board meetings as it is because I'm an outsider there, even if he's been my stepfather for more than half my life, so I keep my attire respectable and high end.

"If you had to seal a deal with the use of your body, would you?" It's not like I could stop her if she said yes. Tara's not mine. Not really. No matter how wonderful it might be to keep her.

"No. I don't think I could stomach it." She covers her face with her hands. "Oh my god, I'm so fucking sorry I just said that too."

"Don't be." I laugh a little to cover up my hurt. "I couldn't stomach it either."

"Then why did you do it?"

I take the first exit and don't speak for a moment. It's better to word this carefully. "I was sixteen when I started. By the time I was nineteen, it was all I knew. I'd dropped out of school. My mom was my only priority. When she died..." I sit at the red light and tip my head back. "Being an escort was all I knew. So, I continued and built my client base. Then I bought a rundown hotel and me, D, Knox, and Vault renovated it. It didn't last long because it wasn't good enough. I sold it, worked harder, and ended up with the Monarch where it is now."

The light turns green. I make a left.

"Know your worth in whatever career you choose, Tara. I charged a high price for the pleasure of my company. I made sure I was worth every fucking cent they paid, too. When I opened the Monarch, I became untouchable. The one thing no one, no matter how much money they offered, could get. That alone brought in big bucks. I went from expensive to priceless."

"Everyone wants what they can't have."

"Exactly." I pull into a cemetery. "And half the time, once they get it, they don't want it anymore."

Tara's laugh is bitter. "That's terrifyingly relatable."

"Isn't it, Butterfly?" I park the car. "Come on. I have someone I want you to meet."

With Tara by my side, I visit my mother's grave for the first time since putting her in the ground...

Pulling myself up the steps, I climb and eventually crawl up to my apartment. After getting hit by that car, my body's one big fucking bruise and the stitches on my chest keep pulling. At least it wasn't worse. I could have broken a bone. Stitches are way cheaper than x-rays and casts. Especially when Dmitri is the one doing the sewing.

Christ, what a day.

My cell was destroyed in the accident, and I'm praying my sim card still works. If I've lost all my contacts, I'll be royally screwed since ninety-nine percent of the people on my list are clients.

"Fuuuck," *I groan, holding my ribs. It hurts to breathe. If Dmitri wasn't so used to getting his ass kicked in the cage, I'm not sure what I would have done. D thinks I've cracked a couple ribs.*

Better than my skull, I guess.

Shoving my key in the lock, I twist and push things open. "I'm home."

Natalie walks out of my mom's bedroom. Her eyes are puffy and bloodshot. The tip of her pointy nose is red.

My stomach plummets. "Mom!" *I hobble into her bedroom and fall to my knees.* "No."

Natalie's voice carries behind me. "I'm so sorry, Ry."

"No, no, no." *The room starts spinning.* "Mom, no!" *I crawl across the floor like a rat to reach the side of her bed.* "Call 9-1-1."

"Ryker, she's gone."

"CALL 9-1-1!" *She's not gone. She's sleeping. My mother wouldn't dare die on me. Not after all this time. She's fought so hard. I've done everything I possibly could to keep her okay.* "Call an ambulance!"

My cell. Where's my fucking cell. DAMNIT! It's fucked!

"Ryker, she's gone." *Natalie pulls me away before I can start chest compressions.* "She's gone, baby."

Baby. I'm not her baby. "This can't be happening right now. She can't die on me."

I'm not ready to let go.

"She already has."

No. I refuse to believe it. "When?"

"About two hours ago."

"Two..." *I fall to my knees. Two hours ago, I was chasing my girlfriend across the street, begging for her to listen to my sorry ass excuses about why I'm a sex worker.* "Two hours ago. Why didn't you fucking call me, Nat?"

"I did," *she says as tears fall from her face, too.* "You didn't answer."

Because my cell was crushed.

Oh my god. This can't be happening. Gripping the sides of my head, I scream until white dots burst in my vision.

"I'm sorry," *she cries.* "I'm so, so, so sorry, Ryker."

"Sorry for what? For making me a whore? For making my mother an addict to pain killers? For making me take clients so you can get a third of my payout?"

Natalie slaps me so hard, blood wells in my mouth.

"She's dead," *I spit out like it's her fault my life's a wreck.*

"It was a mercy," *she says in a low, shaky tone.*

Mercy? MERCY?

All the chaos in me stills as I latch onto that one word. Dread pulls me to my feet. "Natalie." *My fists clench.* "What the fuck do you mean it was a mercy?"

She looks over at my mother laying still in the bed. Then her eyes flutter as she meets my gaze. "I was just trying to help her, Ry."

My hands fly up to my mouth. I'm going to vomit.

"She was in so much pain. She was wasting away in here. This is a mercy for both of you." *Natalie cries, stepping back from me and working her way out of the room.* "I'm so sorry." *She runs out of my apartment while I let her confession sink in.*

One week later, I'm standing beside a dirt hole while my mother's casket is lowered into it. I didn't have a funeral service. The only ones at her burial are me, D, Knox, his pops, and Vault. Her tombstone is a beautiful dark grey with her favorite flowers etched into it. I did that so I never have to come back here and lay real ones on her grave.

Dmitri claps me on the back once the service is over. I have no clue how long I've stood here, but everyone except D is gone. It's sunny. Hot. I'm sweating in my suit. "What are you going to do now, Ry?"

"I don't know," *I say numbly.* "Natalie's gone."

She packed her shit and skipped town after admitting she killed my mom. Mercy my ass. It was murder and nothing else. I hate her. If I find her, I'm going to kill her with my bare fucking hands. I swore I'd never lay an angry hand on a woman, but Natalie will be my exception. She's a monster.

"You can come live with me."

I shake my head. I can't live with Dmitri. I want to run off a cliff and die.

"Will you live at the apartment still, then?"

Not a chance in hell. I'm not staying in that shithole another night. "No. I've got other arrangements."

"Want me to drive you home?"

"No." *I want him to stop asking me questions and hovering over my ass like he's on suicide watch.* "I'll call you later, okay?"

D nods and stuffs his hands in his pockets. But he doesn't leave my mother's graveside. I suspect he has things he wants to tell her. So do I, but I'll never say them now. She can't fucking hear me.

Pulling my cell out, I scroll down the list of contacts and rearrange my brain chemistry just enough to solidify my decision on what my next steps will be. I have no future here. I have no future anywhere. But I've built a network of hungry animals and since I'm what they like to eat...

I'll let them feast until they choke.

By the time I make it back to my apartment, I'm someone else. Someone colder. Someone with nothing left to lose. Using my key, I open Natalie's door and see her shit's still gone, and she's not there. Fucking cunt. Locking it back up, I climb another flight before I have to sit down. My chest hurts. My lungs don't seem to want to work.

Pulling out a switchblade I carry for protection, I flick it open and palm the handle. The urge to slit my wrists isn't strong anymore. Not like it was a week ago. Or a year ago. Or even three years ago. No, that was the old Ryker.

This new Ryker Hudson is in a nice suit, shiny shoes, and has nothing left to lose.

And everything to gain.

Palming my knife, I carve "You're worth more than this" into the windowsill that looks out at the park. It's the truth. I am worth more than what those fuckers have been paying. Just like my mother was worth more than what life gave her.

I'm worth everything.

Even if it's only me who pays the price.

I'll never find love. That much, I know. If Kenzie could throw me away so easily, it'll be the same for everyone else I meet. I don't blame them. I'm garbage.

And now I'm going to become a very expensive piece of meat.

Today is the first day of my new life and I'm getting this date inked onto my chest the first chance I get, so I'm always reminded of the moment Ryker the whore became Ryker the monster. Let everyone who wants a piece of me now choke to death on the first motherfucking bite they take...

"You built an empire."

Tara's voice brings me back to the present. "Yeah. I guess I did alright for myself."

"Alright? You've made *millions*, Ryker." Tara grabs my hand and squeezes it. "You should be proud."

"How much champagne did you have at brunch?" And how much did I actually say out loud while strolling down painful memory lane?

"You never found Natalie?"

"Nope. Natalie wasn't her real name. And the apartment wasn't her only residence. She told me both those things after I started working with her, so finding her was never a possibility once she ghosted."

"I'm glad you had friends with you."

We cut across the grass and I'm a little ashamed to admit I'm struggling to remember where my mother's grave is. That day she went in the ground is a blur for me. "Yeah, me too. They're amazing." And just as broken as me in some ways. "I think she's over here." I double back and go a different direction. "No. Wait."

"Stop." Tara grabs my shoulders and looks up at me. "It's okay if you can't find her."

Fuck. She knows. It makes me want to find my mother faster to prove I'm not a complete piece of shit. "I just need to figure my surroundings out."

"What's her name?"

"Ashley Hudson." I walk faster, feeling frantic as I snake through the graves. "She's got a dark tombstone with flowers carved all over it."

It's like we're on a fucking treasure hunt, only instead of finding jewels, I'll get a corpse.

I question my sanity and whether I came to the right cemetery when Tara hollers, "Over here!"

Sprinting to where she stands, I stare at the grave. It's like no time has passed. Someone's taken care of her stone and when I see the limp daisy looking flower laying in the grass, I know who it is.

"Dmitri used to always pick my mom weeds that had blooms on them." I can't believe he still does this. "I've been a horrible son."

"You've been a grieving son."

"I never came back."

"You're here now."

Why does she excuse my behavior? "I'm not sure why I'm back."

"Yes, you do." Tara bends down and runs her hand over the top of the tombstone. "Hi. I'm Tara. Your son has grown into a great man." She looks back at me and smiles. "And he's missed you very much, Ashley."

I want to throw myself off a fucking bridge.

"I'll leave you two alone for a minute." She keeps her head down and walks away, leaving me alone to face the consequences of my actions.

I have no clue why I brought Tara here. Maybe it was to introduce her to my reasons for everything. Maybe it was because I had no clue where else to go.

Maybe it's because I've missed my mother terribly and it was time.

Ever since Tara stepped into my world, it's been upside down. This is one more snowflake in my globe, whirling around me.

"I love you," I say, falling to my knees. Gripping the top of her stone, I fight too many emotions assaulting me at once. "I miss you so much." My throat tightens. "I'm so sorry I wasn't there for you when I should have been." I say a dozen more things that seem to tumble out of my mouth in a jumble of pathetic words. My eyes burn. My chest feels like someone's stabbed it with a railway spike.

Hundreds of memories flood me. Some bad. Some good. Some beautiful and innocent and wonderful because they were before she got sick and deteriorated on me. My heart clenches because I miss the sound of her laugh. God, I'd give up everything I have just to hear her laugh one more time.

Or to taste her spaghetti again.

I hated it when I was a kid because I knew every time she made it, we'd be eating the leftovers for a week. The number of attempts I've made to recreate her sauce since she's been gone is countless.

"I think I've found someone," I whisper to her stone.

Look, I know my mom's not here. And I'm not sure if I believe in Heaven or Hell or even God because what the fuck kind of creator would have my mom suffer her whole damn life—surviving one tragedy to battle another and another? But it feels good to talk to her. I haven't done that. Ever.

"I have no idea how long it'll last, but she makes me do all the things you said would happen."

My mom once told me I'll know I've found my person when they simultaneously make me feel the chaos of every emotion under the sun while bringing me complete peace. I said the dosage of her meds was too high, and that she needed to cut them in half. She threw a pillow at me and said, "You'll see. If they don't make you a little crazy and a little calm at the same time, they're not it."

"Tara's it." Searching across the cemetery for her, I spot my girl leaning against a tree, looking away from me. Her flowery sundress blows in the breeze, and warmth fills my hollow chest.

I'm done sabotaging myself and our potential.

Marching across the graves with my sight trained on her, I know what I want and by God, I'm fucking taking it.

She must hear me trampling through the grass because she turns around with a smile.

I grab her face and smash my mouth to hers. Lifting on her toes, Tara sinks her hands in my hair and runs them down my neck, holding me captive. Our bodies press together, and my impenetrable glass enclosure shatters, spilling a lifetime of heartache, anger, hunger, depravity, and grief all over the ground. Each of my snowflake terrors slide and scatter, melting in the warmth of her touch.

It's like being gutted and resurrected at the same time.

Pressing her back against the tree, I deepen this kiss for all I'm worth.

And I'm worth a fucking lot.

Our tongues twirl around one another. We breathe the same air. Her body presses completely against mine and it's like being fused to passion itself. I can't get enough of her. I want to feel every inch of her sweet skin. I want to fuck us both into oblivion.

She doesn't make me forget my pain, but Tara quiets the storm inside me. I simultaneously love and abhor it. The storm is all I've known. To see a ray of sunshine almost hurts because it's so fucking precious. I've been afraid to look at it, feel it, embrace it.

There's been a lot of push and pull between us. I'm done pushing. I'm done pulling. I want to take her. *Keep* her.

"Come on," I say, carrying her away from the

tree.

"Where are we going?"

"Home." I want to bring Tara to *my* safe place. "We're going home."

Chapter 34

Tara

We pull up to a brownstone that must be worth a mint. I'm so proud of Ryker for all of his accomplishments. Talk about making the most of a shit situation.

Still, my heart aches for him. My rags to riches story is a fairytale cartoon compared to his horror story. It makes me want to hunt down every person who's ever hurt him and beat them with a steel pipe.

It also makes me wary.

Ryker's different again. Each time he has some kind of breakdown, he changes and I'm fearful of what it means. Look, I'm not delusional enough to think my pussy is so powerful it can fix a damaged man. But I do think having someone who can not only take your savagery, but also your sweetness, isn't a bad thing.

Stepping into Ryker's home, I look around in shock. "Wow."

He shuts the door behind me. "Wow, good or wow, bad?"

My gaze sails around the living room that's decked out with comfy sofas, a beautiful fireplace with a TV mounted above the mantel, and shiny wood floors. Windows line the far wall, letting in so much light, I squint as we make our way to the kitchen.

"Are you thirsty? Hungry?"

Answers catch on my tongue as I pass a cluster of framed photos. "Is that *Dmitri*?"

Ryker looks at the black-and-white photo I'm referring to. "Yeah. We were about thirteen there."

Dmitri's laughing by a set of concrete steps. His pitch-black hair reaches past his shoulders, and he has a skateboard tucked under his arm. Ryker's sitting on a railing, his head ducked a little as he looks up at the camera with a playful smile.

"And that's Vault and Knox," he says, pointing at another picture. This one's in color. The two of them are sitting on a couch that's definitely seen better days. Vault's chunkier than he is now, but there's no mistaking his smile. It's joker-sized and something I've always found attractive. Knox is so skinny he looks like he has an eating disorder. They're both flipping the camera off.

"Who's this?" I point at another black-and-white photo of a big guy with warm eyes. Ryker's arm is around him and they're clanking two beers together.

"That's me and my friend Carson. We helped a friend of ours launch a new kink app and went out to celebrate afterwards. D took the picture."

"Which app?"

"K!nklink." Ryker sees my expression and laughs. "You're a member, aren't you?"

"Uhhhh yeah. That's, wow. This is a little awkward. And ironic."

He cocks his brow. "How so?"

"I signed up last year but chickened out every time someone sent me a winky thing. I heard it was the best app to find a Dom with, but I'm not good at shopping online. I'm more of an in person, touch and try out before I commit kind of girl."

Ryker's smile goes from casual to predatory. "Oh yeah?" He wraps his arms around my waist and brings me in.

"Mmm hmm."

"How many Doms have you had, Tara?" He playfully rocks me back and forth.

"None." His expression says he doesn't believe me. "Well, none who were real Doms. I tried to find some in college, but that was a complete disaster."

"And dangerous," he chides. "Lots of idiots think barking commands while cracking a whip makes them a Dom. There's a lot of psychology and care that goes into this lifestyle too."

"Good thing I found the Monarch and you, then."

He must have thought I was joking before about the Doms in my life, because his body language shifts. The cocky smirk drops from his face. "Wait. I'm really your first?" His expression morphs from suspicious to dread. "Jesus fucking Christ, I'm your *first*?"

"You say that like it's a bad thing."

"I *am* a bad thing," he snaps back.

"Not to me you're not." He's perfect, amazing, what I've been dreaming of. "You're just want I need."

His gaze roams over my face. Without saying a word, he runs his thumb along my bottom lip, dragging it down to show my teeth. "I'm not what you need."

"Don't speak for me, Ryker."

We just went from casual, to playful, to cautious, to this. God, why can't we ever be consistent?

He tips his head back and looks down his nose at me. "I'm your first."

It's like that fact won't penetrate his thick skull. Leaning into me, Ryker's mouth hovers over mine and he licks the seam of my mouth, sending heat to my pussy. Maybe we work best teetering between cheerful and angry. My body sure loves it.

I really should seek professional help.

"Am I a bastard to be both happy and sickened that I'm your first real Dom?"

"No."

"Wrong answer, Tara." He presses his forehead to mine. "Tell me it's terrible that I feel this way. Tell me it's despicable that I love how only me has had you submit to them so beautifully. Tell me I'm a twisted bastard for the way it makes me feel territorial and protective of you."

Words catch in my throat, along with my breath. I'm not saying shit.

"Say it," he growls. "Say I'm a bastard for the things I want to do to you, especially knowing you've never been dominated by someone like me before." His lips brush mine. The intensity between us is so thick, I can't think straight. "Say it, Tara. Say I'm a bastard. A monster. A depraved animal for the way my dick is rock-hard, knowing I'm the only one you trust enough with your desires."

A weak exhale blows out of me. "You don't even know what my desires are."

"Tell me."

I turn the tables. "What do you want to do to me, Mr. Hudson?"

He growls and just when I think he's going to kiss me, he moves and nips my earlobe instead.

"Careful, Butterfly. You're in my territory now."

That doesn't scare me. It makes me melt like butter. "Tell me what you want to do to me."

Why won't he say it?

Fine. I'll approach this another way.

"Do you enjoy knowing I've only taken orders from you, Mr. Hudson?" My back's against the wall. His arms bracket me, caging me in. "Does it please you, Sir, to know that I stayed on my knees like a good girl that first night for you? That I waited on the floor, just like you told me to, all night long?"

"Fuck." An exhale rattles out of him. "*Yes*, Butterfly."

I love how he reacts to me. There's no denying how much I turn him on and it's thrilling, addictive, and fun as hell. I'd be anything in the world for this man—a powerhouse, a puppy, a princess, or a whore. "I got myself off in front of the camera that night, hoping you were watching."

The possessiveness in his tone sounds dangerous and makes my pussy wet. "I didn't get to see it."

"Pity." My heart's racing a mile a minute. This is so much fun. "I put on quite a show for you. Maybe Dmitri saw it instead. Or Vault." Because we both know someone had to keep their eyes on me that night.

Ryker grinds his teeth. "Fuck, Tara, you're going to make me murder my best friends."

I think he's only half joking. "I'm sure they only watched to make sure I stayed safe."

He growls. "Feel safe now, Butterfly?"

When Ryker presses his forehead to mine again, I'm instantly drawn back to the moment when he did this in the hall after beating the shit out of Dmitri and then ripped me away from Vault, who said he was only trying to protect me.

Pieces click together and I realize how thin the line can be between intense and unhinged.

How precariously is Ryker teetering right now?

What will it take to shove him over the edge?

"Yes," I say, with complete confidence. "I feel safe with you, Sir."

"Good." His voice is deeper. "I'll eat a bullet before I ever hurt a woman. Especially you." Ryker nuzzles my neck, making my body overheat. "But if you beg nicely, Butterfly, I'll bring you pleasure that borders criminal acts of violence."

Ummmm. "I... I don't think I know what that means."

"Did you like how I fucked you at your house, Tara?"

"Yes." The way he was a mindless animal, railing me within an inch of my life? If that's his version of violence, sign me the hell up. "I *loved* that."

Threading his hand through my hair, he tucks some of it behind my ear and whispers, "That was me holding back."

Cue the flood in my panties. "What will it take, Mr. Hudson?" I press my palms against his chest and push back a little so I can see his face. "What will it take to get you to *not* hold back on me?"

Ryker stills. I hold my breath. I don't want him to reject me. I need to feel freedom. Taste victory. For so long I've been the good girl. I bend over backwards to please everyone around me, just to make myself worth liking. Worth keeping. But after today, I just want to be myself, instead of what I'm expected to be.

I want to be fucked apart and kissed back together.

"There's no one here to stop me if I go too far, Tara."

"*I'm* here to stop you." We don't need a security team. "I'll call Red if it's too much."

He shakes his head a fraction of an inch. Then swallows hard. "Tara, this could get dangerous. I'm not in my right mind when I fuck the way I like."

"You'll stop when I say Red."

"You trust me to do that?"

"I trust you to keep me safe and give me what I want. I wouldn't have chosen you if I didn't, Ryker."

He steps back as if I've punched him in the gut. "Do you trust yourself?"

His mouth falls open, then closes. He swallows again. "Yes."

That didn't sound convincing. Cupping his face, I look him dead in the eye and gather all my courage. "As the Butterfly, I get what I want, right?"

"Depends." Ryker's pupils widen. "What is it you want?"

I want you. I want what I keep getting a taste of, and I don't want you to take it away and hide it from me again. "I want you to let go, Ryker."

"I can't." He steps back and hits the other wall. "I might hurt you."

"Then hurt me. Hurt me so good I'll never be able to fuck you out of my system. You like that you're my only Dom? Then mark me. Ruin me for every other man who touches me after you."

Rage conquers his terror, and he's suddenly back on me, pressing me against the wall. "Do *not* bring up other men touching you."

"Ruin me."

"You don't know what you're asking me to do."

"Ruin me."

"If you have any sense, Miss Reed, you will walk out of my fucking house and out of my life."

"I'm not going anywhere."

"Stupid, stupid girl."

Tears blur my sight, but I don't budge. How can he be like this? So desperate for me one minute, and done with me the next? I hate it. "You're the most polarizing fool I've ever met, Ryker Hudson."

"That was your last chance, Miss Reed." He manipulates my steps as he presses his body to mine, forcing me to walk backwards out of the kitchen. "You should have taken it."

"I'd rather take you." We're in the hallway now, and I have no clue where he's guiding me.

A smart woman would put distance between herself and this animal. But I'm not smart when it comes to my desires. I'm just a missile seeking its target and my target, from day one of joining the Monarch, has been Ryker.

Our relationship is temporary and volatile. Addictive and unpredictable. Scorching hot and freezing cold.

What's wrong with me that I love this so much?

I think I'm the real toxic one here.

"You asked what it would take for me to let go and fuck you how I want." He draws up, using his height over me as a dominating tool. My back hits a door, but I don't cower. "Do you still want to know?"

"Yes." Ever since he brutally fucked me in my apartment, I knew he was the right one for me. And if I only have a limited time with him, wasting it being stupid and petty would be a crime. In two weeks, I'll walk out for good. Tonight, I'm staying.

Eyes darkening, he licks his lips and takes several steps back. "Crawl to me."

Humiliation and lust war inside me as I sink down onto his hardwood floor. Slightly humiliated, I crawl to him like a dog. My stomach drops even as my pussy clenches when I look up at him and await his next command.

"Such a good girl," he says, making me wet. "Now beg for my dick."

Chapter 35

Ryker

I'm going to Hell.

I have no business being possessive over a Butterfly. She's a temporary catastrophe in my world, and when her time is up, I'm not sure what I'll do about it. There's no repairing the damage she's done.

Or that I'm about to do.

I meant what I said—she should have walked out of my door, out of my city, and out of my life. That she stayed confuses me. I think she's spoiling for a fight. I think what happened at brunch has royally fucked with her brain.

I might be wrong, but I believe Tara's never had a chance to be herself. The way she acted at brunch, her immediate responses and reactions to things. My girl was groomed somehow, I just don't know for what. It makes me murderous.

She's a people pleaser like me.

Today, she stuck up for herself and walked away from people who didn't deserve her. For that, I'm proud. But she's run into the arms of a monster, seeking comfort. And I'm terrified.

Because I plan to take advantage of it.

I really am a fucking bastard.

And now I have her crawling and begging.

She asked for this. I need to remind myself of that.

She wanted me unleashed. She wanted me to let go and fuck her how I want.

This is it. She can call Red any time.

"What's your color, Tara?"

"Green."

I hate her humility. I bet Tara's had to be a lot of things to please others, or to stay on their good side.

I don't have a good side.

She can be anything she wants with me, and I'll fucking adore it.

"Good girl." I cup her chin so it stops quivering. Shoving my thumb into her mouth, I wait for her to close her lips around it. "That's it, baby. Suck." She draws me in. Her mouth is hot and soft, and I can't wait to fuck it.

Her teeth scrape my knuckle when I pull out and I know damn well she wants to bite me.

It makes my dick hard.

Walking backwards, I crook my finger. "Crawl to me again." She whimpers but obeys me. Her hair falls into her face as she follows me through the house, up the stairs, and into my playroom. Shoving the door open, I let her crawl in first. "What color are you?"

She's too busy gawking at my playroom to respond, so I snap my fingers loudly. "What color are you, Tara?"

"Green."

I believe her. The shame in her eyes has lifted substantially.

Squatting down, I make sure she's fully focused on me. "There's nothing wrong with being turned on by any of this."

"I… know."

Her tone says otherwise. I arch my brow. "Own

what you like." I tip her chin. "I've crawled like a dog for you, too. And I'd do it again in a fucking heartbeat."

Her chest rises and falls with her heaving breaths.

Pressing my thumb on her bottom lip, I smear it, distorting her mouth a little. "First, punishment. Then reward." Walking over to my St. Andrew's cross, I cuff one of my wrists. Tara watches in silent confusion until I say, "Come over here, Butterfly." When she tries to stand, I quickly command, "On your hands and knees."

She crawls to me and waits at my feet.

Tara's so pretty when she's a puppy for my love. "Cuff my other hand."

She runs her hands up my legs, waist, and ribs until she reaches the cuff and buckles it around my waiting wrist. I didn't tell her she could touch me, but I'll let it slide. "What now, Sir?"

"You're going to be a good little slut and sit in front of me."

She sinks to the floor.

"Lift your dress."

Her brow furrows as she obeys. Spreading her legs wider, Tara rucks her flowery dress up to her hips.

"Take your underwear off."

She does.

"Now I want you to listen carefully." Her blue eyes lock onto mine. "You're going to crawl back to me, stuff those soaked panties into my mouth, and then sit back where you are and get yourself off. You're going to show me what I missed that first night, Butterfly, when I was a bastard who left you alone."

I should have never done that. Damage control be damned, I should have given Tara all of my energy and attention the instant she picked me. Fuck that. I should have given her my time and devotion the instant she caught my attention in the club months ago.

"Use anything you want to get off with. Make me pay for neglecting you."

She cocks her brow. "Anything I want?"

"Whatever I have is yours."

I just used humiliation to get her hot and bothered. Now I'm giving her all the power and confidence she needs to punish me and take her power back. The change in Tara is instant.

My girl shimmies out of her pretty red panties and crawls to me like a panther, not a wounded puppy. Keeping eye contact with me the entire time, she scrapes her nails along my thighs and chest, then viciously stuffs her underwear in my mouth. I think she might have split my damn lip.

Fucking hell, she's perfection.

Tara stands back and regards me like a painting. "I want your shirt unbuttoned," she says.

I nod, giving her consent.

"I want your pants off, too."

Swallowing around the silk in my mouth, I nod again.

I did say she could use whatever she wanted to get off with. If the sight of me naked does it for her, then I'm onboard with that.

I kick off my shoes, letting the cuffs take more of my weight in my arms as she tugs my pants off.

Tara's smile is ten kinds of wicked. Even with

her mascara a little smeared from her tears earlier, this version of her is fiery as hell. I love it. To see a woman own her position of power. To watch her use it to get what she wants, what she needs?

Sign me the fuck up.

Tara's dignity was shredded earlier today. She likely hates me for some of the things I've said and done, too. But she trusts me and that speaks volumes about our connection. For better or worse, we're drawn together like two magnets. I don't want her feeling bad about what she likes. Nor do I want her confused by what it means. She just needs to know that there are levels of trust and submission, and kinks should never be shameful demons in our bed.

Tara sinks to her knees and spreads her legs just a few feet in front of me. Dragging her tongue along her middle finger, she flips me off while wetting it. "I wonder if Dmitri liked hearing me orgasm."

Jealousy has me immediately pulling on my chains. The instinct to attack what threatens me is so natural, I barely notice the way the St. Andrew's cross creaks from the tension I put on it. Damn Tara for shoving Dmitri in my face like this.

God, she's perfect.

"I so badly wanted to make you happy that night, Sir." Tara leans back with her legs spread to give me the perfect view of her cunt as she rubs her clit. "I ached for you."

My dick is so hard it hurts.

Nostrils flaring, I lean forward, desperate to smell her.

"You want this, don't you?" She dips her finger into her sweet hole. "You want to fill this pussy up, Mr. Hudson?"

I groan and nod.

"Well, you have to earn it."

"I paid two million for it," I say with her panties in my mouth, so all my words are muffled. I could just spit them out, but that's not happening. This is part of my punishment. The deprivation of her touch. Her scent. Her taste. Tara's just out of my reach, and I want to scream with how badly I want her.

Denial is both a punishment and an aphrodisiac for a man like me.

"I'm worth more than two million." She fingers herself faster. "I'm worth *everything*." Her pace quickens and I pull on my restraints when Tara whimpers in a little voice. "Fuck, I want you inside me so bad, Ryker." Rubbing her clit again, she closes her eyes and tips her head back, shoving three fingers into her swollen pussy.

My vision tunnels and I snap.

Yanking as hard as I fucking can, the chains on the cuffs break and I pitch forward, falling on my hands and knees. With her red panties still in my mouth, I crawl to her like a deranged animal. My mouth waters. My dick throbs.

Tara stares at me while she gets herself off. "I wanted to be your good girl, so you'd want to keep me," she says breathlessly. "I wanted to be perfect for you."

I groan with her panties in my mouth.

My stomach bottoms out when she sucks in a sharp breath and fucks herself harder. "I want to come for you," she groans. "I want you to want me so bad you can't walk away from me. Look what you've been missing, Ryker Hudson."

She flicks her clit faster. Fingers herself harder.

"I want you to fuck me like you did in my bed. I want you to take every hole I have and use me like I'm your whore, Ryker. Fill me with your cum and hold it inside me until I beg you to let it drip out. I want to be used in so many ways I won't be able to tell up from down. Real from fantasy."

My heart pounds in my ears. I'm inches away from her, but don't dare touch her. I can't until she lets me.

Once she does, I intend to give her everything she's asking for. I'll break Tara in half. Steal the air from her lungs and replace it with mine. I'll brand her body and keep her for life.

If she survives me.

Tara cries out as she climaxes. It's the most beautiful scene I've ever witnessed. Her hair's a mess, her makeup is smudged, her flowery dress is twisted up around her hips, her thighs shake, and chest rises with every ragged breath she takes. By the time Tara finishes riding out her orgasm and closes her legs, I'm wound up tighter than a snare drum with anticipation to see what she'll do next.

"I'm so wet," she whimpers. "My fingers weren't enough."

Bet not.

"I need something bigger, Sir."

My dick will do nicely.

"I want you to fuck me."

Swallowing is harder than it should be.

"Keep my panties in your mouth while you do it."

Jesus Christ. Humiliation isn't a sensation I endure anymore. That emotion left me a long time ago. But the desire to have things I don't deserve is my biggest flaw. It's also one of my biggest turn-ons.

Rising to my feet, I storm over to a box of condoms and grab one.

"What's that for?" she asks from the floor.

Silently, I point at my raging hard on.

"No. I don't think you've earned that privilege yet."

A growl of frustration tears from my chest.

"Fuck me with that," she says, pointing at one of the floggers hanging on my wall. "And after I come around the handle, I want you to clean it off with your tongue, then I'll use it on you."

The condom falls out of my hand and flutters on the floor. For someone who said she didn't have much experience in kinks, Tara sure knows how to play with all of mine. Reaching for the flogger, I also grab a bottle of lube because this handle isn't necessarily the smoothest.

"Crawl," she orders.

My eyes narrow. Tara's testing my patience and tolerance.

Good thing I studied.

Sinking to my knees, I hold the handle side up and make my way over to her, stopping right between her spread legs. My girl's not bashful. Nor should she be. Tara's not only a perfect Butterfly, but a perfect woman. Soft and hard, confident yet cautious, strong but delicate.

To my disappointment, she snatches the lube and flogger from me, making it clear that I don't get to help yet. With a wry smile, she obscenely strokes the handle, nice and slow. "Don't you wish this was your dick about to sink inside me?"

I nod.

Tara lubes the handle and my cock throbs, greedy and jealous like the rest of me. Her hands shake, so I put mine on top as comfort, then I take the flogger from her. Leaning in for a kiss, I stop midway, realizing I can't.

This part of the punishment hurts most because it denies me the very thing I've deprived her of this entire time. What I've forbidden myself to have for so long. A simple kiss on the mouth.

It's my kryptonite.

Tara's nails scrape my chest as she circles all my tattoos playfully. "I want you to want me."

"I do," I mumble, desperate for her to understand just how much.

"Prove it." She lies on the floor and spreads her legs.

Gripping the flogger, I lean down to smell her precious cunt first. With a flick of my wrist, I bring the tassels down on her sensitive flesh, slapping her pussy with a light thud.

Tara gasps and closes her thighs, reflexively.

I shake my head and spread them open again. Then arch my eyebrow at her.

"Green." Tara immediately says. Licking her lips, she lifts onto her elbows to watch. "Do it again, Sir."

I run the tassels along her belly, down one thigh and up the other. Then I strike her pussy again with it. Tara cries out and her legs close halfway from reflex this time. If she can't keep her legs open, she'll never be able to enjoy what I plan to do with her.

Shooting up to my feet, I prowl across the room and grab a spreader bar. Holding it up, I wait for her consent to use it. Fuck, she's gorgeous. Just look at how her mouth's parted and eyes are heavy-lidded with need.

Lusty little thing.

Tara nods, a wry smile playing across her flushed face.

In less than a minute, I've attached her ankles to the bar so she can't close her legs again. She's spread as far as her flexibility will allow. It's obscene and breathtaking. She lays back with her eyes closed, completely trusting me.

"Green," she says when I snap my fingers to get her attention again. "Very green."

No shit. My girl's soaked and swollen.

Her clit's exposed and at my mercy now. Plunging the handle inside makes Tara groan this deep, guttural sound that's music to my motherfucking ears. I alternate between fucking her with the handle and pulling it out to strike her clit with the tassels. Taking my time, I bring her to the brink of pleasure and pain until she cries out, "Please. I can't stand it anymore."

That's not Red.

"I need to come, Sir."

She'll come when I let her. Tara might have me in the submissive role here, but I'm still running this scene. I continue fucking her with the handle, and just when I think she's about to come, I pull it out. She screams in frustration.

Poor Butterfly, her wings are all aflutter.

I sink the handle back into her pussy and fuck her until she's a writhing mess, then I pull it out and hit her clit with the tassels over and over and over and—

She roars with her release, squirting all over the

floor between us.

With her head tipped back, face contorted as she screams, beads of sweat rolling down between her tits, and thighs shaking like electricity is racing through her veins, Tara looks like she's in the thralls of a demonic possession.

Little does she know this devil has only just begun to have fun with her.

Chapter 36

Tara

Laying back on the carpet with my legs spread so wide it borderlines painful, I'm swimming through an ocean of emotions that have me light and heavy. Dizzy yet grounded. Floating and tethered.

I don't notice Ryker's unhooked my ankles from the spreader bar until he scoops me up and cradles me in his lap. A girl could get used to this.

"I'm still very green." I don't want him to think he's hurt me. I sure as shit don't want the scene to end, either. Burying my face in his neck, I don't want to let him go at all. I'll give anything to feel this alive, forever living on the edge of danger, dancing between pleasure and pain.

What a dangerous lifestyle that would be.

I've never been attached to someone like I'm getting with Ryker. How did he ensnare me so quickly?

Easy. It's the way he holds me. The way he looks at me. The way he gives me what I want in ways I didn't realize I needed. I came to the Monarch for sexual discovery. I'm going to leave with a broken heart.

That's okay. Being wrecked by Ryker will feel too good to regret.

When I go, how long will it take before he finds

someone new? Part of me thought I'd cracked him open—especially when he finally kissed me. But now I'm starting to wonder how many times he's done this with a woman. It's hard to believe Ryker would lie and put on this whole act of being a broken, elusive, dark-minded grieving man who's always alone, but this room wouldn't be here unless he has other play partners. He told me he's brought six women to his bed, including me.

We aren't in his bed though.

"How many women have you brought to this room, Ryker?"

He looks down at me and holds up one finger.

Bullshit. I raise an eyebrow. "One?"

He nods and swallows, my panties still stuffed in his mouth.

"So, I'm number two?"

His gorgeous eyes darken as he shakes his head.

My heart slams to a stop. "I'm the *one*?"

He slowly nods.

I can't climb off his lap fast enough. "Are you serious?"

He nods again, making no move to pull my underwear out of his mouth. And he won't, I realize, because he's still in the scene, being my sub.

"Damnit, Ryker." I rip the fabric from between his lips. "Talk to me."

He shrugs. "There's nothing to say. I don't bring women here, Tara. This is my safe space. I have the club for fun, but this is my haven. My sanctuary."

"You really think I'm going to believe you put yourself in shackles and flog your own back?"

"Dmitri does it." He wipes some of the spit off his chin. "I built this space for my own punishment and pleasure. D comes over and puts me in a subspace when I need him to, and sometimes he uses it when I'm not here."

My gaze sails around the room. It's kitted out with so much BDSM equipment, and I'm starting to realize that the Monarch is only an extension of Ryker's sexual tastes, not the hub.

"If I need a companion, I go to their house and make sure to slip out long before they wake up," he admits. "Only the people I trust have seen this space."

He can't trust me. Not enough to give me the ultimate glimpse behind the curtain like this. "Why did you bring me here?"

"Because I trust you, Tara." He swallows hard. "I've told you things I haven't shared with anyone outside my tight circle." He cups my face. "But it feels right." His hand drops to his lap. "A Dom/sub relationship is built on not only trust but mutual respect. You have no reason to trust me outside of a scene, Butterfly, but you do. I see it every time you look at me."

I wish he'd trust me enough to be his raw, real self around me then. Even now, I know he's guarded. He made this entire scene a distraction to prolong what I really want out of him.

His gaze lifts to mine. "I really fucked shit up for us in the beginning. I didn't show you the respect you deserve, and I'll be forever sorry for it." He swipes the tears saturating my cheeks. "I've always prided myself on knowing how to care for and bring pleasure to others. But you've shown me I still have a lot to learn."

No, he doesn't. He just needs to let his guard down. Except he's been through too much for that to be a simple thing to do. I get it.

"You should have picked Dmitri," he whispers. "He's a far better Dom than I will ever be." He huffs a cold laugh. "Ironic, considering I'm the one with the most experience."

"I didn't want him." And I never will. But the way he talks about Dmitri gives me another worry. "Are you two a couple?"

My question catches Ryker off guard. Not sure why since it's an easy assumption to make—especially after my first flogging lesson.

"No." Ryker rubs the back of his neck. "He and I once shared a woman, but we've never been together sexually, just the two of us. Our dynamic is strictly for tension release—not sexual gratification."

I don't understand the difference. "What did I just get?"

His eyes lower to my pussy. "What does it feel like, Butterfly?"

Good question. I'm boneless and lightheaded and completely spent. "Sexual gratification."

He leans over and kisses my forehead. "If Dmitri was here and in control, he'd have you in a subspace another way. You likely wouldn't have orgasmed, but would still feel satisfied in your mind. Your body, however, would be too relaxed to catch a sexual release."

I remember how Dmitri flogged Ryker, putting him into an immediate headspace that calmed his rage. Releases, I guess, come in all shades of red, white, black, and blue. "Would you ever share me with him?"

The possessive growl that rises out of Ryker's chest is nothing short of vicious. It takes a moment for him to say, "If you wanted me to." He freezes. "Fucking Hell, Tara. I don't want to share you with anyone. Ever."

Be still my falling heart. "Why not?"

"As an escort, I've always done whatever my partner asks of me. The few women I've fucked since owning the Monarch, I treated the same way as all my past clients. I gave them the fantasy they asked for. Let them have whatever they wanted from me. I didn't care. I'd share them with anyone because they didn't matter to me. But you?" He crawls closer and gives me a hand necklace. "I want to keep you all to myself. The thought of sharing you with anyone, even my best friend, makes me want to set the world on fire."

Talk about feeling special.

He shakes his head. "You have no idea how hard it was to watch you go from room to room in my club, always holding my breath to see if you'd take someone into a bedroom. The way my heart would race each time you talked to anyone. Including Sophie."

My eyes widen. "Sophie?" Why would he bring that woman up?

"She's the best Fem Domme I have," he explains. "That woman can likely bring pleasures to you that no one else, including me, could give you."

"I'll have to remember that," I tease.

He doesn't find it funny.

This conversation's become too heavy. It's hard to move and breathe in here. The intensity between us is crushing my heart. "Why did you bring me here, Ryker? What makes me so special? A week ago, you were doing all you could to get me out of your hair, and now you've brought me home. Why?"

He doesn't answer.

"Why?" I yell a little louder.

He swallows hard and still doesn't respond.

Damn this man. He keeps giving me breadcrumbs, leading me down a path that will ultimately bring me to a cliff. When we get to the edge, will he push me off or will I fucking jump?

Chapter 37

Ryker

"Why did you bring me here, Ryker?"
I still haven't answered her.

I've always given my partners exactly what they want. Groomed and trained early, I will always be a motherfucking sex worker in some capacity. Tara's gaze drifts to the date tattooed on my chest and the ragged, thick scar just under it only emphasizes the severity of that night for me. All because I became a new man the night my life tumbled into total darkness does not mean I turned a new leaf.

I'm more depraved than ever.

I've spared the world of my volatile nature as best I can, and Tara keeps yanking the chains of my leash to pry the links apart and break me free.

Damn this woman for trying. And damn me for allowing her.

"I'm supposed to be untouchable." My cold words slither out with a hint of venom. "I've built my empire around being the one thing everyone wants and can't have." To go from being used like a toy to what I am now isn't something I'm willing to give up. Ever. "But I..." My voice cracks. "I wanted..."

Tara's gaze softens. She's waiting for me to come out with it, and I don't know if I can. It's too despicable to admit.

Her head tips back and she says, "You wanted to be the one who pays to have the pleasure for once."

If I could jump off a bridge right now, I would. Shame rides up my back and neck, heating my face. "Yes."

She should slap me. Punch me. Beat me to death for admitting that I wanted to be on the opposite end of my past for a little. There's no sense in trying to explain that I can make it good for us both, or that I respect her and want her to have nothing but pleasure out of me, too. But what would be the point? My actions have been nothing but cruel and contradictory since the beginning.

Dmitri was right, I sabotage myself in epic ways. My volatile behavior has nothing to do with Tara as a woman, and *everything* to do with me as a fucked up bastard.

Tara's not a whore. No Butterfly is. And my feelings for her have transformed into something wicked. I don't know what to do about it. She's everything I could want and more. I don't deserve her.

"Use me," she says, cutting through the prickly silence between us.

My eyes snap to hers. "What?"

"Use me. Let go and use me however you want."

There's no way I heard her correctly. "*Tara.*"

"I'm the Butterfly. I get what I want, correct? Take back your power, Ryker, and use me to do it."

I'm too messed up to be trusted this much. "What if I go too far?"

She shrugs, like this is no big deal. "I'll call Red if you do."

Tara doesn't know that she's offering me the

biggest fantasy of my life right now. As a Switch, I'm well versed in power plays and I'm great at holding back and maintaining control in every scene. For once, I want to lose it all. Tara's giving me permission to do that with her. "This is dangerous."

"Maybe." She leans back with nothing but confidence in her body language. "But I trust you, Ryker Hudson."

And that, I fear, will be our downfall.

Damn me straight to Hell, but I can't deny myself, or Tara, of what we both want anymore. "We need rules before we start," I warn.

"No rules, Ryker." Tara sits up, closing her legs and pushing her dress down. "You'll toe the line the whole time. I want you to do anything... *everything*... you want to me."

She has no clue what she's fucking saying. Her naiveness will make me back off before we've even started. "Tara, you don't even know what your hard lines are. Do you have a clue what your soft ones are, at least?"

Her expression tells me no, she doesn't. As her Dom, I need to protect her, not only from me, but from herself.

"I'll call Red," she says again.

"That's not good enough." My dick's limp between my legs. I push off the floor and grab my pants. "We need a perimeter to play in. I need limits." Because I honestly have none.

The notion gives me pause. Who am I to say she must have a line when I don't have one myself?

Fuck. We're too new to each other to be considering going this far yet.

"What do you want to do to me, Sir?"

Squeezing my eyes shut and counting to ten is the only way to calm my rapid heart rate. "Tara, this isn't going to work."

"What do you want to do to me, Ryker?"

There goes my name in her mouth again. It freezes me in place. Tara scissors her legs together, seeking friction for her needy little cunt while she stares up at me. She's so pretty, so precious, so fragile. The monster in me wants to tear her apart and fuck her piece by piece.

"I told you what I wanted from you." She dips her hand between her thighs but hides the view with the hem of her dress. "Return the favor."

Fine. If she wants to hear my desires, so be it. She'll run out of my door, and out of my life for sure.

I think it's the only way we'll both survive.

"I want to tie your legs up and keep them spread." I stay firmly where I'm standing. "I want to spit all over you. Bite you. Claw you."

Her breaths come out in short bursts, making her soft belly flutter. But she doesn't look away from me. She doesn't even look disgusted.

"I want to spread you wide and call you names."

Her mouth parts, and she touches herself. "What kind of names?"

"Slut, whore, fucktoy." My dick hardens again. "I want to fuck your pretty mouth until you can't breathe. I want come all over your face, hair, and tits. I want to shove things into you."

Tara's cheeks flush. "What kind of things?"

I look around the room for anything. I'm not that fucking picky. "The flogger again. A riding crop. The bottle of lube. Anything that will fit."

"And... if it doesn't?"

A smile spreads across my face as I finally let the monster peek out. "We'll make it fit, Tara."

Her breath catches.

"You have every right to tell me no. The scene will stop when you call Red." I'm desperate to see if she'll actually let me do any of this to her.

Tara licks the finger she'd just shoved into her pussy. "What else do you want to do to me, Ryker Hudson?"

Fuuuuck. She's not running. "I want to get you collared on a leash, then put clamps on your cunt and tits."

Her pupils blow wide. "What else?"

"Fuck you in every hole until you can't move." I stare down my nose at her. "Then I want to fuck you some more."

"What if I pass out again?"

She will. I'll make sure of it. "I want to fuck you even when you're unconscious."

The weight of my confession has me downward spiraling. Does she see me now? Does she understand how depraved I am? She can't call Red if she's passed out. She can't make me stop fucking her at all.

"Do it," she says in a deep, sultry voice. "Do your worst."

"Did you not hear what I just fucking said?" I step forward with my jaw clenched. This woman is insane if she thinks this is okay. "Tara. I'm going to fuck you into oblivion and past that. You won't be able to use your safe word or tap me or anything. I'll use you up."

And spit you out.

My raging hard-on throbs with need. And

what's worse is she's so turned on right now, I can see her wet pussy from here. She's soaked through the dress pressed to her core. The thin fabric's saturated and tells me everything I've admitted sounds right down her alley.

I want to promise her I'll stop if it's too much. I want to reassure her I won't mean the nasty things I'll say. I want to explain that it's not her that's trash, it's *me*.

"You have my consent, Ryker." Tara crawls over to me. "You can tie me up, use me, spit and degrade me. Hell, you can fucking piss on me if you want." She stays on her knees once she reaches my feet and my heart stammers. "I know my worth, Mr. Hudson." Tara wraps her hands around my dick. "And when we're through, you'll know yours, too."

Jesus Christ.

My eyes roll back when she takes the head of my cock into her mouth. I snap. "The fuck do you think you're doing, whore?" Her eyes flash when I say that and my heart kicks up into my throat. "Did I say you could touch me?"

Tara pulls back and drops her hands to her lap. "Sorry, Sir."

"Fuck your sorries," I growl. "Crawl over to the bed."

I hate myself already.

Tara doesn't scamper like a puppy in trouble. She prowls on her hands and knees like a goddamn cougar. It's all that holds me together as I say, "I paid a lot of fucking money for your pussy."

"Yes, you did."

"Shut your whore mouth. You only talk when I tell you to." My chest tightens. To ease the ache, I drop to my knees and lift her dress to place a gentle kiss on her soaked cunt. "This needy little pussy likes attention. Look at you, soaked already. You're such a fucking cockslut."

I spit on her pussy.

She doesn't even flinch.

Forcing myself onto my feet, I turn around and run my hands down my face as I walk away from her. I'll have to use Dmitri's stash of toys for this. There's nothing in here for me to pleasure a woman with beyond my body and some impact play tools. That's not good enough.

Heading to the closet, I pull out a large wooden box and lift the lid. Thank God D's tastes are like mine in depravity. I snag the nipple and labia clamps. He's got a couple massive dildos in here too, so I pluck the biggest one out, impressed by the weight of it. Next, I dig through my rope stash and pick out the softest ones I own.

"Ready to be tied up like an animal?"

Nodding, she keeps her eyes locked on mine instead of looking at any of the items I've brought over.

The first thing I do is thread a small ring around a long piece of rope, then I tie it around her waist, just above her belly button. The knot is simple and doesn't look as intimidating as it will be in a fucking minute. Next, I bend her right leg and quickly rig the knots to keep her knee bent. Now her calf and thigh are pressed together, bound by blue cord that's tight enough to sink into her skin which makes some of her cellulite bulge. It's fucking stunning. My hands shake when I tie her other leg the same way.

Without a word, I crawl on top of her, pressing

a trail of hot kisses up her body until I reach her face. Instead of kissing her lips like I want, I keep crawling until my balls are at her throat. Then I smack her cheek and nose with my dick. "You're only good for one thing, little toy. And I'm going to play with you until you fucking *break*." Grabbing her hands, I truss my girl up with a purple rope and tie her bound hands to the eyehook attached to the center of the bed.

Then I shove the head of my dick between her lips. Her hot velvety tongue swirls around me, and my toes fucking curl. "Greedy little bitch." I pull out and spit on her cheek. My heart pounds when I see she hasn't reacted at all. She just stares at me as if enraptured with the fantasies of whatever I'll do next.

I wipe my spit off with my thumb. *Keep your shit together, Ry.*

Straddling her torso, I press my weight down on her lower body, reminding her of my size and power. Then I pluck the nipple clamps up and watch her reaction. Tara doesn't look at them. Her eyes are still deadlocked on mine.

Kneading her tits roughly, I smack the side of one and watch her breasts jiggle before falling towards her armpits. My mouth waters to play with them. I suck one into my mouth, and twirl my tongue around her hard nipple, and place the clamp on the tit I'm not playing with.

Tara's breath hitches.

Rolling her wet nipple between my fingers, pinching and pulling it, I love how responsive she is. Her skin's flushed, goosebumps rippling down her arms and legs. "What color are you?"

"Green," she whimpers as I clamp her other nipple.

They're attached by a chain, which is going to hook to the collar I've also got for her. "Lift your head." I slide my hand around her neck and slip the collar under her hair, buckling it in place before hooking her nipple clamps to the center of it.

Tara's cheeks are bright red, and pupils have swallowed her irises.

So, I slap her cheek. It's not hard enough to hurt, only to shock. "You fucking like this, you filthy little cunt?"

Tara nods.

"You're a disgusting whore." I climb off her and lick my lips, stroking my cock. "You're pathetic. So fucking needy for this dick, you're soaking my sheets."

Tara only wiggles her ass, giving me a cue that she likes this.

Too bad that's about to change.

Chapter 38

Tara

I've never been more turned on in my life. I don't know what it says about me that I enjoy being degraded and spit on, but here I am, so needy for it, I have to concentrate on my breathing in order to not hyperventilate with excitement.

Keeping my gaze locked on Ryker, I use him as my focal point.

All my life I've had to be the good girl. The daughter who listens. The woman who makes you proud. The one who makes life easy for others. The stepdaughter who stayed obedient and sweet so my mother could reap the rewards. For once, I want to be the opposite. I want to be depraved. Loud. Filthy. Chewed up. Spit on. Fucked hard and wrung out. I don't want to prove myself anymore. I don't want to pretend to be something I'm not.

I want to be *me*.

I stare at Ryker, eager for anything he'll do next. The intensity of our connection, mixed with the clamps biting my nipples and ropes digging into my legs, is delicious. I can't move much and that's thrilling too. It means I'm at his mercy.

"Let's pin these wings back, Butterfly."

He grabs something else from the bed and it's only after the first pinch that I look down to see what he's doing.

He's spreading my labia open with metal pincers. There's a delicate chain draping from each one that he attaches to the rope around my legs.

I'm on display. It's obscene. Raw. Vulnerable.

I've never felt sexier.

"Fuuuck, Tara," Ryker whispers once he steps back to admire his work. Grabbing his dick, he strokes it and leans down to drag his tongue along my exposed clit. I jump from how sensitive it is. "Don't fucking move, little slut."

A shock of pain zips up my spine and down my legs. He's just put a clamp on my clit. Lifting his head to look at me, he holds the chain attached to it between his teeth and tilts back a fraction. The slight movement pulls on my clit and pain zaps me again.

Ryker arches his brow.

"Green," I rasp. If it was any tighter, I'd be yellow, though.

"Good girl." He hooks the chain to the small ring that's threaded through the rope tied around my stomach.

If I arch my back, it'll pull my clit.

Holy shit. Any move I make will affect my pussy or tits.

Ryker climbs off to admire me again. I can't imagine what I look like, but I feel beautiful.

Running a hand down his mouth, he grabs the lube and pours it all over his length and starts jerking himself. The wet noises of his strokes are loud in my ears.

When he pours some lube on my pussy, he says, "Let's play, fucktoy."

It drips all over my pussy and over my asshole.

I'm so turned on, I could cry. The need to come is almost dizzying.

"Do you want to use this hole to make men give you things?" He flicks my pussy, causing a cry to tear from my throat. "You think this little cunt will get you what you want, slut?"

Is he talking about me using my body to negotiate deals?

"Answer me, whore," he shoves his dick inside me, ramming me once and then pulls out.

"No."

"*No?*" He rams into me again, making my body jostle, which tugs the chains attached to my clamps. I cry out again.

"N-no."

"My little whore thinks making a deal with me doesn't count?" He strokes himself harder, faster. "You think you're above selling your body for someone else's pleasure?" He pulls the chain between my tits, making my nipples sting.

"Fuck, Ryker!"

He crawls on top of me and slaps his hand over my mouth. "Shut. The fuck. Up." His breaths punch out as his strokes quicken. They become hard, punishing. He peels his hand off my mouth and stares at my lips. The tendons in his neck thicken, the veins in his throat pop out and flutter with his rapid heartbeat. Sitting up, he jerks himself faster and faster. "That's what you did, Butterfly. You made me pay." He orgasms and hot cum jets out in white ropes, splattering all over my face and chest.

Growling, Ryker runs a hand through the mess, smearing it all over my face. "You actually fucking like this, slut?"

I nod. "I love it."

He crawls off the bed and walks around to the foot of it again. His spent dick flops, half flaccid, between his legs. I want to lick it. Savor every bit of his flavor. Get it hard again so he can fuck me. Biting my lip gives me a chance to taste his cum on my mouth. I immediately want more, so I flick my tongue as far as it will stretch and clean my mouth.

Ryker sinks to his knees and tongue-fucks me until I'm sweating. "Please," I beg. "I need to come."

His fingers dig into my legs. "Did I tell you to speak?"

My head falls back, and I squeeze my eyes shut.

Ryker stuffs his fingers inside me. I think it's two. The pressure almost soothes the ache building in my system, but it's not enough for a climax. Damn him. He's torturing me here. The only thing that's keeping me sane is knowing how turned on he is by this. As badly as I want to come, I want to be played with even more.

"You're doing so good for me," he growls from between my legs.

My thighs ache from being pinned in this tight position. My arms hurt, too. I'm overstimulated and deprived at the same time. It's the perfect combo of chaos.

But it's Ryker's intense gaze that drags me back to the precipice of euphoria. He flashes me a smile and tips his head back as something new presses against my pussy. "Breathe," he orders, then shoves the object inside me.

It's *huge*. Tears spill from the corner of my eyes because even though it hurts, it feels good. It's sickening and exciting. I'm gonna come from it.

"That's my good little cock slut." He pumps the thing in and out of me slowly. Carefully. The pain and pleasure combo has my vision tunneling. "Your cunt's so fucking greedy."

He licks my clamped clit. Pain radiates down my thighs and my stomach rolls. My clit's too sensitive for anything to touch it—including his tongue. "More." It hurts too good to stop now. I'm going to pass out.

Ryker fucks me with the big object and all I can do is ride out the sensations wracking me. "Breathe," he barks. "Don't quit on me now, slut. We've only just begun."

He removes the clamp on my clit. I wheeze with relief, only to cry out from a sudden surge of blood flow down there that has my back arching, which pulls on everything else that's still clamped at his mercy. My pussy clenches around the object still inside me. "Fuck."

Ryker licks my clit in slow drags, drawing an orgasm from me that's so strange, so strong, I can't make sense of it. My hips gyrate, but in this trussed up position, I can't move much. Not enough.

"That's it, slut. Come all over that big dick."

Pain and pleasure skate over my body, pulsing around my pussy. My orgasm is ugly and loud. When he pulls the object out of me, I groan.

I wasn't done yet.

Ryker holds this massive purple and blue dildo up for me to see. "Look what that filthy hole did. It's soaked." He shoves the dildo back inside me and starts fucking me harder with it. I manage to find a little purchase with my feet and raise up as much as I can. Only the chains pull on my nipples and pussy lips, making pain radiate through me in a delicious way that has me roaring with my next release.

I squirt all over Ryker, saturating the bedding. He latches onto my pussy while I continue gushing and shoves a finger in my ass. Then he pops his head up, and sprays my come out of his mouth, all over me.

I'm so turned on I cry.

Next, he grabs a riding crop and taps my tits. Sliding it down my body, he almost tickles me with it. I brace for him to smack my over-stimulated clit, but he drags it past that and teases my legs instead before twirling it once and running the handle along my pussy.

Then he taps the top of my foot with the business end.

I squeak. Everything he does only makes me desperate for more.

"What color are you?" His voice is ragged.

"Green."

Ryker shakes his head like that can't be possible.

Standing with his dick pressed against my pussy. His gaze roams all over my body, looking at the mess I am. The mess he's made of me.

"Jesus fucking Christ, Tara."

He releases the clamps on my pussy and goes for my nipples next. Blood rushes back to them and I scream in the painful pressure of relief. He pulls my wrists off the hook, letting my arms down. Straddling me, he looks like this hurts him more than it does me.

"Green," I rush to say. "I'm still green. I swear it."

His brow furrows just before he crawls down my body, laying ardent kisses all over my skin. "I'm untying you," he warns with a cracked voice.

But I don't want this to end. I can't stop yet. I still want more.

Once he unties my wrists, I run my fingers along my chest, brushing my palms against my nipples. It hurts deliciously, making heat rush to my core. "I need more," I confess.

If he wants to reprimand me for talking out of turn, he keeps it to himself. Ryker trembles as he unties all the knots around my thighs. The moment I regain mobility of my right leg, I groan from the ache I have straightening it out.

My body feels so good. Tight but loose. Suspended between pain and pleasure is exactly where I want to be.

Shoving my hand between my legs, I rub my clit carefully, testing if I can handle the stimulation or not. It's both too much and not enough, but a release starts to build between my legs again. Ryker stares at my pussy while deftly unknotting my other leg. Once he frees it, he hooks my leg over his shoulder and kisses the inside of my thigh. "Fucking incredible."

"I need to come again," I beg. "Please. I… I need this."

I need you.

"Greedy little whore." He spreads my legs and slides his cock inside me. I'm so full, I can't stand it. Wrapping my legs around his middle, I lift my ass up and keep lightly stroking my swollen clit.

"You're so goddamn wet, Tara." Ryker grips my hips and thrusts into me.

"I have to come," I say, my body coiling.

He snakes his hand around my neck and smashes his mouth to mine while railing into me. I implode. My orgasm is a heavy, pulsing, head rush.

Ryker eats my screams. Our mouths stay fused together, and he groans when I claw down his back. My entire body shakes from what we're doing.

When he pulls back, I see his bottom lip is bleeding.

Ooops. Sorry, not sorry.

Ryker pulls out and flips me over. "I want inside this ass."

He tips me up and dumps lube all over my crack. I feel something press into me and quickly realize it's his finger. I have no clue how I'm going to take his fat cock back there, but I'm determined to try. "You like playing with your little fucktoy, Mr. Hudson?" I ask with a smile on my face.

Ryker stills, now with two fingers in my ass. "Yes," he growls, then proceeds to finger-fuck me some more.

"How much?"

He bites my shoulder. "Keep talking and I'll gag you."

I'm not sure I want a gag yet, so I keep quiet.

He works my ass open for a long time. All the while, I focus on how good my body feels. By the time he presses his dick to my opening, I'm desperate for him to stuff it inside me.

"Breathe, baby." He runs his hand down my back and over my ass cheeks. "Relax your muscles for me."

I can't though. I'm too scared. Too thrilled. Too everything.

"You can do this." He rubs his head over my hole and presses into it. "You can take it for me. I know you can, slut." He pushes a little further. "That's a good girl." He sucks in air and exhales it with a moan. Little by little, he pushes deeper into me.

I claw the bed. I'm not sure if I like it or not, but it feels…

"That's it, Tara. You're doing so good for me."

I feel like I can totally do this.

Rubbing my clit to keep my body loose, I focus on the St. Andrews cross. I can't believe Ryker pulled the cuffs so hard, he snapped the chains. This man wanted me so badly, he ripped himself from actual chains to get to me.

I come again. "Oh my *God*."

Ryker bottoms out inside my ass. "Fuuuuck, Butterfly, I feel you fluttering."

With my cheek pressed against the mattress, I reach back and grip his thigh. "Fuck me into oblivion. I need you," Jesus, my heart's pounding. "I need to you to break me."

"What color are you?"

I'll be borderline yellow if he doesn't give me what I need right now. "Green, Ry."

"You won't be for much longer." He grips my hips and slams into me until I black out.

Chapter 39

Ryker

I did it. I fucked my girl until she collapsed into a boneless heap of sweat, cum, and tears. Tara passed out just after I unloaded my orgasm into her ass. She held on as long as she could, my brave, sweet girl, but in the end, exhaustion took her. Or pain. I'm not sure which.

Peeling away from her is like taking off a layer of skin. She's a part of me.

After cleaning off my dick in the bathroom, I get a warm, soapy washcloth and wipe the mess off her as best I can. I can't believe I trashed her body this way.

I can't believe she fucking *let* me.

Wiping the fluids off her face, neck and chest makes me question what kind of human I am. Seeing how Tara responded to the things I did, the names I called her, the way I fucked her… she loved it. And I loved it for her. What kind of human does that make her?

My hands shake as I wipe the mess I made between her legs. The clamps have left little red marks on her delicate flesh. Rope burns have marred her wrists too. Fuck, she was stunning all trussed up and spread for me like a butterfly on display.

I've come twice, and it hasn't put a dent in my lust for her. There are twenty-three bite marks, countless scratches, six handprints, and fourteen welts on Tara that I can count at this angle. She begged me to give her each one too.

"You like playing with your little fucktoy, Mr. Hudson?" Her question will haunt me for life.

Yeah, I like it.

Too much.

"I need you one more time, Butterfly," I say, rolling her over. I doubt she's going to wake up. I've put my girl through hell, and she needs time to recuperate. A decent man would walk away and let her sleep.

I'm not a decent man.

Skating my fingertips along her breasts, her belly, the slope of her waist and the cushion of her thighs, I memorize every inch of her sweet body. This may be the last time I ever get to touch it.

No woman in her right mind would come back to a monster like me. Not after the shit I've pulled tonight. Kinks are born from many things, and I've tried to understand why I like what I like, but the truth hurts too much to admit.

The bottom line is I'm damaged. Others may have these same kinks for healthier reasons, but not me. I'm sick. Twisted. Depraved and starved for power and control because I've gone too long with none of it.

"I'll make it feel good for you," I promise, recalling a man saying those exact words to me right before he destroyed my body for a measly fifty bucks.

Crawling on top of Tara, I kiss her cheek before reaching between her legs to stuff my half flaccid dick inside her as best I can.

The air in my lungs burns. My cheeks heat with

shame because taking her like this, and knowing she allowed it in advance, gets me harder than a rock. The way I fill her, the way she's forced to stretch around my size, is a heady fucking drug.

Addiction has set in, and I pump in and out of her wet pussy. The more I do, the better it feels.

"When I'm through with you, Butterfly, your pussy will always remember who it belongs to." Leaning down, I kiss her mouth and she stirs under me.

"Mmph."

"Shhh." I whisper, my voice trembling while I fuck her a little harder. "Sleep through it." *Please sleep through it. I can't stand the idea of you waking up and seeing me this way.*

Tara's mouth opens and my name slips out sleepily. "Ryker."

Her earlier question slides down my spine and grips my dick. *"You like playing with your little fucktoy, Mr. Hudson?"*

I do. And I won't stop. I don't think it's possible. My body is on some kind of autopilot and while my heart has slammed on the brakes, trying its best to reel me in again, my mind zeroes in on the feel of her body taking what I give it.

Sitting up, I grip her thighs and drag her to me. "Let me keep you." *Let me poison you, too. No one will touch you if I make you toxic like me.*

Tara's eyes flutter open.

"No," I say, my hips still thrusting of their own accord. "No, no, no."

Tara wakes fully and locks her eyes with mine.

"*No*," my voice cracks. "Please don't watch."

She tips her head back and groans like this is

good for her, too. But it *can't* be. It *shouldn't* be. Only I feel her pussy grip my cock and it shakes me to the core. She's enjoying what I'm doing.

Tara's raspy voice knocks the sanity out of me. "You like playing with your little fucktoy, Mr. Hudson?"

My chest cracks open. "*Yes*," I admit, even as a tear falls down my motherfucking face.

"I like it, too."

I fuck her harder, driving us both across the bed.

"Come inside me," she says once I'm close. "Dump it all into me, Ryker."

A terrible noise explodes out of me. Pulling her onto my lap, I spring her up and down on my dick until we're a heap of grunts and tangled limbs. I use her like a fuckdoll. Her tits jiggle in my face. Her nails dig into my shoulders. Her fucking hair is in my mouth.

"You like being my toy? You like the way I use you to get off with?"

"Yes." Her inner walls grip me. "God, yes." She crushes her mouth to mine, and I explode.

I come hard and scream ugly. My dick jerks, emptying my release inside her, pumping every bit of toxicity I own into her precious body. Clutching Tara fiercely, I cage her in my arms, squeezing her tight while my dick continues twitching in her cunt.

"That was incredible," she whispers as I press my lips to her neck.

My dick's softer, still crammed inside her, ready for another round. "Let me just…" I lift her off me gingerly but hear her whimper. *Shit.* "How hurt are you?"

My cum seeps out of her pussy and onto my

groin. It makes me feel dirty and confused.

"I'm not hurt, Ry." She peppers me with kisses and each one is a stab in my dead heart.

I hold her close to me again. My head's spinning. Panic is setting in. *Shit, shit, shit.*

"You're shaking," she says, alarmed. "Are you hurt?"

"I've just done depraved things to you, and you're concerned about my health instead of your own?" I don't deserve her.

"I'm fine. Now tell me what's wrong with you." She looks all over my body like there's going to be a knife in my gut or something. "Jesus, Ry, you're pale."

"I'm in a Dom drop." And crashing hard.

"What's that mean?"

"It means…" Fuck, I don't have the capacity to describe it right now. "Please just let me hold you and take care of you."

Tara's brow furrows. "Will taking care of me make you feel better?"

I nod, unable to speak around the bile rising in my throat.

"Okay." She relaxes in my lap. "But please don't feel bad for what we just did. I *loved* it."

My heart cracks into pieces. Tara just let me do all kinds of things to her. She never even called yellow. Her body melted for my touch, no matter how rough it was. It's been that way since the beginning. Tears build in my eyes, but I blink them back. "You're not really a whore or a slut or any of those things I called you."

"I know." She nestles in my lap a little more, tucking her head under my chin. "But I *really* like being your fucktoy."

I know some people like being used. I see it all the time in my club. But it's hard for me to separate my trauma from their pleasure. Using Tara like this tonight was a balm to my soul during the scene, but now that it's over, I feel like I've ripped my darkness open and all that's dripping out of me is regret and shame.

"You're more than a fucktoy, Tara."

"I know."

"You're more than I deserve."

"Agree to disagree." She lifts her head to look at me. "Sorry I bit your lip earlier."

"It felt good."

She drags her thumb over the split in my lip and I playfully nip at her, which makes her giggle.

It's that giggle that lets me think I can survive this.

But will she survive me?

Chapter 40

Tara

After a long soak with bath salts in Ryker's tub, we got dressed and drove back to the club. We were silent the whole ride here. I'm too exhausted to speak, and I think he's too wrapped up in his mind to make words come out of his face.

There's a noticeable difference in his body language as we pull up to the parking lot behind the Monarch. *He's tense again.* You'd think after the session we just had, some of the volatile aggression he carries all the time would have been fucked right out of his system. Clearly, that's not the case. A little insecure voice whispers in my ear that maybe I wasn't good enough for him. It makes my stomach drop.

Stop it, Tara. No way am I letting my past burdens taint what we've done today.

Turning the engine off, Ryker growls, "Don't move. I'll come around and help you out."

"Okay." He wouldn't let me do anything for myself after we fucked at his house, either. I couldn't brush my hair. I couldn't dry myself off. I couldn't get myself dressed. He took care of everything for me.

The aggressive sex followed by soft attention is a complicated combo.

I've fucked rough before. It's *never* turned out like this. I'm both precious and powerful and it's lovely.

Ryker quickly walks around the car, fixing his tie just before making it to my side. His hand is warm in mine when he helps me out. The two wobbly noodles I have for legs collapse immediately.

"I've got you," he says, scooping me into his arms before my knees hit the concrete. He had to carry me to his car when we left his house, too. Why I thought my body would bounce back faster is beyond me.

He stares straight ahead, his jaw clenching, and stuffs his face into the camera attached to the back door. A few seconds later, Dmitri opens it, his icy eyes wide with alarm. "Jesus, Ry."

Ryker doesn't say a word as he slips past Dmitri, through the kitchen, and into the main area of the club. It's ten o'clock at night and the Monarch is in full swing. Dim lights illuminate our path, setting the mood for all the action happening everywhere. It might be my imagination, but I think Ryker's taking the long way back to our suite. Unrushed, he walks us through most of the common areas and down the hall that leads to the elevators. Everyone's looking at us.

Wrapping my arms around his neck, I nuzzle against him and make eye contact with every motherfucking woman we pass. I'd bet ten grand Ryker's doing the same with all the men. Members move out of our way, respectfully.

Others gawk.

Only one jars me, and that's Blake Rittenhouse. He's got this tight smile on his stupid face, and I match it as we pass by. He can look, stare, lust after, and fantasize all he wants, but he'll never have me. We both know it.

Since I'm feeling extra spicy tonight, I flip him the bird as I kiss the side of Ryker's jaw.

Blake's eyes flash with anger and he pretends to go back to whatever conversation he's having with his partner for the night.

Ryker carries me to the Butterfly suite, where Sophie waits at our door. She opens it and whispers casually that she'll have food and drinks brought up.

"Thanks, Soph." That's all Ryker says before kicking the door closed.

"I think you can put me down now."

He clenches his molars again. "Not yet."

I'm not sure if this is still part of his Dom drop, or if he's just become a territorial caveman. Either way, I don't argue. He places me gingerly on the bed with a sigh. "Let me see you again, Butterfly." When I give him a confused look, he adds, "I want to make sure all the marks are gone and you're okay."

I kind of hope a few of them stay. "I'm fine."

"Let me see." He's not going to take no for an answer. Lifting my dress, I spread my legs a little, and my cheeks blaze with embarrassment. I don't feel sexy like this. Not with how concerned Ryker looks. "Lay back for me."

My head hits the pillows and I stare at the ceiling. "I feel like I'm at a gynecologist's office."

He doesn't laugh when he peels my underwear off me. The gentle probe of his finger on my pussy makes me suck in a harsh breath. "Does that hurt?"

"Not really. It's just a little sore."

"There are no abrasions from the clamps," he says, more to himself, I think. He already checked me earlier. Why is he doing it again? "How's your backside?"

"Sore, but also fine."

"Let me see."

"No." Shoving my dress down, I close my legs and look away. "Why are you acting like this?"

"Tara." Ryker sits on the edge of the bed with my panties in his fist. "You're still bleeding."

It's probably normal given how hard we went at it, and for how long. Ryker's dick is fat and long. A little blood should be standard. "I'm sure it's nothing."

"I can't stand the possibility that I hurt you."

"You didn't do anything I didn't want, Ryker." To make my point clear, I scoot to the edge of the bed and stand. "See? I'm good to go." Except walking takes extra effort. By the time I make it to the bathroom doorway, a sheen of sweat covers my chest and forehead.

I was so hyper focused on making it to the finish line, I didn't hear Ryker come up behind me.

"My brave, beautiful girl." His arms band around my waist and he kisses the side of my neck.

Heat pools in my lower region. "The pain's delicious," I admit. "I can see the draw to floggers and clamps now." I'm not sure if I could handle harder, harsher toys, but down the road, I'd be willing to try. "Later, I'd like to experiment more to see where my limit is with them."

"Not tonight," he warns, his mouth pressed to my neck.

"No." I feel all mushy and soft when he kisses me like this. "Not... *fuck*, not tonight."

"That's my good girl." He palms my tits.

"Ryker?" I lean against him while he runs his hands all over me.

"Yes, Butterfly?"

"I want you again."

He freezes. "It's too soon, baby."

His rejection stings. "I think I know my body well enough to say what I can and cannot handle."

"As your Dom, I will override your wishes if I think it's necessary. I just put you through it, Tara. Your body needs time to heal."

"My ass does, but not the rest of me." I think he's created a monster. Between his possessiveness while carrying me, his sensitivity while taking care of me, and his confidence to march through the club with me curled in his arms like he *owns* me... I'm turned-on big time. "I want more."

"So needy," he whispers. "Can we at least eat first?"

Bracing my hands on the doorjamb, he kisses along my shoulder blades and down my back. God, his mouth is phenomenal. "I'm not hungry."

"Well, I am." He bites my ass cheek. It makes me yip.

Someone knocks on the door.

Ryker presses his forehead on the small of my back and sighs. "Don't you dare fucking move."

"Yes, Sir."

He rushes over and opens the door, whispering something quietly to the person on the other side. Then I hear the door shut and lock. Plates and glasses clank on a tray, which he places on the table by the couch, I think. I keep my eyes forward, staring into the dark bathroom, and hold on to the doorjamb so I can stay upright while I wait for his return.

His body heat warms my back again. "Now..." Ryker wraps his arms around me. "Where were we?"

"You were just about to fuck me."

He spanks my ass. "Nice try." Lifting me over his shoulders, we cross the room, and he drops me back on the bed. "But I said food first."

"Does that mean after I eat you'll give me your dick again?"

"We'll see." He retrieves the tray and uncovers the first dish. It's two grilled cheese sandwiches and tomato soup. Ryker shakes his head, chuckling. "This guy."

Pulling one of the melty sandwiches apart, I hand half to Ryker. "You talking about Dmitri?"

"Yeah." He chomps down on his half, and I swear even the way he chews is sexy. "This is my ultimate comfort food."

And Dmitri knew he needed it tonight. "You have an amazing best friend."

Ryker nods and takes another bite. Wiping his mouth with one of the two napkins rolled up on the tray, he says, "Cheap bread, cheap cheese, and butter. It doesn't get much better than this."

"Oh, I don't know about that." Slipping out of my sundress, I rip off little pieces of my sandwich and place them along my belly. "This might make it taste better."

He arches his brow. With a little smirk, he pushes the tray of food aside and eats each piece, bite after buttery bite, off my body. "Fucking delicious."

I'm half tempted to pour the hot soup on me just to watch him lick it off.

"Don't even think about it, Tara." He shakes his head slowly. "That soup will scald you and I'll be a mess about it."

"It might feel nice," I push. "A little burn never

hurt nobody."

"I think if you got a paper cut, I'd go apeshit." Sliding the tray over, he taps the last covered item. "Any guesses what this might be?"

Well, if these are Ryker's ultimate comfort foods, I'm going to guess, "Cookies."

He grins. "Try again."

"Hot fudge sundae?"

He laughs. "Nope."

"I give up. What is it?"

Ryker lifts the lid, revealing two chocolate pudding cups.

"You're *kidding*." I snag one and rip the lid off. "I haven't had one of these in *forever*." Licking the lid brings me back to my childhood...

"Dinner's ready!" I set the glass bowl down on the kitchen table.

Mom comes in, her freshly dyed hair still wet from the rinse. "Ohhh nice." She snags two spoons from the drying rack and hands one to me. We clink our utensils and dig into the vat of chocolate pudding I've had chilling in the fridge since noon.

"Chocolate pudding is top tier deliciousness." I lick the back of my spoon before scooping another mound and shoving it in my face.

Mom giggles. "You're going to turn into pudding one day."

"I'm sure it's already running through my veins." I shove another spoonful into my mouth. "Want to watch another movie tonight?" We've been on an action movie binge for the past month. It's been perfect. Just the two of us eating our weight in junk food, wrapped up in a million blankets on the couch until midnight. "We can start the

Avengers."

"Not tonight, honey. I have plans." She doesn't look at me when she says this.

Which means I know what her plans are.

Mom's on the prowl again. Jesus, why does she always have to go looking for a rich guy? It never works out. My mom's been married twice already, and both ended in divorces that left us with exactly what we started with. Each other and nothing else.

I wish she'd be happy with only me in her life. But she wants more. She's not looking for love, she's looking for gold. Sometimes I wonder if my mom knows how to love anyone but herself.

"Who is he?" The pudding tastes sour in my mouth now.

"His name's William Brisbane. I met him at a networking conference downtown."

She means she served him coffee at the hotel she works at.

"What's he like?"

"Smart, confident, big brown eyes, and a fat wallet." She waggles her eyebrows at me. "He has a son about your age, too."

She's already done some research. Great.

"He's taking me to that five-star restaurant off Lambert Ave at eight."

"Nice." I have no clue what restaurant she's talking about. Staring at the table, I tap my fingers on my thigh while silence spreads in the kitchen. I finally snap. "Why do you always do this?" I didn't mean to ask it out loud. Last time I did, she slapped me and called me ungrateful. "I'm sorry, I – "

"Look around us, Tara." Mom stabs her spoon into the bowl of pudding and crosses her arms. "Do you like what you see?"

Yes. I do. Our apartment is perfect for the two of us. I have friends on the first floor and down the street. I don't have to take the bus to school because it's close enough to walk. I'm happy here, and if she fucks around, it'll end badly — because it always *ends badly — and then she'll want to pack up and move again.*

Two things are concrete with my mother: Her beauty is a weapon, and she's forever on a treasure hunt.

Nothing's good enough for her, including me.

"Yes, mom. I love it here."

"Well, I hate it. We can do so much better than this, Tara."

Says who? "Agree to disagree."

Her cheeks blaze with her temper. "We're in a tiny apartment that my shit paycheck barely covers the rent on!"

That's because she spends most of her money on high-end clothes, so people will notice and "respect" her. She pays the bare minimum for our life. Rebecca Reed invests in only herself.

"Look at us, Tara. We're having pudding for dinner!" Mom shoves the bowl off the table and it crashes onto the floor in a colossal mess. "How much lower can we sink?"

Fury bubbles out of me. I hate you. *Tears burn in my eyes because I can't believe I thought she was going to be different this time.* "Money isn't everything, Mom."

"You are so fucking stupid." She shoves a finger in my face, and I see they're freshly painted red. "One day you'll understand that if you don't have money, you don't have shit."

"You don't need a rich husband to have money." I toss my hands up. "Work your way up at the hotel. Take some classes and learn a new trade."

She laughs, cold, harsh, and ugly. "Jesus, Tara. You think it's that simple? I don't even have a GED. I'm lucky *to have a job at the hotel as it is. No one wants to hire a woman whose background is scrubbing dishes, stocking shelves, and flipping burgers."* The veins in her temples pop out. *"I'd have made something for myself if it hadn't been for you, but that ship sailed when I was sixteen."*

The walls close in on me. "I didn't ask to be born."

"No, you didn't. And I loved you enough to have you, anyway."

Should I be grateful? "But you don't love me enough to just be happy with me."

Why am I not good enough? I get straight As, I'm in all the gifted classes, I have a part-time job and help with the bills, I never get in trouble, and I'm home by curfew, always. I don't even like action movies, but I watch them all the time for her because they're her favorite.

"Baby," her voice softens, the anger quickly fizzling out fast, just like it always does. Reaching across the table, Mom grabs my hand. "Of course, I'm happy with you. But I'm lonely. I want someone to share a life with. To make memories with." She tips her head and offers a little smile. *"Maybe have another baby, too. Wouldn't you like having a sibling?"*

Hell no.

"I'm sorry I snapped at you," she says, wiggling my hand playfully. "I'm just really nervous about my date with William tonight."

"Why?" *my voice cracks.* "It's just a date."

"No baby, this is the first night of our new future together." She stands up and kisses my forehead. *"And when you meet him, I want you to be extra sweet to him, okay? I want him to love you as much as I do."*

What she means is, "Don't fuck it up like you have all my other relationships."

Swallowing my pride, I force a smile onto my face. "I will, Mom. I'll be perfect."

"Annnd she married William a month later," I say.

"Jeez." Ryker's leaning on his side, his tatted hand propping his head up. "That's wild."

"I've spent my entire childhood moving around, shaping myself to be whatever my mom wanted, so her boyfriend, fiancé, husband, or whatever would love me. And when things would go belly up, she'd blame it on me."

"Fuck, Tara. I'm so sorry." He runs his hand over my leg. "And now she's married a real asshole."

"She doesn't care as long as she gets her own black card." I lean back on the pillow. "And she's already moving on. I saw her fucking that guy Travis in the Mercedes when we left."

Ryker's nonresponse means he saw it too and just wasn't going to mention it.

We've laid in bed, talking, touching and petting each other for a while now. It's nice. "What time is it?"

"Going on midnight, I think."

My yawn's so big my jaw pops. "Man."

"Get some rest, Tara." Ryker kisses my forehead.

I keep my eyes open long enough to watch him get up and turn the lights out around the room. "Are you going to leave?"

He pauses by the bedside table. "Is that what you want?"

"No." I bury my face in the pillow and close my eyes. "I still want you to fuck me."

The mattress dips and the heat rolling off him feels good. "Sleep," he orders, lying next to me. "And let me just hold you for now, Butterfly."

I drift off, hoping if he won't fuck me while I'm awake and begging for it, then he'll fuck me when I'm asleep so I can wake up with him already inside me.

Chapter 41

Ryker

I'm not leaving Tara, even though there are a million things that need to be done. It's late, the club is packed, and I feel guilty for staying locked in this room with my gorgeous woman, while my staff are busting their asses downstairs.

Christ, I'm so attached to her, someone will have to dismember me if they want to pry me off my girl.

Running a hand over the slope of her hip, I love how soft Tara is. How pristine. How opposite of me. I'm a canvas of fuckups, scars, and ink. She's a blank canvas. I'm all hard, rigid lines. She's soft curves and dips. I'm a razor. She's a rose petal.

Peppering her arm with tiny kisses, I stroke her thighs, sweeping my hand down between her legs to see if she'll open for me. Her thighs spread, and she rolls onto her back in her sleep. "Mmm."

"Shhhh." I crawl on top of her, kissing her neck, collarbone, left nipple, and work my way down until I reach her pussy. She takes deep, even breaths as I sink my finger into her pussy. Her body instantly grips my digit, and she moans again. Her body wants me even while she's dead to the world.

I flick my tongue against her clit like a deviant.

Tara sucks in a breath before sinking into a deeper sleep. Her breaths are even and heavy.

I lie to myself and say I just need a taste. That's what addicts do, right? Lie and bullshit about their actual intentions? Tara's my motherfucking drug, and I'll happily overdose on her.

Someone should cut my dick off for this.

I pull my belt off without waking her. Then I unzip my pants and shove them down to my knees. Kneeling between her legs, I grip my hard dick and stroke it.

She's so innocent. So pure. So perfect and whole. I want to feel those things too.

Just for a minute. A couple of strokes and that's it.

I push into her opening and realize it's a mistake to think I can ever willingly pull out. Out of her body. Out of her suite. Out of her life.

"Mmmph." Tara stirs in her sleep again.

"Shhhh," I bury myself balls-deep in her wet heat. "I just need to feel you, baby." Moving in and out slowly is torture. Watching the way her body wraps around mine, the glistening coat of her arousal on my dick, the smell of us together... *Fuuuuck.* "Just a little more." I keep my pace steady and slow, relishing how tight she is. How beautiful.

Her pussy clamps down on my cock, making me suck in a harsh breath through my clenched teeth.

"Ryker," Tara whispers.

"Shhhh," I shove into her again. "Just let me have you for a little longer."

Her eyes crack open, and she smiles. "You can have me for life."

My heart trips over itself. I shove into her harder, making her slide up the bed. "I can't get enough of you." My thrusts stay steady and slow, but they're harsher now. "I don't think I'll ever get enough of you, Tara."

Her head tips back, but she doesn't say anything else. Maybe she's fallen back asleep. I hope so. I don't think I'd have the balls to say all this if she was fully alert. "You're mine." Rubbing her clit with my thumb, reading her little cues that tell me if she's hurting or not. I'm scared to death that clamp on her clit might have bruised her earlier, but she truly seems okay. Thank fuck for small miracles.

"Feels... so good." Her back arches, but her arms remain limp by her side.

This woman is putty in my hands. I pleasure her until she comes. Her pussy clamps down on my dick and milks it with her orgasm. "Ffffuck," she squeaks in a sleepy haze.

"Remember this." My release forces the air from my lungs. "Remember who owns this fucking pussy." I grunt, emptying myself into her. "You're mine now."

No one will touch her after tonight. I made a statement carrying her through my club. Every member now knows who she belongs to.

Specifically, Blake Rittenhouse. That smug bastard doesn't have the balls to test my tolerance. I'll cut his throat if he tries.

Pulling out, I shove my finger in her pussy like a plug. "That's my good girl." I kiss her inner thigh. "You're so good to me, baby."

She stirs again and I look up to see her catching me with my hand caught in her cookie jar. "Get back inside me," she whispers. "I want your dick in me while I sleep."

She's got to be kidding.

Joke or not, I'm going to fucking do it. Sliding

against her back, I roll Tara onto her side and drape her leg over my waist. Angling my cock at her entrance, Tara scoots closer and impales herself on me. "Shhh," she says, kissing my forehead. "Go to sleep."

...

My dreams are fractured and confusing. When I wake up, reaching for Tara, the last of my nightmares blow into snowflakes that freeze my heart. "Tara?" She's not here. Ripping the covers off me, I march into the bathroom and flick on the lights. "Tara?" She's not here either. Rushing across the room, I check the closet, the sofa, even under the fucking bed. "TARA!"

Snagging my cell, I quickly dial D's number. He doesn't answer. *Shit.* I snag my pants off the floor and start stuffing my legs in them when my cell goes off. "Tara's gone."

"I'm in your office," she responds on the other end of the line.

With my heart in my throat, I stare up at the surveillance camera in the corner of our suite. "You're in *my* office?"

"Yes."

"Alone?"

"No. Dmitri's here too."

I shove my finger at the camera. "Don't you *fucking* move." Rushing out of the suite, my vision blurs because of how tired I still am. What the fuck even time is it? The club's quiet, so it's after hours. A maid is vacuuming at the other end of the hallway and I almost trip over the cord as I beeline for the elevator.

Calm down. She's in your office. It's fine. She didn't

leave. She's not gone.

If this is what it'll be like to wake up without Tara at the end of the month, I won't survive it.

Storming down the hall, I shove my way through the door and stop dead in my tracks.

Tara's in my chair, a pencil holding her hair in a knot on the top of her head. "Good morning, sleepyhead." She beams me a smile full of sunshine.

The place smells like female and coffee. "You scared the fuck out of me."

"I wanted to give you space. You needed sleep, and I was too restless to stay still." Tara taps my monitor. "I was totally watching you like a creeper, too. You're sexy when you sleep."

Flattery will get her everywhere with me.

And now that I'm back in her orbit, my heart settles and panic lessens. "How long have you been up here?"

"Mmm." She looks at the clock on her laptop. "Only two hours. Dmitri brought me coffee and breakfast."

I'm both jealous and grateful he took care of my girl. I'd thank him if he hadn't already slipped out of here. "Why couldn't you sleep?"

"My head's too buzzy." She shrugs. "I just need to finish what I started, so it's really over."

There's a resignation letter on the screen. Kudos to her for having the spine to stick to her threats. "You're really quitting?"

"I never wanted to be in realty, anyway. I only did it to make my mom and William happy." She hits a button and the document closes. "It's time to be me."

God damn, I'm so fucking proud of her.

"What are you going to do now?" Whatever it

is, I'll help her.

"I don't know, honestly." Tara leans back and takes a sip of her coffee. "I might just take a break. I have money saved, so my bills won't be an issue for a while."

I'll make sure they aren't. I'm not too worried about her making ends meet, though. Getting a new job won't be a problem for her. Tara's smart as a whip and hard working. Any company would be lucky to have her.

Tara's fingers start flying across the keyboard, her brow knitted with concentration. "Annnnd…" She taps the mouse. "Done."

She's sent the letter. I can only imagine the fallout.

"I'm really proud of you," I say, kissing her head.

"Same." Tara runs her nails up my forearm. "So, what should we do today?"

"Whatever you want, Butterfly." The rooms are open and at her disposal. "Paddles. Whips. Chains. Hot wax."

"Whoa," she laughs. "You've been holding out on me, Mr. Hudson."

Yeah, I have. In so many ways. "I won't anymore."

"Good." She drops her laptop in the trashcan. "How about we start with a walk first? I want a clear mind before you blow me to pieces with that big dick of yours again."

God damn, I love this woman. Grabbing her hand, I pull her out of my chair. "Come on, Butterfly. I know the perfect place."

Chapter 42

Tara

After a long hot shower, complete with Ryker eating me for breakfast, we get dressed and head out of the club. No matter how many questions I ask, I can't figure out where he's taking me. The excitement's palpable between us and let me just say, Ryker Hudson has *the best* genuine smile I've ever seen.

Dressed in a charcoal grey t-shirt, dark jeans, and combat boots—he looks scrumptious as we walk over to one of three motorcycles parked in a row.

Ry hands me a helmet. "Put this on, Butterfly."

"I've never ridden on a motorcycle before." I think he likes being part of my first experience with many things, if I'm reading that grin of his correctly.

He climbs on the bike and holds it steady for me to mount up. Badass level unlocked!

I graze his ribs with my nails and hold his shirt while he starts the engine and backs us up. I'm so excited I could squeal.

"Hold on to me tighter than that, Tara." When I don't comply, the bike jerks forward and slams to a stop, making me crash into his back. My ass left the seat! Holy shit, that was scary. My grip tightens around him like an anaconda. "Good girl."

Ryker blazes through traffic, cutting between

cars. Every time I think I know which direction we're heading, I'm wrong. Twenty minutes later, we pull up to a butterfly conservatory. There's only one car in the parking lot.

Leaving my helmet on the seat, we walk towards the front door where there's a big, "CLOSED" sign.

"Damn." I would have loved to see this place. I've never been here before.

Ryker's not disappointed like me. Hell, he doesn't even seem surprised that it's closed. That devious smile is back on his handsome face as he pulls out his cell and texts someone.

I narrow my gaze. "What are you up to, Mr. Hudson?"

"No good." A few seconds tick by and the door opens. "Thanks for this, Max."

"Lock up when you're done." The employee hands him the keys and walks out.

"You got it." Ryker holds the door for me and tips his head. "After you."

Something tells me he had this planned in advance. "Are private tours another club perk?"

"No, it's a Ryker perk." He laces our fingers together and leads me through a lobby with a gift shop, educational posters, and a circular ticket desk. Bumping a black rubbery door with his back, we enter a dark space that's warm and muggy. "I think after this, I'll have entirely bared my soul to you," he says, pushing through another black door.

We step into a jungle.

Huge tropical trees, flowers, and low-lying plants give the vibe of a wild fairy forest. There's a well-worn yellow brick road painted on the concrete floor with little arrows guiding us through the building. A huge black butterfly net drapes two stories above us. It's incredibly humid and colorful. Long, skinny pedestals stick out of the ground with bowls full of watermelon slices and other fruits. Butterflies flutter all over the place—on branches, blooms, and the feeding bowls.

A tiny white one flies over Ryker's head and lands on the railing that keeps visitors from encroaching on their territory.

"That's a cabbage white." Ryker watches it closely. "They only live one to two weeks, usually."

I had no idea butterflies had such short lives. "She's so sweet." There's a tiny black dot on her wings that looks adorable. She takes off only to land on Ryker's head.

This is just too cute.

"That over there," he says, pointing at a blue and black one, "is a red-spotted purple butterfly. It likes to eat dead things, sap, rotten fruit, and shit."

"Tasty." I lean over the railing for a better look. The wings are almost metallic blue and I wonder if they'd feel like velvet. "How long do they live?"

"A week or two," he says, softly.

"Butterflies don't live very long."

"Nothing really does." He pushes away from the railing. The butterfly on his head flies off and heads over to a purple cone-shaped flower. "I used to come here a lot in the beginning."

We take our time strolling through the conservatory. There's so much to see and learn. The only sound in the place is from the mist machines and the trickle of an artificial water feature. It's lovely.

"Knox used to work here in high school. He'd

let me in through the back and I'd sit and just... *be*." Ryker drops onto a bench and stretches his arms over the back of it.

Directly across is a monarch plaque. The black and orange butterflies, however, are nowhere to be seen. Did they all die? Are they sleeping? Hiding?

Orange slices sit untouched on a plate by some rocks.

"What do monarchs eat?" I sit next to him.

"Nectar." His gaze slides over to me and slips down to the apex of my thighs. "They eat and reproduce a lot."

"Sounds like a good life."

Ryker huffs a laugh and looks up. "They like being in clusters."

Well, what do you know, there they are. A bunch flutter their wings slowly on the top of a tree. "They're a family."

He shakes his head, as if my answer is adorable. Resting my head against his shoulder, I close my eyes and let the warm, muggy air sink into my system. Ryker keeps quiet and runs his fingers along my arm.

I've never felt so peaceful before. So safe and content.

That this is only hitting me now has me wanting to say a million things, but I'm not about to ruin this moment with the hauntings of my past. Besides, it doesn't matter anymore.

Ryker kisses the top of my head. "What are you thinking?"

"Nothing."

"Liar."

"I don't want to say."

"This place has heard a lot of secrets, Tara. It's a

judgement free zone."

I can only imagine how many things a younger Ryker has said in this space when no one was around. He's baring his soul, bringing me here, showing me exactly why he named his club the Monarch. It's because life is beautiful and short. And the place where you can show your true nature should be safe and lovely. Judgement free.

Or maybe I'm overthinking it.

"You don't have to share if you really don't want to."

I know. "I was just thinking that this is the first time I've felt peace before."

Ryker's head lifts off mine, and he looks down at me with hard eyes. He clenches his molars.

"My mom had two other husbands before William. They were awful. It always starts out sweet and ends with them screaming at each other. Her boyfriends in between were worse. So much screaming and violence."

"Did..." He stops and takes in a breath. "Did any of them..."

"None of them ever raised a hand to me, if that's what you're worried about." He relaxes considerably. "All but Garret." He tenses again. "Honestly, I don't know if I blame him for hating me."

"He should have never laid a hand on you, Tara."

"Yeah, but I was a bitch to him." I sound like my mother excusing Garret's bad behavior. "Our parents got married when we were fifteen. He hated my mom because she looks a lot like his mother, who passed away a year prior to William dating my mom. I think my mom knew that because she dyed her hair dark when she started dating William and my mother's a natural dirty blonde like me. She never dyed her hair that color before."

"That's..."

"Speculation," I say, quickly. "Also a little unhinged."

"Why does Garret take his hate for her out on you?"

"Oh, I earned it. I slept with his best friend in high school. In his bed. During a party he was throwing."

"Damn."

"I didn't do it to piss him off. I was just curious and reckless and wanted to have fun. It was the first time I got spanked."

Ryker's brow lifts to his hairline. "How was it?"

"It was great. Too great. The harder he spanked, the louder I screamed. That caught Garret's attention, and he barged in just as his friend came all over my face."

He whistles.

"He hated me before, but he made life absolute *hell* after that. He's never stopped, honestly. In retaliation for sleeping with his bestie, the fucker cut the crotch out of all my underwear and wrote slut across my mirrors in black sharpie and on my face while I was sleeping."

"That's juvenile."

"Yeah, well, I put laxatives in his Gatorade sporadically to make up for it."

"You're diabolical."

"Aren't I?" Pride makes me less guilty about it. Fuck Garret. He's done worse to me, but I'm not going to tell Ryker about the worst parts. What's done is done. And now it's over. "Any anger he has now can be redirected elsewhere. I'm not going to take his Daddy's company, and I don't even want the trust fund William set up for me to have after I've put my time into Brisbane Realty. Garret can have it all, just like he's always wanted."

I twist around and straddle Ryker's lap.

I feel free. Untouchable.

Walking away from my troubles is already the best thing I've ever done for myself. And I'm sure the company is already buzzing with the mass email I sent saying goodbye and attaching my resignation letter for everyone to read.

My mother will have an aneurism when she finds out. Too bad, so sad. She'll get over it. I'm done bending over backwards so she can have a "happy life" with someone she "loves". It's bullshit and I'm over it.

"What are you thinking about now?" Ryker runs his hands through my hair, tucking some of it behind my ears.

"About us."

"What about us?"

Our time is up at the end of the month. What happens then? All my questions lodge in my throat.

Ryker holds the back of my head and brings me in for a kiss. "I'm not going anywhere, Butterfly. Are you?"

"No," I whisper, relief rushing through me. "I want to stay."

"Then stay," he whispers against my mouth. "Stay for however long you can."

A zebra striped butterfly lands on the back of the bench by his hand, reminding me how life is so fragile, so fleeting.

Ryker rubs his nose along my neck. He kisses and licks my sensitive skin, massaging the back of my head while he holds me in place on his lap. "Let me keep you."

I close my eyes and let the moment sweep me up into the fantasy that Ryker keeping me is actually possible.

Chapter 43

Ryker

Sitting smack dab in the middle of Heaven with my girl on my lap, her scent in my nose, and her taste on my tongue, I know what love is. It's peace. It's passion. It's bright and dark. It's wild and unshakeable.

I have no idea what part of Tara spoke to my soul first—her negotiation tactics, her innocent eyes, her blind trust, or her brutal honesty. Hell, it doesn't even matter what hooked me. She has me.

For now. For later. For life.

I'll spend every minute of my next ten lifetimes making her happy and showing her that even monsters can love fiercely.

Tara moans against my mouth as she deepens our kiss.

A fever builds between us. We go from peaceful contentment, to starved and unhinged. She scrapes her nails against my scalp, fucking my hair all up. My dick hardens in my jeans. Bent the wrong way makes it hurt and I like it.

She pulls my shirt off and scratches down the backs of my shoulders next. "Fuck, girl. You're killing me."

Tara's all rosy cheeks and red lips. Her pupils have blown wide already. "I want you." She tugs on my belt.

"You want it…" I get it off much faster for her. "Come get it."

Tara sinks to her knees and tugs my pants down to my ankles. Then she kicks off her shoes and shimmies out of her jeans. With my arms stretched across the back of the bench, I feel like a goddamn king.

But when my girl peels her pink panties down and shoves them in my mouth, I feel like a motherfucking god.

Tara sinks to her knees and takes my cock in her mouth. My fucking eyes cross when she deep throats me.

I didn't know she could do that.

Fuuuuck.

There are so many things to still learn about each other and I can't wait to explore us.

Tara reaches up and pulls her underwear out of my mouth slowly. "I want to hear you say my name."

"Make me."

She pulls my balls hard, making me groan. "Shhhiit, woman."

"That's not my name." Tara yanks them again.

"God damn."

"Not my name." She sucks one into her mouth and I groan.

"You feel so fucking good." Tara bites down and I holler, "Fuck!" Goosebumps erupt across my body. My motherfucking nipples are hard. "Bad girl."

She's not at all sorry.

Climbing onto my lap, she angles my dick to her entrance and sinks down slowly. We both groan when I bottom out. "Do you like me bad, Mr. Hudson?"

"I like you every way you want to be, Butterfly." There's no way I want her thinking she has to morph herself into some mold I want. My girl needs to be her authentic self. Always. "I like you just as you are."

Tara's speed slows down on my cock. Rocking back and forth in waves, she closes her eyes and tips her head back. "Fuck, you feel so good." Her breaths ripple out of her. I pull off her shirt so I can suck on her tits. "Oh god, Ryker." She holds my head and this time I let her.

Biting her nipple through her bra, I love how she cries out. The humidity makes sweat drip down our bodies faster. It's hard to breathe. Tara whimpers as she rides me faster, chasing a release.

"Get off on me, baby. Use me."

Her eyes lock with mine and she stills.

"I want you to use me." Submission has never felt so right. "*Please.*"

Tara swallows hard and nods. She knows what this means to me. She knows what I'm handing over to her. I trust her not to break my newfound power. "You feel so good."

I'm glad.

"I feel you in every part of my body." She rolls her hips back and forth. "You're everywhere inside me."

Damn, I hope that's true. Digging my fingers into her ass cheeks, I grind her harder against me and lift my hips to drive into her deeper. Harder.

"Holy fuck." Her nails dig into my shoulders. "I'm so close."

Gripping her throat, I apply just enough pressure to send her over the edge. She shudders as her orgasm grips around my cock. I jack my hips up, slamming into her over and over while holding her throat. "I fucking love you, *Tara*."

She cries out harder.

My release barrels into me because I've never felt so real and raw in my life. There's nothing but honesty. Realness. The pleasure and the promise of this moment. Anything beyond now isn't guaranteed.

Sweat drips down my back as I bounce her on my lap. If I'm being honest, she owns me, not the other way around. I'll follow her through all this life and into the next if she'll let me. Tara pinches my nipples, twisting them, and I come so hard I see stars.

When we're both too exhausted to move anymore, she collapses on my chest. Our hearts smash against one another as we catch our breath. "Holy shit, that was amazing, Ry."

Butterflies flutter, landing all around us. I kiss her forehead and run my hands up and down her back. "I think I could stay like this forever."

"Me too."

Eventually, we manage to peel apart and get dressed. For the next hour and a half, we circle the conservatory, and I tell her about every butterfly in the building. She probably thinks I'm a fucking geek.

She'd be right.

"Thank you for bringing me here," Tara says, once we close things up and get back on my bike.

I wrap her arms around my waist and start the engine. "Where to next, Butterfly?"

Chapter 44

Tara

Relaxing in bed, I stuff a grape in my mouth, and wait for Ryker to get out of the shower. It takes a lot of control to not join him in there, but I need a break. My pussy aches and I don't think I can go another round just yet.

My man's an animal.

I can't wait until everyone knows he's mine.

When he asked where I wanted to go, I told him back to the club because I couldn't wait to get naked with him again.

A familiar sound chimes from under the bed. I have no clue how my cell got under there, but I'm tempted to let it keep ringing. Only I know exactly who it is. I swear my phone sounds more annoying when my mother is calling.

Digging it out from under the bed, I answer with an eye roll. "Hi, Mom."

"Tara Marie Reed. How could you?"

Guilt tries to take hold of my mouth and make me apologize. I stomp it down and tear it to pieces. I have nothing to be sorry about. "What did I do this time?"

"Don't play stupid." I forgot how she likes to call me that when she's extra mad. "You've broken your father's heart."

My laugh comes out in a cackle. "You're so delusional, Mom."

"I raised you better than this, Tara." She huffs into the phone, and I inwardly cringe when she adds, "You're such a disappointment."

Ryker comes out of the shower, still drying his hair. He approaches me cautiously, seeing I'm on the phone. I can't look at him when I'm on this call. It'll mess me up. I'm already fighting my inner demons here and I don't want to have to be braver just to impress Ryker. I want to be braver for myself and only myself.

"You know what, Mom? *You're* the disappointment." I can't believe I just said that. "If William's heartbroken, it's because he finally realizes what a gold-digging, lying, cheating, greedy woman you are."

She doesn't make a sound.

Fine. Because I've got plenty more to say. "Do you understand that I've spent my whole life thinking I'm the hinge on your relationships? I've carried the guilt that every time you broke up with your fool ass men, it was somehow *my* fault."

"It was!"

"Bullshit." I yell, shoving my finger at the floor. "It's been your fault every time. I was just a kid, mom. A kid who did what she was told. I didn't get an opinion. I didn't get anything but the privilege of following your orders so you could land a rich man and have a cushy life. I swear, you loved your wardrobe more than you ever loved me."

Her silence doesn't last long. "How can you say such hateful things to me? I sacrificed everything to have you."

"I know." God, I'm so sick of having this conversation with her. "You never miss an opportunity to remind me."

"And yet you're still so ungrateful."

I hate her. "I took up golf in high school because you wanted me to make a good impression when William took me and Garret out on Sundays for two whole years."

"Yes. And he paid for your golf lessons."

She's missing the point. "I got a fucking business degree and a real estate license."

"And your father gave you a high-paying job and huge bonuses every year."

She's still missing the point. "I never wanted to be in real estate. I never wanted to golf. Jesus, I wanted to be a *chef*, Mom!"

"Oh please. The only thing you've ever made was that damn pudding. You would have failed. Your father gave you success, and that's all thanks to *me*."

"William is *not* my father. Neither was Steve or Randy or any of the other rich dipshits you tried to bag." My heart pounds in my chest and my cheeks tingle. I feel sick. "I've spent my life doing everything you told me to, so *you* would be happy. I'm done. It's over. Me quitting Brisbane Realty isn't the end. I'm never stepping foot in William's house again. He's not my family."

"Why are you doing this?" she screeches. "I don't understand."

That makes me pause. Now I feel terrible because she didn't know what happened at brunch when I stormed out. "William wanted me to fuck whoever I had to so I could get the Greene Street property before the auction."

She's silent. I latch onto the possibility that she finally understands why I've quit. I brace for her to be furious on my behalf. I hold my breath, feeling lighter because maybe now she won't be so mad at me for what I've done. Maybe she's proud of me for sticking up for myself and walking away with my dignity and power.

"Would it kill you to bend a little?"

I almost drop the phone. "*Excuse me?*"

"Tara. Be real. It's just a little nudge. If you can use your assets to help your father land an important piece of property, what's the big deal?"

I'm speechless.

"Honey," she says, like it's cute that I'd be offended by William's demands.

"Fuck you." The words fall out of my mouth. "You're supposed to protect me."

"From what?" She laughs. "Tara, you're not in any danger. This is such a small thing."

No, it's a huge thing. The biggest. "You don't care about me at all, do you?"

"Of course, I do."

Bullshit. "What about when Garret slammed me against the sliding glass door last Christmas?" My eyes narrow. "You *did* see it, didn't you?"

"You pushed him too far."

"Giving him a present is pushing him too far?" What is wrong with her?

"It was your attitude when you gave it to him, Tara. You're always so nasty."

Something deadly grows in my chest. "He tried to strangle me last week."

"What did you to do to piss him off?"

Unbelievable. The deadly calmness inside turns

to numbness.

My voice shakes as I pace across the room. "I've made excuses for you my whole life," I say quietly, while my inner child shrinks. "I took the blame for your problems. I carried the guilt for your actions. I've been miserable, so you can be happy." When she doesn't say a word, I swear that inner voice always telling me everything's my fault and I should try harder to be better for everyone becomes mute.

When that happens, something else grows in my belly. Rage. It spreads like wildfire in my system, pushing lava in my veins, smoke in my heart, flames in my mind.

"You are a shit mother. You're an even shittier wife. All you do is hop off one dick and straight onto another. By the way, how was *Travis*? Let me guess, thin and long, curved like a banana? I know you prefer them hanging to the left. Bet he's promised to take you far away from grumpy old William. Not like you're leaving with anything in your pocket when you divorce. He was just as smart as your last two husbands and had you sign a prenup. But you don't care because you've already got your next target lined up." I shake my head in disgust. "You only switch men when you think you've found a fatter bank account to suck dry." And William probably already knows because he made that awful—and accurate—dig about my mom at brunch.

"I can't believe you're saying this to me. My *god*, Tara. I'm so disappointed."

"That makes both of us, then." I hang up and throw my phone across the room.

Ryker approaches cautiously, dressed in jeans again. "Are you okay?"

"No." Trembling, I cover my face and try to hold myself together. Saying all that to my mom was terrifying and overdue. I'm a mix of guilt and pride about it.

He steps closer. "Can I touch you?"

"Y-yes." I can't breathe. I think I'm going to throw up. "I feel sick."

"Shhhh." He folds me into his chest and holds me tightly. The pressure of his embrace lets me fall to pieces. I scream-cry until the room darkens. It's ugly. Years of rage and hate blast out of me until I'm a sobbing mess in his arms. He sinks us to the floor and rocks me back and forth. "You did so good, baby."

"I feel like the worst daughter in the world."

"You're not." He clasps my cheeks, forcing me to look at him. "You're *not*. You're a brave, strong woman who just did the greatest thing in the world. You took back your power." He kisses my forehead hard. "You stood up for yourself." He kisses my cheeks. "You know your worth and you made damn sure everyone else does, too." He kisses my mouth and the world swirling around us faster and faster finally slows down.

I'm suddenly so exhausted I can barely keep my eyes open. The fight's out of me. I have nothing left to give. At some point, I fall asleep in his lap on the floor, and he carries me to bed.

When I wake up, Ryker's gone.

Chapter 45

Ryker

It's three in the morning. After tucking Tara in bed, I held her for a while and whispered a million things to her while she lightly snored against me. I didn't touch her, except to kiss her forehead before I left. I'm too wired to sleep. There's a tornado of things swirling in my mind.

Knocking on Dmitri's dungeon door, I wait for him to say, "Come in."

His room smells like a light musk, leather, and something unmistakably Dmitri. He's over by a punching bag, swinging his fists which are already bloody. "What's up?"

"I need to go out for a bit. Can you watch over her for me until I get back?"

He punches the bag one more time, then gives me a hard frown. "Yeah. No problem." The bag swings like a hefty pendulum and D stops it before it hits him. "What's going on?"

Too much. "I just need to clear my head."

D's brow digs down, making him look scarier than usual. "Need help with something?"

What a loaded question. "No." My ass drops onto the cot he sleeps on. I'll never understand why D likes to live this way. He's got plenty of money yet lives like he's still the poor kid from Paxton Street. "I saw your flowers on her grave. I didn't know you still went there."

The only emotion he shows is a flinch of his bottom lip. "Yeah, well, I miss her too, you know. You're not the only one who lost a mom that day."

Sometimes I forget how her death affected more than just me. We all dealt with her loss differently. I'd shoved my grief in a hole and kept it buried for so long, I barely recognize it now that it's resurfaced. It doesn't bite and slice anymore. There's just a small pinch that comes and goes. Like a butterfly with razors on her feet, landing on my heart to let me know that the shriveled organ can still feel things. Then she flies off again.

What does it feel like for Dmitri?

Vault and Knox?

Natalie?

"She loved you." My elbows dig into my knees as I lean forward and stare up at him. "She loved all of us. No matter what." We could never do wrong in my mom's eyes. She'd excuse our bad behavior even after she scolded us for it.

D leans against the concrete wall and crosses his arms. Sweat drips down his bare chest, and even in the low light, I can see all his scars. He's been through Hell and there's no telling when he'll crawl out. "Remember when we thought it was a good idea to set fireworks off the rooftop?"

I'll never forget it. Knox almost blew his damn hand off, trying to fuck with one that fell over after he lit it. Vault tackled him backwards just before the thing blew up. We accidentally melted a big hole in the rubber roofing pads and the rocket shot off in the wrong direction, crashing into the side of the brick building across the street. The cops were called. We all hid in my apartment and pretended we were innocent. My mom totally lied for us and said we'd been playing video games all night under her supervision.

I didn't even own a gaming console…

"Have a good night, officer." Mom shuts and locks the door, then spins on us with a mix of anger, fear, and adrenaline. "Don't you ever do that again!"

"Yes, ma'am." Vault holds a paper towel to his hand because he'd cut it shoving Knox out of the way of the rogue firework. "We're sorry."

"Ohhh, you boys are going to be the death of me." Mom marches over with her hands on her hips, glowering at us. Her stern expression melts almost instantly, and she ruffles my hair. "I'm just glad no one was seriously hurt. What would I do without my boys?" She grabs a first aid kit out of the bathroom and helps Vault with his hand while the rest of us devour a bunch of grilled cheese sandwiches. "They were really pretty, though."

Vault's eyes light up because we've all been forgiven. "Did you see the swirly gold one?"

"Yeah, that was amazing." My mom beams him a huge smile. Then her brow bunches up. "Not sure how I feel about you four being pyrotechnicians though."

"I'm not a fan," Knox shivers. "I nearly blew my balls off."

We all start laughing, my mom included, and then she doubles over and winces.

Shit. "You okay, Mom?"

"I'm fine." She holds her hand up to stop me from coming over. "I think I ate something that's upset my stomach."

I don't like how often she says those words. And my

mom hasn't eaten anything all day that I know of. "How about you go to bed. We'll be quiet for you."

"Don't you dare." *She starts coughing, which also makes her hold her stomach.* "Boys are supposed to be loud. I want my home filled with noise. I'll be fine. I'm just going to lie down for a bit."

"Want us to save you a grilled cheese for later, Miss Ashley?" *Knox takes a big bite out of his third one.*

"No, baby. You guys eat those up." *She says goodnight and heads into her room, shutting the door softly...*

A week later she was diagnosed with cancer.

"You know," I say, half grinning. "We're still pretty loud." The club music blasting from upstairs proves it.

What would my mother say if she knew what kind of man I've turned into?

"She'd be proud of you, Ry." Dmitri pushes off the wall and swaggers across the room to snag a water from his mini fridge. "I'm proud of you."

I gotta go. I can't do this yet. I thought I was ready, but I'm not. "I'll be back in a couple hours."

"K."

My molars hurt from how hard I grind them. After grabbing bolt cutters from the basement storage room, I set out for the night. Sometimes when I go for a ride on my bike, my intrusive, suicidal thoughts scream loudly. Tonight, they don't say a word.

The streets turn into a maze for me to snake through, a path that leads me to a finish line I could find in my sleep.

Greene Street is quiet this time of night. It's dark

and eerie. The streetlamps illuminate graffiti painted on the side of my old apartment building, and the alley is filled with trash and broken furniture. Pulling out my bolt cutters, I break the lock on the door and kick it open.

Mildew and stale air invade my nose. My boot steps echo up the stairwell. Stumbling out onto the roof, cool air smacks my face. There's a dead pigeon, some broken beer bottles, and yup, it's still here. The melted spot from the fireworks all those years ago.

Jesus, they never did anything to improve this place. It's a shithole now, just like it was a shithole then.

But it was *home*.

My best and worst memories were built in this brick biohazard building.

Heart pounding, palms sweating, I stalk over to the edge and look down. Wind blows around me, swirling like my thoughts. A car zooms below, blasting music. The traffic lights keep changing even though there's no one around to follow them.

Life, even in the darkest hour, keeps going.

Taking a deep breath, my chest balloons out with a roar I unleash into the night. I scream until there's nothing left in my lungs. Nothing left in me. No fight. No anger. No remorse.

No shame.

All my life, I did the best I could for myself, for my mom, and for my friends. No, it wasn't ideal, but I've made it this far. I need to keep going.

Tara's beautiful face fills my mind. What she did for herself today bolsters my need to do what I've been too scared of for so long. She knows her worth. She might have been afraid to stand up for herself, but she fucking did it, anyway. She's grabbing life by the balls and will have it kneeling at her feet. Whatever she does from here on out, it'll be great.

I can't wait to watch her spread her wings and fly.

Teetering on the ledge, I close my eyes and let the city smog, iridescent lights, and darkness sink into me.

I escorted because I had to.

I run a sex club now because I want to.

There's a difference. Yes, I had a choice in both, but it didn't feel that way when I was younger. Now I have power. Money. Friends who are my family. I've got a good thing going with Tara, too. I've found a woman who balances me out, plays with my demons and lets me play with hers.

Maybe my life was supposed to have all the bad shit happen in the beginning, so the rest of my days would be amazing and *good*.

Would my mother be proud of the man I've become? I hope so. I'm happy. That's all she ever wanted for me. I'm happy, successful, and safe. I've embraced the dark parts of me and built a world to live in that I love.

I truly *love* the Monarch. I love the life I have with my found family. I love that I'm able to give others a safe space to explore themselves. I love that I can provide and protect.

But it isn't enough.

"This is it." I squat down and perch on the ledge, rocking on my heels. If I was a little less stable, I'd fall.

Saliva builds on my tongue.

Tipping my head back, I shoot a load of spit out of my mouth and watch it disappear in the air before it hits the ground.

"Enough."

My thighs burn when I climb down.

"I'm done."

With every step I take away from the ledge, more and more weight lifts off me. I don't even notice the smell of the building when I take the steps all the way to the floor of my old apartment. Halting at the windowsill with the words still etched in the wood, my heart cracks open.

You're worth more than this.

Yeah, I am. Back then, I thought I was only worth what someone would pay for me. I built a life based on that. Now, I know I'm worth more than staying stunted in my anger over a past I cannot change. I'm worth finding happiness. Love. Acceptance.

I'm worth giving myself some motherfucking grace.

It's time to build the life I deserve.

Pulling my cell out, my deft fingers fly across the screen. Knox picks up on the fourth ring, his sleepy voice gravelly. "What the fuck man, you okay?"

"I'll give you the money." My heart thuds heavily in my chest. "However much you need to get your club up and running, it's yours. I'll fund it all."

Muffled shuffling noises fill my ear. I guess Knox is climbing out of bed. "Did you lose Greene Street?"

"No." I laugh, realizing how easy and right this choice is. "I don't want it anymore."

"Ry..."

"I've got a little over a million I can give. If you

need more, I'll figure something out and make it happen."

"Holy shit, Ryker." Now he's fully awake. "I... I can't let you do this. I'll fuck it up."

"No, you won't. You love that club, man. You've put your heart into it." Why's he backpedaling?

"Pop's will fuck it up for me. I know it." Knox's voice is low and shaky. "I appreciate the offer, Ry, but I can't take it. It'll be for nothing."

"I'll have my lawyers draw up a contract. We'll buy it from your father." That way, Knox will never have to put up with that bastard's bullshit again. "He'll sell it to us."

"I'm not sure he will. What if Brisbane Realty has offered more?"

"I'll take care of it." Or rather, me, Vault, and Dmitri will for him.

"Jesus." Knox sighs on the other end. "You sure you want to invest in me like this?"

"Motherfucker, don't ask me dumb questions like that." Besides, I've already given up startup money to get him this far. Me and D split it. "You deserve that club, brother. It's your baby."

Just like the Monarch is mine.

"We've got your back, Knox. The money is yours. And once we're done talking with your pops, that fucking club will be too."

"I... I don't know what to say."

"Say you're happy." I shove off the steps and leave the building.

"I'm... fuck... yeah. If this really happens, I'll be the happiest sonofabitch on this side of the bridge."

"Good. I'll call you after I have the paperwork drawn up. Get some sleep, bro. You're gonna need it."

I hang up on him.

There's a pep in my step when I straddle my bike. The brick structure that's haunted me for over a decade doesn't look so ominous and powerful anymore.

My cell rings again and the dopey smile I get makes my voice draw out in a playful, "Hey, Butterfly."

"Where are you?"

"Just went for a ride."

"Are you okay?"

God love her. "I'm way better than okay, baby. I'm heading home now."

"You know where to find me when you get here."

Fuck right I do. "Be naked for me."

"Already am, Mr. Hudson."

I blow every red light to get home where I belong.

Chapter 46

Tara

I have no clue what happened to Ryker three nights ago, but he's different. There's a goofy smile on his face that won't quit. He's talkative. Happy. Relaxed.

As much as I'd love to take credit for this shift in him, not even my pussy has that much power.

Yesterday we fucked in a room full of mirrors. The day before that, he taught me tricks on a spinning circular bed positioned in the center of a big voyeur room. No one was there to watch us, but I enjoyed imaging we had a full house. Maybe I have an exhibition kink I should explore more.

I've been straddling his lap all morning in his office, feeling content as a house cat while he clicks away on the computer.

The Monarch is heaven on earth. I never want to leave. "You know, I thought thirty days as the Butterfly was a little overkill."

He tips his office chair back and rocks us. "Oh yeah?"

"That's a long time to be with someone."

"Are you saying you're sick of me, Miss Reed?"

On the contrary. "No, I'm saying I *thought* it was overkill, but now I don't think it's long enough."

We haven't discussed what will happen once

my time here is up. I haven't had the courage to discuss it until now.

Ryker's jaw ticks as he stares at me. "Do you want to stay?"

I'm not sure how to take his tone. "Do you *want* me to stay?"

"Answer my question first, Tara."

That's not a yes or a no. He's making me claim what I want for myself first.

My stomach knots. We were supposed to be temporary. This wasn't meant to last. We started this with a negotiation, but I can't wheel and deal with the terms anymore. This isn't a contract, it's love.

Fuck it. I'm going for what I want and damn the consequences. "I want to stay."

"Good, I was afraid I'd have to handcuff you to my bed like my prisoner to keep you."

Be still my fluttering heart. "I mean… no one's stopping you from still doing that."

He flashes me a brilliant smile and smacks my ass. "You keep saying all the right things."

I'm just being honest.

"So…" I arch my brow at him. "Are we a thing now, Mr. Hudson?"

"We're definitely a thing." His hips jack up and he grinds against me. "We're a big thing."

"You're insatiable." And my panties are soaked again. "My god, that dick of yours is going to snap off from overuse."

"I'll just fuck you with my tongue if it does. I'm ready to accept my fate." His cell rings, breaking our spell. "Yeah?" Ryker stares at me while the person on the other end talks. "Perfect. Thanks." He hangs up and dials another number. The sexy smile on his face transforms into a bigger, broader one. It makes him look younger. "It's yours, Knox."

All kinds of loud screaming blasts out and Ryker holds the phone away from his ear. He laughs so hard his face turns red and eyes water.

That kind of happiness hits me square in the feels.

"Alright, alright. Yeah, I'll tell 'em." Ryker rubs his forehead, still chuckling. "Let me ask the boss first." He tugs my hair playfully. "Can we go out to dinner tonight?"

"We can do anything you want every night."

Ryker's eyes twinkle. "She says yes, but you gotta make that fondue I like, or she won't join us." He belts out another laugh and hangs up. Tossing his phone on the desk, he rocks back, grabbing my ass again, still smiling.

"Are you going to tell me what's going on, or is it secret Monarch business and I'm just your means to cheese fondue?"

"I just bought Knox's club for him."

Wait. What? "How, I mean..." There's no way he can afford to do that. "I thought you didn't have the funds to help him and also get Greene Street."

"I don't." His smile gets even bigger. "I'm not bidding on Greene Street anymore."

I'm so confused. "I thought that property was important to you."

"It was." Ryker slides his chair away from the desk and lifts me up. My legs wrap around him like a belt. "But I'm tired of clinging to my past when I can grip better things."

"Like my ass?" I joke, because I have no clue how to handle this news.

"Like a future with you." He sets me down on his desk. The clanking of his belt unbuckling makes my pussy clench.

"A future with me sounds really nice."

"Fuck yeah it does." He pulls his shirt off my body. I'd put it on this morning because it still carries his cologne, and the scent comforts me. "Do you think you can put up with me for longer than thirty days, Butterfly?" He pushes his dick into me, and it slides right in with how wet I am.

"Maybe," I say, breathless from his thrusts. The papers under my ass crinkle and some fall to the floor. "But it'll cost you."

"Name your price, Miss Reed."

"Forever." I clutch his shoulders to stay upright. "My price is *you* forever."

"Done." He smashes his mouth to mine and slams into me harder and harder until we're both screaming through our orgasms. When we sink back into reality, I wait for him to joke around and back-peddle.

He doesn't.

Neither do I.

"We've got a few hours before the Monarch opens." Ryker squats down and spreads my legs. "Anything special you want to do, baby?"

Nnnnope. Especially not when he drags his tongue along my pussy and eats me like I'm pudding. "God, Ry, you're gonna kill me."

Laying back on the desk with my feet perched on his shoulders is a great way to die, though.

"Poor Butterfly can't flutter anymore." He shoves two fingers into my cunt and rubs my g-spot. "Oh, maybe she can."

He drives my lust higher and higher until my soul lifts from my body and hovers over us. My orgasm is hard and messy and exhausting. I'm going to need a nap before dinner. "You keep fucking me up like this, I won't have the strength to walk tonight. I'll be crawling on my hands and knees to dinner with you and Knox."

Ryker groans. "Fuuuck, Tara. Do *not* remind me of that day. You looked so fucking good like that, and I'm not giving Knox another view of your spectacular ass again. I learned my lesson."

I grin. "Well, maybe I'll just crawl for you here before we leave."

"Fuck, woman." He kisses me so hard our teeth clack. Holy shit, his intensity has no limits. I love it.

"Where is dinner tonight?"

"Knox's underground club."

Nice. "What do you want me to wear?"

"Whatever you want, Butterfly."

Again, he's giving me a chance to be myself. I don't have to dress to impress his friends, which is different for me considering I have an entire section of floral prints for when I meet with my stepfather.

"I have the perfect outfit." I've only worn it once, but it made me feel like a million bucks.

"We can go get it from your house in a bit. I just have to finish a few more orders and sign invoices. Shit, I can't forget to make sure the kitchen's—"

"You stay here." I shove him back into his chair. "I'm just gonna grab it and a couple other things, then come right back. I won't be more than an hour."

…

You know what love is? It's blasting songs on the radio with the windows down, while wearing your man's t-shirt, a set of cotton shorts, and a goofy smile on your face. It's breaking speed limits so you can hurry up and get back to him. It's laughing for no reason other than you're insanely happy.

Wow. I can honestly say I've never felt this level of elation before. Not with anyone.

I can't help but think I've made a difference in Ryker, just like he's made one in me. That deal I made to be the Butterfly has turned out to be the best negotiation of my motherfucking life.

Yeah, we both have a long way to go with our personal issues, but this is a great start.

Opening the door to my apartment, I'm distracted by my cell ringing. With a sweet sing-songy tone, I answer. "Yes, Mr. Hudson?"

"Is it pathetic that I miss you already?"

"Very." I giggle. "You're positively *obsessed*." I love that for me. "You need an intervention."

"Are you there yet?"

"Just walked in." I drop my keys on the table and head to my bedroom. "I should only be like fifteen minutes." I rip open my underwear drawer to grab a few lacy ones. My heart stutters with confusion. Holding a pair of silk panties up, my mouth runs dry. "Shit."

"What's wrong?" Ryker's aggressive tone funnels into my ear.

"I…" There's no way I can tell him someone has cut out the crotch to my underwear. *All* of my fucking underwear. Each one I pick up has been shredded. "Oh my god."

"Tara," Ryker growls. "What the fuck's

wrong?"

Fear floods my system. My mouth runs dry. My heart stops.

I turn around and drop my phone.

Garret's sitting on my bed with a knife in his hand.

Chapter 47

Tara

He doesn't look up from the knife he's playing with. "Where have you been, Tara?"

"Get out!" I scream.

How the hell did he get in here? I changed the code. This can't be happening.

"You've been gone a long time, little sister." Garret stands up and cracks his neck. "Where the fuck have you been?"

He lunges to grab me, and I pivot, dashing out of the bedroom, screaming for help. He slams into my back, tackling me to the ground, and I fall flat on my face. Pain radiates down my spine and my nose runs, blood dripping onto the carpet.

Pulling my hair by the roots, he yanks my head back and growls in my ear, "You and I have played this game for way too long. You're such a fucking tease."

"Please don't do this." I don't know if he's going to hurt me or kill me. I'm not giving him a chance to do either. Kicking relentlessly, I manage to get one leg free and smash him in the belly with my heel.

His grip doesn't loosen. "You're just like your mother. A gold-digging, disgusting cunt. Do you know what cunts are for?"

"Garret, stop." I kick him again. "Get away from

me!"

"I'm not going to do anything you don't want me to do, little sister. I know how you like it." He grabs my ankle and drags me back a few feet before I'm able to escape him again.

I scramble to my feet and run into the living room.

He follows me, palming the knife. "You want the sharp end, or the handle inside you first?"

Dizziness makes me sway. "Garret. Please."

"That's a good girl. *Beg for me.*"

Tears spill down my face. I can't get my legs to work anymore. I'm frozen in place. "Listen to me." Tossing my hands up won't block his blows, but it's all I can think of as I back away from him a little more. "I quit! Do you hear me? I walked away from *everything*. I don't want any of Brisbane's money. It's all yours. It's over."

He punches me in the face, making me spin and crash to the floor. My fucking ears ring. He flips me onto my back and straddles me.

"No!" I slap at him, trying to knock the knife out of his hand. "Garret, *stop!*"

His next punch lands square in my stomach, making me curl up and wheeze. White dots burst in my vision. It stuns me so fast, I don't fight when he rips my shorts down. I just keep gasping for air, feebly smacking at him.

"I've been dying to fuck this pussy up since we were fifteen." He presses the blade to me, sharp side up, and terror floods my system. *Oh my god, oh my god.*

"Don't."

"I saw you first." He drags the blade down my inner thigh, slicing me. "You were *mine first.*" He cuts deeper. "Maybe my name on your body will remind you of that."

Searing pain rips me out of my paralyzing fear, turning me into a whirlwind of panic. Kicking, swinging, and clawing, a burst of rage consumes me.

Which makes what happens next absolutely terrifying.

Chapter 48

Ryker

Don't ask me how I make it to Tara's apartment as fast as I do. I don't remember leaving my office. I don't remember calling my boys. I don't remember getting on my bike. I don't remember climbing the steps to her floor. I don't remember kicking down her door.

But I will always remember her face when she sees me.

Tara sits on the floor with a knife in her hands. She's bloody. Shaking. Hyperventilating. When she sees me rushing towards her, my girl scrambles over to me on her hands and knees.

"I'm okay, I'm okay, I'm okay." She claws her way into my arms and wraps herself around me. "I'm okay."

The fuck she is.

All my aggression funnels into a soft, calm, deadly tone. "Where is he, baby?" After a quick scan around the living room, I find the sonofabitch lying flat on his back behind the couch. "Is he dead?"

"I don't think so." Tara's shaking like a leaf. "I hit him in the back of the head with... with..."

I don't think she remembers.

"Shhh." Stroking her hair, my mind races with which action to take first. Kill him or comfort her.

Garret groans from the floor and Tara squirms violently out of my arms. She stumbles around the couch and punt kicks the motherfucker square in the ribs.

It looks like she's done that a few times already, now that I'm closer.

"Fuck you!" She spits on him. "Fuck you!" she screams again. "I *hate* you. You sick *fuck*!"

My girl's unhinged, and she's scared out of her goddamn mind.

That's when I see the blood dripping down her legs.

Fuck. *NO*.

Tara wipes the blood dripping from her nose with the back of her hand. "He didn't touch me," she says loudly. I wonder if her ears are ringing like mine are. "He didn't rape me." Her body trembles. "He… he didn't get the chance. He didn't…"

I'm on her in a flash. "You did so good, baby." I kiss her forehead, driving her backwards with a firm grip on her arms. "I'm so fucking proud of you."

She deftly walks backwards, letting me steer her out of the apartment. "Look at me, Tara." She's not shaking so violently anymore. That's a good sign. "I need you to go outside and wait for D and the others."

Her brow pinches. "Others?"

"Yeah." I roll up my sleeves. "Can you do that for me, Butterfly?"

Her eyes are bloodshot and glassy. "What are you going to do?"

I shake my head. The less she knows, the better.

"Don't kill him," she says, grabbing my arm. Her nails bite into my skin and the sharp pain grounds me a little. "I don't want him dead."

I do. "He's not worth saving, Tara."

"But *you* are." Tears slip down her face. "The fear of you going to jail is way worse than the fear of him coming after me again."

Emotions catch in my throat as a stampede storms up the stairwell and Dmitri busts through the door. Vault and Knox are right behind him.

D's gaze sails down her body, landing on her bloody thighs. "Tara, are you..." The horror in his eyes lances my heart. "Did he..." Fuck, D can't even finish that sentence.

I shake my head, answering for her.

Hearing my girl scream on the other end of the line while I was miles away from her will give me nightmares for the rest of my life. I think the only reason I'm calm right now is because the severity of the situation still hasn't completely sunk in yet.

Dmitri pulls Tara in for a hug. "We've got you, baby girl." He looks over at me and the kindness he shows Tara transforms to cruelty when he asks me, "What do you want to do with him?"

"Carry him out through the back alley and back to the club."

Tara doesn't want me to kill him, but I'll make damn sure this motherfucker wishes he was dead by the time we're through with him.

...

Seven hours later, I think I've made my point. Garret's in and out of consciousness, so I can't really ask him to repeat all the lessons in manners we've taught him.

Our session in the basement took longer than I

realized. Once I started swinging, I couldn't stop. Dmitri and the others had to pry me off the sorry piece of shit several times because they knew I'd turn him to pulp. Fuck, I wanted to kill him so badly, the dimly lit basement hazed red. I couldn't think straight.

"Go to your girl," D ordered, and I obeyed. Splitting my energy between comforting Tara upstairs and protecting her down here might have driven me insane.

I need to see her. Touch her. Kiss every wound and cocoon her in my safe arms.

But halfway up to the Butterfly suite, I stall out. Shit, I should shower and change before I see Tara. She'll know I'm a monster if she sees me covered in this much blood.

A quick pivot and I'm on a detour. My plan to spare her the gory mess fails when I find her in my office with Sophie guarding the door.

My furious gaze says it all. She was supposed to stay with Tara in the Butterfly suite. She should have followed my motherfucking orders.

"I wasn't about to stop her," Sophie says, putting her hands up like this wasn't her idea.

She steps out of my way, and I open the door.

Tara sits in my chair, her beautiful face glowing from the monitors. Her eyes are puffy, and the tip of her nose is red. I don't have to look to know she's watched what we've done to her stepbrother on the surveillance footage.

Fuck.

"I told you I was a monster." And now she knows the lengths I'll go to for her.

Tara doesn't cringe. She doesn't run. Hell, she doesn't even *blink* as she calmly closes the space between us and cups my cheeks with a steady hand. "You're *my* monster."

When it comes to those I love, there's no line I won't cross for them.

"Take me to him, Ry."

Hell no. "That's not a good idea."

"*Ryker*."

Shit. Why deny her request when she's watched the carnage already? Maybe it's better if she sees. Maybe it'll paint a clearer picture of who she belongs to.

Please don't run away when you see what I've done for you.

Silently leading her through the club and down past Dmitri's dungeon, we dump into an old utility room. The scent of blood, sweat, and piss is pungent.

The instant Tara sees her stepbrother tied to a chair, blood pouring out of his swollen face, his arms bent in the wrong direction, and legs cut up, she freezes.

Bringing her down here was a bad fucking idea. D, Vault, and Knox are all glaring at me with *What the fuck is wrong with you* looks on their faces.

Tara quietly prowls closer to Garret. "Which one of you did that to his face?"

We all took turns. She'll have to be more specific about the injury she's referring to. "Does it matter?" I ask.

"Yes." She won't look away from her stepbrother.

"Me," I answer. "The others got their shots in after they dragged me away for a breather."

Tara's exhale rattles out of her. "Is he going to live?"

I hope not, but probably. "Didn't cut anything vital."

She nods and licks her lips. "Dmitri." Tara blindly holds her hand out. "Give me your knife."

"I don't have one."

"I do." Knox lifts his into the air.

I step between them and hand her my switchblade. If she's going to use something, it'll come from me and no one else. "Here."

She takes it calmly. Too calmly. I cross my arms and wait to see what she's going to do with it.

Tara leans down and gets mere inches away from Garret's swollen face. With her chin trembling, she holds the blade to his throat.

"You remember this," she seethes. "You remember this moment, Garret Brisbane. While you're bound and broken and beaten to shit, with piss running down your motherfucking legs, you remember that *I'm* the one who spared you. *Me.*" She presses the blade to his throat harder and blood blooms under it. "You will *never* get another chance, do you understand?"

He groans.

"Do you understand!" she yells in his face.

Garret slowly nods.

"No one from the Brisbane family will *ever* come near me again." Tara grabs him by the hair and pulls it. "Is that clear?"

Blood pours from the injuries we made on his face and neck. "Y-yes."

She removes the blade from his throat and lets go of him. "Now we're going to get you to the hospital and you're going to say you don't know who attacked you because they knocked you out before you could see their face." She palms the handle of my switchblade and shoves the tip against his dick. "And if you *ever* even *whisper* my name, or try to contact me ever again, I'll cut your dick off and feed it to you." Without flinching, my girl shoves the blade down, slicing right through his pants.

He screams like a stuck pig.

I'm pretty sure she's pierced one of his balls.

"Do. You. Understand?" She twists the knife, and he wails louder, frantically nodding his head.

I once said I was the devil and her demons adore me, but after tonight, I think it's the other way around. Fucking hell, I'm so in love with this woman.

Tara snatches Garret by his hair and yanks the blade out of his nuts. Cool as a cucumber, she heads over to me and asks, "Is it too late for that fondue? I'm starving."

What. The. Fuck. Is my girl in shock or just as crazy as me?

"Honey," Knox says, folding his arms. "After tonight, not a single one of us is going to deny you a damn thing. You want fondue? You got it. You can have anything you fucking want."

Tara's gaze remains deadlocked on me. "Anything at all?"

"Whatever you want," I say, wrapping my arms around her.

"Grilled cheese and chocolate pudding."

My heart explodes.

"God damn, you two really are made for each other," Knox says with a laugh.

Dmitri crosses his arms. "Told you."

"Looks like we've got a new member of the family, boys." Vault announces with a big grin.

"What do you say to that, Butterfly?" I press my forehead to hers. "Can I keep you?"

"Yes, please."

I smash my mouth to hers, driving her out of the utility room and away from Garret for good.

"We'll clean up here," D promises. "Take your girl home."

"Yeah," Tara says, her eyes glassy and cheeks flushed. "Take me home, Mr. Hudson."

"Whatever the Butterfly wants, she gets."

Epilogue

Ryker

Two years later...

A lot has changed and yet everything is still the same. Tara never left my side after the day we taught Garret a lesson in manners. Her mother hasn't reached out to her at all. Neither has any other Brisbane for that matter. Garret survived and the cops never came for us. Good to see he's smart enough to keep his mouth shut. I heard it had to be wired for a while though. Oops.

Knox's club is turning a damn good profit. Once he got it all fixed up, Tara asked to run the business end of it for him, which is phenomenal. Knox is thrilled. She is too. Between spending her days there and nights at the Monarch with me, she's always busy, which makes her deliriously happy.

My girl is smart as a whip. Have I said that already? We're about to open another sex club, too. Only this one doesn't cater to the elite. Anyone can join if they meet the criteria and keep to the rules. We'll see how it goes.

Tara named it the Luna club.

Fucking killer, right? And ironic. Did you know Luna moths only live for about a week? Adults don't even have mouths, so they can't eat. They mate, reproduce, then die.

What a life.

My old apartment building on Greene Street was purchased for a cool three-hundred thousand at auction. It got turned into a park, of all things. There's a walking path, basketball courts, a huge playground, and a baseball diamond. I love coming here.

Tipping my head back, I bask in the summer sun and stretch my arms out on the bench. My Butterfly should be here in about a half hour. We have dinner reservations at six to celebrate my birthday, but I got here early to enjoy the peace this place brings me.

"Ryker?"

My head shoots up at the sound of that voice. Standing in front of me is a woman in black leggings, a tank top, and running shoes. "Oh my god, it is you."

Natalie.

Her name sticks in my throat like thorns. I grind my molars, hoping like hell my brain will make my mouth work, but I'm short circuiting. I thought I'd put my anger to bed over my past, but clearly, that's not the case.

"Can I sit with you?"

Why can't I make words come out of my face?

Natalie drops next to me and folds her hands in her lap, sighing.

Is this really happening right now?

"It's been a long time." She looks over at me. "You've done really well for yourself. I see Knox has too. How are Dmitri and Vault?"

"Are you really going to play this bullshit game with me, Natalie?" There we go. Finally. My mouth does work. Now if I can get the rest of me going, I'll be much better off.

"I've wanted to reach out to you but…" She gazes at the pond across from us. "I can't believe they tore down the building and put this in its place."

I stand up.

"Wait." Natalie grabs my hand and I rip away from her.

"Don't fucking touch me." My heart pounds in my chest. "How can you even sit here with me, like we're friends, after what you did?"

Her mouth turns down and eyebrows bunch. "I've thought of a million ways to say I'm sorry to you, Ryker. Sorry for bringing you into sex work. Sorry for the way I treated you. Sorry for not doing a better job of being there for you in the end."

"The end." Is that what she calls murdering my mother? "You ghosted."

"I know."

"You killed her, and you ghosted." I toss my hands up. "Jesus fucking Christ, what are you even doing here, Nat?"

She takes in a deep breath. "I know what you think, but you're wrong." She looks up at me, squinting against the sunlight. "I didn't kill Ashley, Ry."

It takes forever for my mouth to engage. "You said it was a mercy."

"It was." Her voice shakes and it pisses me off. She doesn't get to cry about my mom. "She knew what you were doing."

I suddenly can't feel my feet. Dropping back onto the bench, I sway with dizziness. "What?"

"She knew you were an escort."

She's lying. My mom could never have found out about that. I'd been so careful. "Bullshit."

"I'm telling you the truth. She knew everything, Ry." Natalie sniffles. "She wasn't disappointed in you for your choices. She just didn't want you to have to keep doing it for her sake."

"I'm so tired," Ashley says, struggling to inhale. Her breathing's changed lately, but today is definitely the worst it's ever been.

"Go to sleep, Ash." Sitting on the side of her bed, I mark the page of the novel I'm reading to her and place the book on the foot of the bed. "We can pick it up again tomorrow."

"No." Her chest rises in short little bursts. "I'm tired."

Yep. Got it. "Ryker's gonna be home really soon. I'm surprised he isn't already." I know she likes to wait up for him. It makes the guilt of knowing what he's out there doing so much worse. I'm the one who brought him into this lifestyle. I'm the one who's fucked him up. I was only trying to help, but I now see it was a huge mistake.

Ryker's no longer using escorting to make money. He's relying on it as a distraction.

Ashley's voice sounds raspy. "I know... why he's out... every night." Her eyes are barely open. "I didn't believe... for one minute... that my old company has been... paying our insurance... or that he's... working construction to... pay the bills." She coughs again. "He never comes home dirty."

Ryker would beg to differ on that. But Ashley's version of dirty is not the same as Ryker's.

Guilt has me panicking to change the subject. "Why don't I get you some water, Ash. And maybe another pillow."

"No." Her breaths grow more labored. "Tell me the... truth. Is he... going to be okay?" A tear slides down her sunken face. The hollows of her cheeks have become so much more pronounced over the past two weeks.

My heart cracks into pieces.

"Yes," I tell her. "He'll be okay."

"I'm so tired." Ashley closes her eyes. "Tell him... when he gets home... you tell him... I'm so proud of who he's become... tell him... I love my sweet boy... so much."

Fuck. I can't do this. "Let me call and see where he is."

Ashley's fingers are ice on my hand. She weakly shakes her head. "I'm so tired."

"Then go to sleep," I whisper, finally hearing what Ashley's been saying for months. She's tired, and she's been hanging on for Ryker and can't anymore.

Oh god. Numbness creeps into my system.

"It's okay," I say, quietly. My heart fractures when I climb into bed with her and hold her tight. "You can go to sleep, Ashley. He'll be home soon. He'll be home and..." I swipe my hot tears away. "And he'll know you love him so much. You've been an amazing mom. You should be so proud of him. He's smart and strong and sweet and caring." I know the moment she's gone, but I can't shut up. "He's such a great kid. He's going to be a great man."

I hold her long after she stops breathing.

Long after my heart bursts into a hundred million pieces.

She wasn't just Ryker's mom. She was the closest thing I've had to a best friend. Ashley knew I was an escort and didn't once shame me for it. I'd tell her my wild stories, and we'd laugh with how crazy some of my dates would get. I never once told her Ryker was part of it. If she really does know the truth, I have no clue how she could have possibly found out.

And now, it doesn't matter...

"That's why I told you it was a mercy," she says, swiping the tears off her face. "I didn't kill her, Ry. I just gave her permission to…"

"Let go," we both say at the same time.

I lean back on the bench and scrub my face. Holy hell.

Natalie clears her throat. "It was a mercy to you too, because when she died, you were free to stop escorting. Her death could be a new beginning for you. I should have never let you into my world like that. And you should have never lied to me about your age, either."

I don't say a word. What's done is done.

Natalie sniffles, but she's no longer crying. "I moved back here a couple years ago, and I come to this park every day for a morning run. I had appointments all day and didn't get here until now, otherwise, I'd have never run into you. I guess the universe knew it was time for our paths to cross again."

She's still an escort.

Nat stands up and tucks a few loose strands of hair behind her ear. "She would have really loved this park."

When Natalie walks away, my mouth goes off the rails. "Nat?"

She looks over her shoulder at me.

"Thank you. For everything."

Her shoulders drop. She nods and starts running again, farther, and farther away from me, around the bend, out of my sight.

I wait for rage to surface. Remorse. Regret. I feel none of it.

Only peace.

"Well, hello, Mr. Hudson."

I quickly pinch my eyes, wiping the half-fallen

tears off, and clear my throat. "Hey, Mrs. Hudson."

Did I mention we got married six months ago?

Tara saunters over, looking like a decadent feast for the eyes. "Who was that you were talking to?"

"No one important." My girl knows I'll tell her eventually, so she never pushes. We share trauma only when we're ready. It's part of our ongoing healing process.

I stand up and whistle as Tara gives me some three-sixty spin action. "That dress is killer, Butterfly."

"I was going for a widow maker meets Suzie housewife vibe." She kicks her foot up to reveal their red soles. "I nailed it."

"Mmmm I'd like to nail you." My arms become two anacondas around her waist. "Fuck dinner. I'm eating you instead." She squeals when I haul her over my shoulder. Smacking her ass, I carry her to my car and drop her carefully on the curb. "Grilled cheese in bed?"

Tara fluffs her dress out. "Can I sit on your face while wearing this thing?"

"As if you even have to ask."

"Good. I made chocolate pudding earlier today, too." Tara's smile is brighter than the sun. "Who loves you, baby?"

Tipping her chin with my finger, I smile against her mouth. "You."

"Mmm hmm." She kisses me hard enough to make my toes curl. "Now take me home, Ryker Hudson, and let's celebrate what a great man you are."

God damn, I love my life.

Other Books By This Author

For information on this book, other books in my
backlist, and future releases,
please visit: **www.BrianaMichaels.com**

If you liked this book, please help spread the word
by leaving a review on the site you purchased your
copy, or on a reader site such as Goodreads.

I'd love to hear from readers too, so feel free to send
me an email at: Briana@BrianaMichaels.com
or visit me on Facebook:
www.facebook.com/BrianaMichaelsAuthor

Thank you!

About the Author

Briana Michaels grew up and still lives on the East Coast. When taking a break from the crazy adventures in her head, she enjoys running around with her two children. If there is time to spare, she loves to read, cook, hike in the woods, and sit outside by a roaring fire. She does all of this with the love and support of her amazing husband who always has her back, encouraging her to go for her dreams. Aye, she's a lucky girl indeed.

Printed in Great Britain
by Amazon